PENGUIN BOOKS

THE PALE CRIMINAL

Philip Kerr was born in Edinburgh in 1956 and lives in London. As a freelance journalist he has written for a number of newspapers and magazines, including the *Sunday Times*. He is the author of the novels *March Violets*, *The Pale Criminal* and *A German Requiem* (also published by Penguin in one volume as *Berlin Noir*). He is also the author of *A Philosophical Investigation*, *Dead Meat* and *Gridiron*, and has edited *The Penguin Book of Lies* and *The Penguin Book of Fights, Feuds and Heartfelt Hatreds*.

D1067163

THE PALE CRIMINAL

PHILIP KERR

PENGUIN BOOKS

PENGUIN BOOKS

Published by the Penguin Group
Penguin Books Ltd, 27 Wrights Lane, London W8 5TZ, England
Penguin Books USA Inc., 375 Hudson Street, New York, New York 10014, USA
Penguin Books Australia Ltd, Ringwood, Victoria, Australia
Penguin Books Canada Ltd, 10 Alcorn Avenue, Toronto, Ontario, Canada M4V 3B2
Penguin Books (NZ) Ltd, 182–190 Wairau Road, Auckland 10, New Zealand

Penguin Books Ltd, Registered Offices: Harmondsworth, Middlesex, England

First published by Viking 1990
Published in Penguin Books, 1991
5 7 9 10 8 6 4

Printed in England by Clays Ltd, St Ives plc

To Jane

Much about your good people moves me to disgust, and it is not their evil I mean. How I wish they possessed a madness through which they could perish, like this pale criminal. Truly I wish their madness were called truth or loyalty or justice: but they possess their virtue in order to live long and in a miserable ease.

Nietzsche

PART ONE

You tend to notice the strawberry tart in Kranzler's Café a lot more when your diet forbids you to have any.

Well, lately I've begun to feel much the same way about women. Only I'm not on a diet, so much as simply finding myself ignored by the waitress. There are so many pretty ones about too. Women, I mean, although I could as easily fuck a waitress as any other kind of female. There was one woman a couple of years ago. I was in love with her, only she disappeared. Well, that happens to a lot of people in this city. But since then it's just been casual affairs. And now, to see me on Unter den Linden, head one way and then the other, you would think that I was watching a hypnotist's pendulum. I don't know, maybe it's the heat. This summer, Berlin's as hot as a baker's armpit. Or maybe it's just me, turning forty and going a bit coochie-coo near babies. Whatever the reason, my urge to procreate is nothing short of bestial, which of course women see in your eyes, and then leave you well alone.

Despite that, in the long hot summer of 1938, bestiality was callously enjoying something of an Aryan renaissance.

1

'Just like a fucking cuckoo.'

'What is?'

Bruno Stahlecker looked up from his newspaper.

'Hitler, who else?'

My stomach sank as it sensed another of my partner's profound analogies to do with the Nazis. 'Yes, of course,' I said firmly, hoping that my show of total comprehension would deter him from a more detailed explanation. But it was not to be.

'No sooner has he got rid of the Austrian fledgling from the European nest than the Czechoslovakian one starts to look precarious.' He smacked the newspaper with the back of his hand. 'Have you seen this, Bernie? German troop movements on the border of the Sudetenland.'

'Yes, I guessed that's what you were talking about.' I picked up the morning mail and, sitting down, started to sort through it. There were several cheques, which helped to take the edge off my irritation with Bruno. It was hard to believe, but clearly he'd already had a drink. Normally a couple of stops away from being monosyllabic (which I prefer being a shade taciturn myself) booze always made Bruno chattier than an Italian waiter.

'The odd thing is that the parents don't notice. The cuckoo keeps throwing out the other chicks, and the foster parents keep on feeding it.'

'Maybe they hope that he'll shut up and go away,' I said pointedly, but Bruno's fur was too thick for him to notice. I glanced over the contents of one of the letters and then read it again, more slowly.

'They just don't want to notice. What's in the post?'

'Hmm? Oh, some cheques.'

'Bless the day that brings a cheque. Anything else?'

'A letter. The anonymous kind. Someone wants me to meet him in the Reichstag at midnight.'

'Does he say why?'

'Claims to have information about an old case of mine. A missing person that stayed missing.'

'Sure, I remember them like I remember dogs with tails. Very unusual. Are you going?'

I shrugged. 'Lately I've been sleeping badly, so why not?'

'You mean apart from the fact that it's a burnt-out ruin, and it isn't safe to go inside? Well, for one, it could be a trap. Someone might be trying to kill you.'

'Maybe you sent it, then.'

He laughed uncomfortably. 'Perhaps I should come with you. I could stay out of sight, but within earshot.'

'Or gunshot?' I shook my head. 'If you want to kill a man you don't ask him to the sort of place where naturally he'll be on his guard.' I tugged open the drawer of my desk.

To look at there wasn't much difference between the Mauser and the Walther, but it was the Mauser that I picked up. The pitch of the grip, the general fit of the pistol made it altogether more substantial than the slightly smaller Walther, and it lacked for nothing in stopping-power. Like a fat cheque, it was a gun that always endowed me with a feeling of quiet confidence when I slipped it into my coat pocket. I waved the gun in Bruno's direction.

'And whoever sent me the party invitation will know I'm carrying a lighter.'

'Supposing there's more than one of them?'

'Shit, Bruno, there's no need to paint the devil on the wall. I can see the risks, but that's the business we're in. Newspapermen get bulletins, soldiers get dispatches and detectives get anonymous letters. If I'd wanted sealing-wax on my mail I'd have become a damned lawyer.'

Bruno nodded, tugged a little at his eyepatch and then transferred his nerves to his pipe – the symbol of our partnership's failure. I hate the paraphernalia of pipe-smoking: the tobacco-pouch, the cleaner, the pocket-knife and the special lighter. Pipe-smokers are the grandmasters of fiddling and fidgeting, and as great a blight on our world as a missionary landing on Tahiti with a boxful of brassieres. It wasn't Bruno's fault, for, in spite of his drinking and his irritating little habits, he was still the good detective I'd rescued from the obscurity of an out-of-the-way posting to a Kripo station in Spreewald. No, it was me that was at fault: I had discovered myself to be as temperamentally unsuited to partnership as I would have been to the presidency of the Deutsche Bank.

But looking at him I started to feel guilty.

'Remember what we used to say in the war? If it's got your name and address on it, you can be sure it'll be delivered.'

'I remember,' he said, lighting his pipe and returning to his *Völkischer Beobachter*. I watched him reading it with bemusement.

'You could as well wait for the town-crier as get any real news out of that.'

'True. But I like to read a paper in the morning, even if it is a crock of shit. I've got into the habit.' We were both silent for a moment or two. 'There's another one of those advertisements in here: "Rolf Vogelmann, Private Investigator, Missing Persons a speciality."'

'Never heard of him.'

'Sure you have. There was another ad in last Friday's classified. I read it out to you. Don't you remember?' He took his pipe out of his mouth and pointed the stem at me. 'You know, maybe we should advertise, Bernie.'

'Why? We've got all the business we can handle, and more. Things have never been better, so who needs the extra expense? Anyway, it's reputation that counts in this line of business, not column inches in the Party's newspaper. This Rolf Vogelmann obviously doesn't know what the hell he's doing. Think of all the Jewish business that we get. None of our clients reads that kind of shit.'

'Well, if you don't think we need it, Bernie . . .'

'Like a third nipple.'

'Some people used to think that was a sign of luck.'

'And quite a few who thought it reason enough to burn you at the stake.'

7

'The devil's mark, eh?' He chuckled. 'Hey, maybe Hitler's got one.'

'Just as surely as Goebbels has a cloven hoof. Shit, they're all from hell. Every damn one of them.'

I heard my footsteps ringing on a deserted Königsplatz as I approached what was left of the Reichstag building. Only Bismarck, standing on his plinth, hand on sword, in front of the western doorway, his head turned towards me, seemed prepared to offer some challenge to my being there. But as I recalled he had never been much of an enthusiast for the German parliament – had never even set foot in the place – and so I doubted that he'd have been much inclined to defend the institution on which his statue had, perhaps symbolically, turned its back. Not that there was much about this rather florid, Renaissance-style building that looked worth fighting for now. Its façade blackened by smoke, the Reichstag looked like a volcano which had seen its last and most spectacular eruption. But the fire had been more than merely the burnt offering of the 1918 Republic; it was also the clearest piece of pyromancy that Germany could have been given as to what Adolf Hitler and his third nipple had in store for us.

I walked up to the north side and what had been Portal V, the public entrance, through which I had walked once before, with my mother, more than thirty years ago.

I left my flashlight in my coat pocket. A man with a torch in his hand at night needs only to paint a few coloured circles on his chest to make a better target of himself. And anyway, there was more than enough moonlight shining through what was left of the roof for me to see where I was going. Still, as I stepped through the north vestibule, into what had once been a waiting-room, I worked the Mauser's slide noisily to let whoever was expecting me know that I was armed. And in the eerie, echoing silence, it sounded louder than a troop of Prussian cavalry.

'You won't need that,' said a voice from the galleried floor above me.

'All the same, I'll just hang on to it awhile. There might be rats about.'

The man laughed scornfully. 'The rats left here a long time ago.' A torch beam shone in my face. 'Come on up, Gunther.'

'Seems like I should know your voice,' I said, starting up the stairs.

'I'm the same way. Sometimes I recognize my voice, but I just don't seem to know the man using it. There's nothing unusual in that, is there? Not these days.' I took out my flashlight and pointed it at the man I now saw retreating into the room ahead of me.

'I'm interested to hear it. I'd like to hear you say that sort of thing over at Prinz Albrecht Strasse.' He laughed again.

'So you do recognize me after all.'

I caught up with him beside a great marble statue of the Emperor Wilhelm I that stood in the centre of a great, octagonally-shaped hall, where my torch finally picked out his features. There was something cosmopolitan about these, although he spoke with a Berlin accent. Some might even have said that he looked more than a little Jewish, if the size of his nose was anything to go by. This dominated the centre of his face like the arm on a sundial, and tugged the upper lip into a thin sneer of a smile. His greying, fair hair he wore closely cropped, which had the effect of accentuating the height of his forehead. It was a cunning, wily sort of face, and suited him perfectly.

'Surprised?' he said.

'That the head of Berlin's Criminal Police should send me an anonymous note? No, that happens to me all the time.'

'Would you have come if I had signed it?'

'Probably not.'

'And if I had suggested that you come to Prinz Albrecht Strasse instead of this place? Admit you were curious.'

'Since when has Kripo had to rely on suggestion to get people down to headquarters?'

'You've got a point.' His smirk broadening, Arthur Nebe produced a hip flask from his coat pocket. 'Drink?'

'Thanks. I don't mind if I do.' I swigged a cheekful of the clear grain alcohol thoughtfully provided by the Reichskrim-inaldirektor, and then took out my cigarettes. After I had lit us both I held the match aloft for a couple of seconds.

'Not an easy place to torch,' I said. 'One man, acting on his own: he'd have to have been a fairly agile sort of bugger. And even then I reckon it would have taken Van der Lubbe all night to get this little campfire blazing.' I sucked at my cigarette and added: 'The word is that Fat Hermann had a hand in it. A hand holding a piece of burning tinder, that is.'

'I'm shocked, shocked to hear you make such a scandalous suggestion about our beloved prime minister.' But Nebe was laughing as he said it. 'Poor old Hermann, getting the unofficial blame like that. Oh, he went along with the arson, but it wasn't his party.'

'Whose was it, then?'

'Joey the Cripp. That poor fucking Dutchman was an added bonus for him. Van der Lubbe had the misfortune to have decided to set fire to this place on the same night as Goebbels and his lads. Joey thought it was his birthday, especially as Lubbe turned out to be a Bolshie. Only he forgot that the arrest of a culprit meant a trial, which meant that there would have to be the irritating formality of producing evidence. And of course right from the start it was obvious to a man with his head in a bag that Lubbe couldn't have acted on his own.'

'So why didn't he say something at the trial?'

'They pumped him full of some shit to keep him quiet, threatened his family. You know the sort of thing.' Nebe walked round a huge bronze chandelier that lay twisted on the dirty marble floor. 'Here. I want to show you something.'

He led the way into the great Hall of the Diet, where Germany had last seen some semblance of democracy. Rising high above us was the shell of what had once been the Reichstag's glass dome. Now all the glass was blown out and, against the moon, the copper girders resembled the web of some gigantic spider. Nebe pointed his torch at the scorched, split beams that surrounded the Hall.

'They're badly damaged by the fire, but those half figures supporting the beams – can you see how some of them are also holding up letters of the alphabet?'

'Just about.'

'Yes, well, some of them are unrecognizable. But if you look hard you can still see that they spell out a motto.'

'Not at one o'clock in the morning I can't.'

Nebe ignored me. 'It says "Country before Party".' He repeated the motto almost reverently, and then looked at me with what I supposed to be a meaning.

I sighed and shook my head. 'Oh, that really knocks over the heap. You? Arthur Nebe? The Reichskriminaldirektor? A beefsteak Nazi? Well, I'll eat my broom.'

'Brown on the outside, yes,' he said. 'I don't know what colour I am on the inside, but it's not red – I'm no Bolshevik. But then it's not brown either. I am no longer a Nazi.'

'Shit, you're one hell of a mimic, then.'

'I am now. I have to be to stay alive. Of course, it wasn't always that way. The police force is my life, Gunther. I love it. When I saw it corroded by liberalism during the Weimar years I thought that National Socialism would restore some respect for law and order in this country. Instead, it's worse than ever. I was the one who helped get the Gestapo away from the control of Diels, only to find him replaced with Himmler and Heydrich, and . . .'

'. . . and then the rain really started to come in at the eaves. I get the picture.'

'The time is coming when everyone will have to do the same. There's no room for agnosticism in the Germany that Himmler and Heydrich have got planned for us. It'll be stand up and be counted or take the consequences. But it's still possible to change things from the inside. And when the time is right we'll need men like you. Men on the force who can be trusted. That's why I've asked you here – to try and persuade you to come back.'

'Me? Back in Kripo? You must be joking. Listen, Arthur, I've built up a good business, I make a very good living now. Why should I chuck all that away for the pleasure of being on the force again?'

'You might not have much choice in the matter. Heydrich thinks that you might be useful to him if you were back in Kripo.'

'I see. Any particular reason?'

'There's a case he wants you to handle. I'm sure I don't

have to tell you that Heydrich takes his Fascism very personally. He generally gets what he wants.'

'What's this case about?'

'I don't know what he's got in mind; Heydrich doesn't confide in me. I just wanted to warn you, so that you'd be prepared, so that you didn't do anything stupid like tell him to go to hell, which might be your first reaction. We both have great respect for your abilities as a detective. It just happens that I also want somebody in Kripo that I can trust.'

'Well, what it is to be popular.'

'You'll give it some thought.'

'I don't see how I can avoid it. It'll make a change from the crossword, I suppose. Anyway, thanks for the red light, Arthur, I appreciate it.' I wiped my dry mouth nervously. 'You got any more of that lemonade? I could use a drink now. It's not every day you get such good news.'

Nebe handed me his flask and I went for it like a baby after its mother's tit. Less attractive, but damn near as comforting.

'In your love letter you mentioned you had some information about an old case. Or was that your equivalent of the child-molester's puppy?'

'There was a woman you were looking for a while back. A journalist.'

'That's quite a while back. Nearly two years. I never found her. One of my all too frequent failures. Perhaps you ought to let Heydrich know that. It might persuade him to let me off the hook.'

'Do you want this or not?'

'Well, don't make me straighten my tie for it, Arthur.'

'There's not much, but here it is. A couple of months ago, the landlord of the place where your client used to live decided to redecorate some of the apartments, including hers.'

'Big-hearted of him.'

'In her toilet, behind some kind of false panel, he found a doper's kit. No drugs, but everything you'd need to service a habit – needles, syringes, the works. Now, the tenant who took over the place from your client when she disappeared was a priest, so it didn't seem likely that these needles were his,

12

right? And if the lady was using dope, then that might explain a lot, wouldn't you say? I mean, you never can predict what a doper will do.'

I shook my head. 'She wasn't the type. I'd have noticed something, wouldn't I?'

'Not always. Not if she was trying to wean herself off the stuff. Not if she were a strong sort of character. Well then, it was reported and I thought you'd like to know. So now you can close that file. With that sort of secret there's no telling what else she might have kept from you.'

'No, it's all right. I got a good look at her nipples.'

Nebe smiled nervously, not quite sure if I was telling him a dirty joke or not.

'Good were they – her nipples?'

'Just the two of them, Arthur. But they were beautiful.'

2

Monday, 29 August

The houses on Herbertstrasse, in any other city but Berlin, would each have been surrounded by a couple of hectares of shrub-lined lawn. But as it was they filled their individual plots of land with little or no space for grass and paving. Some of them were no more than the front-gate's width from the sidewalk. Architecturally they were a mixture of styles, ranging from the Palladian to the neo-Gothic, the Wilhelmine and some that were so vernacular as to be impossible to describe. Judged as a whole, Herbertstrasse was like an assemblage of old field-marshals and grand-admirals in full-dress-uniforms obliged to sit on extremely small and inadequate camp stools.

The great wedding-cake of a house to which I had been summoned belonged properly on a Mississippi plantation, an impression enhanced by the black cauldron of a maid who answered the door. I showed her my ID and told her that I was expected. She stared doubtfully at my identification, as if she were Himmler himself.

'Frau Lange didn't say nothing to me about you.'

'I expect she forgot,' I said. 'Look, she only called my office half an hour ago.'

'All right,' she said reluctantly. 'You'd better come in.'

She showed me into a drawing-room that you could have called elegant but for the large and only partially chewed dog-bone that was lying on the carpet. I looked around for the owner but there was no sign of one.

'Don't touch anything,' said the black cauldron. 'I'll tell her you're here.' Then, muttering and grumbling like I'd got her out of the bath, she waddled off to find her mistress. I sat down on a mahogany sofa with dolphins carved on the arm-rests. Next to it was a matching table, the top resting on dolphin-tails. Dolphins were a comic effect always popular with

14

German cabinet-makers, but, personally, I'd seen a better sense of humour in a three-pfennig stamp. I was there about five minutes before the cauldron rolled back in and said that Frau Lange would see me now.

We went along a long, gloomy hallway that was home to a lot of stuffed fish, one of which, a fine salmon, I stopped to admire.

'Nice fish,' I said. 'Who's the fisherman?' She turned impatiently.

'No fisherman here,' she said. 'Just fish. What a house this is for fish, and cats, and dogs. Only the cats is the worst. At least the fish is dead. You can't dust them cats and dogs.'

Almost automatically I ran my finger along the salmon's cabinet. There didn't seem to be a great deal of evidence that any kind of dusting took place; and even on my comparatively short introduction to the Lange household, it was easy to see that the carpets were rarely, if ever, vacuumed. After the mud of the trenches a bit of dust and a few crumbs on the floor don't offend me that much. But all the same, I'd seen plenty of homes in the worst slums of Neukölln and Wedding that were kept cleaner than this one.

The cauldron opened some glass doors and stood aside. I went into an untidy sitting-room which also seemed to be part office, and the doors closed behind me.

She was a large, fleshy orchid of a woman. Fat hung pendulously on her peach-coloured face and arms, making her look like one of those stupid dogs that is bred to have a coat several sizes too large for it. Her own stupid dog was altogether more shapeless than the ill-fitting Sharpei she resembled.

'It's very good of you to come and see me at such short notice,' she said. I uttered a few deferential noises, but she had the sort of clout you can only get from living in a fancy address like Herbertstrasse.

Frau Lange sat down on a green-coloured chaise longue and spread her dog's fur on her generous lap like a piece of knitting she intended to work on while explaining her problem to me. I supposed her to be in her middle fifties. Not that it mattered. When women get beyond fifty their age ceases to be of interest to anyone other than themselves. With men the situation is entirely the opposite.

She produced a cigarette case and invited me to smoke, adding as a proviso: 'They're menthol.'

I thought it was curiosity that made me take one, but as I sucked my first lungful I winced, realizing that I had merely forgotten how disgusting a menthol tastes. She chuckled at my obvious discomfort.

'Oh, put it out man, for God's sake. They taste horrible. I don't know why I smoke them, really I don't. Have one of your own or I'll never get your attention.'

'Thanks,' I said, stubbing it out in a hub-cap of an ashtray, 'I think I will.'

'And while you're at it, you can pour us both a drink. I don't know about you but I could certainly do with one.' She pointed to a great Biedermeier secretaire, the top section of which, with its bronze Ionic columns, was an ancient Greek temple in miniature.

'There's a bottle of gin in that thing,' she said. 'I can't offer you anything but lime juice to put in it. I'm afraid it's the only thing I ever drink.'

It was a little early for me, but I mixed two anyway. I liked her for trying to put me at my ease, even though that was supposed to be one of my own professional accomplishments. Except that Frau Lange wasn't in the least bit nervous. She looked like the kind of lady who had quite a few professional accomplishments of her own. I handed her the drink and sat down on a creaking leather chair that was next to the chaise.

'Are you an observant man, Herr Gunther?'

'I can see what's happening in Germany, if that's what you mean.'

'It wasn't, but I'm glad to hear it anyway. No, what I meant was, how good are you at seeing things?'

'Come now, Frau Lange, there's no need to be the cat creeping around the hot milk. Just walk right up and lap it.' I waited for a moment, watching her grow awkward. 'I'll say it for you if you like. You mean, how good a detective am I.'

'I'm afraid I know very little of these matters.'

'No reason why you should.'

'But if I am to confide in you I feel I ought to have some idea of your credentials.'

I smiled. 'You'll understand that mine is not the kind of business where I can show you the testimonials of several satisfied customers. Confidentiality is as important to my clients as it is in the confessional. Perhaps even more important.'

'But then how is one to know that one has engaged the services of someone who is good at what he does?'

'I'm very good at what I do, Frau Lange. My reputation is well-known. A couple of months ago I even had an offer for my business. Rather a good offer, as it happened.'

'Why didn't you sell?'

'In the first place the business wasn't for sale. And in the second I'd make as bad an employee as I would an employer. All the same, it's flattering when that sort of thing happens. Of course, all this is quite beside the point. Most people who want the services of a private investigator don't need to buy the firm. Usually they just ask their lawyers to find someone. You'll find that I'm recommended by several law firms, including the ones who don't like my accent or my manners.'

'Forgive me, Herr Gunther, but in my opinion the law is a much overrated profession.'

'I can't argue with you there. I never met a lawyer yet that wasn't above stealing his mother's savings and the mattress she was keeping them under.'

'In nearly all business matters I have found my own judgement to be a great deal more reliable.'

'What exactly is your business, Frau Lange?'

'I own and manage a publishing company.'

'The Lange Publishing Company?'

'As I said, I haven't often been wrong by trusting my own judgement, Herr Gunther. Publishing is all about taste, and to know what will sell one must appreciate something of the tastes of the people to whom one is selling. Now, I'm a Berliner to my fingertips, and I believe I know this city and its people as well as anyone does. So with reference to my original

17

question, which was to do with your being observant, you will answer me this: if I were a stranger in Berlin, how would you describe the people of this city to me?'

I smiled. 'What's a Berliner, eh? That's a good question. No client's ever asked me to leap through a couple of hoops to see how clever a dog I am before. You know, mostly I don't do tricks, but in your case I'll make an exception. Berliners like people to make exceptions for them. I hope you're paying attention now because I've started my act. Yes, they like to be made to feel exceptional, although at the same time they like to keep up appearances. Mostly they've got the same sort of look. A scarf, hat and shoes that could walk you to Shanghai without a corn. As it happens, Berliners like to walk, which is why so many of them own a dog: something vicious if you're masculine, something cute if you're something else. The men comb their hair more than the women, and they also grow moustaches you could hunt wild pig in. Tourists think that a lot of Berlin men like dressing-up as women, but that's just the ugly women giving the men a bad name. Not that there are many tourists these days. National Socialism's made them as rare a sight as Fred Astaire in jackboots.

'The people of this town will take cream with just about anything, including beer, and beer is something they take very seriously indeed. The women prefer a ten-minute head on it, just like the men, and they don't mind paying for it themselves. Nearly everyone who drives a car drives much too fast, but nobody would ever dream of running a red light. They've got rotten lungs because the air is bad, and because they smoke too much, and a sense of humour that sounds cruel if you don't understand it, and even crueller if you do. They buy expensive Biedermeier cabinets as solid as blockhouses, and then hang little curtains on the insides of the glass doors to hide what they've got in there. It's a typically idiosyncratic mixture of the ostentatious and the private. How am I doing?'

Frau Lange nodded. 'Apart from the comment about Berlin's ugly women, you'll do just fine.'

'It wasn't pertinent.'

'Now there you're wrong. Don't back down or I shall stop

liking you. It was pertinent. You'll see why in a moment. What are your fees?'

'Seventy marks a day, plus expenses.'

'And what expenses might there be?'

'Hard to say. Travel. Bribes. Anything that results in information. You get receipts for everything except the bribes. I'm afraid you have to take my word for those.'

'Well, let's hope that you're a good judge of what is worth paying for.'

'I've had no complaints.'

'And I assume you'll want something in advance.' She handed me an envelope. 'You'll find a thousand marks in cash in there. Is that satisfactory to you?' I nodded. 'Naturally I shall want a receipt.'

'Naturally,' I said, and signed the piece of paper she had prepared. Very businesslike, I thought. Yes, she was certainly quite a lady. 'Incidentally, how did you come to choose me? You didn't ask your lawyer, and,' I added thoughtfully, 'I don't advertise, of course.'

She stood up and, still holding her dog, went over to the desk.

'I had one of your business cards,' she said, handing it to me. 'Or at least my son did. I acquired it at least a year ago from the pocket of one of his old suits I was sending to the Winter Relief.' She referred to the welfare programme that was run by the Labour Front, the DAF. 'I kept it, meaning to return it to him. But when I mentioned it to him I'm afraid he told me to throw it away. Only I didn't. I suppose I thought it might come in useful at some stage. Well, I wasn't wrong, was I?'

It was one of my old business cards, dating from the time before my partnership with Bruno Stahlecker. It even had my previous home telephone number written on the back.

'I wonder where he got it,' I said.

'I believe he said that it was Dr Kindermann's.'

'Kindermann?'

'I'll come to him in a moment, if you don't mind.' I thumbed a new card from my wallet.

19

'It's not important. But I've got a partner now, so you'd better have one of my new ones.' I handed her the card, and she placed it on the desk next to the telephone. While she was sitting down her face adopted a serious expression, as if she had switched off something inside her head.

'And now I'd better tell you why I asked you here,' she said grimly. 'I want you to find out who's blackmailing me.' She paused, shifting awkwardly on the chaise longue. 'I'm sorry, this isn't very easy for me.'

'Take your time. Blackmail makes anyone feel nervous.' She nodded and gulped some of her gin.

'Well, about two months ago, perhaps a little more, I received an envelope containing two letters that had been written by my son to another man. To Dr Kindermann. Of course I recognized my son's handwriting, and although I didn't read them, I knew that they were of an intimate nature. My son is a homosexual, Herr Gunther. I've known about it for some time, so this was not the terrible revelation to me that this evil person had intended. He made that much clear in his note. Also that there were several more letters like the ones I had received in his possession, and that he would send them to me if I paid him the sum of 1,000 marks. Were I to refuse he would have no alternative but to send them to the Gestapo. I'm sure I don't have to tell you, Herr Gunther, that this government takes a less enlightened attitude towards these unfortunate young men than did the Republic. Any contact between men, no matter how tenuous, is these days regarded as punishable. For Reinhard to be exposed as a homosexual would undoubtedly result in his being sent to a concentration camp for up to ten years.

'So I paid, Herr Gunther. My chauffeur left the money in the place I was told, and a week or so later I received not a packet of letters as I had expected, but only one letter. It was accompanied by another anonymous note which informed me that the author had changed his mind, that he was poor, that I should have to buy the letters back one at a time, and that there were still ten of them in his possession. Since then I have received four back, at a cost of almost 5,000 marks. Each time he asks for more than the last.'

'Does your son know about this?'

'No. And for the moment at least I can see no reason why we should both suffer.' I sighed, and was about to voice my disagreement when she stopped me.

'Yes, you're going to say that it makes catching this criminal more difficult, and that Reinhard may have information which might help you. You're absolutely right, of course. But listen to my reasons, Herr Gunther.

'First of all, my son is an impulsive boy. Most likely his reaction would be to tell this blackmailer to go to the devil, and not pay. This would almost certainly result in his arrest. Reinhard is my son, and as his mother I love him very dearly, but he is a fool, with no understanding of pragmatism. I suspect that whoever is blackmailing me has a shrewd appreciation of human psychology. He understands how a mother, a widow, feels for her only son – especially a rich and rather lonely one like myself.

'Second, I myself have some appreciation of the world of the homosexual. The late Dr Magnus Hirschfeld wrote several books on the subject, one of which I'm proud to say I published myself. It's a secret and rather treacherous world, Herr Gunther. A blackmailer's charter. So it may be that this evil person is actually acquainted with my son. Even between men and women, love can make a good reason for blackmail – more so when there is adultery involved, or race defilement, which seems to be more a cause for concern to these Nazis.

'Because of this, when you have discovered the blackmailer's identity, I will tell Reinhard, and then it will be up to him what is to be done. But until then he will know nothing of this.' She looked at me questioningly. 'Do you agree?'

'I can't fault your reasoning, Frau Lange. You seem to have thought this thing through very clearly. May I see the letters from your son?' Reaching for a folder by the chaise she nodded, and then hesitated.

'Is that necessary? Reading his letters, I mean.'

'Yes it is,' I said firmly. 'And do you still have the notes from the blackmailer?' She handed me the folder.

'Everything is in there,' she said. 'The letters and the anonymous notes.'

'He didn't ask for any of them back?'

'No.'

'That's good. It means we're dealing with an amateur. Someone who had done this sort of thing before would have told you to return his notes with each payment. To stop you accumulating any evidence against him.'

'Yes, I see.'

I glanced at what I was optimistically calling evidence. The notes and envelopes were all typewritten on good quality stationery without any distinctive features, and posted at various districts throughout west Berlin – W.35, W.40, W.50 – the stamps all commemorating the fifth anniversary of the Nazis coming to power. That told me something. This anniversary had taken place on 30 January, so it didn't look like Frau Lange's blackmailer bought stamps very often.

Reinhard Lange's letters were written on the heavier weight of paper that only people in love bother to buy – the kind that costs so much it just has to be taken seriously. The hand was neat and fastidious, even careful, which was more than could be said of the contents. An Ottoman bath-house attendant might not have found anything particularly objectionable about them, but in Nazi Germany, Reinhard Lange's love-letters were certainly sufficient to earn their cheeky author a trip to a KZ wearing a whole chestful of pink triangles.

'This Dr Lanz Kindermann,' I said, reading the name on the lime-scented envelope. 'What exactly do you know about him?'

'There was a stage when Reinhard was persuaded to be treated for his homosexuality. At first he tried various endocrine preparations, but these proved ineffective. Psychotherapy seemed to offer a better chance of success. I believe several high-ranking Party members, and boys from the Hitler Youth, have undergone the same treatment. Kindermann is a psychotherapist, and Reinhard first became acquainted with him when he entered Kindermann's clinic in Wannsee seeking a cure. Instead he became intimately involved with Kindermann, who is himself homosexual.'

'Pardon my ignorance, but what exactly is psychotherapy? I thought that sort of thing was no longer permitted.'

Frau Lange shook her head. 'I'm not exactly sure. But I think that the emphasis is on treating mental disorders as part of one's overall physical health. Don't ask me how that differs from that fellow Freud, except that he's Jewish, and Kindermann is German. Kindermann's clinic is strictly Germans only. Wealthy Germans, with drink and drug problems, those for whom the more eccentric end of medicine has some appeal – chiropracty and that sort of thing. Or those just seeking an expensive rest. Kindermann's patients include the Deputy Führer, Rudolf Hess.'

'Have you ever met Dr Kindermann?'

'Once. I didn't like him. He's a rather arrogant Austrian.'

'Aren't they all?' I murmured. 'Think he'd be the type to try a little blackmail? After all, the letters were addressed to him. If it isn't Kindermann, then it has to be somebody who knows him. Or at least somebody who had the opportunity to steal the letters from him.'

'I confess that I hadn't suspected Kindermann for the simple reason that the letters implicate both of them.' She thought for a moment. 'I know it sounds silly, but I never gave any thought as to how the letters came to be in somebody else's possession. But now you come to mention it, I suppose that they must have been stolen. From Kindermann I would think.'

I nodded. 'All right,' I said. 'Now let me ask you a rather more difficult question.'

'I think I know what you're going to say, Herr Gunther,' she said, heaving a great sigh. 'Have I considered the possibility that my own son might be the culprit?' She looked at me critically, and added: 'I wasn't wrong about you, was I? It's just the sort of cynical question that I hoped you would ask. Now I know I can trust you.'

'For a detective being a cynic is like green fingers in a gardener, Frau Lange. Sometimes it gets me into trouble, but mostly it stops me from underestimating people. So you'll forgive me I hope if I suggest that this could be the best reason of all for not involving him in this investigation, and that you've already thought of it.' I saw her smile a little, and

added: 'You see how I don't underestimate you, Frau Lange.'
She nodded. 'Could he be short of money, do you think?'

'No. As a board director of the Lange Publishing Company he draws a substantial salary. He also has income from a large trust that was set up for him by his father. It's true, he likes to gamble. But worse than that, for me, is that he is the owner of a perfectly useless title called *Urania*.'

'Title?'

'A magazine. About astrology, or some such rubbish. It's done nothing but lose money since the day he bought it.' She lit another cigarette and sucked at it with lips puckered like she was going to whistle a tune. 'And he knows that if he were ever really short of money, then he would only have to come and ask me.'

I smiled ruefully. 'I know I'm not what you might call cute, but have you ever thought of adopting someone like me?' She laughed at that, and I added: 'He sounds like a very fortunate young man.'

'He's very spoiled, that's what he is. And he's not so young any more.' She stared into space, her eyes apparently following her cigarette smoke. 'For a rich widow like myself, Reinhard is what people in business call "a loss leader". There is no disappointment in life that begins to compare with one's disappointment in one's only son.'

'Really? I've heard it said that children are a blessing as one gets older.'

'You know, for a cynic you're beginning to sound quite sentimental. I can tell you've no children of your own. So let me put you right about one thing, Herr Gunther. Children are the reflection of one's old age. They're the quickest way of growing old I know. The mirror of one's decline. Mine most of all.'

The dog yawned and jumped off her lap as if having heard it many times before. On the floor it stretched and ran towards the door where it turned and looked back expectantly at its mistress. Unperturbed at this display of canine hubris, she got up to let the brute out of the room.

'So what happens now?' she said, coming back to her chaise longue.

'We wait for another note. I'll handle the next cash delivery. But until then I think it might be a good idea if I were to check into Kindermann's clinic for a few days. I'd like to know a little more about your son's friend.'

'I suppose that's what you mean by expenses, is it?'

'I'll try to make it a short stay.'

'See that you do,' she said, affecting a schoolmistressy sort of tone. 'The Kindermann Clinic is a hundred marks a day.'

I whistled. 'Very respectable.'

'And now I must excuse myself, Herr Gunther,' she said. 'I have a meeting to prepare for.' I pocketed my cash and then we shook hands, after which I picked up the folder she had given me and pointed my suit at the door.

I walked back along the dusty corridor and through the hall. A voice barked: 'You just hang on there. I got to let you out. Frau Lange don't like it if I don't see her guests out myself.'

I put my hand on the doorknob and found something sticky there. 'Your warm personality, no doubt.' I jerked the door open irritatedly as the black cauldron waddled across the hall. 'Don't trouble,' I said inspecting my hand. 'You just get on back to whatever it is that you do around this dustbowl.'

'Been a long time with Frau Lange,' she growled. 'She never had no complaints.'

I wondered if blackmail came into it at all. After all, you have to have a good reason to keep a guard-dog that doesn't bark. I couldn't see where affection might possibly fit into it either – not with this woman. It was more probable that you could grow attached to a river crocodile. We stared at each other for a moment, after which I said, 'Does the lady always smoke that much?'

The black thought for a moment, wondering whether or not it was a trick question. Eventually she decided that it wasn't. 'She always has a nail in her mouth, and that's a fact.'

'Well, that must be the explanation,' I said. 'With all that cigarette smoke around her, I bet she doesn't even know you're there.' She swore under her searing breath and slammed the door in my face.

I had lots to think about as I drove back along Kurfürstendamm towards the city centre. I thought about Frau Lange's case and then her thousand marks in my pocket. I thought about a short break in a nice comfortable sanitarium at her expense, and the opportunity it offered me, temporarily at least, to escape Bruno and his pipe; not to mention Arthur Nebe and Heydrich. Maybe I'd even sort out my insomnia and my depression.

But most of all I thought of how I could ever have given my business card and home telephone number to some Austrian flower I'd never even heard of.

3

Wednesday, 31 August

The area south of Königstrasse, in Wannsee, is home to all
sorts of private clinics and hospitals – the smart shiny kind,
where they use as much ether on the floors and windows as
they do on the patients themselves. As far as treatment is
concerned they are inclined to be egalitarian. A man could be
possessed of the constitution of an African bull elephant and
still they would be happy to treat him like he was shell-
shocked, with a couple of lipsticked nurses to help him with
the heavier brands of toothbrush and lavatory paper, always
provided he could pay for it. In Wannsee, your bank balance
matters more than your blood pressure.

Kindermann's clinic stood off a quiet road in a large but
well-behaved sort of garden that sloped down to a small backwater off the main lake and included, among the many elm
and chestnut trees, a colonnaded pier, a boathouse and a
Gothic folly that was so neatly built as to take on a rather
more sensible air. It looked like a medieval telephone
kiosk.

The clinic itself was such a mixture of gable, half-timber,
mullion, crenellated tower and turret as to be more Rhine
castle than sanitarium. Looking at it I half expected to see a
couple of gibbets on the rooftop, or hear a scream from a
distant cellar. But things were quiet, with no sign of anyone
about. There was only the distant sound of a four-man crew
on the lake beyond the trees to provoke the rooks to raucous
comment.

As I walked through the front door I decided that there
would probably be more chance of finding a few inmates
creeping around outside about the time when the bats were
thinking of launching themselves into the twilight.

My room was on the third floor, with an excellent view of
the kitchens. At eighty marks a day it was the cheapest they

had, and skipping around it I couldn't help but wonder if for an extra fifty marks a day I wouldn't have rated something a little bigger, like a laundry-basket. But the clinic was full. My room was all they had available, said the nurse who showed me up there.

She was a cute one. Like a Baltic fishwife but without the quaint country conversation. By the time she had turned down my bed and told me to get undressed I was almost breathless with excitement. First Frau Lange's maid, and then this one, as much a stranger to lipstick as a pterodactyl. It wasn't as if there weren't prettier nurses about. I'd seen plenty downstairs. They must have figured that with a very small room the least they could do would be to give me a very large nurse in compensation.

'What time does the bar open?' I said. Her sense of humour was no less pleasing than her beauty.

'There's no alcohol allowed in here,' she said, snatching the unlit cigarette from my lips. 'And strictly no smoking. Dr Meyer will be along to see you presently.'

'So what's he, the second-class deck? Where's Dr Kindermann?'

'The doctor is at a conference in Bad Neuheim.'

'What's he doing there, staying at a sanitarium? When does he come back here?'

'The end of the week. Are you a patient of Dr Kindermann, Herr Strauss?'

'No, no I'm not. But for eighty marks a day I had hoped I would be.'

'Dr Meyer is a very capable physician, I can assure you.' She frowned at me impatiently, as she realized that I hadn't yet made a move to get undressed, and started to make a tutting noise that sounded like she was trying to be nice to a cockatoo. Clapping her hands sharply, she told me to hurry up and get into bed as Dr Meyer would wish to examine me. Judging that she was quite capable of doing it for me, I decided not to resist. Not only was my nurse ugly, but she was also possessed of a bedside manner that must have been acquired in a market garden.

When she'd gone I settled down to read in bed. Not the kind of read you would describe as gripping, so much as incredible. Yes, that was the word: incredible. There had always been weird, occult magazines in Berlin, like *Zenit* and *Hagal*, but from the shores of the Maas to the banks of the Memel there was nothing to compare with the grabbers that were writing for Reinhard Lange's magazine, *Urania*. Leafing through it for just fifteen minutes was enough to convince me that Lange was probably a complete spinner. There were articles entitled 'Wotanism and the Real Origins of Christianity', 'The Superhuman Powers of the Lost Citizens of Atlantis', 'The World Ice Theory Explained', 'Esoteric Breathing Exercises for Beginners', 'Spiritualism and Race Memory', 'The Hollow-Earth Doctrine', 'Anti-Semitism as Theocratic Legacy', etc. For a man who could publish this sort of nonsense, the blackmail of a parent, I thought, was probably the sort of mundane activity that occupied him between ariosophical revelations.

Even Dr Meyer, himself no obvious testament to the ordinary, was moved to remark upon my choice of reading matter.

'Do you often read this kind of thing?' he asked, turning the magazine over in his hands as if it had been a variety of curious artefact dug from some Trojan ruin by Heinrich Schliemann.

'No, not really. It was curiosity that made me buy it.'

'Good. An abnormal interest in the occult is often an indication of an unstable personality.'

'You know, I was just thinking the same thing myself.'

'Not everyone would agree with me in that, of course. But the visions of many modern religious figures – St Augustine, Luther – are most probably neurotic in their origins.'

'Is that so?'

'Oh yes.'

'What does Dr Kindermann think?'

'Oh, Kindermann holds some very unusual theories. I'm not sure I understand his work, but he's a very brilliant man.' He picked up my wrist. 'Yes indeed, a very brilliant man.'

The doctor, who was Swiss, wore a three-piece suit of green

tweed, a great moth of a bow-tie, glasses and the long white chin-beard of an Indian holy man. He pushed up my pyjama sleeve and hung a little pendulum above the underside of my wrist. He watched it swing and revolve for a while before pronouncing that the amount of electricity I was giving off indicated that I was feeling abnormally depressed and anxious about something. It was an impressive little performance, but none the less bullet-proof, given that most of the folk who checked into the clinic were probably depressed or anxious about something, even if it was only their bill.

'How are you sleeping?' he said.

'Badly. Couple of hours a night.'

'Do you ever have nightmares?'

'Yes, and I don't even like cheese.'

'Any recurring dreams?'

'Nothing specific.'

'And what about your appetite?'

'I don't have one to speak of.'

'Your sex life?'

'Same as my appetite. Not worth mentioning.'

'Do you think much about women?'

'All the time.'

He scribbled a few notes, stroked his beard, and said: 'I'm prescribing extra vitamins and minerals, especially magnesium. I'm also going to put you on a sugar-free diet, lots of raw vegetables and kelp. We'll help get rid of some of the toxins in you with a course of blood-purification tablets. I also recommend that you exercise. There's an excellent swimming-pool here, and you may even care to try a rainwater bath, which you'll find to be most invigorating. Do you smoke?' I nodded. 'Try giving up for a while.' He snapped his notebook shut. 'Well, that should all help with your physical well-being. Along the way we'll see if we can't effect some improvement in your mental state with psychotherapeutic treatment.'

'Exactly what is psychotherapy, Doctor? Forgive me, but I thought that the Nazis had branded it as decadent.'

'Oh no, no. Psychotherapy is not psychoanalysis. It places no reliance on the unconscious mind. That sort of thing is all right for Jews, but it has no relevance to Germans. As you yourself will now appreciate, no psychotherapeutic treatment is ever pursued in isolation from the body. Here we aim to relieve the symptoms of mental disorder by adjusting the attitudes that have led to their occurrence. Attitudes are conditioned by personality, and the relation of a personality to its environment. Your dreams are only of interest to me to the extent that you are having them at all. To treat you by attempting to interpret your dreams, and to discover their sexual significance is, quite frankly, nonsensical. Now that is decadent.' He chuckled warmly. 'But that's a problem for Jews, and not you, Herr Strauss. Right now, the most import-ant thing is that you enjoy a good night's sleep.' So saying he picked up his medical bag and took out a syringe and a small bottle which he placed on the bedside table.

'What's that?' I said uncertainly.

'Hyoscine,' he said, rubbing my arm with a pad of surgical spirit.

The injection felt cold as it crept up my arm, like embalming fluid. Seconds after recognizing that I would have to find another night on which to snoop around Kindermann's clinic, I felt the ropes mooring me to consciousness slacken, and I was adrift, moving slowly away from the shore, Meyer's voice already too far away for me to hear what he was saying.

After four days in the clinic I was feeling better than I had felt in four months. As well as my vitamins, and my diet of kelp and raw vegetables, I'd tried hydrotherapy, naturotherapy and a solarium treatment. My state of health had been further diagnosed through examination of my irises, my palms and my fingernails, which revealed me as calcium-deficient; and a technique of autogenic relaxation had been taught to me. Dr Meyer was making progress with his Jungian 'totality ap-proach', as he called it, and was proposing to attack my depression with electrotherapy. And although I hadn't yet managed to search Kindermann's office, I did have a new nurse, a real beauty called Marianne, who remembered Rein-hard Lange staying at the clinic for several months, and had

31

already demonstrated a willingness to discuss her employer and the affairs of the clinic.

She woke me at seven with a glass of grapefruit juice and an almost veterinary selection of pills.

Enjoying the curve of her buttocks and the stretch of her pendulous breasts, I watched her draw back the curtains to reveal a fine sunny day, and wished that she could have revealed her naked body as easily.

'And how are you this beautiful day?' I said.

'Awful,' she grimaced.

'Marianne, you know it's supposed to be the other way around, don't you? I'm the one who is supposed to feel awful, and you're the one who should ask after my health.'

'I'm sorry, Herr Strauss, but I am bored as hell with this place.'

'Well, why don't you jump in here beside me and tell me all about it. I'm very good at listening to other people's problems.'

'I'll bet you're very good at other things as well,' she said, laughing. 'I shall have to put bromide in your fruit-juice.'

'What would be the point of that? I've already got a whole pharmacy swilling around inside of me. I can't see that another chemical would make much difference.'

'You'd be surprised.'

She was a tall, athletic-looking blonde from Frankfurt with a nervous sense of humour and a rather self-conscious smile that indicated a lack of personal confidence. Which was strange, given her obvious attractiveness.

'A whole pharmacy,' she scoffed. 'A few vitamins and something to help you sleep at night. That's nothing compared with some of the others.'

'Tell me about it.'

She shrugged. 'Something to help them wake up, and stimulants to help combat depression.'

'What do they use on the pansies?'

'Oh, them. They used to give them hormones, but it didn't work. So now they try aversion therapy. But despite what they

32

say at the Goering Institute about it being a treatable disorder, in private all the doctors say that the basic condition is hard to influence. Kindermann should know. I think he might be a bit warm himself. I've heard him tell a patient that psychotherapy is only helpful in dealing with the neurotic reactions that may arise from homosexuality. That it helps the patient to stop deluding himself.'

'So then all he has to worry about is Section 175.'

'What's that?'

'The section of the German penal code which makes it a criminal offence. Is that what happened to Reinhard Lange? He was just treated for associated neurotic reactions?' She nodded, and sat herself on the edge of my bed. 'Tell me about this Goering Institute. Any relation to Fat Hermann?'

'Matthias Goering is his cousin. The place exists to provide psychotherapy with the protection of the Goering name. If it weren't for him there would be very little mental health in Germany worthy of the name. The Nazis would have destroyed psychiatric medicine merely because its leading light is a Jew. The whole thing is the most enormous piece of hypocrisy. A lot of them continue privately to subscribe to Freud, while denouncing him in public. Even the so-called Orthopaedic Hospital for the SS near Ravensbrück is nothing but a mental hospital for the SS. Kindermann is a consultant there, as well as being one of the Goering Institute's founding members.'

'So who funds the Institute?'

'The Labour Front, and the Luftwaffe.'

'Of course. The prime minister's petty-cash box.'

Marianne's eyes narrowed. 'You know, you ask a lot of questions. What are you, a bull or something like that?'

I got out of bed and slipped into my dressing-gown. I said: 'Something like that.'

'Are you working on a case here?' Her eyes widened with excitement. 'Something Kindermann could be involved in?'

I opened the window and leant out for a moment. The morning air was good to breathe, even the stuff coming up from the kitchens. But a cigarette was better. I brought my last packet in from the window ledge and lit one. Marianne's eyes lingered disapprovingly on the cigarette in my hand.

'You shouldn't be smoking, you know.'

'I don't know if Kindermann is involved or not,' I said. 'That's what I was hoping to find out when I came here.'

'Well, you don't have to worry about me,' she said fiercely. 'I couldn't care what happens to him.' She stood up with her arms folded, her mouth assuming a harder expression. 'The man is a bastard. You know, just a few weeks ago I worked a whole weekend because nobody else was available. He said he'd pay me double-time in cash. But he still hasn't given me my money. That's the kind of pig he is. I bought a dress. It was stupid of me, I should have waited. Well, now I'm behind with the rent.'

I was debating with myself whether or not she was trying to sell me a story when I saw the tears in her eyes. If it was an act it was a damn good one. Either way it deserved some kind of recognition.

She blew her nose, and said: 'Would you give me a cigarette, please?'

'Sure.' I handed her the pack and then thumbed a match.

'You know, Kindermann knew Freud,' she said, coughing a little with her first smoke. 'At the Vienna Medical School, when he was a student. After graduating he worked for a while at the Salzburg Mental Asylum. He's from Salzburg originally. When his uncle died in 1930, he left him this house, and he decided to turn it into a clinic.'

'It sounds like you know him quite well.'

'Last summer his secretary was sick for a couple of weeks. Kindermann knew I had some secretarial experience and asked me to fill in a while while Tarja was away. I got to know him reasonably well. Well enough to dislike him. I'm not going to stay here much longer. I've had enough, I think. Believe me, there are plenty of others here who feel much the same way.'

'Oh? Think anyone would want to get back at him? Anyone who might have a grudge against him?'

'You're talking about a serious grudge, aren't you? Not just a bit of unpaid overtime.'

34

'I suppose so,' I said, and flicked my cigarette out of the open window.

Marianne shook her head. 'No, wait,' she said. 'There was someone. About three months ago Kindermann dismissed one of the male nurses for being drunk. He was a nasty piece of work, and I don't think anyone was sad to see him go. I wasn't there myself, but I heard that he used some quite strong language to Kindermann when he left.'

'What was his name, this male nurse?'

'Hering, Klaus Hering I think.' She looked at her watch. 'Hey, I've got to be getting on with my work. I can't stay talking to you all morning.'

'One more thing,' I said. 'I need to take a look around Kindermann's office. Can you help?' She started to shake her head. 'I can't do it without you, Marianne. Tonight?'

'I don't know. What if we get caught?'

'The "we" part doesn't come into it. You keep a look-out, and if someone finds you, you say that you heard a noise, and that you were investigating. I'll have to take my chances. Maybe I'll say I was sleepwalking.'

'Oh, that's a good one.'

'Come on, Marianne, what do you say?'

'All right, I'll do it. But leave it until after midnight, that's when we lock up. I'll meet you in the solarium at around 12.30.'

Her expression changed as she saw me slide a fifty from my wallet. I crushed it into the breast pocket of her crisp white uniform. She took it out again.

'I can't take this,' she said. 'You shouldn't.' I held her fist shut to stop her returning the note.

'Look, it's just something to help tide you over, at least until you get paid for your overtime.' She looked doubtful.

'I don't know,' she said. 'It doesn't seem right somehow. This is as much as I make in a week. It'll do a lot more than just tide me over.'

'Marianne,' I said, 'it's nice to make ends meet, but it's even nicer if you can tie a bow.'

4

Monday, 5 September

'The doctor told me that the electrotherapy has the temporary side-effect of disturbing the memory. Otherwise I feel great.'

Bruno looked at me anxiously. 'You're sure?'

'Never felt better.'

'Well, rather you than me, being plugged in like that.' He snorted. 'So whatever you managed to find out while you were in Kindermann's place is temporarily mislaid inside your head, is that it?'

'It's not quite that bad. I managed to take a look around his office. And there was a very attractive nurse who told me all about him. Kindermann is a lecturer at the Luftwaffe Medical School, and a consultant at the Party's private clinic in Bleibtreustrasse. Not to mention his membership of the Nazi Doctors Association, and the Herrenklub.'

Bruno shrugged. 'The man is gold-plated. So what?'

'Gold-plated, but not exactly treasured. He isn't very popular with his staff. I found out the name of someone who he sacked and who might be the type to bear him a grudge.'

'It's not much of a reason, is it? Being sacked?'

'According to my nurse, Marianne, it was common knowledge that he got the push for stealing drugs from the clinic dispensary. That he was probably selling them on the street. So he wasn't exactly the Salvation Army type, was he?'

'This fellow have a name?'

I thought hard for a moment, and then produced my notebook from my pocket. 'It's all right,' I said, 'I wrote it down.'

'A detective with a crippled memory. That's just great.'

'Slow your blood down, I've got it. His name is Klaus Hering.'

'I'll see if the Alex has anything on him.' He picked up the telephone and made the call. It only took a couple of minutes. We paid a bull fifty marks a month for the service. But Klaus Hering was clean.

'So where is the money supposed to go?'

He handed me the anonymous note which Frau Lange had received the previous day and which had prompted Bruno to telephone me at the clinic.

'The lady's chauffeur brought it round here himself,' he explained, as I read over the blackmailer's latest composition of threats and instructions. 'A thousand marks to be placed in a Gerson carrier-bag and left in a wastepaper basket outside the Chicken House at the Zoo, this afternoon.'

I glanced out of the window. It was another warm day, and without a doubt there would be plenty of people at the Zoo.

'It's a good place,' I said. 'He'll be hard to spot and even harder to tail. There are, as far as I remember, four exits to the Zoo.' I found a map of Berlin in my drawer and spread it out on the desk. Bruno came and stood over my shoulder.

'So how do we play it?' he asked.

'You handle the drop, I'll play the sightseer.'

'Want me to wait by one of the exits afterwards?'

'You've got a four-to-one chance. Which way would you choose?'

He studied the map for a minute and then pointed to the canal exit. 'Lichtenstein Bridge. I'd have a car waiting on the other side in Rauch Strasse.'

'Then you'd better have a car there yourself.'

'How long do I wait? I mean, the Zoo's open until nine o'clock at night, for Christ's sake.'

'The Aquarium exit shuts at six, so my guess is that he'll show up before then, if only to keep his options open. If you haven't seen us by then, go home and wait for my call.'

I stepped out of the airship-sized glass shed that is the Zoo Station, and walked across Hardenbergplatz to Berlin Zoo's main entrance, which is just a short way south of the Planetarium. I bought a ticket that included the Aquarium, and a guidebook to make myself look more plausibly a tourist, and made my way first to the Elephant House. A strange man sketching there covered his pad secretively and shied away at my approach. Leaning on the rail of the enclosure I watched this curious behaviour repeated again and again as other visitors came over, until by and by the man found himself standing next to me again. Irritated at the presumption that I should be at all interested in his miserable sketch, I craned my neck over his shoulder, waving my camera close to his face.

'Perhaps you should take up photography,' I said brightly. He snarled something and cowered away. One for Dr Kindermann, I thought. A real spinner. At any kind of show or exhibition, it is always the people that present you with the most interesting spectacle.

It was another fifteen minutes before I saw Bruno. He hardly seemed to see me or the elephants as he walked by, holding the small Gerson store carrier-bag that contained the money under his arm. I let him get well in front, and then followed.

Outside the Chicken House a small red-brick, half-timbered building covered in ivy, which looked more like a village beer-cellar than a home to wild fowl, Bruno stopped, glanced around him, and then dropped the bag into a wastepaper basket that was beside a garden-seat. He walked quickly away, east, and in the direction of his chosen station at the exit on the Landwehr Canal.

A high crag of sandstone, the habitat of a herd of Barbary sheep, was situated opposite the Chicken House. According to the guidebook it was one of the Zoo's landmarks, but I thought it looked too theatrical to be a good imitation of the sort of place that would have been inhabited by these trotting rags in the wild. It was more like something you would have found on the stage of some grossly overblown production of *Parsifal*, if such a thing were humanly possible. I hovered there awhile, reading about the sheep and finally taking several photographs of these supremely uninteresting creatures.

Behind Sheep Rock was a high viewing tower from which it was possible to see the front of the Chicken House, indeed the whole of the Zoo, and I thought it looked like ten pfennigs well-spent for anyone wanting to make sure that he wasn't about to walk into a trap. With this thought in mind I was meandering away from the Chicken House, and towards the lake when a youth of about eighteen, with dark hair and a grey sports jacket, appeared from the far side of the Chicken House. Without even looking around he quickly picked the Gerson bag out of the wastepaper basket and dropped it into another carrier, this one from the Ka-De-We store. Then he walked briskly past me and, after a decent interval, I followed.

Outside the Moorish-style Antelope House the youth paused briefly beside the group of bronze centaurs that stood there, and, giving the appearance of one engrossed in his guidebook, I walked straight on to the Chinese Temple, where, hidden by several people, I stopped to watch him out of the corner of my eye. He came on again, and I guessed that he was making for the Aquarium and the south exit.

Fish were the last thing that you expected to see in the great green building that connects the Zoo with Budapester Strasse. A life-sized stone Iguanadon towered predatorily beside the door, above which was the head of yet another dinosaur. Elsewhere, the walls of the Aquarium were covered with murals and stone reliefs that depicted the kind of prehistoric beasts which would have swallowed a shark whole. It was to the Aquarium's other inhabitants, the reptiles, that these antediluvian decorations were in fact preferable.

Seeing my man disappear through the front door, and realizing that the Aquarium's dark interior would make it easy to lose him, I quickened my pace. Once inside I saw how much more probable than possible this actually was, since the sheer number of visitors made it difficult to see where he had gone.

Assuming the worst, I hurried towards the other door that led out on to the street, and almost collided with the youth as he turned away from a tank that contained a creature that looked more like a floating mine than a fish. For a few seconds he hesitated at the foot of the great marble stairs that led up to the reptiles before walking down to the exit, and out of the Aquarium and the Zoo.

Outside on Budapester Strasse I fell in behind a group of

schoolchildren as far as Ansbacher Strasse, where I got rid of the guidebook, slipped into the raincoat I was carrying, and turned up the brim of my hat. Minor alterations to your appearance are essential when following someone. There's that, and staying in the open. It's only when you start to cower in doorways that your man will get suspicious. But this fellow never even looked back as he crossed Wittenberg Platz, and went through the front door of Kaufhaus des Westens, the Ka-De-We, Berlin's biggest department store.

I had thought that he had used the other carrier only to throw a tail off, somebody who might have been waiting at one of the exits on the look out for a man carrying a Gerson bag. But now I realized that we were also in for a switch.

The beer-restaurant on Ka-De-We's third floor was full of lunchtime drinkers. They sat stolidly facing plates of sausage, and glasses of beer that were the height of table lamps. The youth carrying the money wandered among the tables as if looking for someone, and finally sat down opposite a man wearing a blue suit, sitting alone. He placed the carrier-bag with the money beside another just like it on the floor.

Finding an empty table I sat down just in sight of them, and picked up a menu which I affected to study. A waiter appeared. I told him I hadn't made up my mind, and he went away again.

Now the man in the blue suit stood up, laid some coins on the table and, bending down, picked up the carrier bag with the money. Neither one of them said a word.

When the blue suit went out of the restaurant I followed him, obeying the cardinal rule of all cases involving ransom: you always go after the money.

With its massive arched portico and twin, minaret-like towers, there was a monolithic, almost Byzantine quality about the Metropol Theatre on Nollendorfplatz. Appearing on reliefs at the foot of the great buttresses were intertwined as many as twenty naked figures, and it seemed like the ideal kind of place to try your hand at a spot of virgin sacrifice. On the righthand side of the theatre was a big wooden gateway, and through it the car park, as big as a football pitch, which backed on to several tall tenements.

It was to one of these buildings that I followed Blue Suit and the money. I checked the names on the mailboxes in the downstairs hall, and was pleased to find a K. Hering residing at number nine. Then I called Bruno from a phone box at the U-Bahn station across the road.

When my partner's old DKW pulled up at the wooden gate, I got into the passenger seat and pointed across to the other side of the car park, nearest to the tenements, where there were still quite a few spaces left, the ones nearer the theatre itself having been taken by those going to the eight o'clock show.

'That's our man's place there,' I said. 'On the second floor. Number nine.'

'Did you get a name?'

'It's our friend from the clinic, Klaus Hering.'

'That's nice and tidy. What does he look like?'

'He's about my height, thin, wiry build, fair hair, rimless glasses, aged about thirty. When he went in he was wearing a blue suit. If he leaves see if you can't get in there and find the pansy's love letters. Otherwise just stay put. I'm going to see the client for further instructions. If she's got any I'll be back tonight. If not, then I'll relieve you at six o'clock tomorrow morning. Any questions?' Bruno shook his head. 'Want me to ring the wife?'

'No thanks. Katia's used to my odd hours by now, Bernie. Anyway, me not being there will help to clear the air. I had another argument with my boy Heinrich when I got back from the Zoo.'

'What was it this time?'

'He's only gone and joined the motorized Hitler Youth, that's all.'

I shrugged. 'He would have to have joined the regular Hitler Youth sooner or later.'

'The little swine didn't have to be in such a damned hurry to join, that's all. He could have waited to be taken in, like the rest of the lads in his class.'

41

'Come on, look on the bright side. They'll teach him how to drive and look after an engine. They'll still turn him into a Nazi, of course, but at least he'll be a Nazi with a skill.'

Sitting in a taxi back to Alexanderplatz where I had left my car, I reflected that the prospect of his son acquiring mechanical skills probably wasn't much of a consolation to a man who, at the same age as Heinrich, had been a junior cycling champion. And he was right about one thing: Heinrich really was a perfect little swine.

I didn't call Frau Lange to let her know I was coming, and although it was only eight o'clock by the time I got to Herbert-strasse, the house looked dark and uninviting, as if those living there were out, or had retired to bed. But that's one of the more positive aspects of this job. If you've cracked the case then you are always assured of a warm welcome, no matter how unprepared they are for your arrival.

I parked the car, went up the steps to the front door and pulled the bell. Almost immediately a light came on in the window above the door, and after a minute or so the door opened to reveal the black cauldron's ill-tempered face.

'Do you know what time it is?'

'It's just gone eight,' I said. 'The curtains are going up at theatres all over Berlin, diners in restaurants are still scrutinizing the menu and mothers are just thinking that it's about time their children were in bed. Is Frau Lange at home?'

'She's not dressed for no gentlemen callers.'

'Well that's all right. I haven't brought her any flowers or chocolates. And I'm certainly not a gentleman.'

'You spoke the truth there all right.'

'That one was for free. Just to put you in a good enough mood to do as you're told. This is business, urgent business, and she'll want to see me or know the reason why I wasn't let in. So why don't you run along and tell her I'm here.'

I waited in the same room on the sofa with the dolphin armrests. I didn't like it any better the second time, not least because it was now covered with the ginger hairs of an enormous cat, which lay asleep on a cushion underneath a long oak sideboard. I was still picking the hairs off my trousers when Frau Lange came into the room. She was wearing a green silk dressing-gown of the sort that left the tops of her big breasts on show like the twin humps of some pink sea-monster, matching slippers, and she carried an unlit cigarette in her fingers. The dog stood dumbly at her corn-plastered heel, its nose wrinkling at the overpowering smell of English lavender that trailed off Frau Lange's body like an old feather-boa. Her voice was even more masculine than I had remembered.

'Just tell me that Reinhard had nothing to do with it,' she said imperiously.

'Nothing at all,' I said.

The sea-monster sank a little as she breathed a sigh of relief. 'Thank God for that,' she said. 'And do you know who it is that has been blackmailing me, Herr Gunther?'

'Yes. A man who used to work at Kindermann's clinic. A male nurse called Klaus Hering. I don't suppose that the name will mean much to you, but Kindermann had to dismiss him a couple of months ago. My guess is that while he was working there he stole the letters that your son wrote to Kindermann.'

She sat down and lit her cigarette. 'But if his grudge was against Kindermann, why pick on me?'

'I'm just guessing, you understand, but I'd say that a lot has to do with your wealth. Kindermann's rich, but I doubt he's a tenth as rich as you, Frau Lange. What's more, it's probably mostly tied up in that clinic. He's also got quite a few friends in the SS, so Hering may have decided that it was simply safer to squeeze you. On the other hand, he may have already tried Kindermann and failed to get anywhere. As a psychotherapist he could probably easily explain your son's letters as the fantasies of a former patient. After all, it's not uncommon for a patient to grow attached to his doctor, even somebody as apparently loathsome as Kindermann.'

'You've met him?'

'No, but that's what I hear from some of the staff working at the clinic.'

'I see. Well, now what happens?'

'As I remember, you said that would be up to your son.'

43

'All right. Supposing that he wants you to go on handling things for us. After all, you've made pretty short work of it so far. What would your next course of action be?'

'Right now my partner, Herr Stahlecker, is keeping our friend Hering under surveillance at his apartment on Nollendorfplatz. As soon as Hering goes out, Herr Stahlecker will try and break in and recover your letters. After that you have three possibilities. One is that you can forget all about it. Another is that you can put the matter in the hands of the police, in which case you run the risk of Hering making allegations against your son. And then you can arrange for Hering to get a good old-fashioned hiding. Nothing too severe, you understand. Just a good scare to warn him off and teach him a lesson. Personally I always favour the third choice. Who knows? It might even result in your recovering some of your money.'

'Oh, I'd like to get my hands on that miserable man.'

'Best leave that sort of thing to me, eh? I'll call you tomorrow and you can tell me what you and your son have decided to do. With any luck we may even have recovered the letters by then.'

I didn't exactly need my arm twisted to have the brandy she offered me by way of celebration. It was excellent stuff that should have been savoured a little. But I was tired, and when she and the sea-monster joined me on the sofa I felt it was time to be going.

About that time I was living in a big apartment on Fasanenstrasse, a little way south of Kurfürstendamm, and within easy reach of all the theatres and better restaurants I never went to.

It was a nice quiet street, all white, mock porticoes and Atlantes supporting elaborate façades on their well-muscled shoulders. Cheap it wasn't. But that apartment and my partner had been my only two luxuries in two years.

The first had been rather more successful for me than the second. An impressive hallway with more marble than the Pergamon Altar led up to the second floor where I had a suite of rooms with ceilings that were as high as trams. German architects and builders were never known for their penny-pinching.

My feet aching like young love, I ran myself a hot bath.

I lay there for a long time, staring up at the stained-glass window which was suspended at right angles to the ceiling, and which served, quite redundantly, to offer some cosmetic division of the bathroom's higher regions. I had never ceased to puzzle as to what possible reason had prompted its construction.

Outside the bathroom window a nightingale sat in the yard's solitary but lofty tree. I felt that I had a lot more confidence in his simple song than the one that Hitler was singing.

I reflected that it was the kind of simplistic comparison my beloved pipe-smoking partner might have relished.

5

Tuesday, 6 September

In the darkness the doorbell rang. Drunk with sleep I reached across to the alarm clock and picked it off the bedside table. It said 4.30 in the morning with still nearly an hour to go before I was supposed to wake up. The doorbell rang again, only this time it seemed more insistent. I switched on a light and went out into the hall.

'Who is it?' I said, knowing well enough that generally it's only the Gestapo who take a pleasure in disturbing people's sleep.

'Haile Selassie,' said a voice. 'Who the fuck do you think it is? Come on, Gunther, open up, we haven't got all night.'

Yes, it was the Gestapo all right. There was no mistaking their finishing-school manners.

I opened the door and allowed a couple of beer barrels wearing hats and coats to barge past me.

'Get dressed,' said one. 'You've got an appointment.'

'Shit, I am going to have to have a word with that secretary of mine,' I yawned. 'I forgot all about it.'

'Funny man,' said the other.

'What, is this Heydrich's idea of a friendly invitation?'

'Save your mouth to suck on your cigarette, will you? Now climb into your suit or we'll take you down in your fucking pyjamas.'

I dressed carefully, choosing my cheapest German Forest suit and an old pair of shoes. I stuffed my pockets with cigarettes. I even took along a copy of the *Berlin Illustrated News*. When Heydrich invites you for breakfast it's always best to be prepared for an uncomfortable and possibly indefinite visit.

Immediately south of Alexanderplatz, on Dircksenstrasse, the Imperial Police Praesidium and the Central Criminal Courts faced each other in an uneasy confrontation: legal administration versus justice. It was like two heavyweights standing toe to toe at the start of a fight, each trying to stare the other down.

Of the two, the Alex, also sometimes known as 'Grey Misery', was the more brutal looking, having a Gothic-fortress design with a dome-shaped tower at each corner, and two smaller towers atop the front and rear façades. Occupying some 16,000 square metres it was an object lesson in strength if not in architectural merit.

The slightly smaller building that housed the central Berlin courts also had the more pleasing aspect. Its neo-Baroque sandstone façade possessed something rather more subtle and intelligent than its opponent.

There was no telling which one of these two giants was likely to emerge the winner; but when both fighters have been paid to take a fall it makes no sense to stick around and watch the end of the contest.

Dawn was breaking as the car drew into Alex's central courtyard. It was still too early for me to have asked myself why Heydrich should have had me brought here, instead of Sipo, the Security Service headquarters in the Wilhelmstrasse, where Heydrich had his own office.

My two male escorts ushered me to an interview room and left me alone. There was a good deal of shouting going on in the room next door and that gave me something to think about. That bastard Heydrich. Never quite did it the way you expected. I took out a cigarette and lit it nervously. With the cigarette burning in a corner of my sour-tasting mouth I stood up and went over to the grimy window. All I could see were other windows like my own, and on the rooftop the aerial of the police radio station. I ground the cigarette into the Mexico Mixture coffee-tin that served as an ashtray and sat down at the table again.

I was supposed to get nervous. I was meant to feel their power. That way Heydrich would find me all the more inclined to agree with him when eventually he decided to show up. Probably he was still fast asleep in his bed.

If that was how I was supposed to feel I decided to do it differently. So instead of breakfasting on my fingernails and wearing out my cheap shoes pacing round the room, I tried a little self-relaxation, or whatever it was that Dr Meyer had called it. Eyes closed, breathing deeply through my nose, my mind concentrated on a simple shape, I managed to remain calm. So calm I didn't even hear the door. After a while I opened my eyes and stared into the face of the bull who had come in. He nodded slowly.

'Well, you're a cool one,' he said, picking up my magazine.

'Aren't I just?' I looked at my watch. Half an hour had gone by. 'You took your time.'

'Did I? I'm sorry. Glad you weren't bored though. I can see you expected to be here a while.'

'Doesn't everyone?' I shrugged, watching a boil the size of a wheel-nut rub at the edge of his greasy collar.

When he spoke his voice came from deep within him, his scarred chin dipping down to his broad chest like a cabaret tenor.

'Oh yes,' he said. 'You're a private detective, aren't you? A professional smart-ass. Do you mind me asking, what kind of a living do you people make?'

'What's the matter, the bribes not coming in regular enough for you?' He forced himself to smile through that one. 'I do all right.'

'Don't you find that it gets lonely? I mean, you're a bull down here, you've got friends.'

'Don't make me laugh. I've got a partner, so I get all the friendly shoulder to cry on I need, right?'

'Oh yes. Your partner. That would be Bruno Stahlecker, wouldn't it?'

'That's right. I could give you his address if you like, but I think he's married.'

'All right, Gunther. You've proved you're not scared. No need to make a performance out of it. You were picked up at 4.30. It's now seven –'

'Ask a policeman if you want the right time.'

'– but you still haven't asked anyone why you're here.'

48

'I thought that's what we were talking about.'

'Were we? Assume I'm ignorant. That shouldn't be too difficult for a smart-ass like you. What did we say?'

'Oh shit, look, this is your sideshow, not mine, so don't expect me to bring up the curtain and work the fucking lights. You go right ahead with your act and I'll just try to laugh and clap in the right places.'

'Very well,' he said, his voice hardening. 'So where were you last night?'

'At home.'

'Got an alibi?'

'Yeah. My teddy bear. I was in bed, asleep.'

'And before that?'

'I was seeing a client.'

'Mind telling me who?'

'Look, I don't like this. What are we trawling for? Tell me now, or I don't say another lousy word.'

'We've got your partner downstairs.'

'What's he supposed to have done?'

'What he's done is get himself killed.'

I shook my head. 'Killed?'

'Murdered, to be rather more precise. That's what we usually call it in these sort of circumstances.'

'Shit,' I said, closing my eyes again.

'That's my act, Gunther. And I do expect you to help me with the curtain and the lights.' He jabbed a forefinger against my numb chest. 'So let's have some fucking answers, eh?'

'You stupid bastard. You don't think I had anything to do with it, do you? Christ, I was the only friend he had. When you and all your cute friends here at the Alex managed to have him posted out to some backwater in Spreewald, I was the one who came through for him. I was the one who appreciated that despite his awkward lack of enthusiasm for the Nazis, he was still a good bull.' I shook my head bitterly, and swore again.

'When did you last see him?'

'Last night, around eight o'clock. I left him in the car park behind the Metropol on Nollendorfplatz.'

'Was he working?'

'Yes.'

'Doing what?'

'Tailing someone. No, keeping someone under observation.'

'Someone working in the theatre or living in the apartments?'

I nodded.

'Which was it?'

'I can't tell you. At least, not until I've discussed it with my client.'

'The one you can't tell me about either. Who do you think you are, a priest? This is murder, Gunther. Don't you want to catch the man who killed your partner?'

'What do you think?'

'I think that you ought to consider the possibility that your client had something to do with it. And then suppose he says, "Herr Gunther, I forbid you to discuss this unfortunate matter with the police." Where does that get us?' He shook his head. 'No fucking deal, Gunther. You tell me or you tell the judge.' He stood up and went to the door. 'It's up to you. Take your time. I'm not in any hurry.'

He closed the door behind him, leaving me with my guilt for ever having wished ill to Bruno and his harmless pipe.

About an hour later the door opened and a senior SS officer came into the room.

'I was wondering when you'd show up,' I said.

Arthur Nebe sighed and shook his head.

'I'm sorry about Stahlecker,' he said. 'He was a good man. Naturally you'll want to see him.' He motioned me to follow him. 'And then I'm afraid you'll have to see Heydrich.'

Beyond an outer office and an autopsy-theatre where a pathologist stood working on the naked body of an adolescent girl was a long, cool room with rows of tables stretching out in front of me. On a few of them lay human bodies, some naked, some covered with sheets, and some like Bruno still clothed and looking more like items of lost luggage than anything human.

I walked over and took a long hard look at my dead partner.

The front of his shirt looked as though he had spilt a whole bottle of red wine on himself, and his mouth gaped open like he'd been stabbed sitting in a dentist's chair. There are lots of ways of winding up a partnership, but they didn't come much more permanent than this one.

'I never knew he wore a plate,' I said absently, catching the glint of something metallic inside Bruno's mouth. 'Stabbed?'

'Once, through the pump. They reckon under the ribs and up through the pit of the stomach.'

I picked up each of his hands and inspected them carefully. 'No protection cuts,' I said. 'Where did they find him?'

'Metropol Theatre car park,' said Nebe.

I opened his jacket, noticing the empty shoulder-holster, and then unbuttoned the front of his shirt, which was still sticky with his blood, to inspect the wound. It was difficult to tell without seeing him cleaned up a bit, but the entry looked split, as if the knife had been rocked inside him.

'Whoever did it knew how to kill a man with a knife,' I said. 'This looks like a bayonet wound.' I sighed and shook my head. 'I've seen enough. There's no need to put his wife through this, I'll make the formal identification. Does she know yet?'

Nebe shrugged. 'I don't know.' He led the way back through the autopsy-theatre. 'But I expect someone will tell her soon enough.'

The pathologist, a young fellow with a large moustache, had stopped work on the girl's body to have a smoke. The blood from his gloved hand had stained the cigarette paper and there was some of it on his lower lip. Nebe stopped and regarded the scene before him with more than a little distaste.

'Well?' he said angrily. 'Is it another one?'

The pathologist exhaled lazily and pulled a face. 'At this early stage, it certainly looks that way,' he said. 'She's wearing all the right accessories.'

'I see.' It was easily apparent that Nebe didn't much care for the young pathologist. 'I trust your report will be rather more detailed than the last one. Not to mention more accurate.' He turned abruptly and walked quickly away, adding loudly over his shoulder, 'And make sure I have it as soon as possible.'

In Nebe's staff-car, on the way to the Wilhelmstrasse, I asked him what it was all about. 'Back there, in the autopsy-theatre, I mean.'

'My friend,' he said, 'I think that's what you're about to find out.'

The headquarters of Heydrich's SD, the Security Service, at number 102 Wilhelmstrasse, seemed innocuous enough from the outside. Even elegant. At each end of an Ionic colonnade was a square, two-storey gatehouse. and an archway that led into a courtyard behind. A screen of trees made it difficult to see what lay beyond, and only the presence of two sentries told you that here was an official building of some sort.

We drove through the gate, past a neat shrub-lined lawn about the size of a tennis-court, and stopped outside a beautiful, three-storey building with arched windows that were as big as elephants. Stormtroopers jumped to open the car doors and we got out.

The interior wasn't quite what I had expected of Sipo HQ. We waited in a hall, the central feature of which was an ornate gilt staircase, decorated with fully-formed caryatids, and enormous chandeliers. I looked at Nebe, allowing my eyebrows to inform him that I was favourably impressed.

'It's not bad, is it?' he said, and taking me by the arm he led me to the French windows which looked out on to a magnificent landscaped garden. Beyond this, to the west, could be seen the modern outline of Gropius's Europa Haus, while to the north, the southern wing of Gestapo headquarters on Prinz Albrecht Strasse was clearly visible. I had good reason to recognize it, having once been detained there awhile at Heydrich's order.

At the same time, appreciating the difference between the SD, or Sipo as the Security Service was sometimes called, and the Gestapo was a rather more elusive matter, even for some of the people who worked for these two organizations. As far as I could understand the distinction, it was just like Bockwurst and Frankfurter: they have their special names, but they look and taste exactly the same.

What was easy to perceive was that with this building, the Prinz Albrecht Palais, Heydrich had done very well for himself. Perhaps even better than his putative master, Himmler, who now occupied the building next door to Gestapo headquarters, in what was formerly the Hotel Prinz Albrecht Strasse. There was no doubt that the old hotel, now called SS-Haus, was bigger than the Palais. But as with sausage, taste is seldom a question of size.

I heard Arthur Nebe's heels click, and looking round I saw that the Reich's crown prince of terror had joined us at the window.

Tall, skeletally thin, his long, pale face lacking expression, like some plaster of Paris death-mask, and his Jack Frost fingers clasped behind his ramrod-straight back, Heydrich stared outside for a moment or two, saying nothing to either of us.

'Come, gentlemen,' he said eventually, 'it's a beautiful day. Let's walk a bit.' Opening the windows he led the way into the garden, and I noticed how large were his feet and how bandy his legs, as if he had been riding a lot: if the silver Horseman's Badge on his tunic pocket was anything to go by, he probably had.

In the fresh air and sunshine he seemed to become more animated, like some kind of reptile.

'This was the summer house of the first Friedrich Wilhelm,' he said expansively. 'And more recently the Republic used it for important guests such as the King of Egypt, and the British prime minister. Ramsay MacDonald of course, not that idiot with the umbrella. I think it's one of the most beautiful of all the old palaces. I often walk here. This garden connects Sipo with Gestapo headquarters, so it's actually very convenient for me. And it's especially pleasant at this time of year. Do you have a garden, Herr Gunther?'

'No,' I said. 'They've always seemed like a lot of work to me. When I stop work, that's exactly what I do – stop work, not start digging in a garden.'

'That's too bad. At my home in Schlactensee we have a fine garden with its own croquet lawn. Are either of you familiar with the game?'

'No,' we said in unison.

'It's an interesting game; I believe it's very popular in England. It provides an interesting metaphor for the new Germany. Laws are merely hoops through which the people must be driven, with varying degrees of force. But there can be no movement without the mallet – croquet really is a perfect game for a policeman.' Nebe nodded thoughtfully, and Heydrich himself seemed pleased with this comparison. He began to talk quite freely. In brief about some of the things he hated – Freemasons, Catholics, Jehovah's Witnesses, homo-sexuals and Admiral Canaris, the head of the Abwehr, Ger-man Military Secret Intelligence; and at length about some of the things that gave him pleasure – the piano and the cello, fencing, his favourite nightclubs and his family.

'The new Germany,' he said, 'is all about arresting the decline of the family, you know, and establishing a national community of blood. Things are changing. For instance, there are now only 22,787 tramps in Germany, 5,500 fewer than at the start of the year. There are more marriages, more births and half as many divorces. You might well ask me why the family is so important to the Party. Well, I'll tell you. Children. The better our children, the better the future for Germany. So when something threatens those children, then we had better act quickly.'

I found a cigarette and started to pay attention. It seemed like he was coming to the point at last. We stopped at a park bench and sat down, me between Heydrich and Nebe, the chicken-liver in the black-bread sandwich.

'You don't like gardens,' he said thoughtfully. 'What about children? Do you like them?'

'I like them.'

'Good,' he said. 'It's my own personal opinion that it is essential to like them, doing what we do – even the things we must do that are hard because they seem distasteful to us – for otherwise we can find no expression for our humanity. Do you understand what I mean?'

I wasn't sure I did, but I nodded anyway.

'May I be frank with you?' he said. 'In confidence?'

'Be my guest.'

'A maniac is loose on the streets of Berlin, Herr Gunther.'

I shrugged. 'Not so as you would notice,' I said.

Heydrich shook his head impatiently.

'No, I don't mean a stormtrooper beating up some old Jew. I mean a murderer. He's raped and killed and mutilated four young German girls in as many months.'

'I haven't seen anything in the newspapers about it.'

Heydrich laughed. 'The newspapers print what we tell them to print, and there's an embargo on this particular story.'

'Thanks to Streicher and his anti-Semitic rag, it would only get blamed on the Jews,' said Nebe.

'Precisely so,' said Heydrich. 'The last thing I want is an anti-Jewish riot in this city. That sort of thing offends my sense of public order. It offends me as a policeman. When we do decide to clear out the Jews it will be in a proper way, not with a rabble to do it. There are the commercial implications too. A couple of weeks ago some idiots in Nuremberg decided to tear down a synagogue. One that just happened to be well-insured with a German insurance company. It cost them thousands of marks to settle the claim. So you see, race riots are very bad for business.'

'So why tell me?'

'I want this lunatic caught, and caught soon, Gunther.' He looked drily at Nebe. 'In the best traditions of Kripo a man, a Jew, has already confessed to the murders. However, since he was almost certainly in custody at the time of the last murder, it seems that he might actually be innocent, and that an over-zealous element in Nebe's beloved police force may quite simply have framed this man.

'But you, Gunther, you have no racial or political axe to grind. And what is more you have considerable experience in this field of criminal investigation. After all it was you, was it not, who apprehended Gormann, the strangler? That may have been ten years ago, but everyone still remembers the case.' He paused and looked me straight in the eye – an uncomfortable sensation. 'In other words, I want you back, Gunther. Back in Kripo, and tracking down this madman before he kills again.'

I flicked my cigarette-butt into the bushes and stood up. Arthur Nebe stared at me dispassionately, almost as if he disagreed with Heydrich's wish to have me back on the force and leading the investigation in preference to any of his own men. I lit another cigarette and thought for a moment.

'Hell, there must be other bulls,' I said. 'What about the one who caught Kürten, the Beast of Dusseldorf. Why not get him?'

'We've already checked up on him,' said Nebe. 'It would seem that Peter Kürten just gave himself up. Prior to that it was hardly the most efficient investigation.'

'Isn't there anyone else?'

Nebe shook his head.

'You see, Gunther,' said Heydrich, 'we come back to you again. Quite frankly I doubt that there is a better detective in the whole of Germany.'

I laughed and shook my head. 'You're good. Very good. That was a nice speech you made about children and the family, General, but of course we both know that the real reason you're keeping the lid on this thing is because it makes your modern police force look like a bunch of incompetents. Bad for them, bad for you. And the real reason you want me back is not because I'm such a good detective, but because the rest are so bad. The only sort of crimes that today's Kripo is capable of solving are things like race-defilement, or telling a joke about the Führer.'

Heydrich smiled like a guilty dog, his eyes narrowing.

'Are you refusing me, Herr Gunther?' he said evenly.

'I'd like to help, really I would. But your timing is poor. You see, I've only just found out that my partner was murdered last night. You can call me old-fashioned, but I'd like to find out who killed him. Ordinarily I'd leave it to the boys in the Murder Commission, but given what you've just told me it doesn't sound too promising, does it? They've all but accused me of killing him, so who knows, maybe they'll

56

force me to sign a confession, in which case I'll have to work for you in order to escape the guillotine.'

'Naturally I'd heard about Herr Stahlecker's unfortunate death,' he said, standing up again. 'And of course you'll want to make some inquiries. If my men can be of any assistance, no matter how incompetent, then please don't hesitate. However, assuming for a moment that this obstacle were removed, what would be your answer?'

I shrugged. 'Assuming that if I refused I would lose my private investigator's licence –'

'Naturally . . .'

'– gun permit, driving licence –'

'No doubt we'd find some excuse . . .'

'– then probably I would be forced to accept.'

'Excellent.'

'On one condition.'

'Name it.'

'That for the duration of the investigation, I be given the rank of Kriminalkommissar and that I be allowed to run the investigation any way I want.'

'Now wait a minute,' said Nebe. 'What's wrong with your old rank of inspector?'

'Quite apart from the salary,' said Heydrich, 'Gunther is no doubt keen that he should be as free as possible from the interference of senior officers. He's quite right of course. He'll need that kind of rank in order to overcome the prejudices that will undoubtedly accompany his return to Kripo. I should have thought of it myself. It is agreed.'

We walked back to the Palais. Inside the door an SD officer handed Heydrich a note. He read it and then smiled.

'Isn't that a coincidence?' he smiled. 'It would seem that my incompetent police force has found the man who murdered your partner, Herr Gunther. I wonder, does the name Klaus Hering mean anything to you?'

'Stahlecker was keeping a watch on his apartment when he was killed.'

'That is good news. The only sand in the oil is that this Hering fellow would appear to have committed suicide.' He looked at Nebe and smiled. 'Well, we had better go and take a look, don't you think, Arthur? Otherwise Herr Gunther here will think that we have made it up.'

It is difficult to form any clear impression of a man who has been hanged that is not grotesque. The tongue, turgid and protruding like a third lip, the eyes as prominent as a racing dog's balls – these things tend to colour your thoughts a little. So apart from the feeling that he wouldn't be winning the local debating-society prize, there wasn't much to say about Klaus Hering except that he was about thirty years old, slimly built, fair-haired and, thanks in part to his necktie, getting on for tall.

The thing looked clear-cut enough. In my experience hanging is almost always suicide: there are easier ways to kill a man. I have seen a few exceptions, but these were all accidental cases, where the victim had encountered the mishap of vagal inhibition while going about some sado-masochistic perversion. These sexual nonconformists were usually found naked or clothed in female underwear with a spread of pornographic literature to sticky hand, and were always men.

In Hering's case there was no such evidence of death by sexual misadventure. His clothes were such as might have been chosen by his mother; and his hands, which were loose at his sides, were unfettered eloquence to the effect that his homicide had been self-inflicted.

Inspector Strunck, the bull who had interrogated me back at the Alex, explained the matter to Heydrich and Nebe.

'We found this man's name and address in Stahlecker's pocket,' he said. 'There's a bayonet wrapped in newspaper in the kitchen. It's covered in blood, and from the look of it I'd say it was the knife that killed him. There's also a blood-stained shirt that Hering was probably wearing at the time.'

'Anything else?' said Nebe.

'Stahlecker's shoulder-holster was empty, General,' said Strunck. 'Perhaps Gunther might like to tell us if this was his gun or not. We found it in a paper bag with the shirt.'

He handed me a Walther PPK. I put the muzzle to my nose

58

and sniffed the gun-oil. Then I worked the slide and saw that there wasn't even a bullet in the barrel, although the magazine was full. Next I pulled down the trigger-guard. Bruno's initials were scratched neatly on the black metal.

'It's Bruno's gun, all right,' I said. 'It doesn't look like he even got his hand on it. I'd like to see that shirt please.'

Strunck glanced at his Reichskriminaldirektor for approval.

'Let him see it, Inspector,' said Nebe.

The shirt was from C & A, and heavily bloodstained around the stomach area and the right cuff, which seemed to confirm the general set-up.

'It does look as though this was the man who murdered your partner, Herr Gunther,' said Heydrich. 'He came back here and, having changed his clothes, had a chance to reflect upon what he'd done. In a fit of remorse he hanged himself.'

'It would seem so,' I said, without much uncertainty. 'But if you don't mind, General Heydrich, I'd like to take a look round the place. On my own. Just to satisfy my curiosity about one or two things.'

'Very well. Don't be too long, will you?'

With Heydrich, Nebe and the police gone from the apartment, I took a closer look at Klaus Hering's body. Apparently he had tied a length of electrical cord to the banister, slipped a noose over his head, and then simply stepped off the stair. But only an inspection of Hering's hands, wrists and neck itself could tell me if that had really been what happened. There was something about the circumstances of his death, something I couldn't quite put my finger on, that I found questionable. Not least was the fact that he had chosen to change his shirt before hanging himself.

I climbed over the banister on to a small shelf that was made by the top of the stairwell's wall, and knelt down. Leaning forward, I had a good view of the suspension point behind Hering's right ear. The level of tightening of the ligature is always higher and more vertical with a hanging than with a case of strangulation. But here there was a second and altogether more horizontal mark just below the noose which seemed to confirm my doubts. Before hanging himself, Klaus Hering had been strangled to death.

I checked that Hering's shirt collar was the same size as the bloodstained shirt I had examined earlier. It was. Then I climbed back over the banister and stepped down a few stairs. Standing on tiptoe I reached up to examine his hands and wrists. Prising the right hand open I saw the dried blood and then a small shiny object, which seemed to be sticking into the palm. I pulled it out of Hering's flesh and laid it carefully on to the flat of my hand. The pin was bent, probably from the pressure of Hering's fist, and although encrusted with blood, the death's-head motif was unmistakable. It was an SS cap badge.

I paused briefly, trying to imagine what might have happened, certain now that Heydrich must have had a hand in it. Back in the garden at the Prinz Albrecht Palais, had he not asked me himself what my answer to his proposition would be if 'the obstacle' that was my obligation to find Bruno's murderer, were 'removed'? And wasn't this as completely removed as it was possible to achieve? No doubt he had anticipated what my answer would be and had already ordered Hering's murder by the time we went for our stroll.

With these and other thoughts I searched the apartment. I was quick but thorough, lifting mattresses, examining cisterns, rolling back rugs and even leafing through a set of medical textbooks. I managed to find a whole sheet of the old stamps commemorating the fifth anniversary of the Nazis coming to power which had consistently appeared on the blackmail notes to Frau Lange. But of her son's letters to Dr Kindermann there was no sign.

6

Friday, 9 September

It felt strange being back in a case-meeting at the Alex, and even stranger hearing Arthur Nebe refer to me as Kommissar Gunther. Five years had elapsed since the day in June 1933 when, no longer able to tolerate Goering's police purges, I had resigned my rank of Kriminalinspektor in order to become the house detective at the Adlon Hotel. Another few months and they would have probably fired me anyway. If anyone had said then that I'd be back at the Alex as a member of Kripo's upper officer class while a National Socialist government was still in power, I'd have said that he was crazy.

Most of the people seated round the table would almost certainly have expressed the same opinion, if their faces were anything to go by now: Hans Lobbes, the Reichskriminal-direktor's number three and head of Kripo Executive; Count Fritz von der Schulenberg, deputy to Berlin's Police President, and representing the uniformed boys of Orpo. Even the three officers from Kripo, one from Vice and two from the Murder Commission who had been assigned to a new investigating team that was, at my own request, to be a small one, all regarded me with a mixture of fear and loathing. Not that I blamed them much. As far as they were concerned I was Heydrich's spy. In their position I would probably have felt much the same way.

There were two other people in attendance at my invitation, which compounded the atmosphere of distrust. One of these, a woman, was a forensic psychiatrist from the Berlin Charité Hospital. Frau Marie Kalau vom Hofe was a friend of Arthur Nebe, himself something of a criminologist, and attached officially to police headquarters as a consultant in matters of criminal psychology. The other guest was Hans Illmann, Professor of Forensic Medicine at the Friedrich Wilhelm University in Berlin, and formerly senior pathologist at the Alex until his cool hostility to Nazism had obliged Nebe to retire him. Even by Nebe's own admission, Illmann was better than any of the pathologists currently working at the Alex, and so at my request he had been invited to take charge of the forensic medical aspects of the case.

A spy, a woman and a political dissident. It needed only the stenographer to stand and sing 'The Red Flag' for my new colleagues to believe that they were the subject of a practical joke.

Nebe finished his long-winded introduction of me and the meeting was in my hands.

I shook my head. 'I hate bureaucracy,' I said. 'I loathe it. But what is required here is a bureaucracy of information. What is relevant will become clear later on. Information is the lifeblood of any criminal investigation, and if that information is contaminated then you poison the whole investigative body. I don't mind if a man's wrong about something. In this game we're nearly always wrong until we're right. But if I find a member of my team knowingly submitting wrong information, it won't be a matter for a disciplinary tribunal. I'll kill him. That's information you can depend on.

'I'd also like to say this. I don't care who did it. Jew, nigger, pansy, stormtrooper, Hitler Youth Leader, civil servant, motorway construction worker, it's all the same to me. Just as long as he did do it. Which leads me to the subject of Josef Kahn. In case any of you have forgotten, he's the Jew who confessed to the murders of Brigitte Hartmann, Christiane Schulz, and Zarah Lischka. Currently he's a Paragraph Fifty-one in the municipal lunatic asylum at Herzeberge, and one of the purposes of this meeting is to evaluate that confession in the light of the fourth murdered girl, Lotte Winter.

'At this point let me introduce you to Professor Hans Illmann, who has kindly agreed to act as the pathologist in this case. For those of you who don't know him, he's one of the best pathologists in the country, so we're very fortunate to have him working with us.'

Illmann nodded by way of acknowledgement, and carried on with his perfect roll-up. He was a slight man with thin, dark hair, rimless glasses and a small chin beard. He finished licking the paper and poked the roll-up into his mouth, as good as any machine-made cigarette. I marvelled quietly. Medical brilliance counted for nothing beside this kind of subtle dexterity.

'Professor Illmann will take us through his findings after Kriminalassistant Korsch has read the relevant case note.' I nodded at the dark, stocky young man sitting opposite me. There was something artificial about his face, as if it had been made up for him by one of the police artists from Sipo Technical Services, with three definite features and very little else: eyebrows joined in the middle and perched on his over-hanging brows like a falcon preparing for flight; a wizard's long, crafty chin; and a small, Fairbanks-style moustache. Korsch cleared his throat and began speaking in a voice that was an octave higher than I was expecting.

'Brigitte Hartmann,' he read. 'Aged fifteen, of German parents. Disappeared 23 May 1938. Body found in a potato sack on an allotment in Siesdorf, 10 June. She lived with her parents on the Britz Housing Estate, south of Neukölln, and had walked from her home to catch the U-Bahn at Parchimerallee. She was going to visit her aunt in Reinickdorf. The aunt was supposed to meet her at Holzhauser Strasse station, only Brigitte never arrived. The station master at Parchimer didn't remember her getting on the train, but said that he'd had a night on the beer and probably wouldn't have remembered anyway.' This drew a guffaw from along the table.

'Drunken bastard,' snorted Hans Lobbes.

'This is one of the two girls who have since been buried,' said Illmann quietly. 'I don't think there's anything I can add to the findings of the autopsy there. You may proceed, Herr Korsch.'

'Christiane Schulz. Aged sixteen, of German parents. Disappeared 8 June 1938. Body found 2 July, in a tramway tunnel that connects Treptower Park on the righthand bank of the Spree, with the village of Stralau on the other. Half way along the tunnel there's a maintenance point, little more than a recessed archway. That's where the trackman found her body, wrapped in an old tarpaulin.

'Apparently the girl was a singer and often took part in the BdM, the League of German Girls, evening radio programme. On the night of her disappearance she had attended the Funkturm Studios on Masuren-Strasse, and sang a solo – the Hitler Youth song – at seven o'clock. The girl's father works as an engineer at the Arado Aircraft Works in Brandenburg-Neuendorf, and was supposed to pick her up on his way home, at eight o'clock. But the car had a flat tyre and he was twenty minutes late. By the time he got to the studios Christiane was nowhere to be seen and, supposing that she had gone home on her own, he drove back to Spandau. When by 9.30 she still hadn't arrived, and having contacted her closest friends, he called the police.'

Korsch glanced up at Illmann, and then myself. He smoothed the vain little moustache and turned to the next page in the file that lay open in front of him.

'Zarah Lischka,' he read. 'Aged sixteen, of German parents. Disappeared 6 July 1938, body found 1 August, down a drain in the Tiergarten, close to the Siegessäule. The family lived in Antonstrasse, Wedding. The father works at the slaughterhouse on Landsbergerallee. The girl's mother sent her down to some shops located on Lindowerstrasse, close to the S-Bahn station. The shopkeeper remembers serving her. She bought some cigarettes, although neither one of her parents smokes, some Blueband and a loaf of bread. Then she went to the pharmacy next door. The owner also remembers her. She bought some Schwarzkopf Extra Blonde hair colourant.'

Sixty out of every hundred German girls use it, I told myself almost automatically. It was funny the sort of junk I was remembering these days. I don't think I could have told you much of what was really important in the world other than what was happening in the German Sudeten areas – the riots, and the nationality conferences in Prague. It remained to be seen whether or not what was happening in Czechoslovakia was the only thing that really mattered after all.

Illmann stubbed out his cigarette and began to read his findings.

'The girl was naked, and there were signs that her feet had been bound. She had sustained two knife wounds to the throat. Nevertheless there existed strong indications that she had also been strangled, probably to silence her. It is likely that she was unconscious when the murderer cut her throat. The bruising bisected by the wounds suggests as much. And this is interesting. From the amount of blood still in her feet, and the crusted blood found inside her nose and on her hair, as well as the fact that the feet had been very tightly bound, it is my finding that the girl was hanging upside down when her throat was cut. Like a pig.'

'Jesus,' said Nebe.

'From my examination of the case notes of the previous two victims, it seems highly probable that the same *modus operandi* was applied there too. The suggestion made by my predecessor that these girls had their throats cut while they lay flat on the ground is patently nonsense, and takes no account of the abrasions to the ankles, or the amount of blood left in the feet. Indeed, it seems nothing short of negligent.'

'That is noted,' said Arthur Nebe, writing. 'Your predecessor is, in my opinion also, an incompetent.'

'The girl's vagina was undamaged and not penetrated,' continued Illmann. 'However, the anus gaped wide, permitting the passage of two fingers. Tests for spermatozoa proved positive.'

Somebody groaned.

'The stomach was flacid and was empty. Apparently Brigitte ate apfelkraut and bread-and-butter for lunch before going to the station. All food had been digested at the time of death. But apple is not easily digested, absorbing water as it does. Thus I would put this girl's death at between six and eight hours after she ate lunch, and therefore a couple of hours after she was reported missing. The obvious conclusion is that she was abducted and then later killed.'

I looked at Korsch. 'And the last one please, Herr Korsch.'

'Lotte Winter,' he said. 'Aged sixteen, of German parents.

Disappeared 18 July 1938, her body found 25 August. She lived in Pragerstrasse, and attended the local grammar school where she was studying for her Middle Standard. She left home to have a riding lesson with Tattersalls at the Zoo, and never arrived. Her body was found inside the length of an old canoe in a boathouse near Muggel Lake.'

'Our man gets around, doesn't he?' said Count von der Schulenberg quietly.

'Like the Black Death,' said Lobbes.

Illmann took over once again.

'Strangled,' he said. 'Resulting in fractures of voice box, hyoid, thyroid cornua and alae, indicating a greater degree of violence than in the case of the Schulz girl. This girl was stronger, being more athletically inclined in the first place. She may have put up more of a fight. Suffocation was the cause of death here, although the carotid artery on the right side of her neck had been slashed. As before, the feet showed signs of having been tied together, and there was blood in the hair and nostrils. Undoubtedly she was hanging upside down when her throat was cut, and similarly her body was almost drained of blood.'

'Sounds like a fucking vampire,' exclaimed one of the detectives from the Murder Commission. He glanced at Frau Kalau vom Hofe. 'Sorry,' he added. She shook her head.

'Any sexual interference?' I asked.

'Because of the disagreeable odour, the girl's vagina had to be irrigated,' announced Illmann to more groans, 'and so no sperm could be found. However, the vaginal entrance did show scratch marks, and there was a trace of bruising to the pelvis, indicating that she had been penetrated – and forcibly.'

'Before her throat was cut?' I asked. Illmann nodded. The room was silent for a moment. Illmann set about fixing another roll-up.

'And now another girl has disappeared,' I said. 'Is that not correct, Inspector Deubel?'

Deubel shifted uncomfortably in his chair. He was a big, blond fellow with grey, haunted eyes that looked as though they had seen too much late-night police-work of the kind that requires you to wear thick leather protective gloves.

66

'Yes, sir,' he said. 'Her name is Irma Hanke.'

'Well, since you are the investigating officer, perhaps you would care to tell us something about her.'

He shrugged. 'She's from a nice German family. Aged seventeen, lives in Schloss Strasse, Steglitz.' He paused as his eye flicked down his notes. 'Disappeared Wednesday, 24 August, having left the house to collect for the Reich Economy Programme, on behalf of the BdM.' He paused again.

'And what was she collecting?' said the count.

'Old toothpaste tubes, sir. I believe that the metal is –'

'Thank you, Inspector, I know what the scrap value of toothpaste tubes is.'

'Yes, sir.' He glanced at his notes again. 'She was reported as having been seen on Feuerbachstrasse, Thorwaldsenstrasse, and Munster Damm. Munster Damm runs south beside a cemetery, and the sexton there says he saw a BdM girl answering Irma's description walking there at about 8.30 p.m. He thought she was heading west, in the direction of Bismarckstrasse. She was probably returning home, having said to her parents that she would be back at around 8.45. She never arrived, of course.'

'Any leads?' I asked.

'None, sir,' he said firmly.

'Thank you, Inspector.' I lit a cigarette, and then held the match to Illmann's roll-up. 'Very well then,' I puffed. 'So what we have are five girls, all of them about the same age, and all of them conforming to the Aryan stereotype that we know and love so well. In other words, they all had blonde hair, naturally or otherwise.

'Now, after our third Rhine maiden is murdered, Josef Kahn gets himself arrested for the attempted rape of a prostitute. In other words, he tried to leave without paying.'

'Typical Jew,' said Lobbes. There were a few laughs at that.

'As it happened, Kahn was carrying a knife, quite a sharp one at that, and he even has a minor criminal record for small theft and indecent assault. Very convenient. So the arresting officer at Grolmanstrasse Police Station, namely one Inspector Willi Oehme, decides to turn a few cards and see if he can't

67

make twenty-one. He has a chat with young Josef, who's a bit soft in the head, and what with his honey-tongue and his thick knuckles, Willi manages to persuade Josef to sign a confession.

'Gentlemen, here I'd like to introduce you all to Frau Kalau vom Hofe. I say "Frau", as she's not allowed to call herself a doctor, although she is one, because she is very evidently a woman, and we all know, don't we, that a woman's place is in the home, producing recruits for the Party, and cooking the old man's dinner. She is in fact a psychotherapist, and is an acknowledged expert on that unfathomable little mystery that we refer to as the Criminal Mind.'

My eyes looked and licked at the creamy woman who sat at the far end of the table. She wore a magnolia skirt and a white marocain blouse, and her fair hair was pinned up in a tight bun at the back of her finely sculpted head. She smiled at my introduction and took a file out of her briefcase and opened it in front of her.

'When Josef Kahn was a child,' she said, 'he contracted acute encephalitis lethargica, which occurred in epidemic form among children in Western Europe between 1915 and 1926. This produced a gross change in his personality. After the acute phase of the illness, children may become increasingly restless, irritable, aggressive even, and appear to lose all moral sense. They beg, steal, lie and are often cruel. They talk incessantly and become unmanageable at school and at home. Abnormal sexual curiosity and sexual problems are often observed. Post-encephalitic adolescents sometimes show certain features of this syndrome, especially the lack of sexual restraint, and this is certainly true in Josef Kahn's case. He is also developing Parkinsonism, which will result in his increased physical debilitation.'

Count von der Schulenberg yawned and looked at his wristwatch. But the doctor was not deterred. Instead she seemed to find his bad manners amusing.

'Despite his apparent criminality,' she said, 'I do not think that Josef killed any of these girls. Having discussed the forensic evidence with Professor Illmann, I am of the opinion that these killings show a level of premeditation of which

Kahn is simply incapable. Kahn is capable only of the kind of frenzied murder that would have had him leave the victim where she fell.'

Illmann nodded. 'An analysis of his statement reveals a number of discrepancies with the known facts,' he said. 'His statement says that he used a stocking for the strangulations. The evidence, however, shows quite clearly that bare hands were used. He says that he stabbed his victims in the stomach. The evidence shows that none of them was stabbed, that they were all slashed across the throat. Then there is the fact that the fourth murder must have occurred while Kahn was in custody. Could this murder be the work of a different killer, someone copying the first three? No. Because there has been no press coverage of the first three to copy. And no, because the similarities between all four murders are too strong. They are all the work of the same man.' He smiled at Frau Kalau vom Hofe. 'Is there anything you wish to add to that, madam?'

'Only that that man could not possibly be Josef Kahn,' she said. 'And that Josef Kahn has been the subject of a form of fraud that one might have thought was impossible in the Third Reich.' There was a smile on her mouth as she closed her file and sat back in her chair, opening her cigarette case. Smoking, like being a doctor, was something else that women weren't supposed to do, but I could see that it wasn't the sort of thing that would have given her too many qualms.

It was the count who spoke next.

'In the light of this information, may one inquire of the Reichskriminaldirektor if the ban on news-reporting that has applied in this case will now be lifted?' His belt creaked as he leant across the table, apparently eager to hear Nebe's reply. The son of a well-known general who was now the ambassador to Moscow, young von der Schulenberg was impeccably well-connected. When Nebe didn't answer, he added: 'I don't see how one can possibly impress upon the parents of girls in Berlin the need for caution without some sort of official statement in the newspapers. Naturally I will make sure that every Anwärter on the force is made aware of the need for vigilance on the street. However, it would be easier for my

69

men in Orpo if there were some assistance from the Reich Ministry of Propaganda.'

'It's an accepted fact in criminology,' said Nebe smoothly, 'that publicity can act as an encouragement to a murderer like this, as I'm sure Frau Kalau vom Hofe will confirm.'

'That's correct,' she said. 'Mass murderers do seem to like to read about themselves in the newspapers.'

'However,' Nebe continued, 'I will make a point of telephoning the Muratti building today, and asking them if there is not some propaganda that can be directed towards young girls being made more aware of the need to be careful. At the same time, any such campaign would have to receive the blessing of the Obergruppenführer. He is most anxious that there is nothing said which might create a panic amongst German women.'

The count nodded. 'And now,' he said, looking at me, 'I have a question for the Kommissar.'

He smiled, but I wasn't about to place too much reliance on it. He gave every impression of having attended the same school in supercilious sarcasm as Obergruppenführer Heydrich. Mentally I lifted my guard in readiness for the first punch.

'As the detective who ingeniously solved the celebrated case of Gormann the strangler, will he share with us now his initial thoughts in this particular case?'

The colourless smile persisted beyond what might have seemed comfortable, as if he was straining at his tight sphincter. At least, I assumed it was tight. As the deputy of a former SA man, Count Wolf von Helldorf, who was reputed to be as queer as the late SA boss Ernst Röhm, Schulenberg might well have had the kind of arse that would have tempted a short-sighted pickpocket.

Sensing that there was even more to be made of this disingenuous line of inquiry, he added: 'Perhaps an indication as to the kind of character we might be looking for?'

'I think I can help the administrative president there,' said Frau Kalau vom Hofe. The count's head jerked irritatedly in her direction.

She reached down into her briefcase and laid a large book on to the table. And then another, and another, until there was a pile as high as one of von der Schulenberg's highly polished jackboots.

'Anticipating just such a question, I took the liberty of bringing along several books dealing with the psychology of the criminal,' she said. 'Heindl's *Professional Criminal*, Wulffen's excellent *Handbook of Sexual Delinquency*, Hirschfeld's *Sexual Pathology*, F. Alexander's *The Criminal and his Judges* –'

This was too much for him. He collected his papers off the table and stood up, smiling nervously.

'Another time perhaps, Frau vom Hofe,' he said. Then he clicked his heels, bowed stiffly to the room and left.

'Bastard,' muttered Lobbes.

'It's quite all right,' she said, adding some copies of the German Police Journal to the pile of textbooks. 'You can't teach Hans what he won't learn.' I smiled, appreciating her cool resilience, as well as the fine breasts which strained at the material of her blouse.

After the meeting was concluded, I lingered there a little in order to be alone with her.

'He asked a good question,' I said. 'One to which I didn't have much of an answer. Thanks for coming to my assistance when you did.'

'Please don't mention it,' she said, starting to return some of her books to the briefcase. I picked one of them up and glanced at it.

'You know, I'd be interested to hear your answer. Can I buy you a drink?'

She looked at her watch. 'Yes,' she smiled. 'I'd like that.'

Die Letze Instanz, at the end of Klosterstrasse on the old city wall, was a local bar much favoured by bulls from the Alex and court officials from the nearby court of last instance, from which the place took its name.

Inside it was all dark-brown wood-panelled walls and flagged floors. Near the bar, with its great draught pump of yellow ceramic, on top of which stood the figure of a seventeenth-century soldier, was a large seat made of green, brown and yellow tiles, all with moulded figures and heads. It had the look of a very cold and uncomfortable throne, and on it sat the bar's owner, Warnstorff, a pale-skinned, dark-haired man wearing a collarless shirt and a capacious leather apron that was also his bag of change. When we arrived he greeted me warmly and showed us to a quiet table in the back, where he brought us a couple of beers. At another table a man was dealing vigorously with the biggest piece of pig's knuckle either of us had ever seen.

'Are you hungry?' I asked her.

'Not now I've seen him,' she said.

'Yes, I know what you mean. It does put you off rather, doesn't it? You'd think he was trying to win the Iron Cross the way he's battling that joint.'

She smiled, and we were silent for a moment. Eventually she said, 'Do you think there's going to be a war?'

I stared into the top of my beer as if expecting the answer to float to the surface. I shrugged and shook my head.

'I haven't really been keeping that close an eye on things lately,' I said, and explained about Bruno Stahlecker and my return to Kripo. 'But shouldn't I be asking you? As the expert on criminal psychology you should have a better appreciation of the Führer's mind than most people. Would you say his behaviour was compulsive or irresistible within the definition of Paragraph Fifty-one of the Criminal Code?'

It was her turn to search for inspiration in a glass of beer.

'We don't really know each other well enough for this kind of conversation, do we?' she said.

'I suppose not.'

'I will say this, though,' she said lowering her voice. 'Have you ever read *Mein Kampf*?'

'That funny old book they give free to all newlyweds? It's the best reason to stay single I can think of.'

'Well, I have read it. And one of the things I noticed was that there is one passage, as long as seven pages, in which Hitler makes repeated references to venereal disease and its effects. Indeed, he actually says that the elimination of venereal disease is The Task that faces the German nation.'

'My God, are you saying that he's syphilitic?'

'I'm not saying anything. I'm just telling you what is written in the Führer's great book.'

'But the book's been around since the mid-twenties. If he's had a hot tail since then his syphilis would have to be tertiary.'

'It might interest you to know,' she said, 'that many of Josef Kahn's fellow inmates at the Herzeberge Asylum are those whose organic dementia is a direct result of their syphilis. Contradictory statements can be made and accepted. The mood varies between euphoria and apathy, and there is general emotional instability. The classic type is characterized by a demented euphoria, delusions of grandeur and bouts of extreme paranoia.'

'Christ, the only thing you left out was the crazy moustache,' I said. I lit a cigarette and puffed at it dismally. 'For God's sake change the subject. Let's talk about something cheerful, like our mass-murdering friend. Do you know, I'm beginning to see his point, I really am. I mean, these are tomorrow's young mothers he's killing. More childbearing machines to produce new Party recruits. Me, I'm all for these by-products of the asphalt civilization they're always on about – the childless families with eugenically dud women, at least until we've got rid of this regime of rubber truncheons. What's one more psychopath among so many?'

'You say more than you know,' she said. 'We're all of us capable of cruelty. Every one of us is a latent criminal. Life is just a battle to maintain a civilized skin. Many sadistic killers find that it's only occasionally that it comes off. Peter Kurten for example. He was apparently a man of such a kindly disposition that nobody who knew him could believe that he was capable of such horrific crimes as he committed.'

She rummaged in her briefcase again and, having wiped the table, she laid a thin blue book between our two glasses.

'This book is by Carl Berg, a forensic pathologist who had the opportunity of studying Kurten at length following his arrest. I've met Berg and respect his work. He founded the

Düsseldorf Institute of Legal and Social Medicine, and for a while he was the medico-legal officer of the Düsseldorf Criminal Court. This book, *The Sadist*, is probably one of the best accounts of the mind of the murderer that has ever been written. You can borrow it if you like.'

'Thanks, I will.'

'That will help you to understand,' she said. 'But to enter into the mind of a man like Kurten, you should read this.' Again she dipped into the bag of books.

'*Les Fleurs du mal*,' I read, 'by Charles Baudelaire.' I opened it and looked over the verses. 'Poetry?' I raised an eyebrow.

'Oh, don't look so suspicious, Kommissar. I'm being perfectly serious. It's a good translation, and you'll find a lot more in it than you might expect, believe me.' She smiled at me.

'I haven't read poetry since I studied Goethe at school.'

'And what was your opinion of him?'

'Do Frankfurt lawyers make good poets?'

'It's an interesting critique,' she said. 'Well, let's hope you think better of Baudelaire. And now I'm afraid I must be going.' She stood up and we shook hands. 'When you've finished with the books you can return them to me at the Goering Institute on Budapesterstrasse. We're just across the road from the Zoo Aquarium. I'd certainly be interested to hear a detective's opinion of Baudelaire,' she said.

'It will be my pleasure. And you can tell me your opinion of Dr Lanz Kindermann.'

'Kindermann? You know Lanz Kindermann?'

'In a way.'

She gave me a judicious sort of look. 'You know, for a police Kommissar you are certainly full of surprises. You certainly are.'

7

Sunday, 11 September

I prefer my tomatoes when they've still got some green left in them. Then they're sweet and firm, with smooth, cool skins, the sort you would choose for a salad. But when a tomato has been around for a while, it picks up a few wrinkles as it grows too soft to handle, and even begins to taste a little sour.

It's the same with women. Only this one was perhaps a shade green for me, and possibly rather too cool for her own good. She stood at my front door and gave me an impertinent sort of north-to-south-and-back-again look, as if she was trying to assess my prowess, or lack of it, as a lover.

'Yes?' I said. 'What do you want?'

'I'm collecting for the Reich,' she explained, playing games with her eyes. She held a bag of material out, as if to corroborate her story. 'The Party Economy Programme. Oh, the concierge let me in.'

'I can see that. Exactly what would you like?'

She raised an eyebrow at that and I wondered if her father thought she wasn't still young enough for him to spank.

'Well, what have you got?' There was a quiet mockery in her tone. She was pretty, in a sulky, sultry sort of way. In civilian clothes she might have passed for a girl of twenty, but with her two pigtails, and dressed in the sturdy boots, long navy skirt, trim white blouse and brown leather jacket of the BdM – the League of German Girls – I guessed her to be no more than sixteen.

'I'll have a look and see what I can find,' I said, half amused at her grown-up manner, which seemed to confirm what you sometimes heard of BdM girls, which was that they were sexually promiscuous and just as likely to get themselves pregnant at Hitler Youth Camp as they were to learn needlework, first aid and German folk history. 'I suppose you had better come in.'

The girl sauntered through the door as if she were trailing a mink wrap and gave the hall a cursory examination. She didn't seem to be much impressed. 'Nice place,' she murmured quietly.

I closed the door and laid my cigarette in the ashtray on the hall table. 'Wait here,' I told her.

I went into the bedroom and foraged under the bed for the suitcase where I kept old shirts and threadbare towels, not to mention all my spare house dust and carpet fluff. When I stood up and brushed myself off she was leaning in the doorway and smoking my cigarette. Insolently she blew a perfect smoke-ring towards me.

'I thought you Faith-and-Beauty girls weren't supposed to smoke,' I said, trying to conceal my irritation.

'Is that a fact?' she smirked. 'There are quite a few things we're not encouraged to do. We're not supposed to do this, we're not supposed to do that. Just about everything seems to be wicked these days, doesn't it? But what I always say is, if you can't do the wicked things when you're still young enough to enjoy them, then what's the point of doing them at all?' She jerked herself away from the wall and stalked out.

Quite the little bitch, I thought, following her into the sitting-room next door.

She inhaled noisily, like she was sucking at a spoonful of soup, and blew another smoke-ring in my face. If I could have caught it I would have wrapped it round her pretty little neck.

'Anyway,' she said, 'I hardly think one little drummer is going to knock over the heap, do you?'

I laughed. 'Do I look like the sort of dog's ear who would smoke cheap cigarettes?'

'No, I suppose not,' she admitted. 'What's your name?'

'Plato.'

'Plato. It suits you. Well, Plato, you can kiss me if you want.'

'You don't creep around it, do you?'

'Haven't you heard the nicknames they have for the BdM? The German Mattress League? Commodities for German Men?' She put her arms about my neck and performed a

76

variety of coquettish expressions she'd probably practised in front of her dressing-table mirror.

Her hot young breath tasted stale, but I let myself equal the competence in her kiss, just to be affable, my hands squeezing at her young breasts, kneading the nipples with my fingers. Then I cupped her chubby behind in both my moistening palms, and drew her closer to what was increasingly on my mind. Her naughty eyes went round as she pressed herself against me. I can't honestly say I wasn't tempted.

'Do you know any good bedtime stories, Plato?' she giggled.

'No,' I said, tightening my grip on her. 'But I know plenty of bad ones. The kind where the beautiful but spoilt princess gets boiled alive and eaten up by the wicked troll.'

A vague glimmer of doubt began to grow in the bright blue iris of each corrupt eye, and her smile was no longer wholly confident as I hauled up her skirt and started to tug her pants down.

'Oh, I could tell you lots of stories like that,' I said darkly. 'The sort of stories that policemen tell their daughters. Horrible gruesome stories that give girls the kind of nightmares which their fathers can be glad of.'

'Stop it,' she laughed nervously. 'You're frightening me.' Certain now that things weren't going quite to plan, she reached desperately for her pants as I yanked them down her legs, exposing the fledgling that nestled in her groin.

'They're glad because it means that their pretty little daughters will be much too scared to ever go into a strange man's house, just in case he should turn into a wicked troll.'

'Please, mister, don't,' she said.

I smacked her bare bottom and pushed her away.

'So it's lucky for you, princess, that I'm a detective and not a troll, otherwise you'd be ketchup.'

'You're a policeman?' she gulped, tears welling up in her eyes.

'That's right, I'm a policeman. And if I ever find you playing the apprentice snapper again, I'll see to it that your father takes a stick to you, understand?'

'Yes,' she whispered, and quickly pulled up her pants.

I picked up the pile of old shirts and towels from where I had dropped them on the floor, and pushed them into her arms.

'Now get out of here before I do the job myself.' She ran into the hall and out of the apartment in terror, as if I had been Niebelung himself.

After I'd closed the door on her, the smell and touch of that delicious little body, and the frustrated desire of it, remained with me for as long as it took to pour myself a drink and take a cold bath.

That September it seemed that passion everywhere, already smouldering like a rotten fuse-box, was easily ignited, and I wished that the hot blood of Sudeten Germans in Czechoslovakia could have been as easily dealt with as was my own excitation.

As a bull you learn to expect an increase in crime during hot weather. In January and February even the most desperate criminals stay home in front of the fire.

Reading Professor Berg's book, *The Sadist*, later on that same day, I wondered how many lives had been saved simply because it was too cold or too wet for Kürten to venture out of doors, Still, nine murders, seven attempted murders and forty acts of arson was an impressive enough record.

According to Berg, Kürten, the product of a violent home, had come to crime at an early age, committing a string of petty larcenies and enduring several periods of imprisonment until, at the age of thirty-eight, he had married a woman of strong character. He had always had sadistic impulses, being inclined to torture cats and other dumb animals, and now he was obliged to keep these tendencies in a mental straitjacket. But when his wife was not at home Kürten's evil demon at times grew too powerful to restrain, and he was driven to commit the terrible and sadistic crimes for which he was to become infamous.

This sadism was sexual in its origin, Berg explained. Kürten's home circumstances had rendered him predisposed to a deviation of the sexual urge, and his early experiences had all helped to condition the direction of that urge.

In the twelve months that separated Kürten's capture and his execution, Berg had met frequently with Kürten and found him to be a man of notable character and talent. He was possessed of considerable charm and intelligence, an excellent memory and keen powers of observation. Indeed, Berg was moved to remark upon the man's accessibility. Another outstanding characteristic was Kürten's vanity, which manifested itself in his smart, well-cared for appearance and in his delight at having outwitted the Düsseldorf police for as long as he had cared to do so.

Berg's conclusion was not a particularly comfortable one for any civilized member of society: Kürten was not mad within the terms of Paragraph Fifty-one, in that his acts were neither completely compulsive nor wholly irresistible, so much as pure, unadulterated cruelty.

If that wasn't bad enough, reading Baudelaire left me feeling as comfortable in my soul as a bullock in an abattoir. It didn't require a superhuman effort of imagination to accept Frau Kalau vom Hofe's suggestion that this rather Gothic French poet provided an explicit articulation of the mind of a Landru, a Gormann or a Kürten.

Yet there was something more here. Something deeper and more universal than merely a clue as to the psyche of the mass murderer. In Baudelaire's interest in violence, in his nostalgia for the past and through his revelation of the world of death and corruption, I heard the echo of a Satanic litany that was altogether more contemporary, and saw the pale reflection of a different kind of criminal, one whose spleen had the force of law.

I don't have much of a memory for words. I can barely remember the words of the national anthem. But some of these verses stayed in my head like the persistent smell of mingled musk and tar.

That evening I drove down to see Bruno's widow Katia at their home in Berlin-Zehlendorf. This was my second visit since Bruno's death, and I brought some of his things from the office, as well as a letter from my insurance company acknowledging receipt of the claim I had made on Katia's behalf.

There was even less to say now than before, but nevertheless I stayed for a full hour, holding Katia's hand and trying to swallow the lump in my throat with several glasses of schnapps.

'How's Heinrich taking it?' I said uncomfortably, hearing the unmistakable sound of the boy singing in his bedroom.

'He hasn't talked about it yet,' said Katia, her grief giving way a little to embarrassment. 'I think he sings because he wants to escape from having to face up to it.'

'Grief affects people very differently,' I said, scraping around for some sort of excuse. But I didn't think this was true at all. To my own father's premature death, when I hadn't been much older than Heinrich was now, had been appended as its brutal corollary the inescapable logic that I was myself not immortal. Ordinarily I would not have been insensitive to Heinrich's situation, 'But why must he sing that song?'

'He's got it into his head that the Jews had something to do with his father's death.'

'That's absurd,' I said.

Katia sighed and shook her head. 'I've told him that, Bernie. But he won't listen.'

On my way out I lingered at the boy's doorway, listening to his strong young voice.

'"Load up the empty guns, And polish up the knives, Let's kill the Jewish bastards, Who poison all our lives."'

For a moment I was tempted to open the door and belt the young thug on the jaw. But what was the point? What was the point of doing anything but leave him alone? There are so many ways of escaping from that which one fears, and not the least of these is hatred.

8

Monday, 12 September

A badge, a warrant card, an office on the third floor and, apart from the number of SS uniforms there were about the place, it almost felt like old times. It was too bad that there were not many happy memories, but happiness was never an emotion in plentiful supply at the Alex, unless your idea of a party involved working on a kidney with a chair-leg. A couple of times men I knew from the old days stopped me in the corridor to say hallo, and how sorry they were to hear about Bruno. But mostly I got the kind of looks that might have greeted an undertaker in a cancer ward.

Deubel, Korsch and Becker were waiting for me in my office. Deubel was explaining the subtle technique of the cigarette punch to his junior officers.

'That's right,' he said. 'When he's putting the nail in his guzzler, you give him the uppercut. An open jaw breaks real easy.'

'How nice to hear that criminal investigation is keeping up with modern times,' I said as I came through the door. 'I suppose you learned that in the Freikorps, Deubel.'

The man smiled. 'You've been reading my school-report, sir.'

'I've been doing a lot of reading,' I said, sitting down at my desk.

'Never been much of a reader myself,' he said.

'You surprise me.'

'You've been reading that woman's books, sir?' said Korsch. 'The ones that explain the criminal mind?'

'This one doesn't take much explanation,' said Deubel. 'He's a fucking spinner.'

'Maybe,' I said. 'But we're not about to catch him with blackjacks and brass knuckles. You can forget all your usual methods – cigarette punches and things like that.' I stared hard at Deubel. 'A killer like this is difficult to catch because, for most of the time at least, he looks and behaves like an ordinary citizen. And with none of the hallmarks of criminality, and no obvious motive, we can't rely on informers to help us get on his track.'

Kriminalassistent Becker, on loan from Department VB3 – Vice – shook his head.

'If you'll forgive me, sir,' he said, 'that's not quite true. Dealing with sexual deviants, there are a few informers. Buttfuckers and dolly-boys, it's true, but now and again they do come up with the goods.'

'I'll bet they do,' Deubel muttered.

'All right,' I said. 'We'll talk to them. But first there are two aspects to this case that I want us all to consider. One is that these girls disappear and then their bodies are found all over the city. Well, that tells me that our killer is using a car. The other aspect is that as far as I am aware, we've never had any reports of anyone witnessing the abduction of a victim. No reports of a girl being dragged kicking and screaming into the back of a car. That seems to me to indicate that maybe they went willingly with the killer. That they weren't afraid. Now it's unlikely that they all knew the killer, but quite possibly they might have trusted him because of what he was.'

'A priest, maybe,' said Korsch. 'Or a youth leader.'

'Or a bull,' I said. 'It's quite possible he could be any one of those things. Or all of them.'

'You think he might be disguising himself?' said Korsch.

I shrugged. 'I think that we have to keep an open mind about all of these things. Korsch, I want you to check through the records and see if you can't match anyone with a record for sexual assault with either a uniform, a church or a car licence plate.' He sagged a little. 'It's a big job, I know, so I've spoken to Lobbes in Kripo Executive, and he's going to get you some help.' I looked at my wristwatch. 'Kriminaldirektor Müller is expecting you over in VC1 in about ten minutes, so you'd better get going.'

'Nothing on the Hanke girl yet?' I said to Deubel, when Korsch had gone.

'My men have looked everywhere,' he said. 'The railway embankments, the parks, waste ground. We've dragged the Teltow Canal twice. There's not a lot more we can do.' He lit a cigarette and grimaced. 'She's dead by now. Everyone knows it.'

'I want you to conduct a door-to-door inquiry throughout the area where she disappeared. Speak to everyone, and I mean everyone, including the girl's schoolfriends. Somebody must have seen something. Take some photographs to jog a few memories.'

'If you don't mind me saying, sir,' he growled, 'that's surely a job for the uniformed boys in Orpo.'

'Those mallet-heads are good for arresting drunks and garter-handlers,' I said. 'But this is a job requiring intelligence. That's all.'

Pulling another face, Deubel stubbed out his cigarette in a way that let me know he wished the ashtray could have been my face, and dragged himself reluctantly out of my office.

'Better mind what you say about Orpo to Deubel, sir,' said Becker. 'He's a friend of Dummy Daluege's. They were in the same Stettin Freikorps regiment.' The Freikorps were para-military organizations of ex-soldiers which had been formed after the war to destroy Bolshevism in Germany and to protect German borders from the encroachments of the Poles. Kurt 'Dummy' Daluege was the chief of Orpo.

'Thanks, I read his file.'

'He used to be a good bull. But these days he works an easy shift and then pushes off home. All Eberhard Deubel wants out of life is to live long enough to collect his pension and see his daughter grow up to marry the local bank manager.'

'The Alex has got plenty like him,' I said. 'You've got children, haven't you, Becker?'

'A son, sir,' he said proudly. 'Norfried. He's nearly two.'

'Norfried, eh? That sounds German enough.'

'My wife, sir. She's very keen on this Aryan thing of Dr Rosenberg's.'

'And how does she feel about you working in Vice?'

'We don't talk much about what happens in my job. As far as she is concerned, I'm just a bull.'

'So tell me about these sexual-deviant informers.'

'While I was in Section M2, the Brothel Surveillance Squad, we only used one or two,' he explained. 'But Meisinger's Queer Squad use them all the time. He depends on informers. A few years ago there was a homosexual organization called the Friendship League, with about 30,000 members. Well, Meisinger got hold of the entire list and still leans on a name now and then for information. He also has the confiscated subscription lists of several pornographic magazines, as well as the names of the publishers. We might try a couple of them, sir. Then there is Reichsführer Himmler's ferris-wheel. It's an electrically powered rotating card-index with thousands and thousands of names on it, sir. We could always see what came up on that.'

'It sounds like something a gypsy fortune-teller would use.'

'They say that Himmler's keen on that shit.'

'And what about a man who's keen on nudging something? Where are all the bees in this city now that all the brothels have been closed down?'

'Massage parlours. You want to give a girl some bird, you've got to let her rub your back first. Kuhn – he's the boss of M2 – he doesn't bother them much. You want to ask a few snappers if they'd had to massage any spinners lately, sir?'

'It's as good a place to start as any I can think of.'

'We'll need an E-warrant, a search for missing persons.'

'Better go and get one, Becker.'

Becker was tall, with small, bored, blue eyes, a thin straw-hat of yellow hair, a doglike nose, and a mocking, almost manic smile. His looked a cynical sort of face, which was indeed the case. In Becker's everyday conversation there was more blasphemy against the divine beauty of life than you would have found among a pack of starving hyenas.

Reasoning that it was still too early for the massage-trade, we decided to try the dirty-book brigade first, and from the Alex we drove south to Hallesches Tor.

Wende Hoas was a tall, grey building close to the S-Bahn railway. We went up to the top floor where, with manic smile firmly in place, Becker kicked in one of the doors.

A tubby, prim little man with a monocle and a moustache looked up from his chair and smiled nervously as we walked into his office. 'Ah, Herr Becker,' he said. 'Come in, come in. And you've brought a friend with you. Excellent.'

There wasn't much room in the musty-smelling room. Tall stacks of books and magazines surrounded the desk and filing cabinet. I picked up a magazine and started to flick through it.

'Hallo, Helmut,' Becker chuckled, picking up another. He grunted with satisfaction as he turned the pages. 'This is filthy,' he laughed.

'Help yourselves, gentlemen,' said the man called Helmut. 'If there's anything special you're looking for, just ask. Don't be shy.' He leant back in his chair and from the pocket of his dirty grey waistcoat he produced a snuff box which he opened with a flick of his dirty thumbnail. He helped himself to a pinch, an indulgence which was effected with as much offence to the ear as any of the printed matter that might have been available was to the eye.

In close but poorly photographed gynaecological detail, the magazine I was looking at was partly given over to text that was designed to strain the fly-buttons. If it was to be believed, young German nurses copulated with no more thought than the average alley-cat.

Becker tossed his magazine on to the floor and picked up another. '"The Virgin's Wedding Night",' he read.

'Not your sort of thing, Herr Becker,' Helmut said.

'"The Story of a Dildo"?'

'That one's not at all bad.'

'"Raped on the U-Bahn".'

'Ah, now that is good. There is a girl in that one with the juiciest plum I've ever seen.'

'And you've seen a few, haven't you, Helmut?'

The man smiled modestly, and looked over Becker's shoulder as he gave the photographs close attention.

'Rather a nice girl-next-door type, don't you think?'

Becker snorted. 'If you happen to live next door to a fucking dog kennel.'

'Oh, very good,' Helmut laughed, and started to clean his monocle. As he did so, a long and extremely grey length of his lank brown hair disengaged itself from a poorly disguised bald-patch, like a quilt slipping off a bed, and dangled ridiculously beside one of his transparent red ears.

'We're looking for a man who likes mutilating young girls,' I said. 'Would you have anything catering for that sort of pervert?'

Helmut smiled and shook his head sadly. 'No, sir, I'm afraid not. We don't much care to deal for the sadistic end of the market. We leave the whipping and bestiality to others.'

'Like hell you do,' Becker sneered.

I tried the filing cabinet, which was locked.

'What's in here?'

'A few papers, sir. The petty-cash box. The account books, that sort of thing. Nothing to interest you, I think.'

'Open it.'

'Really, sir, there's nothing of any interest —' The words dried in his mouth as he saw the cigarette lighter in my hand. I thumbed the bezel and held it underneath the magazine I'd been reading. It burned with a slow blue flame.

'Becker. How much would you say this magazine was?'

'Oh, they're expensive, sir. At least ten Reichsmarks each.'

'There must be a couple of thousands' worth of stock in this rat-hole.'

'Easily. Be a shame if there was a fire.'

'I hope he's insured.'

'You want to see inside the cabinet?' said Helmut. 'You only had to ask.' He handed Becker the key as I dropped the blazing magazine harmlessly into the metal wastepaper bin.

There was nothing in the top drawer besides a cash box, but in the bottom drawer was another pile of pornographic magazines. Becker picked one up and turned back the plain front cover.

'"Virgin Sacrifice",' he said, reading the title page. 'Take a look at this, sir.'

He showed me a series of photographs depicting the degradation and punishment of a girl, who looked to be of high-school age, by an old and ugly man wearing an ill-fitting toupee. The weals his cane had left on her bare backside seemed very real indeed.

'Nasty,' I said.

'You understand, I am merely the distributor,' Helmut said, blowing his nose on a filthy handkerchief, 'not the manufacturer.'

One photograph was particularly interesting. In it the naked girl was bound hand and foot, and lying on a church altar like a human sacrifice. Her vagina had been penetrated with an enormous cucumber. Becker looked fiercely at Helmut.

'But you know who produced it, don't you?' Helmut remained silent only until Becker grabbed him by the throat and started to slap him across the mouth.

'Please don't hit me.'

'You're probably enjoying it, you ugly little pervert,' he snarled, warming to his work. 'Come on, talk to me, or you'll talk to this.' He snatched a short rubber truncheon from his pocket, and pressed it against Helmut's face.

'It was Poliza,' shouted Helmut. Becker squeezed his face.

'Say again?'

'Theodor Poliza. He's a photographer. He has a studio on Schiffbauerdamm, next to the Comedy Theatre. He's the one you want.'

'If you're lying to us, Helmut,' said Becker, grinding the rubber against Helmut's cheek, 'we'll be back. And we'll not only set fire to your stock, but you with it. I hope you've got that.' He pushed him away.

Helmut dabbed at his bleeding mouth with the handkerchief, 'Yes, sir,' he said, 'I understand.'

When we were outside again I spat into the gutter.

'Gives you a nasty taste in the mouth, doesn't it, sir? Makes me glad I didn't have a daughter, really it does.'

I'd like to have said that I agreed with him there. Only I didn't. We drove north.

What a city it was for its public buildings, as immense as

grey granite mountains. They built them big just to remind you of the importance of the state and the comparative insignificance of the individual. That just shows you how this whole business of National Socialism got started. It's hard not to be overawed by a government, any government, that is accommodated in such grand buildings. And the long wide avenues that ran straight from one district to another seemed to have been made for nothing else but columns of marching soldiers.

Quickly recovering my stomach I told Becker to stop the car at a cooked-meat shop on Friedrichstrasse and bought us both a plate of lentil soup. Standing at one of the little counters, we watched Berlin housewives lining up to buy their sausage, which lay coiled on the long marble counter like the rusted springs from some enormous motor car, or grew off the tiled walls in great bunches, like overripe bananas.

Becker may have been married, but he hadn't lost his eye for the ladies, passing some sort of nearly obscene comment about most of the women who came into the shop while we were there. And it hadn't escaped my attention that he'd helped himself to a couple of pornographic magazines. How could it have? He didn't try to hide them. Slap a man's face, make his mouth bleed, threaten him with an india rubber, call him a filthy degenerate and then help yourself to some of his dirty books – that's what being in Kripo was all about.

We went back to the car.

'Do you know this Poliza character?' I said.

'We've met,' he said. 'What can I tell you about him except that he's shit on your shoe?'

The Comedy Theatre on Schiffbauerdamm was on the north side of the Spree, a tower-topped relic ornamented with alabaster tritons, dolphins and assorted naked nymphs, and Poliza's studio was in a basement nearby.

We went down some stairs and into a long alleyway. Outside the door to Poliza's studio we were met by a man wearing a cream-coloured blazer, a pair of green trousers, a cravat of lime silk and a red carnation. No amount of care or expense had been spared with his appearance, but the overall effect was so lacking in taste that he looked like a gypsy grave.

Poliza took one look at us and decided that we weren't there selling vacuum-cleaners. He wasn't much of a runner. His bottom was too big, his legs were too short and his lungs were probably too hard. But by the time we realized what was happening he was nearly ten metres down the alley.

'You bastard,' muttered Becker.

The voice of logic must have told Poliza he was being stupid, that Becker and I were easily capable of catching him, but it was probably so hoarsened by fear that it sounded as disquietingly unattractive as we ourselves must have appeared.

There was no such voice for Becker, hoarse or otherwise. Yelling at Poliza to stop, he broke into a smooth and powerful running action. I struggled to keep up with him, but after only a few strides he was well ahead of me. Another few seconds and he would have caught the man.

Then I saw the gun in his hand, a long-barrelled Parabellum, and yelled at both men to stop.

Almost immediately Poliza came to a halt. He began to raise his arms as if to cover his ears against the noise of the gunshot, turning as he collapsed, blood and aqueous humour spilling gelatinously from the bullet's exit wound in his eye, or what was left of it.

We stood over Poliza's dead body.

'What is it with you?' I said breathlessly. 'Have you got corns? Are your shoes too tight? Or maybe you didn't think your lungs were up to it? Listen, Becker, I've got ten years on you and I could have caught this man if I'd been wearing a deep-sea-diver's suit.'

Becker sighed and shook his head.

'Christ, I'm sorry, sir,' he said. 'I only meant to wing him.' He glanced awkwardly at his pistol, almost as if he didn't quite believe it could have just killed a man.

'Wing him? What were you aiming at, his earlobe? Listen, Becker, when you try and wing a man, unless you're Buffalo Bill you aim at his legs, not try and give him a fucking haircut.' I looked around, embarrassed, almost expecting a crowd to have gathered, but the alley stayed empty. I nodded down at his pistol. 'What is that cannon, anyway?'

Becker raised the gun. 'Artillery Parabellum, sir.'

'Shit, haven't you ever heard of the Geneva Convention? That's enough gun to drill for oil.'

I told him to go and telephone the canned-meat wagon, and while he was away I took a look around Poliza's studio.

There wasn't much to see. An assortment of open-crotch shots drying on a line in the darkroom. A collection of whips, chains, manacles and an altar complete with candlesticks, of the sort that I had seen in the photographed series of the girl with the cucumber. A couple of piles of magazines like the ones we had found back at Helmut's office. Nothing to indicate that Poliza might have murdered five schoolgirls.

When I went outside again I found that Becker had returned with a uniformed policeman, a sergeant. The pair of them stood looking at Poliza's body like two small boys regarding a dead cat in the gutter, the sergeant even poking at Poliza's side with the toe of his boot.

'Right through the window,' I heard the man say, with what sounded like admiration. 'I never realized there was so much jelly in there.'

'It's a mess, isn't it?' said Becker without much enthusiasm.

They looked up as I walked towards them.

'Wagon coming?' Becker nodded. 'Good. You can make your report later.' I spoke to the sergeant. 'Until it arrives, you'll stay here with the body, sergeant?'

He straightened up. 'Yes, sir.'

'You finished admiring your handiwork?'

'Sir,' said Becker.

'Then let's go.'

We walked back to the car.

'Where are we going?'

'I'd like to check on a couple of these massage parlours.'

'Evona Wylezynska's the one to talk to. She owns several places. Takes 25 per cent of everything the girls make. Most likely she'll be at her place on Richard Wagner Strasse.'

'Richard Wagner Strasse?' I said. 'Where the hell is that?'

'It used to be Sesenheimerstrasse, running on to Spree-strasse. You know, where the Opera House is.'

'I suppose that we should count ourselves lucky that it's opera Hitler loves, and not football.'

Becker grinned. Driving there he seemed to recover some of his spirits.

'Do you mind if I ask you a really personal question, sir?'

I shrugged. 'Go right ahead. But if it works out, I might have to put my answer in an envelope and mail it to you instead.'

'Well it's this: have you ever fucked a Jew, sir?'

I looked at him, trying to catch his eye, but he kept both of them determinedly on the road.

'No, I can't say I have. But it certainly wasn't the race laws that prevented it. I guess I just never met one who wanted to fuck me.'

'So you wouldn't object if you got the chance?'

I shrugged. 'I don't suppose I would.' I paused, waiting for him to go on, but he didn't, so I said, 'Why do you ask, as a matter of fact?'

Becker smiled over the steering-wheel.

'There's a little Jewish snapper at this rub-joint we're going to,' he said enthusiastically. 'A real scorcher. She's got a plum that's like the inside of a conger-eel, just one long piece of suction muscle. The kind to suck you in like a minnow and blow you right out of her arse. Best bit of damned plum I've ever had.' He shook his head doubtfully. 'I don't reckon there's anything to beat a nice ripe Jewess. Not even a nigger-woman, or a Chink.'

'I never knew you were so broad-minded, Becker,' I said, 'or so damned cosmopolitan. Christ, I bet you've even read Goethe.'

Becker laughed at that one. He seemed to have quite forgotten Poliza. 'One thing about Evona,' he said. 'She won't talk unless we relax a little, if you know what I mean. Have a drink, take things easy. Act like we're not in a hurry. The minute we start to act like a couple of official stiffs in our trousers she'll haul down the shutters and start polishing the mirrors in the bedrooms.'

'Well, there's a lot of people like that these days. Like I

91

always say, people won't put their fingers near the stove if they figure you're stewing a broth.'

Evona Wylezynska was a Pole with an Eton crop smelling lightly of Macassar oil, and a dangerous crevasse of cleavage. Although it was only the mid-afternoon she wore a peignoir of peach-coloured voile over a matching heavy satin slip, and high-heeled slippers. She greeted Becker like he was there with a rent rebate.

'Darling Emil,' she cooed. 'Such a long time since we seen you here. Where have you been hiding?'

'I'm off Vice now,' he explained, kissing her on the cheek.

'What a shame. And you were so good at it.' She gave me a litmus-paper sort of look, as if I was something that might stain the expensive carpet. 'And who is this you've brought us?'

'It's all right, Evona. He's a friend.'

'Does your friend have a name? And does he not know to take his hat off when he comes into a lady's house?'

I let that one go, and took it off. 'Bernhard Gunther, Frau Wylezynska,' I said, and shook her hand.

'Pleased to meet you, darling, I'm sure.' Her thickly accented, languorous voice seemed to start somewhere near the bottom of her corset, the faint outline of which I could just about make out underneath her slip. By the time it got to her pouting mouth it had more tease than a fairy's kitten. The mouth was giving me quite a few problems too. It was the kind of mouth that can eat a five-course dinner at Kempinski's without spoiling its lipstick, only on this occasion I seemed to be the preoccupation of its taste-buds.

She ushered us into a comfortable sitting-room that wouldn't have embarrassed a Potsdam lawyer, and stalked towards the enormous drinks tray.

'What will you have, gentlemen? I have absolutely everything.'

Becker guffawed loudly. 'There's no doubt about that,' he said.

I smiled thinly. Becker was starting to irritate me badly. I asked for a scotch whisky, and as Evona handed me my glass her cold fingers touched mine.

She took a mouthful of her own drink as if it were unpleasant medicine to be hurried down, and tugged me on to a big leather sofa. Becker chuckled and sat down on an armchair beside us.

'And how is my old friend Arthur Nebe?' she asked. Noting my surprise, she added: 'Oh yes, Arthur and I have known each other for many years. Ever since 1920 in fact, when he first joined Kripo.'

'He's much the same,' I said.

'Tell him to come and visit me sometime,' she said. 'He can storm free with me any time he wants. Or just a nice massage. Yes, that's it. Tell him to come here for a nice rub. I give it to him myself.' She laughed loudly at the idea and lit a cigarette.

'I'll tell him,' I said, wondering if I would, and wondering if she really cared one way or the other.

'And you, Emil. Maybe you would like a little company? Maybe you would both like a rub yourselves, eh?'

I was about to broach the real purpose of our visit, but found that Becker was already clapping his hands and chuckling some more.

'That's it,' he said, 'let's relax a little. Be nice and friendly.' He glanced at me meaningfully. 'We're not in a hurry are we, sir?'

I shrugged and shook my head.

'Just as long as we don't forget why we came,' I said, trying not to sound like a prig.

Evona Wylezynska stood up and pressed a bell on the wall behind a curtain. She made a tutting noise, and said: 'Why not just forget everything? That's why most of my gentlemen come here, to forget about their cares.'

While her back was turned Becker frowned and shook his head at me. I wasn't sure exactly what he meant.

Evona took the nape of my neck in the palm of her hand and began to knead the flesh there with fingers that were as strong as blacksmith's pincers.

'There's a lot of tension here, Bernhard,' she informed me seductively.

'I don't doubt it. You should see the cart they've got me pulling down at the Alex. Not to mention the number of passengers I've been asked to take.' It was my turn to glance meaningfully at Becker. Then I took Evona's fingers away from my neck and kissed them amicably. They smelt of iodine soap, and there are better olfactory aphrodisiacs than that.

Evona's girls walked slowly into the room like a troupe of circus horses. Some were wearing just slips and stockings, but mostly they were naked. They took up positions around Becker and myself, and started to smoke or to help themselves to drinks, almost as if we hadn't been there at all. It was more female flesh than I had seen in a long time, and I have to admit that my eyes would have branded the bodies of any ordinary women. But these girls were used to being eyed, and remained coolly undisturbed by our prurient stares. One picked up a dining chair and, setting it down in front of me, sat astride it so that I had as perfect a view of her genitals as I could have been expected to have wished for. She started flexing her bare buttocks against the seat of the chair for good measure.

Almost immediately Becker was on his feet and rubbing his hands together like the keenest of street-traders.

'Well, this is very nice, isn't it?' Becker put his arms around a couple of the girls, his face growing redder with excitement. He glanced around the room and, not finding the face he was looking for, said: 'Tell me, Evona, where is that lovely little child-bearing machine of a Jewess who used to work for you?'

'You mean Esther. I'm afraid she had to go away.' We waited, but there was no sign of anything other than smoke coming from Evona's mouth to expand upon what she had said.

'That's too bad,' said Becker. 'I was telling my friend here just how nice she was.' He shrugged. 'Never mind. Plenty more where she came from, eh?' Ignoring the look on my face, and still supported like a drunk by the two snappers, he turned and walked down the creaking corridor and into one of the bedrooms, leaving me alone with the rest of them.

'And what is your preference, Bernhard?' Evona snapped her fingers and waved one of her girls forward. 'This one and Esther are very much alike,' she said, taking hold of the girl's bare backside and turning it towards my face, smoothing it with the palm of her hand. 'She has two vertebrae too many, so that her behind is a long way from her waist. Very beautiful, do you not think?'

'Very beautiful,' I said, and patted the girl's marble-cool bottom politely. 'But to be honest, I'm the old-fashioned type. I like a girl to have all her mind on me and not my wallet.'

Evona smiled. 'No, I did not think you were the type.' She smacked the girl's behind like a favourite dog. 'Go on, off you go. All of you.'

I watched them troop silently out of the room and felt something close to disappointment that I wasn't more like Becker. She seemed to sense this ambivalence.

'You are not like Emil. He is attracted to any girl who will show him her fingernails. I think that one would fuck a cat with a broken back. How's your drink?'

I swirled it demonstratively. 'Just fine,' I said.

'Well, is there anything else that I can get you?'

I felt her bosom press against my arm and smiled down at what was hanging in the gallery. I lit a cigarette and looked her in the eye.

'Don't pretend to be disappointed if I say that all I'm after is some information.'

She smiled, checking her advance, and reached for her drink. 'What kind of information?'

'I'm looking for a man, and before you rip a hole for the joke, the man I'm after is a killer, with four goals on the score-sheet.'

'How can I help you? I run a whorehouse, not a private detective agency.'

'It's not uncommon for a man to use one of your girls roughly.'

'There's none of them wears velvet gloves, Bernhard, I'll tell you that much. Quite a lot of them figure that just because they've paid for the privilege, it gives them a licence to tear a girl's underwear.'

'Someone who went beyond what is considered to be a normal hazard of the profession, then. Maybe one of your girls has had such a client. Or heard of someone who has.'

'Tell me more about your killer.'

'I don't know much,' I sighed. 'I don't know his name, where he lives, where he came from or what he looks like. What I do know is that he likes tying up schoolgirls.'

'Lots of men like tying girls up,' Evona said. 'Don't ask me what they get out of it. There are even some who like to whip girls, although I don't permit that sort of thing. That kind of pig should be locked away.'

'Look, anything might help. Right now there's not a great deal to go on.'

Evona shrugged, and stubbed out her cigarette. 'What the hell,' she said. 'I was a schoolgirl myself once. You said four girls.'

'It may even be five. All aged about fifteen or sixteen. Nice families, and bright futures until this maniac kidnaps them, rapes them, cuts their throats and then dumps their naked bodies.'

Evona looked thoughtful. 'There was something,' she said carefully. 'Of course you realize that it's unlikely that the sort of man who comes to my place or any place like it is not the sort of man who preys on young girls. I mean, the point of a place like this is to take care of a man's needs.'

I nodded, but I was thinking of Kürten, and of how his case contradicted her. I decided not to press the point.

'Like I said, it's a long shot.'

Evona stood up and excused herself for a moment. When she returned she was accompanied by the girl whose elongated backside I had been obliged to admire. This time she was wearing a gown, and seemed more nervous clothed than she had been while naked.

'This is Helene,' Evona said, sitting down again. 'Helene, sit down and tell the Kommissar about the man who tried to kill you.'

The girl sat down on the chair where Becker had been sitting. She was pretty in a tired sort of way, as if she didn't sleep enough, or was using some sort of drug. Hardly daring to look me in the eye she chewed her lip and tugged at a length of her long red hair.

'Well, go on,' Evona urged. 'He won't eat you. He had that chance earlier on.'

'The man we're looking for likes to tie girls up,' I told her, leaning forward encouragingly. 'Then he strangles them, or cuts their throats.'

'I'm sorry,' she said after a minute. 'This is hard for me. I wanted to forget all about it, but Evona says that some school-girls have been murdered. I want to help, really I do, but it's hard.'

I lit a cigarette and offered her the packet. She shook her head. 'Take your time, Helene,' I said. 'Is this a customer we're talking about? Someone who came for a massage?'

'I won't have to go to court, will I? I'm not saying anything if it means standing up in front of a magistrate and saying I'm a party-girl.'

'The only person you'll have to tell is me.'

The girl sniffed without much enthusiasm.

'Well, you seem all right, I suppose.' She shot a look at the cigarette in my hand. 'Can I change my mind about that nail?'

'Sure,' I said, and held out the packet.

The first drag seemed to galvanize her. She smarted as she told the story, embarrassed a little, and probably a bit scared as well.

'About a month ago I had a client in one evening. I gave him a massage and when I asked him if he wanted me to dial his number he asked me if he could tie me up and then get himself frenched. I said that it would cost him another twenty, and he agreed. So there I was, trussed up like a roast chicken, having finished frenching him, and I ask him to untie me. He gets this funny look in his eye, and calls me a dirty whore, or something like that. Well you get used to men going mean on you when you've finished, like they're ashamed of themselves, but I could see that this one was different, so I tried to stay calm. Then he got the knife out and start to lay it flat on my neck like he wanted me to be scared. Which I was. Fit to scream my lungs out of my throat, only I didn't want to scare him into cutting me right away, thinking that I might be able to talk him out of it.' She took another tremulous drag on her cigarette.

'But that was just his cue to start throttling me, him thinking that I was about to scream, I mean. He grabbed hold of my windpipe and starts to choke me. If one of the other girls hadn't walked in there by mistake he'd have scratched me out and no mistake. I had the bruises on my neck for almost a week afterwards.'

'What happened when the other girl came in?'

'Well, I couldn't say for sure. I was more concerned with drawing breath than seeing that he got a taxi home all right, you know what I mean? As far as I know he just snatched up his things and got his smell out the door.'

'What did he look like?'

'He had a uniform on.'

'What kind of uniform? Can you be a little more specific?'

She shrugged. 'Who am I, Hermann Goering? Shit, I don't know what kind of uniform it was.'

'Well was it green, black, brown or what? Come on, girl, think. It's important.'

She took a fierce drag and shook her head impatiently.

'An old uniform. The sort they used to wear.'

'You mean like a war veteran?'

'Yes, that's the sort of thing, only a bit more – Prussian, I suppose. You know, the waxed moustache, the cavalry boots. Oh yes, I nearly forgot, he had spurs on.'

'Spurs?'

'Yes, like to ride a horse.'

'Anything else you remember?'

'He had a wineskin, on a string which he slung over his shoulder, so that it looked like a bugle at his hip. Only he said that it was full of schnapps.'

I nodded, satisfied, and leant back on the sofa, wondering what it would have been like to have had her after all. For the first time I noticed the yellowish discoloration of her hands which wasn't nicotine, jaundice or her temperament, but a clue that she'd been working in a munitions factory. In the same way I'd once identified a body pulled out of the Landwehr. Another thing I had learned from Hans Illmann.

'Hey, listen,' said Helene, 'if you get this bastard, make sure that he gets all the usual Gestapo hospitality, won't you? Thumbscrews and rubber truncheons?'

'Lady,' I said, standing up, 'you can depend on it. And thanks for helping.'

Helene stood up, her arms folded, and shrugged. 'Yes, well, I was a schoolgirl myself once, you know what I mean?'

I glanced at Evona and smiled. 'I know what you mean.' I jerked my head at the bedrooms along the corridor. 'When Don Juan's concluded his investigations, tell him that I went to question the head-waiter at Peltzers. Then maybe I thought I'd talk to the manager at the Winter Garden and see what I could get out of him. After that I might just head back to the Alex and clean my gun. Who knows, I may even find time to do a little police work along the way.'

9

Friday, 16 September

'Where are you from, Gottfried?'

The man smiled proudly. 'Eger, in the Sudetenland. Another few weeks and you can call it Germany.'

'Foolhardy is what I call it,' I said. 'Another few weeks and your Sudetendeutsche Partei will have us all at war. Martial law has already been declared in most SDP districts.'

'Men must die for what they believe in.' He leant back on his chair and dragged a spur along the floor of the interrogation room. I stood up, loosening my shirt collar, and moved out of the shaft of sunlight that shone through the window. It was a hot day. Too hot to be wearing a jacket, let alone the uniform of an old Prussian cavalry officer. Gottfried Bautz, arrested early that same morning, didn't seem to notice the heat, although his waxed moustache was beginning to show signs of a willingness to stand easy.

'What about women?' I asked. 'Do they have to die as well?'

His eyes narrowed. 'I think that you had better tell me why I have been brought here, don't you, Herr Kommissar?'

'Have you ever been to a massage parlour on Richard Wagner Strasse?'

'No, I don't think so.'

'You're a difficult man to forget, Gottfried. I doubt that you could have made yourself look any easier to remember than if you had rode up the stairs on a white stallion. Incidentally, why do you wear the uniform?'

'I served Germany, and I'm proud of it. Why shouldn't I wear a uniform?'

I started to say something about the war being over, but there didn't seem like much point, what with another one on the way, and Gottfried being such a spinner.

'So,' I said. 'Were you at the massage parlour on Richard Wagner Strasse, or not?'

'Maybe. One doesn't always remember the exact locations of places like that. I don't make a habit of –'

'Spare me the character reference. One of the girls there says that you tried to kill her.'

'That's preposterous.'

'She's quite adamant, I'm afraid.'

'Has this girl made a complaint against me?'

'Yes, she has.'

Gottfried Bautz chuckled smugly. 'Come now, Herr Kommissar. We both know that's not true. In the first place there hasn't been an identification parade. And in the second, even if there was, there's not a snapper in the whole of Germany who would report so much as a lost poodle. No complaint, no witness, and I fail to see why we're having this conversation at all.'

'She says that you tied her up like a hog, nudged her mouth and then tried to strangle her.'

'She says, she says. Look, what is this shit? It's my word against hers.'

'You're forgetting the witness, aren't you, Gottfried? The girl who came in while you were squeezing the shit out of the other one? Like I said, you're not an easy man to forget.'

'I'm prepared to let a court decide who is telling the truth here,' he said. 'Me, a man who fought for his country, or a couple of stupid little honeybees. Are they prepared to do the same?' He was shouting now, sweat starting off his forehead like pastry-glaze. 'You're just pecking at vomit, and you know it.'

I sat down again and aimed my forefinger at the centre of his face.

'Don't get smart, Gottfried. Not in here. The Alex breaks more skin that way than Max Schmelling, and you don't always get to go back to your dressing-room at the end of the fight.' I folded my hands behind my head, leant back and looked nonchalantly up at the ceiling. 'Take my word for it, Gottfried. This little bee isn't so dumb that she won't do exactly what I tell her to do. If I tell her to french the magistrate in open court she'll do it. Understand?'

'You can go fuck yourself, then,' he snarled. 'I mean, if you're going to custom-build me a cage then I don't see that you need me to cut you a key. Why the hell should I answer any of your questions?'

'Please yourself. I'm not in any hurry. Me, I'll go back home, take a nice hot bath, get a good night's sleep. Then I'll come back here and see what kind of an evening you've had. Well, what can I say? They don't call this place Grey Misery for nothing.'

'All right, all right,' he groaned. 'Go ahead and ask your lousy questions.'

'We searched your room.'

'Like it?'

'Not as much as the bugs you share with. We found some rope. My inspector thinks it's the special strangling kind you buy at Ka-De-We. On the other hand it could be the kind you use to tie someone up.'

'Or it could be the sort of rope I use in my job. I work for Rochling's Furniture Removals.'

'Yes, I checked. But why take a length of rope home with you? Why not just leave it in the van?'

'I was going to hang myself.'

'What changed your mind?'

'I thought about it awhile, and then things didn't seem quite so bad. That was before I met you.'

'What about the bloodstained cloth we found in a bag underneath your bed?'

'That? Menstrual blood. An acquaintance of mine, she had a small accident. I meant to burn it, but I forgot.'

'Can you prove that? Will this acquaintance corroborate your story?'

'Unfortunately I can't tell you very much about her, Kommissar. A casual thing, you understand.' He paused. 'But surely there are scientific tests which will substantiate what I say?'

'Tests will determine whether or not it is human blood. But

I don't think there's anything as precise as you are suggesting. I can't say for sure, I'm not a pathologist.'

I stood up again and went over to the window. I found my cigarettes and lit one.

'Smoke?' He nodded and I threw the packet on to the table. I let him get his first breath of it before I tossed him the grenade. 'I'm investigating the murders of four, possibly five young girls,' I said quietly. 'That's why you're here now. Assisting us with our inquiries, as they say.'

Gottfried stood up quickly, his tongue tamping down his lower lip, the cigarette rolling on the table where he had thrown it. He started to shake his head and didn't stop.

'No, no, no. No, you've got the wrong man. I know absolutely nothing of this. Please, you've got to believe me. I'm innocent.'

'What about that girl you raped in Dresden, in 1931? You were in the cement for that, weren't you, Gottfried? You see, I've checked your record.'

'It was statutory rape. The girl was under age, that's all. I didn't know. She consented.'

'Now let's see, how old was she again? Fifteen? Sixteen? That's about the same age as the girls who've been murdered. You know, maybe you just like them young. You feel ashamed of what you are, and transfer your guilt to them. How can they make you do these things?'

'No, it's not true, I swear it –'

'How can they be so disgusting? How can they provoke you so shamelessly?'

'Stop it, for Christ's sake –'

'You're innocent. Don't make me laugh. Your innocence isn't worth shit in the gutter, Gottfried. Innocence is for decent, law-abiding citizens, not the kind of sewer-rat like you who tries to strangle a girl in a massage parlour. Now sit down and shut up.'

He rocked on his heels for a moment, and then sat down heavily. 'I didn't kill anyone,' he muttered. 'Whichever way you want to cut it, I'm innocent, I tell you.'

'That you may be,' I said. 'But I'm afraid I can't plane a

piece of wood without dropping a few shavings. So, innocent or not, I've got to keep you for a while. At least until I can check you out.' I picked up my jacket and walked to the door.

'One last question for the moment,' I said. 'I don't suppose you own a car, do you?'

'On my pay? You are joking, aren't you?'

'What about the furniture van. Are you the driver?'

'Yes. I'm the driver.'

'Ever use it in the evenings?' He stayed silent. I shrugged and said: 'Well, I suppose I can always ask your employer.'

'It's not allowed, but sometimes I do use it, yes. Do a bit of private contracting, that sort of thing.' He looked squarely at me. 'But I never used it to kill anyone in, if that's what you were suggesting.'

'It wasn't, as it happens. But thanks for the idea.'

I sat in Arthur Nebe's office and waited for him to finish his telephone call. His face was grave when finally he replaced the receiver. I was about to say something when he raised his finger to his lips, opened his desk drawer and took out a tea-cosy with which he covered the phone.

'What's that for?'

'There's a wire on the telephone. Heydrich's, I suppose, but who can tell? The tea-cosy keeps our conversation private.' He leant back in his chair underneath a picture of the Führer and uttered a long and weary sigh. 'That was one of my men calling from the Berchtesgaden,' he said. 'Hitler's talks with the British prime minister don't seem to be going particularly well. I don't think our beloved Chancellor of Germany cares if there's war with England or not. He's conceding absolutely nothing.

'Of course he doesn't give a damn about these Sudeten Germans. This nationalist thing is just a cover. Everyone knows it. It's all that Austro-Hungarian heavy industry that he wants. That he needs, if he's going to fight a European war. God, I wish he had to deal with someone stronger than Chamberlain. He brought his umbrella with him you know. Bloody little bank manager.'

'Do you think so? I'd say the umbrella denotes quite a sensible sort of man. Can you really imagine Hitler or Goebbels ever managing to stir up a crowd of men carrying umbrellas? It's the very absurdity of the British which makes them so impossible to radicalize. And why we should envy them.'

'It's a nice idea,' he said, smiling reflectively. 'But tell me about this fellow you've arrested. Think he might be our man?'

I glanced around the room for a moment, hoping to find greater conviction on the walls and the ceiling, and then lifted my hands almost as if I meant to disclaim Gottfried Bautz's presence in a cell downstairs.

'From a circumstantial point of view, he could fit the laundry list.' I rationed myself to one sigh. 'But there's nothing that definitely connects him. The rope we found in his room is the same type as the rope that was used to bind the feet of one of the dead girls. But then it's a very common type of rope. We use the same kind here at the Alex.

'Some cloth we found underneath his bed could be stained with blood from one of his victims. Equally, it could be menstrual blood, as he claims. He has access to a van in which he could have transported and killed his victims relatively easily. I've got some of the boys checking it over now, but so far it appears to be as clean as a dentist's fingers.

'And then of course there is his record. We've locked his door once before for a sexual offence – a statutory rape. More recently he probably tried to strangle a snapper he'd first persuaded to be tied up. So he could fit the psychological bill of the man we're looking for.' I shook my head. 'But that's more "could-be" than Fritz fucking Lang. What I want is some real evidence.'

Nebe nodded sagely and put his boots on the desk. Tapping his fingers' ends together, he said: 'Could you build a case? Break him?'

'He's not stupid. It will take time. I'm not that good an interrogator, and I'm not about to take any short-cuts either. The last thing I want on this case is broken teeth on the charge sheet. That's how Josef Kahn got himself folded away and put in the costume-hire hospital.' I helped myself from the box of American cigarettes on Nebe's desk and lit one with an enormous brass table lighter, a present from Goering. The prime minister was always giving away cigarette lighters to people who had done him some small service. He used them like a nanny uses boiled sweets.

'Incidentally, has he been released yet?'

Nebe's lean face adopted a pained expression. 'No, not yet,' he said.

'I know it's considered only a small detail, the fact that he hasn't actually murdered anyone, but don't you think it's time he should be let out? We still have some standards left, don't we?'

He stood up and came round the desk to stand in front of me.

'You're not going to like this, Bernie,' he said. 'No more than I do myself.'

'Why should this be an exception? I figure that the only reason there aren't any mirrors in the lavatories is so that nobody has to look himself in the eye. They're not going to release him, right?'

Nebe leant against the side of the desk, folded his arms and stared at the toes of his boots for a minute.

'Worse than that, I'm afraid. He's dead.'

'What happened?'

'Officially?'

'You can give it a shot.'

'Josef Kahn took his own life while the balance of his mind was disturbed.'

'I can see how that would read nicely. But you know different, right?'

'I don't know anything for certain.' He shrugged. 'So call it informed guesswork. I hear things, I read things and I make a few reasonable conclusions. Naturally as Reichskriminaldirektor I have access to all kinds of secret decrees in the Ministry of the Interior.' He took a cigarette and lit it. 'Usually these are camouflaged with all sorts of neutral-sounding bureaucratic names.

'Well then, at the present moment there's a move to establish a new committee for the research of severe constitutional disease –'

'You mean like what this country is suffering from?'

'– with the aim of encouraging "positive eugenics, in accordance with the Führer's thoughts on the subject".' He waved his cigarette at the portrait on the wall behind him. 'Whenever you read that phrase "the Führer's thoughts on the subject", one knows to pick up one's well-read copy of his book. And there you will find that he talks about using the most modern medical means at our disposal to prevent the physically degenerate and mentally sick from contaminating the future health of the race.'

'Well, what the hell does that mean?'

'I had assumed it meant that such unfortunates would simply be prevented from having families. I mean, that does seem sensible, doesn't it? If they are incapable of looking after themselves then they can hardly be fit to bring up children.'

'It doesn't seem to have deterred the Hitler Youth leaders.'

Nebe snorted and went back round his desk. 'You're going to have to watch your mouth, Bernie,' he said, half-amused.

'Get to the funny bit.'

'Well, it's this. A number of recent reports, complaints if you like, made to Kripo by those related to institutionalized people leads me to suspect that some sort of mercy-killing is already being unofficially practised.'

I leant forward and grasped the bridge of my nose.

'Do you ever get headaches? I get headaches. It's smell that really sets them off. Paint smells pretty bad. So does formaldehyde in the mortuary. But the worst are those rotten pissing places you get where the dozers and rum-sweats sleep rough. That's a smell I can recall in my worst nightmares. You know, Arthur, I thought I knew every bad smell there was in this city. But that's last month's shit fried with last year's eggs.'

Nebe pulled open a drawer and took out a bottle and two glasses. He said nothing as he poured a couple of large ones.

I threw it back and waited for the fiery spirit to seek out what was left of my heart and stomach. I nodded and let him pour me another. I said: 'Just when you thought that things couldn't get any worse, you find out that they've always been a lot worse than you thought they were. And then they get worse.' I drained the second glass and then surveyed its empty shape. 'Thanks for telling me straight, Arthur.' I dragged myself to my feet. 'And thanks for the warmer.'

'Please keep me informed about your suspect,' he said. 'You might consider letting a couple of your men work a friend-and-foe shift on him. No rough stuff, just a bit of the old-fashioned psychological pressure. You know the sort of thing I mean. Incidentally, how are you getting on with your team? Everything working out there? No resentments, or anything like that?'

I could have sat down again and given him a list of faults there that were as long as a Party rally, but really he didn't need it. I knew that Kripo had a hundred bulls who were worse than the three I had in my squad. So I merely nodded and said that everything was fine.

But at the door to Nebe's office I stopped and uttered the words automatically, without even thinking. I said it, and not out of obligation, in response to someone else, in which situation I might have consoled myself with the excuse that I was just keeping my head down and avoiding the trouble of giving offence. I said it first.

'Heil Hitler.'

'Heil Hitler.' Nebe didn't look up from whatever it was that he had started writing as he mumbled his reply, so he didn't see my expression. I couldn't say what it would have looked like. But whatever my expression, it was born of the realization that the only real complaint I had at the Alex was going to be against myself.

10

The telephone rang. I wrestled my way across from the other side of the bed and answered it. I was still registering the time while Deubel was speaking. It was two a.m.

'Say that again.'

'We think we've found the missing girl, sir.'

'Dead?'

'Like a mouse in a trap. There's no positive identification yet, but it looks like all the rest of them, sir. I've called Professor Illmann. He's on his way now.'

'Where are you, Deubel?'

'Zoo Bahnhof.'

It was still warm outside when I went down to the car, and I opened the window to enjoy the night air, as well as to help wake me up. For everyone but Herr and Frau Hanke asleep at their home in Steglitz, it promised to be a nice day.

I drove east along Kurfürstendamm with its geometric-shaped, neon-lit shops, and turned north up Joachimstaler Strasse, at the top of which loomed the great luminous green-house that was the Zoo Station. In front were several police vans, a redundant ambulance and a few drunks still intent on making a night of it, being moved on by a bull.

Inside, I walked across the floor of the central ticket hall towards the police barrier that had been erected in front of the lost property and left-luggage areas. I flashed my badge at the two men guarding the barrier and carried on through. As I rounded the corner Deubel met me half way.

'What have we got?' I said.

'Body of a girl in a trunk, sir. From the look and smell of her she's been in there sometime. The trunk was in the left-luggage office.'

'The professor here yet?'

'Him and the photographer. They haven't done much more than give her a dirty look. We wanted to wait for you.'

'I'm touched by your thoughtfulness. Who found the mortal remains?'

'I did, sir, with one of the uniformed sergeants in my squad.'

'Oh? What did you do, consult a medium?'

'There was an anonymous telephone call, sir. To the Alex. He told the desk sergeant where to find the body, and the desk sergeant told my sergeant. He rang me and we came straight down here. We located the trunk, found the girl and then I called you.'

'An anonymous caller you say. What time was this?'

'About twelve. I was just going off shift.'

'I'll want to speak to the man who took that call. You better get someone to check he doesn't go off duty either, at least not until he's made his report. How did you get in here?'

'The night station-master, sir. He keeps the keys in his office when they close the left luggage.' Deubel pointed at a fat greasy-looking man standing a few metres away, chewing the skin on the palm of his hand. 'That's him over there.'

'Looks like we're keeping him from his supper. Tell him I want the names and addresses of everyone who works in this section, and what time they start work in the morning. Regardless of what hours they work, I want to see them all here at the normal opening time, with all their records and paperwork.' I paused for a moment, steeling myself for what was about to follow.

'All right,' I said. 'Show me where.'

In the left-luggage office, Hans Illmann sat on a large parcel labelled 'Fragile', smoking one of his roll-ups and watching the police photographer set up his flashlights and camera-tripods.

'Ah, the Kommissar,' he said, eyeing me and standing. 'We're not long here ourselves, and I knew you'd want us to wait for you. Dinner's a little overcooked, so you'll need these.' He handed me a pair of rubber gloves, and then looked querulously at Deubel. 'Are you sitting down with us, inspector?'

Deubel grimaced. 'I'd rather not, if you don't mind, sir. Normally I would, but I've got a daughter about that age myself.'

I nodded. 'You'd better wake up Becker and Korsch and get them down here. I don't see why we should be the only ones to lose our rat.'

Deubel turned to go.

'Oh, inspector,' said Illmann, 'you might ask one of our uniformed friends to organize some coffee. I work a great deal better when I'm awake. Also, I need someone to take notes. Can your sergeant write legibly, do you think?'

'I assume he does, sir.'

'Inspector, the one assumption that it is safe to make with regard to the educational standards that prevail in Orpo is that which allows only of the man being capable of completing a betting-slip. Find out for sure, if you wouldn't mind. I'd rather do it myself than later have to decipher the cyrillic scrawl of a more primitive life-form.'

'Yes, sir.' Deubel smiled thinly and went to carry out his orders.

'I didn't think he was the sensitive type,' Illmann commented, watching him go. 'Imagine a detective not wanting to see the body. It's like a wine merchant declining to try a Burgundy he's about to purchase. Unthinkable. Wherever do they find these face-slappers?'

'Simple. They just go out and shanghai all the men wearing leather shorts. It's what the Nazis call natural selection.'

On the floor at the back of the left-luggage office lay the trunk containing the body, covered with a sheet. We pulled up a couple of large parcels and sat down.

Illmann drew back the sheet, and I winced a little as the animal-house smell rose up to greet me, turning my head automatically towards the better air that lay behind my shoulder.

'Yes, indeed,' he murmured, 'it's been a warm summer.'

It was a full-sized steamer trunk, and made of good quality blue leather, with brass locks and studs – the kind you see being loaded on to those high-class passenger liners that sail between Hamburg and New York. For its solitary occupant, a naked girl of about sixteen years old, there was only one kind of journey, the more final kind, which remained to be embarked upon. Partly swathed in what looked like a length of brown curtain material, she lay on her back with her legs folded to the left, a bare breast arching upwards as if there was something underneath her. The head lay at an impossibly contradictory angle to the rest of her body, the mouth open and almost smiling, the eyes half closed and, but for the dried blood in her nostrils and the rope around her ankles, you might almost have thought the girl was in the first stages of awakening from a long sleep.

Deubel's sergeant, a burly fellow with less neck than a hip-flask and a chest like a sandbag, arrived with a notebook and pencil, and sat a little way apart from Illmann and me, sucking a sweet, his legs crossed almost nonchalantly, apparently undisturbed at the sight which lay before us.

Illmann looked appraisingly at him for a moment and then nodded, before beginning to describe what he saw.

'An adolescent female,' he said solemnly, 'about sixteen years of age, naked, and lying inside a large trunk of quality manufacture. The body is covered partially with a length of brown cretonne, and the feet are bound with a piece of rope.' He spoke slowly, with pauses between the phrases in order to allow the sergeant's handwriting to keep pace with him.

'Pulling the fabric away from the body reveals the head almost completely severed from the torso. The body itself shows signs of advancing decomposition, consistent with it having been in the trunk for at least four to five weeks. The hands show no signs of defence wounds, and I'm wrapping them for further examination of the fingers in the laboratory, although since she clearly bit her nails I expect I'll be wasting my time.' He took two thick paper bags out of his case and I helped him secure them over the dead girl's hands.

'Hallo, what's this? Do my eyes deceive me, or is this a bloodstained blouse which I see before me?'

'It looks like her BdM uniform,' I said, watching him pick up first the blouse, and then a navy skirt.

'How extraordinarily thoughtful of our friend to send us her laundry. And just when I thought he was becoming just a little bit predictable. First an anonymous telephone call to the Alex, and now this. Remind me to consult my diary and check that it's not my birthday.'

Something else caught my eye, and I leant forward and picked the small square piece of card out of the trunk.

'Irma Hanke's identity card,' I said.

'Well that saves me the trouble, I suppose.' Illmann turned his head towards the sergeant. 'The trunk also contained the dead girl's clothing and her identity card,' he dictated.

Inside the card was a smudge of blood.

'Could that be a fingermark, do you think?' I asked him.

He took the card out of my hand and looked carefully at the mark. 'Yes, it could. But I don't see the relevance. An actual fingerprint would be a different story. That would answer a lot of our prayers.'

I shook my head. 'It's not an answer. It's a question. Why would a psycho bother to look at his victim's identity? I mean, the blood indicates that she was probably already dead, assuming it's hers. So why does our man feel obliged to find out her name?'

'Perhaps in order that he might name her in his anonymous call to the Alex?'

'Yes, but then why wait several weeks before making the call? Doesn't that strike you as strange?'

'You have a point there, Bernie.' He bagged the identity card and placed it carefully in his case, before looking back into the trunk. 'And what have we here?' He lifted up a small but heavy-looking sack and glanced inside. 'How's this for strange?' He held it open for my inspection. It was the empty toothpaste tubes that Irma Hanke had been collecting for the Reich Economy Programme. 'Our killer does seem to have thought of everything.'

'It's almost as if the bastard were defying us to catch him. He gives us everything. Think how smug he'll be if we still can't nail him.'

Illmann dictated some more notes to the sergeant and then

pronounced that he was finished with the preliminary scene-of-crime investigation, and that it was now the photographer's turn. Pulling our gloves off we moved away from the trunk and found that the station-master had provided coffee. It was hot and strong and I needed it to take away the taste of death that was coating my tongue. Illmann rolled a couple of cigarettes and handed me one. The rich tobacco tasted like barbecued nectar.

'Where does this leave your crazy Czech?' he said. 'The one who thinks he's a cavalry officer.'

'It seems that he really was a cavalry officer,' I said. 'Got a bit shell-shocked on the Eastern Front and never quite recovered. All the same, he's no hop and skip, and frankly, unless I get some hard evidence I'm not confident of making anything stick to him. And I'm not about to send anyone up on an Alexanderplatz-style confession. Not that he's saying anything, mind. He's been questioned the whole weekend and still maintains his innocence. I'll see if somebody from the left-luggage office here can identify him as the coat that left the trunk, but if not then I'll have to let him go.'

'I imagine that will upset your sensitive inspector,' chuckled Illmann. 'The one with the daughter. From what he was saying to me earlier, he was quite sure that it was only a matter of time before you had a case against him.'

'Almost certainly. He views the Czech's conviction for statutory rape as the best reason why I should let him take the fellow into a quiet cell and tap dance all over him.'

'So strenuous, these modern police methods. Wherever do they find the energy?'

'That's all they find energy for. This is well past Deubel's bedtime, as he's already reminded me. Some of these bulls think they're working banking hours.' I waved him over. 'Have you ever noticed how most of Berlin's crimes seem to happen during the day?'

'Surely you're forgetting the early-morning knock-up from your friendly neighbourhood Gestapo man.'

'You never get anyone more senior than a Kriminalassistent doing the A1 Red Tabs. And only then if it's someone important.'

114

I turned to face Deubel, who was doing his best to act dog-tired and ready for a hospital bed.

'When the photographer has finished his portrait, tell him I want a couple of shots of the trunk with the lid closed. What's more I want the prints ready by the time the left-luggage staff turns up. It'll be something to help refresh their memories. The professor here will be taking the trunk back to the Alex as soon as the snaps are done.'

'What about the girl's family, sir? It is Irma Hanke, isn't it?'

'They'll need to make a formal identification, of course, but not until the professor's had his way with her. Maybe even smartened her up a bit for her mother?'

'I'm not a mortician, Bernie,' he said coolly.

'Come on. I've seen you sew up a bag of minced beef before now.'

'Very well,' Illmann sighed. 'I'll see what I can do. I shall need most of the day, however. Possibly until tomorrow.'

'Have as long as you like, but I want to tell them the news this evening, so see if at least you can nail her head back on to her shoulders by then will you?'

Deubel yawned loudly.

'All right, inspector, you've passed the audition. The role of the tired man in need of his bed is yours. God knows you've worked hard enough for it. As soon as Becker and Korsch turn up you can go home. But I want you to set up an identity parade later on this morning. See if the men who work in this office can't remember our Sudeten friend.'

'Right, sir,' he said, already more alert now that his going home was imminent.

'What's the name of that desk sergeant? The one who took the anonymous call.'

'Gollner.'

'Not old Tanker Gollner?'

'Yes, sir. You'll find him at the police barracks, sir. Apparently he said he'd wait for us there as he'd been pissed around by Kripo before and didn't want to have to sit around all night waiting for us to show up.'

'Same old Tanker,' I smiled. 'Right, I'd best not keep him

waiting, had I?'

'What shall I tell Korsch and Becker to do when they arrive?' Deubel asked.

'Get Korsch to go through the rest of the junk in this place. See if we might not have been left any other kind gifts.'

Illmann cleared his throat. 'It might be an idea if one of them were present to observe the autopsy,' he said.

'Becker can help you. He seems to enjoy being around the female body. Not to mention his excellent qualifications in the matter of violent death. Just don't leave him alone with your cadaver, Professor. He's just liable to shoot her or fuck her, depending on the way he's feeling.'

Kleine Alexander Strasse ran north-east towards Horst Wessel Platz and was where the police barracks for those stationed at the nearby Alex was situated. It was a big building, with small apartments for married men and senior officers, and single rooms for the rest.

Despite the fact that he was no longer married, Wachmeister Fritz 'Tanker' Gollner had a small one-bedroom apartment at the back of the barracks on the third floor, in recognition of his long and distinguished service record.

A well-tended window box was the apartment's only concession to homeliness, the walls being bare of anything except a couple of photographs in which Gollner was being decorated. He waved me to the room's solitary armchair and sat himself on the edge of the neatly made bed.

'Heard you was back,' he said quietly. Leaning forwards he pulled out a crate from under the bed. 'Beer?'

'Thanks.'

He nodded reflectively as he pushed off the bottle-tops with his bare thumbs.

'And it's Kommissar now, I hear. Resigns as an inspector. Reincarnated as a Kommissar. Makes you believe in fucking magic, doesn't it? If I didn't know you better I'd say you were in somebody's pocket.'

'Aren't we all? In one way or another.'

'Not me. And unless you've changed, not you either.' He

swigged his beer thoughtfully.

Tanker was an East Fresian from Emsland where, it is said, brains are as rare as fur on fish. While he may not have been able to spell Wittgenstein, let alone explain his philosophy, Tanker was a good policeman, one of the old school of uniformed bulls, the firm but fair sort, enforcing the law with a friendly box on the ear for young rowdies, and less inclined to arrest a man and haul him off to the cells than give him an effective and administratively simple bedtime-story with his encyclopaedia-sized fist. It was said of Tanker that he was the toughest bull in Orpo and, looking at him sitting opposite me now, in his shirt sleeves, his great belt creaking under the weight of his even greater belly, I didn't find this hard to believe. Certainly time had stood still with his prognathous features – somewhere around one million years BC. Tanker could not have looked less civilized than if he had been wearing the skin of a sabre-toothed tiger.

I found my cigarettes and offered him one. He shook his head and took out his pipe.

'If you ask me,' I said, 'we're every one of us in the back pocket of Hitler's trousers. And he means to slide down a mountain on his arse.'

Tanker sucked at the bowl of his pipe and started to fill it with tobacco. When he'd finished he smiled and raised his bottle.

'Then here's to stones under the fucking snow.'

He belched loudly and lit his pipe. The clouds of pungent smoke that rolled towards me like Baltic fog reminded me of Bruno. It even smelt like the same foul mixture that he had smoked.

'You knew Bruno Stahlecker, didn't you, Tanker?'

He nodded, still drawing on the pipe. Through clenched teeth, he said: 'That I did. I heard about what happened. Bruno was a good man.' He removed the pipe from his leathery old mouth and surveyed the progress of his smoke. 'Knew him quite well, really. We were both in the infantry together. Saw a fair bit of action, too. Of course, he wasn't much more than a spit of a lad then, but it never seemed to

117

bother him much, the fighting I mean. He was a brave one.'

'The funeral was last Thursday.'

'I'd have gone too if I could have got the time.' He thought for a moment. 'But it was all the way down in Zehlendorf. Too far.' He finished his beer and opened another two bottles. 'Still, they got the piece of shit who killed him I hear, so that's all right then.'

'Yes, it certainly looks like it,' I said. 'Tell me about this telephone call tonight. What time was this?'

'Just before midnight, sir. Fellow asks for the duty sergeant. You're speaking to him, I says. Listen carefully, he says. The missing girl, Irma Hanke, he says, is to be found in a large blue-leather trunk in the left-luggage at Zoo Bahnhof. Who's this, I asks, but he'd hung up.'

'Can you describe his voice?'

'I'd say it was an educated sort of voice, sir. And used to giving an order and having it carried out. Rather like an officer.' He shook his large head. 'Couldn't tell you how old, though.'

'Any accent?'

'Just the trace of Bavarian.'

'You sure about that?'

'My late wife was from Nuremberg, sir. I'm sure.'

'And how would you describe his tone? Agitated? Disturbed at all?'

'He didn't sound like a spinner, if that's what you mean, sir. He was as cool as the piss out of a frozen eskimo. As I said, just like an officer.'

'And he asked to speak to the duty sergeant?'

'Those were his actual words, sir.'

'Any background noise? Traffic? Music? That sort of thing?'

'Nothing at all.'

'What did you do then? After the call.'

'I telephoned the operator at the Central Telephone Office on Französische Strasse. She traced the number to a public telephone box outside Bahnhof West Kreuz. I sent a squad car round there to seal it off until a team from 5D could get down there and have it checked out for piano players.'

'Good man. And then you called Deubel?'

'Yes, sir.'

I nodded and started on my second bottle of beer.

'I take it Orpo knows what this is all about?'

'Von der Schulenberg had all the Hauptmanns into the briefing-room at the start of last week. They passed on to us what a lot of the men already suspected. That there was another Gormann on the streets of Berlin. Most of the lads figure that's why you're back on the force. Most of the civils we've got now couldn't detect coal on a slag heap. But that Gormann case. Well, it was a good piece of work.'

'Thanks, Tanker.'

'All the same, sir, it doesn't look like this little Sudeten spinner you're holding could have done it, does it? If you don't mind me saying so.'

'Not unless he had a telephone in his cell, no. Still, we'll see if the left-luggage people at Zoo Bahnhof like the look of him. You never know, he might have had an associate on the outside.'

Tanker nodded. 'That's true enough,' he said. 'Anything is possible in Germany just as long as Hitler shits in the Reich Chancellery.'

Several hours later I was back at Zoo Bahnhof, where Korsch had already distributed photographs of the trunk to the assembled left-luggage staff. They stared and stared, shook their heads and scratched their grizzly chins, and still none of them could remember anyone leaving a blue-leather trunk.

The tallest of them, a man wearing the longest khaki-coloured boiler coat, and who seemed to be in charge of the rest, collected a notebook from under the metal-topped counter and brought it over to me.

'Presumably you record the names and addresses of those leaving luggage with you,' I said to him, without much enthusiasm. As a general rule, killers leaving their victims as left-luggage at railway stations don't normally volunteer their real names and addresses.

The man in the khaki coat, whose bad teeth resembled the blackened ceramic insulators on tram cables, looked at me with quiet confidence and tapped the hard cover of his register with the quick of a fingernail.

'It'll be in here, the one who left your bloody trunk.'

He opened his book, licked a thumb that a dog would have refused, and began to turn the greasy pages.

'On the trunk in your photograph there's a ticket,' he said. 'And on that ticket is a number, same one as what's chalked on the side of the item. And that number will be in this book, alongside a date, a name and an address.' He turned several more pages and then traced down the page with his forefinger.

'Here we are,' he said. 'The trunk was deposited here on Friday, 19 August.'

'Four days after she disappeared,' Korsch said quietly.

The man followed his finger along a line to the facing page. 'Says here that the trunk belongs to a Herr Heydrich, initial "R", of Wilhelmstrasse, number 102.'

Korsch snorted with laughter.

'Thank you,' I said to the man. 'You've been most helpful.'

'I don't see what's funny,' grumbled the man as he walked away.

I smiled at Korsch. 'Looks like someone has a sense of humour.'

'Are you going to mention this in the report, sir?' he grinned.

'It's material, isn't it?'

'It's just that the general won't like it.'

'He'll be beside himself, I should think. But you see, our killer isn't the only one who enjoys a good joke.'

Back at the Alex I received a call from the head of what was ostensibly Illmann's department – VD1, Forensics. I spoke to an SS-Hauptsturmführer Dr Schade, whose tone was predictably obsequious, no doubt in the belief that I had some influence with General Heydrich.

The doctor informed me that a fingerprint team had removed a number of prints from the telephone box at West

Kreuz in which the killer had apparently called the Alex. These were now a matter for VCI, the Records Department. As to the trunk and its contents, he had spoken to Kriminal-assistent Korsch and would inform him immediately if any fingerprints were discovered there.

I thanked him for his call, and told him that my investigation was to receive top priority, and that everything else would have to take second place.

Within fifteen minutes of this conversation, I received another telephone call, this time from the Gestapo.

'This is Sturmbannführer Roth here,' he said. 'Section 4BI. Kommissar Gunther, you are interfering with the progress of a most important investigation.'

'4BI? I don't think I know that department. Are you calling from within the Alex?'

'We are based at Meinekestrasse, investigating Catholic criminals.'

'I'm afraid I know nothing of your department, Sturmbann-führer. Nor do I wish to. Nevertheless, I cannot see how I can possibly be interfering with one of your investigations.'

'The fact remains that you are. It was you who ordered SS-Hauptsturmführer Dr Schade to give your own investigation priority over any other?'

'That's right, I did.'

'Then you, a Kommissar, should know that the Gestapo takes precedence over Kripo where the services of VDI are required.'

'I know of no such thing. But what great crime has been committed that might require your department to take prece-dence over a murder investigation? Charging a priest with a fraudulent transubstantiation perhaps? Or trying to pass off the communion wine as the blood of Christ?'

'Your levity is quite out of order, Kommissar,' he said. 'This department is investigating most serious charges of homosexuality among the priesthood.'

'Is that so? Then I shall certainly sleep more soundly in my bed tonight. All the same, my investigation has been given top priority by General Heydrich himself.'

'Knowing the importance that he attaches to apprehending religious enemies of the state, I find that very hard to believe.'

'Then may I suggest that you telephone the Wilhelmstrasse and have the general explain it to you personally.'

'I'll do that. No doubt he will also be greatly disturbed at your failure to appreciate the menace of the third international conspiracy dedicated to the ruin of Germany. Catholicism is no less a threat to Reich security than Bolshevism and World Jewry.'

'You forgot men from outer space,' I said. 'Frankly, I don't give a shit what you tell him. VD1 is part of Kripo, not the Gestapo, and in all matters relating to this investigation Kripo is to take priority in the services of our own department. I have it in writing from the Reichskriminaldirektor, as does Dr Schade. So why don't you take your so-called case and shove it up your arse. A little more shit in there won't make much of a difference to the way you smell.'

I slammed the receiver down on to its cradle. There were, after all, a few enjoyable aspects to the job. Not least of these was the opportunity it afforded to piss on the Gestapo's shoes.

At the identity parade later that same morning, the left-luggage staff failed to identify Gottfried Bautz as the man who had deposited the trunk containing Irma Hanke's body, and to Deubel's disgust I signed the order releasing him from custody.

It's the law that all strangers arriving in Berlin must be reported to a police station by their hotelier or landlord within six days. In this way the Resident Registration Office at the Alex is able to give out the address of anyone resident in Berlin for the price of fifty pfennigs. People imagine that this law must be part of the Nazi Emergency Powers, but in truth it has existed for a while. The Prussian police was always so efficient.

My office was a few doors down from the Registration Office in room 350, which meant that the corridor was always noisy with people, and obliged me to keep my door shut. No doubt this had been one of the reasons why I had been put here, as far away from the offices of the Murder Commission as it was possible to be. I suppose the idea was that my presence should be kept out of the way of other Kripo personnel, for fear that I might contaminate them with some of my more anarchic attitudes to police investigation. Or perhaps they had hoped that my insubordinate spirit might be broken by first being dramatically lowered. Even on a sunny day like this one was, my office had a dismal aspect. The olive-green metal desk had more thread-catching edges than a barbed-wire fence, and had the single virtue of matching the worn linoleum and the dingy curtains, while the walls were a couple of thousand cigarettes' shade of yellow.

Walking in there after snatching a few hours of sleep back at my apartment, and presented with the sight of Hans Illmann waiting patiently for me with a dossier of photographs, I didn't think that the place was about to get any more pleasant. Congratulating myself on having had the foresight to eat something before what promised to be an unappetizing meeting, I sat down and faced him.

'So this is where they've been hiding you,' he said.

'It's supposed to be only temporary,' I explained, 'just like me. But frankly, it suits me to be out of the way of the rest of Kripo. There's less chance of becoming a permanent fixture here again. And I dare say that suits them too.'

'One would not have thought it possible to cause such aggravation throughout Kripo Executive from such a bureaucratic dungeon as this.' He laughed, and stroking his chin-beard added: 'You, and a Sturmbannführer from the Gestapo, have caused all sorts of problems for poor Dr Schade. He's had telephone calls from lots of important people. Nebe, Müller, even Heydrich. How very satisfying for you. No, don't shrug modestly like that. You have my admiration, Bernie, you really do.'

I pulled open a drawer in my desk and took out a bottle and a couple of glasses.

'Let's drink to it,' I said.

'Gladly. I could use one after the day I've had.' He picked

up the full glass and sipped it gratefully. 'You know, I had no idea that there was a special department in the Gestapo to persecute Catholics.'

'Nor had I. But I can't say that it surprises me much. National Socialism permits only one kind of organized belief.' I nodded at the dossier on Illmann's lap. 'So what have you got?'

'Victim number five is what we have got.' He handed me the dossier and started to roll himself a cigarette.

'These are good,' I said flicking through its contents. 'Your man takes a nice photograph.'

'Yes, I thought you'd appreciate them. That one of the throat is particularly interesting. The right carotid artery is almost completely severed thanks to one perfectly horizontal knife cut. That means that she was flat on her back when he cut her. All the same, the greater part of the wound is on the right-hand side of the throat, so in all probability our man is right-handed.'

'It must have been some knife,' I said, observing the depth of the wound.

'Yes. It severed the larynx almost completely.' He licked his cigarette paper. 'Something extremely sharp, like a surgical curette I should say. At the same time, however, the epiglottis was strongly compressed, and between that and the oesophagus on the right were haematomas as big as an orange pip.'

'Strangled, right?'

'Very good,' Illmann grinned. 'But half-strangled, in actual fact. There was a small quantity of blood in the girl's partially inflated lungs.'

'So he throttled her into silence, and later cut her throat?'

'She bled to death, hanging upside down like a butchered calf. Same as all the others. Do you have a match?'

I tossed my book across the desk. 'What about her important little places? Did he fuck her?'

'Fucked her, and tore her up a bit in the process. Well, you'd expect that. The girl was a virgin, I should imagine. There were even imprints of his fingernails on the mucous membrane. But more importantly I found some foreign pubic hairs, and I don't mean that they were imported from Paris.'

124

'You've got a hair colour?'

'Brown. Don't ask me for a shade, I can't be that specific.'

'But you're sure they're not Irma Hanke's?'

'Positive. They stood out on her perfectly Aryan fair-haired little plum like shit in a sugar-bowl.' He leaned back and blew a cloud into the air above his head. 'You want me to try and match one with a cutting from the bush of your crazy Czech?'

'No, I released him at lunchtime. He's in the clear. And as it happens his hair was fair.' I leafed through the typewritten pages of the autopsy report. 'Is that it?'

'Not quite.' He sucked at his cigarette and then crushed it into my ashtray. From his tweed hunting-jacket pocket he produced a sheet of folded newspaper which he spread out on the desk. 'I thought you ought to see this.'

It was the front page of an old issue of *Der Stürmer*, Julius Streicher's anti-Semitic publication. A flash across the top left-hand corner of the paper advertised it as 'A Special Ritual Murder Number'. Not that one needed reminding. The pen-and-ink illustration said it eloquently enough. Eight naked, fair-haired German girls hanging upside-down, their throats slit, and their blood spilling into a great Communion plate that was held by an ugly caricature Jew.

'Interesting, don't you think?' he said.

'Streicher's always publishing this sort of crap,' I said. 'Nobody takes it seriously.'

Illmann shook his head, and reclaimed his cigarette. 'I'm not for one minute saying that it should be. I no more believe in ritual murder than I believe in Adolf Hitler the Peacemaker.'

'But there is this drawing, right?' He nodded. 'Which is remarkably similar to the method with which five German girls have already been killed.' He nodded again.

I glanced down the page at the article that accompanied the drawing, and read: 'The Jews are charged with enticing Gentile children and Gentile adults, butchering them and draining their blood. They are charged with mixing this blood into their masses (unleavened bread) and using it to practise super-stitious magic. They are charged with torturing their victims, especially the children; and during this torture they scream threats, curses and cast magic spells against the Gentiles. This systematic murder has a special name. It is called Ritual Murder.'

'Are you suggesting that Streicher might have had something to do with these murders?'

'I don't know that I'm suggesting anything, Bernie. I merely thought I ought to bring it to your attention.' He shrugged. 'But why not? After all, he wouldn't be the first district Gauleiter to commit a crime. Governor Kube of Kurmark for example.'

'There are quite a few stories about Streicher that one hears,' I said.

'In any other country Streicher would be in prison.'

'Can I keep this?'

'I wish you would. It's not the sort of thing that one likes to leave lying on the coffee-table.' He crushed out yet another cigarette and stood up to leave. 'What are you going to do?'

'About Streicher? I don't exactly know.' I looked at my watch. 'I'll think about it after the formal ID. Becker's on his way back here with the girl's parents by now. We'd better get down to the mortuary.'

It was something that Becker said that made me drive the Hankes home myself after Herr Hanke had positively identified the remains of his daughter.

'It's not the first time I've had to break bad news to a family,' he had explained. 'In a strange way they always hope against hope, clinging on to the last straw right up until the end. And then when you tell them, that's when it really hits them. The mother breaks down, you know. But somehow these two were different. It's difficult to explain what I mean, sir, but I got the impression that they were expecting it.'

'After four weeks? Come on, they had just resigned themselves to it, that's all.'

Becker frowned and scratched the top of his untidy head.

'No,' he said slowly, 'it was stronger than that, sir. Like they already knew, for sure. I'm sorry, sir, I'm not explaining it very well. Perhaps I shouldn't have mentioned it at all. Perhaps I am imagining it.'

'Do you believe in instinct?'

'I suppose so.'

'Good. Sometimes it's the only thing a bull has got to go on. And then he's got no choice but to trust in it. A bull that doesn't trust a few hunches now and then doesn't ever take any chances. And without taking them you can't ever hope to solve a case. No, you were right to tell me.'

Sitting beside me now, as I drove south-west to Steglitz, Herr Hanke, an accountant with the AEG works on Seestrasse, seemed anything but resigned to his only daughter's death. All the same, I didn't discount what Becker had told me. I was keeping an open mind until I could form my own opinion.

'Irma was a clever girl,' Hanke sighed. He spoke with a Rhineland accent, with a voice that was just like Goebbels'. 'Clever enough to stay on at school and get her Abitur, which she'd wanted to do. But she was no book-buffalo. Just bright, and pretty with it. Good at sports. She had just won her Reich Sports Badge and her swimming certificate. She never did any harm to anyone.' His voice was breaking as he added: 'Who could have killed her, Kommissar? Who would do such a thing?'

'That's what I intend to find out,' I said. But Hanke's wife sitting in the back seat believed she already had the answer.

'Isn't it obvious who is responsible?' she said. 'My daughter was a good BdM girl, praised in her racial-theory class as the perfect example of the Aryan type. She knew her Horst Wessel and could quote whole pages of the Führer's great book. So who do you think killed her, a virgin, but the Jews? Who else but the Jews would have done such things to her?'

Herr Hanke turned in his seat and took his wife by the hand.

'We don't know that, Silke, dear,' he said. 'Do we, Kommissar?'

'I think it's very unlikely,' I said.

'You see, Silke? The Kommissar doesn't believe it, and neither do I.'

'I see what I see,' she hissed. 'You're both wrong. It's as plain as the nose on a Jew's face. Who else but the Jews? Don't you realize how obvious it is?'

'The accusation is loudly raised immediately, anywhere in the world, when a body is found which bears the marks of ritual murder. This accusation is raised only against the Jews.' I remembered the words of the article in *Der Stürmer* which I had folded in my pocket, and as I listened to Frau Hanke it occurred to me that she was right, but in a way she could hardly have dreamt of.

11

Thursday, 22 September

A whistle shrieked, the train jolted, and then we pulled slowly out of Anhalter Station on the six-hour journey that would take us to Nuremberg. Korsch, the compartment's only other occupant, was already reading his newspaper.

'Hell,' he said, 'listen to this. It says here that the Soviet foreign minister, Maxim Litvinoff declared in front of the League of Nations in Geneva that his government is determined to fulfil its existing treaty of alliance with Czechoslovakia, and that it will offer military help at the same time as France. Christ, we'll really be in for it then, with an attack on both fronts.'

I grunted. There was less chance of the French offering any real opposition to Hitler than there was of them declaring Prohibition. Litvinoff had chosen his words carefully. Nobody wanted war. Nobody but Hitler, that is. Hitler the syphilitic.

My thoughts returned to a meeting I had had the previous Tuesday with Frau Kalau vom Hofe at the Goering Institute.

'I brought your books back,' I explained. 'The one by Professor Berg was particularly interesting.'

'I'm glad you thought so,' she said. 'How about the Baudelaire?'

'That too, although it seemed much more applicable to Germany now. Especially the poems called "Spleen".'

'Maybe now you're ready for Nietzsche,' she said, leaning back in her chair.

It was a pleasantly furnished, bright office with a view of the Zoo opposite. You could just about hear the monkeys screaming in the distance.

Her smile persisted. She was better looking than I remembered. I picked up the solitary photograph that sat on her desk and stared at a handsome man and two little boys.

'Your family?'

'Yes.'

'You must be very happy.' I returned the picture to its position. 'Nietzsche,' I said, changing the subject. 'I don't know about that. I'm not really much of a reader, you see. I don't seem to be able to find the time. But I did look up those pages in *Mein Kampf* – the ones about venereal disease. Mind you, it meant that for a while I had to use a brick to wedge the bathroom window open.' She laughed. 'Anyway, I think you must be right.' She started to speak but I raised my hand. 'I know, I know, you didn't say anything. You were just telling me what is written in the Führer's marvellous book. Not offering a psychotherapeutic analysis of him through his writing.'

'That's right.'

I sat down and faced her across the desk.

'But that sort of thing is possible?'

'Oh, yes indeed.'

I handed her the page from *Der Stürmer*.

'Even with something like this?'

She looked at me levelly, and then opened her cigarette box. I helped myself to one, and then lit us both.

'Are you asking me officially?' she said.

'No, of course not.'

'Then I should say that it would be possible. In fact I should say that *Der Stürmer* is the work of not one but several psychotic personalities. The so-called editorials, these illustrations by Fino – God only knows what effect this sort of filth is having on people.'

'Can you speculate a little? The effect, I mean.'

She pursed her beautiful lips. 'Hard to evaluate,' she said after a pause. 'Certainly for weaker personalities, this sort of thing, regularly absorbed, could be corrupting.'

'Corrupting enough to make a man a murderer?'

'No,' she said, 'I don't think so. It wouldn't make a killer out of a normal man. But for a man already disposed to kill, I think it's quite possible that this kind of story and drawing might have a profound effect on him. And as you know from your own reading of Berg, Kürten himself was of the opinion that the more salacious kind of crime reporting had very definitely affected him.'

She crossed her legs, the sibilance of her stockings drawing my thoughts to their tops, to her garters and finally to the lacy paradise that I imagined existed there. My stomach tightened at the thought of running my hand up her skirt, at the thought of her stripped naked before me, and yet still speaking intelligently to me. Exactly where is the beginning of corruption?

'I see,' I said. 'And what would be your professional opinion of the man who published this story? I mean Julius Streicher.'

'A hatred like this is almost certainly the result of a great mental instability.' She paused for a moment. 'Can I tell you something in confidence?'

'Of course.'

'You know that Matthias Goering, the chairman of this institute, is the prime minister's cousin?'

'Yes.'

'Streicher has written a lot of poisonous nonsense about medicine as a Jewish conspiracy, and psychotherapy in particular. For a while the future of mental health in this country was in jeopardy because of him. Consequently Dr Goering has good reason to wish Streicher out of the way, and has already prepared a psychological evaluation of him at the prime minister's orders. I'm sure that I could guarantee the cooperation of this institute in any investigation involving Streicher.'

I nodded slowly.

'Are you investigating Streicher?'

'In confidence?'

'Of course.'

'I don't honestly know. Right now let's just say that I'm curious about him.'

'Do you want me to ask Dr Goering for help?'

I shook my head. 'Not at this stage. But thanks for the offer. I'll certainly bear it in mind.' I stood up, and went to the door. 'I'll bet you probably think quite highly of the prime minister, him being the patron of this institute. Am I right?'

'He's been good to us, it's true. Without his help I doubt

there would be an institute. Naturally we think highly of him for that.'

'Please don't think I'm blaming you, I'm not. But hasn't it ever occurred to you that your beneficent patron is just as likely to go and shit in someone else's garden, as Streicher is in yours? Have you ever thought about that? It stikes me as how it's a dirty neighbourhood we're living in, and that we're all going to keep finding crap on our shoes until someone has the sense to put all the stray dogs in the public kennel.' I touched the brim of my hat to her. 'Think about it.'

Korsch twisted his moustache absently as he continued reading his newspaper. I supposed that he had grown it in an effort to look more of a character, in the same way as some men will grow a beard: not because they dislike shaving – a beard requires just as much grooming as a clean-shaven face – but because they think it will make them seem like someone to be taken seriously. But with Korsch the moustache, little more than the stroke of an eyebrow-pencil, merely served to under-score his shifty mien. It made him look like a pimp, an effect at odds with his character however, which in a period of less than two weeks, I had discovered to be a willing and reliable one.

Noticing my attention, he was moved to inform me that the Polish foreign minister, Josef Beck, had demanded a solution to the problem of the Polish minority in the Olsa region of Czechoslovakia.

'Just like a bunch of gangsters, isn't it, sir?' he said. 'Every-one wants his cut.'

'Korsch,' I said, 'you missed your vocation. You should have been a newsreader on the radio.'

'Sorry, sir,' he said, folding away his paper. 'Have you been to Nuremberg before?'

'Once. Just after the war. I can't say I like Bavarians much, though. How about you?'

'First time. But I know what you mean about Bavarians. All that quaint conservatism. It's a lot of nonsense, isn't it?' He looked out of the window for a minute at the moving picture that was the German countryside. Facing me again he said:

'Do you really think Streicher could have something to do with these killings, sir?'

'We're not exactly tripping over the leads in this case, are we? Nor would it appear that the Gauleiter of Franconia is what you would call popular. Arthur Nebe even went so far as to tell me that Julius Streicher is one of the Reich's greatest criminals, and that there are already several investigations pending against him. He was keen that we should speak to the Nuremberg Police President personally. Apparently there's no love lost between him and Streicher. But at the same time we have to be extremely careful. Streicher runs his district like a Chinese warlord. Not to mention the fact that he's on first-name terms with the Führer.'

When the train reached Leipzig a young SA naval company leader joined our compartment, and Korsch and I went in search of the dining car. By the time we had finished eating the train was in Gera, close to the Czech border, but despite the fact that our SA travelling companion got off at that stop, there was no sign of the troop concentrations we had heard about. Korsch suggested that the naval SA man's presence there meant that there was going to be an amphibious attack, and this, we both agreed, would be the best thing for everyone, given that the border was largely mountainous.

It was early evening by the time that the train got into the Haupt Station in central Nuremberg. Outside, by the equestrian statue of some unknown aristocrat, we caught a taxi which drove us eastwards along Frauentorgraben and parallel to the walls of the old city. These are as high as seven or eight metres, and dominated at intervals by big square towers. This huge medieval wall, and a great, dry, grassy moat that is as wide as thirty metres, help to distinguish the old Nuremberg from the new, which, with a singular lack of obtrusion, surrounds it.

Our hotel was the Deutscher Hof, one of the city's oldest and best, and our rooms commanded excellent views across the wall to the steep, pitched rooftops and regiments of chimney-pots which lay beyond.

At the beginning of the eighteenth century, Nuremberg was

the largest city in the ancient kingdom of Franconia, as well as one of the principal marts of trade between Germany, Venice and the East. It was still the chief commercial and manufacturing city of southern Germany, but now it had a new importance, as the capital of National Socialism. Every year, Nuremberg played host to the great Party rallies which were the brainchild of Hitler's architect, Speer.

As thoughtful as the Nazis were, naturally you didn't have to go to Nuremberg to see one of these over-orchestrated events, and in September people stayed away from cinemas in droves for fear of having to sit through the newsreels which would be made up of virtually nothing else.

By all accounts, sometimes there were as many as a hundred thousand people at the Zeppelin Field to wave their flags. Nuremberg, like any city in Bavaria as I recall, never did offer much in the way of real amusement.

Since we weren't appointed to meet Martin, the Nuremberg Chief of Police, until ten o'clock the following morning, Korsch and I felt obliged to spend the evening in search of whatever entertainment there was. Especially because Kripo Executive was footing the bill. It was a thought that had particular appeal for Korch.

'This isn't bad at all,' he said enthusiastically. 'Not only is the Alex paying for me to stay in a cock-smart hotel, but I'm also getting the overtime.'

'Make the most of it,' I said. 'It's not often that fellows like you and me get to play the Party bigshot. And if Hitler gets his war, we may have to live on this little memory for quite a while.'

A lot of bars in Nuremberg had the look of places which might have been the headquarters of smaller trade guilds. These were filled with militaria and other relics of the past, and the walls were often adorned with old pictures and curious souvenirs collected by generations of proprietors, which were of no more interest to us than a set of logarithm tables. But at least the beer was good, you could always say that about Bavaria, and at the Blaue Flasche on Hall Platz, where we ended up for dinner, the food was even better.

Back at the Deutscher Hof we called in at the hotel's café restaurant for a brandy and were met by an astonishing sight. Sitting at a corner table, loudly drunk, was a party of three that included a couple of brainless-looking blondes and, wearing the single-breasted light-brown tunic of an NSDAP political leader, the Gauleiter of Franconia, Julius Streicher himself.

The waiter returning with our drinks smiled nervously when we asked him to confirm that it was indeed Julius Streicher sitting in the corner of the café. He said that it was, and quickly left as Streicher started to shout for another bottle of champagne.

It wasn't difficult to see why Streicher was feared. Apart from his rank, which was powerful enough, the man was built like a bare-fist fighter. With hardly any neck at all, his bald head, small ears, solid-looking chin and almost invisible eyebrows, Streicher was a paler version of Benito Mussolini. His apparent belligerence was given greater force by an enormous rhino-whip which lay on the table before him like some long black snake.

He thumped the table with his fist so that all the glasses and cutlery rattled loudly.

'What the fuck does a man have to do to get some fucking service around here?' he yelled at the waiter. 'We're dying of thirst.' He pointed at another waiter. 'You, I told you to keep a fucking eye on us, you little cunt, and the minute you saw an empty bottle to bring us another. What, are you stupid or something?' Once again he banged the table with his fist, much to the amusement of his two companions, who squealed with delight, and persuaded Streicher to laugh at his own ill-temper.

'Who does he remind you of?' said Korsch.

'Al Capone,' I said without thinking, and then added: 'Actually, they all remind me of Al Capone.' Korsch laughed.

We sipped our brandies and watched the show, which was more than we could have hoped for so early in our visit, and by midnight Streicher's and our own were the only parties left in the café, the others having been driven away by the

Gauleiter's incessant cursing. Another waiter came to wipe our table and empty our ashtray.

'Is he always this bad?' I asked him.

The waiter laughed bitterly. 'This? This is nothing,' he said. 'You should have seen him ten days ago after the Party rallies were finally over. He tore hell out of this place.'

'Why do you let him come in here, then?' said Korsch.

The waiter looked at him pityingly. 'Are you kidding? You just try stopping him. The Deutscher is his favourite watering-hole. He'd soon find some pretext on which to close us down if we ever kicked him out. Maybe worse than that, who knows? They say he often goes up to the Palace of Justice on Furtherstrasse and whips young boys in the cells there.'

'Well, I'd hate to be a Jew in this town,' said Korsch.

'Too right,' said the waiter. 'Last month he persuaded a crowd of people to burn down the synagogue.'

Streicher now began to sing, and accompanied himself with a percussion that was provided with his knife and fork and the table-top, from which he had thoughtfully removed the table-cloth. The combination of his drumming, accent, drunkenness and complete inability to hold a tune, not to mention the screeches and giggles of his two guests, made it impossible for either Korsch or myself to recognize the song. But you could bet that it wasn't by Kurt Weill, and it did have the effect of driving the two of us off to bed.

The next morning we walked a short way north to Jakob's Platz, where opposite a fine church stands a fortress built by the old order of Teutonic knights. At its south-eastern point, it includes a domed edifice that is the Elisabeth-Kirche, while at the south-western point, on the corner of Schlotfegergasse, is the old barracks, now police headquarters. As far as I was aware, there wasn't another police HQ in the whole of Germany which had the facility of its own Catholic church.

'That way they're sure to wring a confession out of you one way or the other,' Korsch joked.

SS-Obergruppenführer Dr Benno Martin, whose predecessors as police president of Nuremberg included Heinrich

Himmler, greeted us in his baronial top-storey office. The look of the place was such that I half expected him to have a sabre in his hand; and indeed, when he turned to one side I noticed that he had a duelling scar on his cheek.

'And how is Berlin?' he asked quietly, offering us a cigarette from his box. His own smoke he fitted into a rosewood holder that was more like a pipe and which held the cigarette vertically, at a right-angle to his face.

'Things are quiet,' I said. 'But that's because everyone is holding their breath.'

'Quite so,' he said, and waved at the newspaper on his desk. 'Chamberlain has flown to Bad Godesberg for more talks with the Führer.'

Korsch pulled the paper towards him and glanced at the headline. He pushed it back again.

'There's too much damned talk, if you ask me,' said Martin.

I grunted non-committally.

Martin grinned and laid his square chin on his hand. 'Arthur Nebe tells me that you've got a psychopath stalking the streets of Berlin, raping and cutting the flower of German maidenhood. He also tells me that you've a mind to take a look at Germany's most infamous psychopath and see if they might at least be holding hands. I refer of course to that pig's sphincter, Streicher. Am I right?'

I met his cold, penetrating gaze and held it. I was willing to bet that the general was no altar boy himself. Nebe had described Benno Martin as an extremely capable administrator. For a police chief in Nazi Germany that could have meant just about anything up to, and including, a Torquemada.

'That's right, sir,' I said, and showed him the *Der Stürmer* front page. 'This illustrates exactly how five girls have been murdered. With the exception of the Jew catching the blood in the plate of course.'

'Of course,' said Martin. 'But you haven't ruled out the Jews as a possibility.'

'No, but –'

'But it's the very theatricality of this same mode of killing that makes you doubt that it could be them. Am I right?'

'That and the fact that none of the victims has been Jewish.'

'Maybe he just prefers more attractive girls,' Martin grinned. 'Maybe he just prefers blonde, blue-eyed girls to depraved Jewish mongrels. Or maybe it's just coincidence.' He caught my raised eyebrow. 'But you're not the kind of man who believes much in coincidence, Kommissar, are you?'

'Not where murder is concerned, sir, no. I see patterns where other people see coincidence. Or at least I try to.' I leant back in my chair, crossing my legs. 'Are you acquainted with the work of Carl Jung on the subject, sir?'

He snorted with derision. 'Good God, is that what Kripo gets up to in Berlin these days?'

'I think he'd have made rather a good policeman, sir,' I said, smiling affably, 'if you don't mind me saying so.'

'Spare me the psychology lecture, Kommissar,' Martin sighed. 'Just tell me which particular pattern you see that might involve our beloved Gauleiter here in Nuremberg.'

'Well sir, it's this. It has crossed my mind that someone might be trying to sew the Jews into a very nasty body-bag.'

Now the general raised an eyebrow.

'Do you really care what happens to the Jews?'

'Sir, I care what happens to fifteen-year-old girls on their way home from school tonight.' I handed the general a sheet of typewritten paper. 'These are the dates on which the five girls disappeared. I hoped that you might be able to tell me if Streicher or any of his associates were in Berlin on any of these occasions.'

Martin glanced down the page. 'I suppose that I can find out,' he said. 'But I can tell you now that he is virtually *persona non grata* there. Hitler keeps him down here, out of harm's way, so that the only people he can annoy are the ones of no account, like myself. Of course, that's not to say that Streicher doesn't visit Berlin in secret sometimes. He does. The Führer enjoys Streicher's after-dinner conversation, though I cannot imagine why, since he also apparently enjoys my own.'

He turned to the trolley of telephones that stood by his desk and called up his adjutant, telling him to establish Streicher's whereabouts on the dates I had provided.

'I was given to understand that you also had certain information regarding Streicher's criminal behaviour,' I said.

Martin got up and went over to his filing cabinet. Laughing quietly he took out a file that was as thick as a shoe box, and brought it back to the desk.

'There's virtually nothing I don't know about that bastard,' he snarled. 'His SS guards are my men. His telephone is tapped, and I have listening devices in all of his homes. I even have photographers on constant vigil in a shop opposite a room where he sees a prostitute from time to time.'

Korsch breathed a curse that was both admiration and surprise.

'So, where do you want to start? I could occupy one whole department with what that bastard gets up to in this town. Rape charges, paternity suits, assaults on young boys with that whip he carries, bribery of public officials, misappropriation of Party funds, fraud, theft, forgery, arson, extortion – we are talking about a gangster, gentlemen. A monster, terrorizing the people of this town, never paying his bills, driving businesses into bankruptcy, wrecking the careers of honourable men who had the courage to cross him.'

'We had a chance to see him for ourselves,' I said. 'Last night, at the Deutscher Hof. He was boozing it up with a couple of ladies.'

The general's look was scathing. 'Ladies. You're joking, of course. They'd have certainly been nothing more than common prostitutes. He introduces them to people as actresses, but prostitutes is what they are. Streicher is behind most of the organized prostitution in this city.' He opened his box-file and started to leaf through the complaint-sheets.

'Indecent assaults, criminal damage, hundreds of charges of corruption – Streicher runs this city like his personal kingdom, and gets away with it.'

'The rape charges sound interesting,' I said. 'What happened there?'

'No evidence offered. The victims were either bullied or bought. You see, Streicher is a very rich man. Quite apart from what he makes as a district governor, selling favours, offices even, he makes a fortune off that lousy newspaper of his. It's got a circulation of half a million, which at thirty pfennigs a copy adds up to 150,000 Reichsmarks a week.' Korsch whistled. 'And that's not counting what he makes from the advertising. Oh yes, Streicher can buy himself an awful lot of favours.'

'Anything more serious than the rape charges?'

'You mean, has he murdered anyone?'

'Yes.'

'Well, we won't count the lynchings of the odd Jew here and there. Streicher likes to organize a nice pogrom for himself now and then. Quite apart from anything else, it gives him a chance to pick up a bit of extra loot. And we'll discount the girl who died in his house at the hands of a backstreet angel-maker. Streicher wouldn't be the first senior Party member to procure an illegal abortion. That leaves two unsolved homicides which point the finger at his having been involved.

'One, a waiter at a party Streicher went to, who decided to choose that occasion to commit suicide. A witness saw Streicher walking in the grounds with the waiter less than twenty minutes before the man was found drowned in the pond. The other, a young actress acquainted with Streicher, whose naked body was found in Luitpoldhain Park. She had been flogged to death with a leather whip. You know, I saw the body. There wasn't a centimetre of skin left on her.'

He sat down again, apparently satisfied with the effect his revelations had had on Korsch and myself. Even so he could not resist adding a few more salacious details as they occurred to him.

'And then there is Streicher's collection of pornography, which he boasts is the largest in Nuremberg. Boasting is what Streicher is best at: the number of illegitimate children he has fathered, the number of wet-dreams he's had that week, how many boys he has whipped that day. It's even the sort of detail he includes in his public speeches.'

I shook my head and heard myself sigh. How did it ever get to be this bad? How was it that a sadistic monster like Streicher got to a position of virtually absolute power? And how many others like him were there? But perhaps the most surprising thing was that I still had the capacity to be surprised at what was happening in Germany.

'What about Streicher's associates?' I said. 'The writers on *Der Stürmer*. His personal staff. If Streicher is trying to hang one on the Jews he could be using someone else to do the dirty work.'

General Martin frowned. 'Yes, but why do it in Berlin? Why not do it here?'

'I can think of a couple of good reasons,' I said. 'Who are Streicher's main enemies in Berlin?'

'With the exception of Hitler, and possibly Goebbels, you can take your pick.' He shrugged. 'Goering most of all. Then Himmler, and Heydrich.'

'That's what I thought you'd say. There's your first reason. Five unsolved murders in Berlin would cause maximum embarrassment to at least two of his worst enemies.'

He nodded. 'And your second reason?'

'Nuremberg has a history of Jew-baiting,' I said. 'Pogroms are common enough here. But Berlin is still comparatively liberal in its treatment of Jews. So if Streicher were to bring down the blame for these murders on to the heads of Berlin's Jewish community, then that would make things even harder for them as well. Perhaps for Jews all over Germany.'

'There might be something in that,' he admitted, picking another cigarette and screwing it into his curious little holder. 'But it's going to take time to organize this kind of investigation. Naturally I assume that Heydrich will ensure the full cooperation of the Gestapo. I think that the highest level of surveillance is warranted, don't you, Kommissar?'

'That's certainly what I'll be writing in my report, sir.'

The telephone rang. Martin answered it and then handed me the receiver.

'Berlin,' he said. 'For you.'

It was Deubel.

'There's another girl missing,' he said.

'When?'

'Around nine last night. Blonde, blue-eyed, same age as the others.'

141

'No witnesses?'

'Not so far.'

'We'll catch the afternoon train back.' I handed the receiver to Martin.

'It looks as if our killer was busy again last night,' I explained. 'Another girl disappeared around the time that Korsch and myself were sitting in the café at the Deutscher Hof giving Streicher an alibi.'

Martin shook his head. 'It would have been too much to hope that Streicher could have been absent from Nuremberg on all your dates,' he said. 'But don't give up. We may even yet manage to establish some sort of coincidence affecting Streicher and his associates which satisfies you, and me, not to mention this fellow Jung.'

12

Saturday, 24 September

Steglitz is a prosperous, middle-class suburb in south-west Berlin. The red bricks of the town hall mark its eastern side, and the Botanical Gardens its west. It was at this end, near the Botanical Museum and the Planzen Physiological Institute, that Frau Hildegard Steininger lived with her two children, Emmeline aged fourteen, and Paul aged ten.

Herr Steininger, the victim of a fatal car crash, had been some brilliant bank official with the Privat Kommerz, and the type that was insured up to his hair follicles, leaving his young widow comfortably off in a six-room apartment in Lepsius Strasse.

At the top of a four-storey building, the apartment had a large wrought-iron balcony outside a small, brown-painted French window, and not one but three skylights in the sitting-room ceiling. It was a big, airy sort of place, tastefully furnished and decorated, and smelling strongly of the fresh coffee she was making.

'I'm sorry to make you go through all this again,' I told her. 'I just want to make absolutely sure we didn't miss anything.'

She sighed and sat down at the kitchen table, opening her crocodile-leather handbag and finding a matching cigarette box. I lit her and watched her beautiful face tense a little. She spoke like she'd rehearsed what she was saying too many times to play the part well.

'On Thursday evenings Emmeline goes to a dancing class with Herr Wiechert in Potsdam. Grosse Weinmeisterstrasse if you want to know the address. That's at eight o'clock, so she always leaves here at seven, and catches a train from Steglitz Station which takes thirty minutes. There's a change at Wannsee I think. Well, at exactly ten minutes past eight, Herr Wiechert telephoned me to see if Emmeline was sick, as she hadn't arrived.'

143

I poured the coffee and set two cups down on the table before sitting opposite her.

'Since Emmeline is never, ever late, I asked Herr Wiechert to call again as soon as she arrived. And indeed he did call again, at 8.30, and at nine o'clock, but on each occasion it was to tell me that there was still no sign of her. I waited until 9.30 and called the police.'

She sipped her coffee with a steady hand, but it wasn't hard to see that she was upset. There was a wateriness in her blue eyes, and in the sleeve of her blue-crepe dress could be seen a sodden-looking lace handkerchief.

'Tell me about your daughter. Is she a happy sort of girl?'

'As happy as any girl can be who's recently lost her daddy.' She moved her blonde hair away from her face, something she must have done not once but fifty times while I was there, and stared blankly into her coffee cup.

'It was a stupid question,' I said. 'I'm sorry.' I found my cigarettes and filled the silence with the scrape of a match and my embarrassed breath of satisfying tobacco smoke. 'She attends the Paulsen Real Gymnasium School, doesn't she? Is everything all right there? No problems with exams, or anything like that? No school bullies giving her any trouble?'

'She's not the brightest in her class, perhaps,' said Frau Steininger, 'but she's very popular. Emmeline has lots of friends.'

'And the BdM?'

'The what?'

'The League of German Girls.'

'Oh, that. Everything's fine there too.' She shrugged, and then shook her head exasperatedly. 'She's a normal child, Kommissar. Emmeline isn't the kind to run away from home, if that's what you're implying.'

'Like I said, I'm sorry to have to ask these questions, Frau Steininger. But they have to be asked, I'm sure you understand. It's best that we know absolutely everything.' I sipped my coffee and then contemplated the grounds on the bottom of my cup. What did a shape like a scallop shell denote? I wondered. I said: 'What about boyfriends?'

She frowned. 'She's fourteen years old, for God's sake.' Angrily, she stubbed out her cigarette.

'Girls grow up earlier than boys. Earlier than we like, perhaps.' Christ, what did I know about it? Listen to me, I thought, the man with all the goddamned children.

'She's not interested in boys yet.'

I shrugged. 'Just tell me when you get tired of answering these questions, lady, and I'll get out of your way. I'm sure you've got lots more important things to do than help me to find your daughter.'

She stared at me hard for a minute, and then apologized.

'Can I see Emmeline's room, please?'

It was a normal room for a fourteen-year-old girl, at least normal for one who attended a fee-paying school. There was a large bill-poster for a production of *Swan Lake* at the Paris Opéra in a heavy black frame above the bed, and a couple of well-loved teddy bears sitting on the pink quilt. I lifted the pillow. There was a book there, a ten-pfennig romance of the sort you could buy on any street corner. Not exactly *Emil and the Detectives*.

I handed the book to Frau Steininger.

'Like I said, girls grow up early.'

'Did you speak to the technical boys?' I came through the door of my office at the same time as Becker was coming out. 'Is there anything on that trunk yet? Or that length of curtain material?'

Becker turned on his heel and followed me to my desk.

'The trunk was made by Turner & Glanz, sir.' Finding his notebook, he added, 'Friedrichstrasse, number 193a.'

'Sounds cock-smart. They keep a sales list?'

'I'm afraid not, sir. It's a popular line apparently, especially with all the Jews leaving Germany for America. Herr Glanz reckons that they must sell three or four a week.'

'Lucky him.'

'The curtain material is cheap stuff. You can buy it any-where.' He started to search through my in-tray.

'Go on, I'm listening.'

'You haven't read my report yet then?'

'Does it sound like I have?'

'I spent yesterday afternoon at Emmeline Steininger's school – the Paulsen Real Gymnasium.' He found his report and waved it in front of my face.

'That must have been nice for you. All those girls.'

'Perhaps you should read it now, sir.'

'Save me the trouble.'

Becker grimaced and looked at his watch.

'Well actually, sir, I was just about to go off. I'm supposed to be taking my children to the funfair at Luna Park.'

'You're getting as bad as Deubel. Where's he, as a matter of interest? Doing a bit of gardening? Shopping with the wife?'

'I think he's with the missing girl's mother, sir.'

'I've just come from seeing her myself. Never mind. Tell me what you found out and then you can clear off.'

He sat down on the edge of my desk and folded his arms.

'I'm sorry, sir, I was forgetting to tell you something else first.'

'Were you indeed? It seems to me that bulls forget quite a lot round the Alex these days. In case you need reminding, this is a murder investigation. Now get off my desk and tell me what the hell is going on.'

He sprang off my desk and stood to attention.

'Gottfried Bautz is dead, sir. Murdered, it looks like. His landlady found the body in his apartment early this morning. Korsch has gone over there to see if there's anything in it for us.'

I nodded quietly. 'I see.' I cursed, and then glanced up at him again. Standing there in front of my desk like a soldier, he was managing to look quite ridiculous. 'For God's sake, Becker, sit down before rigor mortis sets in and tell me about your report.'

'Thank you, sir.' He drew up a chair, turned it around and sat with his forearms leaning on the back.

'Two things,' he said. 'First, most of Emmeline Steininger's classmates thought she had spoken about running away from home on more than one occasion. Apparently she and her stepmother didn't get along too well –'

146

'Her stepmother? She never mentioned that.'

'Apparently her real mother died about twelve years ago. And then the father died recently.'

'What else?'

Becker frowned.

'You said that there were two things.'

'Yes, sir. One of the other girls, a Jewish girl, remembered something that happened a couple of months back. She said that a man wearing a uniform stopped his car near the school gate and called her over. He said that if she answered some questions he'd give her a lift home. Well, she says that she went and stood by his car, and the man asked her what her name was. She said that it was Sarah Hirsch. Then the man asked her if she was a Jew, and when she said that she was he just drove off without another word.'

'Did she give you a description?'

He pulled a face and shook his head. 'Too scared to say much at all. I had a couple of uniformed bulls with me and I think they put her off.'

'Can you blame her? She probably thought you were going to arrest her for soliciting or something. Still, she must be a bright one if she's at a Gymnasium. Maybe she would talk if her parents were with her, and if there weren't any dummies with you. What do you think?'

'I'm sure of it, sir.'

'I'll do it myself. Do I strike you as the avuncular type, Becker? No, you'd better not answer that.'

He grinned amiably.

'All right, that's all. Enjoy yourself.'

'Thank you, sir.' He stood up and went to the door.

'And Becker?'

'Yes, sir?'

'Well done.'

When he'd gone I sat staring into space for quite a while wishing that it was me who was going home to take my children out for a Saturday afternoon at Luna Park. I was overdue for some time off myself, but when you're alone in the world, that sort of thing doesn't seem to matter as much. I was balanced precariously on the edge of a pool of self-pity when there was knock at my door and Korsch came into the room.

'Gottfried Bautz has been murdered, sir,' he said immediately.

'Yes, I heard. Becker said you went to take a look. What happened?'

Korsch sat down on the chair recently occupied by Becker. He was looking more animated than I had ever seen him before, and clearly something had got him very excited.

'Someone thought his brains were lacking a bit of air, so they gave him a special blow-hole. A real neat job. Between the eyes. The forensic they had down there reckoned it was probably quite a small gun. Probably a six millimetre.' He shifted on his chair. 'But this is the interesting part, sir. Whoever plugged him first knocked him cold. Gottfried's jaw was broken clean in two. And there was a cigarette end in his mouth. Like he'd bitten his smoke in half.' He paused, waiting for me to pass it between my ears a little. 'The other half was on the floor.'

'Cigarette punch?'

'Looks like it, sir.'

'Are you thinking what I'm thinking?'

Korsch nodded deliberately. 'I'm afraid I am. And here's another thing. Deubel keeps a six-shot Little Tom in his jacket pocket. He says that it's just in case he ever loses his Walther. A Little Tom fires the same size of round as killed the Czech.'

'Does he?' I raised my eyebrows. 'Deubel was always convinced that even if Bautz had had nothing to do with our case, he still belonged in the cement.'

'He tried to persuade Becker to have a word with some of his old friends in Vice. He wanted Becker to get them to red tab Bautz on some pretext and have him sent to a KZ. But Becker wasn't having any of it. He said that they couldn't do it, not even on the evidence of the snapper he tried to cut.'

'I'm very glad to hear it. Why wasn't I told about this before?' Korsch shrugged. 'Have you mentioned any of this to the team investigating Bautz's death? I mean about Deubel's cigarette punch and the gun?'

'Not yet, sir.'

'Then we'll handle it ourselves.'

'What are you going to do?'

'That all depends on whether or not he still has that gun. If you'd pierced Bautz's ears, what would you do with it?'

'Find the nearest pig-iron smelter.'

'Precisely. So if he can't show me that gun for examination then he's off this investigation. That might not be enough for a court, but it will satisfy me. I've no use for murderers on my team.'

Korsch scratched his nose thoughtfully, narrowly avoiding the temptation to pick it.

'I don't suppose you've any idea where Inspector Deubel is, do you?'

'Someone looking for me?' Deubel sauntered through the open door. The beery stink that accompanied him was enough to explain where he had been. An unlit cigarette in the corner of his crooked mouth, he stared belligerently at Korsch and then, with unsteady distaste, at me. He was drunk.

'Been in the Café Kerkau,' he said, his mouth refusing to move quite as he would have normally expected. 'It's all right, you know. It's all right, I'm off duty. Least for another hour, anyway. Be fine by then. Don't you worry about me. I can take care of myself.'

'What else have you been taking care of?'

He straightened like a puppet jerking back on its unsteady legs.

'Been asking questions at the station where the Steininger girl went missing.'

'That's not what I meant.'

'No? No? Well, what did you mean, Herr Kommissar?'

'Someone murdered Gottfried Bautz.'

'What, that Czech bastard?' He uttered a laugh that was part belch and part spit.

'His jaw was broken. There was a cigarette end in his mouth.'

'So? What's that to do with me?'

'That's one of your little specialities, isn't it? The cigarette punch? I've heard you say so yourself.'

'There's no fucking patent on it, Gunther.' He took a long drag on the dead cigarette and narrowed his bleary eyes. 'You accusing me of canning him?'

'Can I see your gun, Inspector Deubel?'

For several seconds Deubel stood sneering at me before reaching for his shoulder holster. Behind him Korsch was slowly reaching for his own gun, and he kept his hand on its handle until Deubel had laid the Walther PPK on my desk. I picked it up and sniffed the barrel, watching his face for some sign that he knew Bautz had been killed with a gun of a much smaller calibre.

'Shot, was he?' He smiled.

'Executed, more like,' I said. 'It looks like someone put one between his eyes while he was out cold.'

'I'm choked.' Deubel shook his head slowly.

'I don't think so.'

'You're just pissing on the wall, Gunther, and hoping that some of it will splash my fucking trousers. Sure, I didn't like that little Czech, just like I hate every pervert that touches kids and hurts women. But that doesn't mean that I had anything to do with his murder.'

'There's an easy way of convincing me of that.'

'Oh? And what's that?'

'Show me that garter-gun you keep on you. The Little Tom.'

Deubel raised his hands innocently.

'What garter gun? I haven't got a gun like that. The only lighter I'm carrying is there on the table.'

'Everyone who's worked with you knows about that gun. You've bragged about it often enough. Show me the gun and you're in the clear. But if you're not carrying it, then I'll figure it's because you had to get rid of it.'

'What are you talking about? Like I said, I don't have —'

Korsch stood up. He said: 'Come on, Eb. You showed that gun to me only a couple of days ago. You even said that you were never without it.'

'You piece of shit. Take his side against one of your own, would you? Can't you see? He's not one of us. He's one of Heydrich's fucking spies. He doesn't give two farts about Kripo.'

'That's not the way I see it,' Korsch said quietly. 'So how about it? Do we get to see the gun or not?'

Deubel shook his head, smiled and wagged a finger at me.

'You can't prove anything. Not a thing. You know that, don't you?'

I pushed my chair away with the backs of my legs. I needed to be on my feet to say what I was going to say.

'Maybe so. All the same, you're off this case. I don't particularly give a damn what happens to you, Deubel, but as far as I'm concerned you can slither back to whichever excremental corner of this place you came from. I'm choosy about who I have to work with. I don't like killers.'

Deubel bared his yellow teeth even further. His grin looked like the keyboard of an old and badly out of tune piano. Hitching up his shiny flannel trousers he squared his shoulders and pointed his belly in my direction. It was all I could do to resist slamming my fist right into it, but starting a fight like that would probably have suited him very well.

'You want to open your eyes, Gunther. Take a walk down to the cells and the interrogation rooms and see what's happening in this place. Choosy about who you work with? You poor swine. There are people being beaten to death here, in this building. Probably as we speak. Do you think anyone really gives a damn about what happens to some cheap little pervert? The morgue is full of them.'

I heard myself reply, with what sounded even to me like almost hopeless naïveté, 'Somebody has to give a damn, otherwise we're no better than criminals ourselves. I can't stop other people from wearing dirty shoes, but I can polish my own. Right from the start you knew that was the way I wanted it. But you had to do it your own way, the Gestapo way, that says a woman's a witch if she floats and innocent if she sinks. Now get out of my sight before I'm tempted to see if my clout with Heydrich goes as far as kicking your arse out of Kripo.'

Deubel sniggered. 'You're a renthole,' he said, and having stared Korsch out until his boozy breath obliged him to turn away, Deubel lurched away.

Korsch shook his head. 'I never liked that bastard,' he said, 'but I didn't think he was –' He shook his head again.

I sat down wearily and reached for the desk drawer and the bottle I kept there.

'Unfortunately he's right,' I said, filling a couple of glasses. I met Korsch's quizzical stare and smiled bitterly. 'Charging a Berlin bull with murder . . .' I laughed. 'Shit, you might just as well try and arrest drunks at the Munich beer festival.'

13

Sunday, 25 September

'Is Herr Hirsch at home?'

The old man answering the door straightened and then nodded. 'I am Herr Hirsch,' he said.

'You are Sarah Hirsch's father?'

'Yes. Who are you?'

He must have been at least seventy, bald, with white hair growing long over the back of his collar, and not very tall, stooped even. It was hard to imagine this man having fathered a fifteen-year-old daughter. I showed him my badge.

'Police,' I said. 'Please don't be alarmed. I'm not here to make any trouble for you. I merely wish to question your daughter. She may be able to describe a man, a criminal.'

Recovering a little of his colour after the sight of my credentials, Herr Hirsch stood to one side and silently ushered me into a hall that was full of Chinese vases, bronzes, blue-patterned plates and intricate balsa-wood carvings in glass cases. These I admired while he closed and locked the front door, and he mentioned that in his youth he had been in the German navy and had travelled widely in the Far East. Aware now of the delicious smell that filled the house, I apologized and said that I hoped I wasn't disturbing the family meal.

'It will be a while yet before we sit down and eat,' said the old man. 'My wife and daughter are still working in the kitchen.' He smiled nervously, no doubt unaccustomed to the politeness of public officials, and led me into a reception room.

'Now then,' he said, 'you said that you wished to speak to my daughter Sarah. That she may be able to identify a criminal.'

'That's right,' I said. 'One of the girls from your daughter's school has disappeared. It's quite possible she was abducted. One of the men, questioning some of the girls in your daughter's class, discovered that several weeks ago Sarah was herself approached by a strange man. I should like to see if she can remember anything about him. With your permission.'

'But of course. I'll go and fetch her,' he said, and went out.

Evidently this was a musical family. Beside a shiny black Bechstein grand were several instrument cases, and a number of music-stands. Close to the window which looked out on to a large garden was a harp, and in most of the family photographs on the sideboard, a young girl was playing a violin. Even the oil painting above the fireplace depicted something musical – a piano recital I supposed. I was standing looking at it and trying to guess the tune when Herr Hirsch returned with his wife and daughter.

Frau Hirsch was much taller and younger than her husband, perhaps no more than fifty – a slim, elegant woman with a set of pearls to match. She wiped her hands on her pinafore and then grasped her daughter by her shoulders, as if wishing to emphasize her parental rights in the face of possible interference from a state which was avowedly hostile to her race.

'My husband says that a girl is missing from Sarah's class at school,' she said calmly. 'Which girl is it?'

'Emmeline Steininger,' I said.

Frau Hirsch turned her daughter towards her a little.

'Sarah,' she scolded, 'why didn't you tell us that one of your friends had gone missing?'

Sarah, an overweight but healthy, attractive adolescent, who could not have conformed less to Streicher's racist stereotype of the Jew, being blue-eyed and fair-haired, gave an impatient toss of her head, like a stubborn little pony.

'She's run away, that's all. She was always talking about it. Not that I care much what's happened to her. Emmeline Steininger's no friend of mine. She's always saying bad things about Jews. I hate her, and I don't care if her father is dead.'

'That's enough of that,' her father said firmly, probably not caring to hear much about fathers who were dead. 'It doesn't matter what she said. If you know something that will help the Kommissar to find her, then you must tell him. Is that clear?'

Sarah pulled a face. 'Yes, Daddy,' she yawned, and threw herself down into an armchair.

'Sarah, really,' said her mother. She smiled nervously at me. 'She's not normally like this, Kommissar. I must apologize.'

'That's all right,' I smiled, sitting down on the footstool in front of Sarah's chair.

'On Friday, when one of my men spoke to you, Sarah, you told him you remembered seeing a man hanging around near your school, perhaps a couple of months ago. Is that right?' She nodded. 'Then I'd like you to try and tell me everything that you can remember about him.'

She chewed her fingernail for a moment, and inspected it thoughtfully. 'Well, it was quite a while ago,' she said.

'Anything you might recall could help me. For instance, what time of day was it?' I took out my notebook and laid it on my thigh.

'It was going-home time. As usual I was going home by myself.' She turned her nose up at the memory of it. 'Anyway, there was this car near the school.'

'What kind of car?'

She shrugged. 'I don't know makes of cars, or anything like that. But it was a big, black one, with a driver in the front.'

'Was he the one who spoke to you?'

'No, there was another man in the back seat. I thought they were policemen. The one sitting in the back had the window down and he called to me as I came through the gate. I was by myself. Most of the other girls had gone already. He asked me to come over, and when I did he told me that I was —' She blushed a little and stopped.

'Go on,' I said.

'— that I was very beautiful, and that he was sure my father and mother were very proud to have a daughter like me.' She glanced awkwardly at her parents. 'I'm not making it up,' she said with something approaching amusement. 'Honestly, that's what he said.'

'I believe you, Sarah,' I said. 'What else did he say?'

'He spoke to his driver and said, wasn't I a fine example of German maidenhood, or something stupid like that.' She laughed. 'It was really funny.' She caught a look from her father that I didn't see, and settled down again. 'Anyway, it was something like that. I can't remember exactly.'

'And did the driver say anything back to him?'

'He suggested to his boss that they could give me a ride home. Then the one in the back asked me if I'd like that. I said that I'd never ridden in one of those big cars before, and that I'd like to –'

Sarah's father sighed loudly. 'How many times have we told you, Sarah, not to –'

'If you don't mind, sir,' I said firmly, 'perhaps that can wait until later.' I looked back at Sarah. 'Then what happened?'

'The man said that if I answered some questions correctly, he'd give me a ride, just like a movie-star. Well, first he asked me my name, and when I told him he just sort of looked at me, as if he were shocked. Of course it was because he realized that I was Jewish, and that was his next question: was I Jewish? I almost told him I wasn't, just for the fun of it. But I was scared he would find out and that I would get into trouble, and so I told him I was. Then he leant back in his seat, and told the chauffeur to drive on. Not another word. It was very strange. As if I had vanished.'

'That's very good, Sarah. Now tell me: you said you thought they were policemen. Were they wearing uniforms?'

She nodded hesitantly.

'Let's start with the colour of these uniforms.'

'Sort of green-coloured, I suppose. You know, like a policeman, only a bit darker.'

'What were their hats like? Like policemen's hats?'

'No, they were peaked hats. More like officers. Daddy was an officer in the navy.'

'Anything else? Badges, ribbons, collar insignia? Anything like that?' She kept shaking her head. 'All right. Now the man who spoke to you. What was he like?'

Sarah pursed her lips and then tugged at a length of her hair. She glanced at her father. 'Older than the driver,' she said. 'About fifty-five, sixty. Quite heavy-looking, not much hair, or maybe it was just closely cropped, and a small moustache.'

'And the other one?'

She shrugged. 'Younger. A bit pale-looking. Fair-haired. I can't remember much about him at all.'

'Tell me about his voice, this man sitting in the back of the car.'

'You mean his accent?'

'Yes, if you can.'

'I don't know for sure,' she said. 'I find accents quite difficult to place. I can hear that they're different, but I can't always say where the person is from.' She sighed deeply, and frowned as she tried hard to concentrate. 'It could have been Austrian. But I suppose it could just as easily have been Bavarian. You know, old-fashioned.'

'Austrian or Bavarian,' I said, writing in my notebook. I thought about underlining the word 'Bavarian' and then thought better of it. There was no point in giving it more emphasis than she had done, even if Bavarian suited me better. Instead I paused, saving my last question until I was sure that she had finished her answer.

'Now think very clearly, Sarah. You're standing by the car. The window is down and you're looking straight into the car. You see the man with the moustache. What else can you see?'

She shut her eyes tight, and licking her lower lip she bent her brain to squeeze out one last detail.

'Cigarettes,' she said after a minute. 'Not like Daddy's.' She opened her eyes and looked at me. 'They had a funny smell. Sweet, and quite strong. Like bay-leaves, or oregano.'

I scanned my notes and when I was sure that she had nothing left to add I stood up.

'Thank you, Sarah, you've been a great help.'

'Have I?' she said gleefully. 'Have I really?'

'You certainly have.' We all smiled, and for a moment the four of us forgot who and what we were.

Driving from the Hirsch home, I wondered if any of them realized that for once Sarah's race had been to her advantage – that being Jewish had probably saved her life.

I was pleased with what I had learned. Her description was the first real piece of information in the case. In the matter of accents her description tallied with that of Tanker, the desk sergeant who had taken the anonymous call. But what was more important it meant that I was going to have to get the dates on which Streicher had been in Berlin from General Martin in Nuremberg, after all.

14

Monday, 26 September

I looked out of the window of my apartment at the backs of the adjoining buildings, and into several sitting-rooms where each family was already grouped expectantly round the radio. From the window at the front of my apartment I could see that Fasanenstrasse was deserted. I walked into my own sitting-room and poured myself a drink. Through the floor I could hear the sound of classical music coming from the radio in the pension below. A little Beethoven provided a nice top and tail for the radio speeches of the Party leaders. It's just what I always say: the worse the picture, the more ornate the frame.

Ordinarily I'm no listener to Party broadcasts. I'd sooner listen to my own wind. But tonight's was no ordinary Party broadcast. The Führer was speaking at the Sportspalast on Potsdamerstrasse, and it was widely held that he would declare the true extent of his intentions towards Czechoslovakia and the Sudetenland.

Personally, I had long ago come to the conclusion that for years Hitler had been deceiving everyone with his speeches about peace. And I'd seen enough westerns at the cinema to know that when the man in the black hat picks on the little fellow standing next to him at the bar, he's really spoiling for a fight with the sheriff. In this case the sheriff just happened to be French, and it didn't take much to see that he wasn't much inclined to do anything but stay indoors and tell himself that the gunshots he could hear across the street were just a few fire-crackers.

In the hope that I was wrong about this, I turned on the radio, and like 75 million other Germans, waited to find out what would become of us.

A lot of women say that whereas Goebbels merely seduces, Hitler positively fascinates. It's difficult for me to comment on this. All the same, there is no denying the hypnotic effect that the Führer's speeches seem to have on people. Certainly the crowd at the Sportspalast seemed to appreciate it. I expect you had to be there to get the real atmosphere. Like a visit to a sewage plant.

For those of us listening at home, there was nothing to appreciate, no hope in anything that the number one carpet-chewer said. There was only the dreadful realization that we were a little closer to war than we had been the day before.

Tuesday, 27 September

The afternoon saw a military parade on Unter den Linden, one which looked more ready for war than anything ever seen before on the streets of Berlin. This was a mechanized division in full field equipment. But to my astonishment, there were no cheers, no salutes and no waving of flags. The reality of Hitler's belligerence was in everyone's mind and seeing this parade, people just turned and walked away.

Later that same day, when at his own request I met Arthur Nebe away from the Alex, at the offices of Gunther & Stahl-ecker, Private Investigators – the door was still awaiting the sign-writer to come and change the name back to the original – I told him what I had seen.

Nebe laughed. 'What would you say if I told you that the division you saw were this country's probable liberators?'

'Is the army planning a *putsch*?'

'I can't tell you very much except to say that high officers of the Wehrmacht have been in contact with the British prime minister. As soon as the British give the order, the army will occupy Berlin and Hitler will be brought to trial.'

'When will that be?'

'As soon as Hitler invades Czechoslovakia the British will declare war. That will be the time. Our time, Bernie. Didn't I tell you that Kripo would be needing men like you?'

I nodded slowly. 'But Chamberlain has been negotiating with Hitler, hasn't he?'

'That's the British way, to talk, to be diplomatic. It wouldn't be cricket if they didn't try to negotiate.'

'Nevertheless, he must believe that Hitler will sign some sort of treaty. More importantly, both Chamberlain and Daladier must themselves be prepared to sign some sort of treaty.'

'Hitler won't walk away from the Sudeten, Bernie. And the British aren't about to renege on their own treaty with the Czechs.'

I went over to the drinks cabinet and poured a couple.

'If the British and French intended to keep their treaty, then there would be nothing to talk about,' I said, handing Nebe a glass. 'If you ask me, they're doing Hitler's work for him.'

'My God, what a pessimist you are.'

'All right, let me ask you this. Have you ever been faced with the prospect of fighting someone you didn't want to fight? Someone larger than you, perhaps? It may be that you think you'll get a good hiding. It may be that you simply haven't got the stomach for it. You try and talk your way out of the situation, of course. The man who talks too much doesn't want to fight at all.'

'But we are not larger than the British and the French.'

'But they don't have the stomach for it.'

Nebe raised his glass. 'To the British stomach, then.'

'To the British stomach.'

Wednesday, 28 September

'General Martin has supplied the information about Streicher, sir.' Korsch looked at the telegraph he was holding. 'On the five dates in question it would seem that Streicher was known to be in Berlin on at least two of them. With regard to the other two that we don't know about, Martin has no idea where he was.'

'So much for his boast about his spies.'

'Well, there is one thing, sir. Apparently on one of the dates, Streicher was seen coming from the Furth aerodrome in Nuremberg.'

'What's the flying time between here and Nuremberg?'

'Couple of hours at the most. Do you want me to check with Tempelhof airport?'

'I've got a better idea. Get on to the propaganda boys at the Muratti. Ask them to supply you with a nice photograph of Streicher. Better ask for one of all the Gauleiters so as not to draw too much attention to yourself. Say it's for security up at the Reichs Chancellery, that always sounds good. When you've got it, I want you to go and talk to the Hirsch girl. See if she can't identify Streicher as the man in the car.'

'And if she does?'

'If she does, then you and I are going to find that we have made a lot of new friends. With one notable exception.'

'That's what I was afraid of.'

Thursday, 29 September

Chamberlain returned to Munich. He wanted to talk again. The Sheriff came too but it seemed that he was only going to look the other way when the shooting started. Mussolini polished his belt and his head and turned up to offer support to his spiritual ally.

While these important men came and went, a young girl, of little or no account in the general scheme of things, disappeared while doing the family shopping at the local market.

Moabit Market was on the corner of Bremerstrasse and Arminius Strasse. A large red-brick building, about the same size as a warehouse, it was where the working class of Moabit – which means everyone who lived in the area – bought their cheese, fish, cooked meats and other fresh provisions. There were even one or two places where you could stand and drink a quick beer and eat a sausage. The place was always busy and there were at least six ways in and out of the place. It's not somewhere that you just wander round. Most people are in a hurry, with little time to stand and stare at things they cannot afford; and anyway, there is none of those sort of goods in Moabit. So my clothes and unhurried demeanour marked me out from the rest.

We knew that Liza Ganz had disappeared from there because that was where a fishmonger had found a shopping bag which Liza's mother later identified as belonging to her.

Apart from that, nobody saw a damn thing. In Moabit, people don't pay you much attention unless you're a policeman looking for a missing girl, and even then it's just curiosity.

Friday, 30 September

In the afternoon I was summoned to Gestapo headquarters on Prinz Albrecht Strasse.

Glancing up as I passed through the main door, I saw a statue sitting on a truck-tyre of a scroll, working at a piece of embroidery. Flying over her head were two cherubs, one scratching his head and the other wearing a generally puzzled sort of expression. My guess was that they were wondering why the Gestapo should have chosen that particular building to set up shop. On the face of it, the art school formerly occupying number eight Prinz Albrecht Strasse and the Gestapo, who were currently resident there, didn't seem to have much in common beyond the rather obvious joke that everyone made about framing things. But that particular day I was more puzzled as to why Heydrich should have summoned me there, instead of to the Prinz Albrecht Palais on nearby Wilhelmstrasse. I didn't doubt that he had a reason. Heydrich had a reason for doing everything, and I felt sure that I would dislike this one just as much as all the others I'd ever heard.

Beyond the main door you went through a security check, and walking on again you found yourself at the foot of a staircase that was as big as an aqueduct. At the top of the flight you were in a vaulted waiting hall, with three arched windows that were of locomotive proportions. Beneath each window was a wooden bench of the kind you see in church and it was there that I waited, as instructed.

Between each window, on plinths, sat busts of Hitler and Goering. I wondered a bit at Himmler leaving Fat Hermann's head there, knowing how much they hated each other. Maybe

Himmler just admired it as a piece of sculpture. And then maybe his wife was the Chief Rabbi's daughter.

After nearly an hour Heydrich finally emerged from the two double doors facing me. He was carrying a briefcase and shooed away his SS adjutant when he caught sight of me.

'Kommissar Gunther,' he said, appearing to find some amusement at the sound of my rank in his own ears. He ushered me forwards along the gallery. 'I thought we could walk in the garden once again, like the last time. Do you mind accompanying me back to the Wilhelmstrasse?'

We went through an arched doorway and down another massive set of stairs to the notorious south wing, where what had once been sculptors' workshops were now Gestapo prison cells. I had good reason to remember these, having once been briefly detained there myself, and I was quite relieved when we emerged through a door and stood in the open air once again. You never knew with Heydrich.

He paused there for a moment, glancing at his Rolex. I started to say something, but he raised his forefinger and, almost conspiratorially, pressed his finger to his thin lips. We stood and waited, but for what I had no idea.

A minute or so later a volley of shots rang out, echoing away across the gardens. Then another; and another. Heydrich checked his watch again, nodded and smiled.

'Shall we?' he said, striding on to the gravel pathway.

'Was that for my benefit?' I said, knowing full well that it was.

'The firing squad?' He chuckled. 'No, no, Kommissar Gunther. You imagine too much. And anyway, I hardly think that you of all people require an object lesson in power. It's just that I am particular about punctuality. With kings this is said to be a virtue, but with a policeman this is merely the hallmark of administrative efficiency. After all, if the Führer can make the trains run on time, the least I ought to be able to do is make sure that a few priests are liquidated at the proper appointed hour.'

So it was an object lesson after all, I thought. Heydrich's way of letting me know that he was aware of my disagreement with Sturmbannführer Roth from 4B1.

'Whatever happened to being shot at dawn?'

'The neighbours complained.'

'You did say priests, didn't you?'

'The Catholic Church is no less of an international conspiracy than Bolshevism or Judaism, Gunther. Martin Luther led one Reformation, the Führer will lead another. He will abolish Roman authority over German Catholics, whether the priests permit him or not. But that is another matter, and one best left to those who are well versed in its implementation.

'No, I wanted to tell you about the problem I have, which is that I am under a certain amount of pressure from Goebbels and his Muratti hacks that this case you are working on be given publicity. I'm not sure how much longer I can stave them off.'

'When I was given this case, General,' I said, lighting a cigarette, 'I was against a ban on publicity. Now I'm convinced that publicity is exactly what our killer has been after all along.'

'Yes, Nebe said you were working on the theory that this might be some sort of conspiracy engineered by Streicher and his Jew-baiting pals to bring down a pogrom on the heads of the capital's Jewish community.'

'It sounds fantastic, General, only if you don't know Streicher.'

He stopped, and thrusting his hands deep inside his trouser pockets, he shook his head.

'There is nothing about that Bavarian pig that could possibly surprise me.' He kicked at a pigeon with the toe of his boot, and missed. 'But I want to hear more.'

'A girl has identified a photograph of Streicher as possibly the man who tried to pick her up outside a school from which another girl disappeared last week. She thinks that the man might have had a Bavarian accent. The desk sergeant who took an anonymous call tipping us off where exactly to find the body of another missing girl said that the caller had a Bavarian accent.

'Then there's motive. Last month the people of Nuremberg burnt down the city's synagogue. But here in Berlin there are only ever a few broken windows and assaults at the very worst. Streicher would love to see the Jews in Berlin getting some of what they've had in Nuremberg.

'What is more, *Der Stürmer*'s obsession with ritual murder leads me to make comparisons with the killer's *modus operandi*. You add all that to Streicher's reputation and it starts to look like something.'

Heydrich accelerated ahead of me, his arms stiff at his sides as if he were riding in the Vienna Riding School, and then turned to face me. He was smiling enthusiastically.

'I know one person who would be delighted to see Streicher's downfall. That stupid bastard has been making speeches all but accusing the prime minister of being impotent. Goering is furious about it. But you don't really have enough yet, do you?'

'No, sir. For a start my witness is Jewish.' Heydrich groaned. 'And of course the rest is largely theoretical.'

'Nevertheless, I like your theory, Gunther. I like it very much.'

'I'd like to remind the general that it took me six months to catch Gormann the Strangler. I haven't yet spent a month on this case.'

'We don't have six months, I'm afraid. Look here, get me a shred of evidence and I can keep Goebbels off my back. But I need something soon, Gunther. You've got another month, six weeks at the outside. Do I make myself clear?'

'Yes, sir.'

'Well, what do you need from me?'

'Round the clock Gestapo surveillance of Julius Streicher,' I said. 'A full undercover investigation of all his business activities and known associates.'

Heydrich folded his arms and took his long chin in his hand. 'I'll have to speak to Himmler about that. But it should be all right. The Reichsführer hates corruption even more than he loathes the Jews.'

'Well, that's certainly comforting, sir.'

We walked on towards the Prinz Albrecht Palais.

'Incidentally,' he said, as we neared his own headquarters,

'I've just had some important news that affects us all. The British and French have signed an agreement at Munich. The Führer has got the Sudeten.' He shook his head in wonder. 'A miracle, isn't it?'

'Yes indeed,' I muttered.

'Well, don't you understand? There isn't going to be a war. At least, not for the present time.'

I smiled awkwardly. 'Yes, it's really good news.'

I understood perfectly. There wasn't going to be a war. There wasn't going to be any signal from the British. And without that, there wasn't going to be any army *putsch* either.

PART TWO

15

Monday, 17 October

The Ganz family, what remained of it following a second anonymous call to the Alex informing us where the body of Liza Ganz was to be found, lived south of Wittenau in a small apartment on Birkenstrasse, just behind the Robert Koch Hospital where Frau Ganz was employed as a nurse. Herr Ganz worked as a clerk at the Moabit District Court, which was also nearby.

According to Becker they were a hard-working couple in their late thirties, both of them putting in long hours, so that Liza Ganz had often been left by herself. But never had she been left as I had just seen her, naked on a slab at the Alex, with a man stitching up those parts of her he had seen fit to cut open in an effort to determine everything about her, from her virginity to the contents of her stomach. Yet it had been the contents of her mouth, easier of access, which had confirmed what I had begun to suspect.

'What made you think of it, Bernie?' Illmann had asked.

'Not everyone rolls up as good as you, Professor. Sometimes a little flake will stay on your tongue, or under your lip. When the Jewish girl who said she saw our man said he was smoking something sweet-smelling, like bay-leaves or oregano, she had to be talking about hashish. That's probably how he gets them away quietly. Treats them all grown-up by offering them a cigarette. Only it's not the kind they're expecting.'

Illmann shook his head in apparent wonder.

'And to think that I missed it. I must be getting old.'

Becker slammed the car door and joined me on the pavement. The apartment was above a pharmacy. I had a feeling I was going to need it.

We walked up the stairs and knocked on the door. The man who opened it was dark and bad-tempered looking. Recognizing Becker he uttered a sigh and called to his wife. Then he glanced back inside and I saw him nod grimly.

'You'd better come in,' he said.

I was watching him closely. His face remained flushed, and as I squeezed past him I could see small beads of perspiration on his forehead. Further into the place I caught a warm, soapy smell, and I guessed that he'd only recently finished taking a bath.

Closing the door, Herr Ganz overtook and led us into the small sitting-room where his wife was standing quietly. She was tall and pale, as if she spent too much time indoors, and clearly she had not long stopped crying. The handkerchief was still wet in her hand. Herr Ganz, shorter than his wife, put his arm around her broad shoulders.

'This is Kommissar Gunther, from the Alex,' said Becker.

'Herr and Frau Ganz,' I said, 'I'm afraid you must prepare yourselves for the worst possible news. We found the body of your daughter Liza early this morning. I'm very sorry.' Becker nodded solemnly.

'Yes,' said Ganz. 'Yes, I thought so.'

'Naturally there will have to be an identification,' I told him. 'It needn't be right away. Perhaps later on, when you've had a chance to draw yourselves together.' I waited for Frau Ganz to dissolve, but for the moment at least she seemed inclined to remain solid. Was it because she was a nurse, and rather more immune to suffering and pain? Even her own? 'May we sit down?'

'Yes, please do,' said Ganz.

I told Becker to go and make some coffee for us all. He went with some alacrity, eager to be out of the grief-stricken atmosphere, if only for a moment or two.

'Where did you find her?' said Ganz.

It wasn't the sort of question I felt comfortable answering. How do you tell two parents that their daughter's naked body was found inside a tower of car tyres in a disused garage on Kaiser Wilhelm Strasse? I gave him the sanitized version, which included no more than the location of the garage. At this there occurred a very definite exchange of looks.

Ganz sat with his hand on his wife's knee. She herself was quiet, vacant even, and perhaps less in need of Becker's coffee than I was.

'Have you any idea who might have killed her?' he said.

'We're working on a number of possibilities, sir,' I said, finding the old police platitudes coming back to me once again. 'We're doing everything we can, believe me.'

Ganz's frown deepened. He shook his head angrily. 'What I fail to understand is why there has been nothing in the newspapers.'

'It's important that we prevent any copy-cat killings,' I said. 'It often happens in this sort of case.'

'Isn't it also important that you stop any more girls from being murdered?' said Frau Ganz. Her look was one of exasperation. 'Well, it's true, isn't it? Other girls have been murdered. That's what people are saying. You may be able to keep it out of the papers, but you can't stop people from talking.'

'There have been propaganda drives warning girls to be on their guard,' I said.

'Well, they obviously didn't do any good, did they?' said Ganz. 'Liza was an intelligent girl, Kommissar. Not the kind to do anything stupid. So this killer must be clever too. And the way I see it, the only way to put girls properly on their guard is to print the story, in all its horror. To scare them.'

'You may be right, sir,' I said unhappily, 'but it's not up to me. I'm only obeying orders.' That was the typically German excuse for everything these days, and I felt ashamed using it.

Becker put his head round the kitchen door.

'Could I have a word, sir?'

It was my turn to be glad to leave the room.

'What's the matter?' I said bitterly. 'Forgotten how to boil a kettle?'

He handed me a newspaper cutting, from the *Beobachter*. 'Take a look at this, sir. I found it in the drawer here.'

It was an advertisement for a 'Rolf Vogelmann, Private Investigator, Missing Persons a Speciality', the same advertisement that Bruno Stahlecker had used to plague me with.

Becker pointed to the date at the top of the cutting: '3 October,' he said. 'Four days after Liza Ganz disappeared.'

'It wouldn't be the first time that people got tired waiting for the police to come up with something,' I said. 'After all, that's how I used to make a comparatively honest living.'

Becker collected some cups and saucers and put them on to a tray with the coffee pot. 'Do you suppose that they might have used him, sir?'

'I don't see any harm in asking.'

Ganz was unrepentant, the sort of client I wouldn't have minded working for myself.

'As I said, Kommissar, there was nothing in the newspapers about our daughter, and we saw your colleague here only twice. So as time passed we wondered just what efforts were being made to find our daughter. It's the not knowing that gets to you. We thought that if we hired Herr Vogelmann then at least we could be sure that someone was doing his best to try and find her. I don't mean to be rude, Kommissar, but that's the way it was.'

I sipped my coffee and shook my head.

'I quite understand,' I said. 'I'd probably have done the same thing myself. I just wish this Vogelmann had been able to find her.'

You had to admire them, I thought. They could probably ill-afford the services of a private investigator and yet they had still gone ahead and hired one. It might even have cost them whatever savings they had.

When we had finished our coffee and were leaving I suggested that a police car might come round and bring Herr Ganz down to the Alex to identify the body early the following morning.

'Thank you for your kindness, Kommissar,' said Frau Ganz, attempting a smile. 'Everyone's been so kind.'

Her husband nodded his agreement. Hovering by the open door, he was obviously keen to see the back of us.

'Herr Vogelmann wouldn't take any money from us. And now you're arranging a car for my husband. I can't tell you how much we appreciate it.'

I squeezed her hand sympathetically, and then we left.

In the pharmacy downstairs I bought some powders and swallowed one in the car. Becker looked at me with disgust.

'Christ, I don't know how you can do that,' he said, shuddering.

'It works faster that way. And after what we just went through I can't say that I notice the taste much. I hate giving bad news.' I swept my mouth with my tongue for the residue. 'Well? What did you make of that? Get the same hunch as before?'

'Yes. He was giving her all sorts of meaningful little looks.'

'So were you, for that matter,' I said, shaking my head in wonder.

Becker grinned broadly. 'She wasn't bad, was she?'

'I suppose you're going to tell me what she'd be like in bed, right?'

'More your type I'd have thought, sir.'

'Oh? What makes you say that?'

'You know, the type that responds to kindness.'

I laughed, despite my headache. 'More than she responds to bad news. There we are with our big feet and long faces and all she can do is look like she was in the middle of her period.'

'She's a nurse. They're used to handling bad news.'

'That crossed my mind, but I think she'd done her crying already, and quite recently. What about Irma Hanke's mother? Did she cry?'

'God, no. As hard as Jew Süss that one. Maybe she did sniff a little when I first showed up. But they were giving off the same sort of atmosphere as the Ganzes.'

I looked at my watch. 'I think we need a drink, don't you?'

We drove to the Café Kerkau, on Alexanderstrasse. With sixty billiard tables, it was where a lot of bulls from the Alex went to relax when they came off duty.

I bought a couple of beers and carried them over to a table where Becker was practising a few shots.

'Do you play?' he said.

'Are you stretching me out? This used to be my sitting-room.' I picked up a stick and watched Becker shoot the cue ball. It hit the red, banked off the cushion and hit the other white ball square.

'Care for a little bet?'

'Not after that shot. You've got a lot to learn about working a line. Now if you'd missed it –'

'Lucky shot, that's all,' Becker insisted. He bent down and cued a wild one which missed by half a metre.

I clicked my tongue. 'That's a billiard cue you're holding, not a white stick. Stop trying to lay me down, will you? Look, if it makes you happy, we'll play for five marks a game.'

He smiled slightly and flexed his shoulders.

'Twenty points all right with you?'

I won the break and missed the opening shot. After that I might just as well have been baby-sitting. Becker hadn't been in the Boy Scouts when he was young, that much was certain. After four games I tossed a twenty on to the felt and begged for mercy. Becker threw it back.

'It's all right,' he said. 'You let me lay you down.'

'That's another thing you've got to learn. A bet's a bet. You never ever play for money unless you mean to collect. A man that lets you off might expect you to let him off. It makes people nervous, that's all.'

'That sounds like good advice.' He pocketed the money.

'It's like business,' I continued. 'You never work for free. If you won't take money for your work then it can't have been worth much.' I returned my cue to the rack and finished my beer. 'Never trust anyone who's happy to do the job for nothing.'

'Is that what you've learnt as a private detective?'

'No, it's what I've learnt as a good businessman. But since you mention it, I don't like the smell of a private investigator who tries to find a missing schoolgirl and then waives his fee.'

'Rolf Vogelmann? But he didn't find her.'

'Let me tell you something. These days a lot of people go missing in this town, and for lots of different reasons. Finding one is the exception, not the rule. If I'd torn up the bill of every disappointed client I had, I'd have been washing dishes by now. When you're private, there's no room for sentiment. The man who doesn't collect, doesn't eat.'

'Maybe this Vogelmann character is just more generous than you were, sir.'

I shook my head. 'I don't see how he can afford to be,' I said, unfolding Vogelmann's advertisement and looking at it again. 'Not with these overheads.'

16

Tuesday, 18 October

It was her, all right. There was no mistaking that golden head and those well-sculpted legs. I watched her struggle out of Ka-De-We's revolving door, laden with parcels and carrier-bags, looking like she was doing her last-minute Christmas shopping. She waved for a taxi, dropped a bag, bent down to retrieve it and looked up to find that the driver had missed her. It was difficult to see how. You'd have noticed Hildegard Steininger with a sack over your head. She looked as though she lived in a beauty parlour.

From inside my car I heard her swear and, drawing up at the curb, I wound down the passenger window.

'Need a lift somewhere?'

She was still looking around for another taxi when she answered. 'No, it's all right,' she said, as if I had cornered her at a cocktail party and she had been glancing over my shoulder to see if there might be someone more interesting coming along. There wasn't, so she remembered to smile, briefly, and then added: 'Well, if you're sure it's no trouble.'

I jumped out to help her load the shopping. Millinery stores, shoe shops, a perfumers, a fancy Friedrichstrasse dress-designer, and Ka-De-We's famous food hall: I figured she was the type for whom a cheque-book provided the best kind of panacea for what was troubling her. But then, there are lots of women like that.

'It's no trouble at all,' I said, my eyes following her legs as they swung into the car, briefly enjoying a view of her stocking tops and garters. Forget it, I told myself. This one was too pricey. Besides, she had other things on her mind. Like whether the shoes matched the handbag, and what had happened to her missing daughter.

'Where to?' I said. 'Home?'

She sighed like I'd suggested the Palme doss-house on

Frobelstrasse, and then, smiling a brave little smile, she nodded. We drove east towards Bülowstrasse.

'I'm afraid that I don't have any news for you,' I said, fixing a serious expression to my features and trying to concentrate on the road rather than the memory of her thighs.

'No, I didn't think you did,' she said dully. 'It's been almost four weeks now, hasn't it?'

'Don't give up hope.'

Another sigh, rather more impatient. 'You're not going to find her. She's dead, isn't she? Why doesn't somebody just admit it?'

'She's alive until I find out different, Frau Steininger.' I turned south down Potsdamerstrasse and for a while we were both silent. Then I became aware of her shaking her head and breathing like she had walked up a flight of stairs.

'Whatever must you think of me, Kommissar?' she said. 'My daughter missing, probably murdered, and here I am spending money as if I hadn't a care in the world. You must think me a heartless sort of woman.'

'I don't think anything of the kind,' I said, and started telling her how people dealt with these things in different ways, and that if a bit of shopping helped to take her mind off her daughter's disappearance for a couple of hours then that was perfectly all right, and that nobody would blame her. I thought I made a convincing case, but by the time we reached her apartment in Steglitz, Hildegard Steininger was in tears.

I took hold of her shoulder and just squeezed it, letting her go a bit before I said, 'I'd offer you my handkerchief if I hadn't wrapped my sandwiches in it.'

Through her tears she tried a smile. 'I have one,' she said, and tugged a square of lace from out of her sleeve. Then she glanced over at my own handkerchief and laughed. 'It does look as if you'd wrapped your sandwiches in it.'

After I'd helped to carry her purchases upstairs, I stood outside her door while she found her key. Opening it, she turned and smiled gracefully.

'Thank you for helping, Kommissar,' she said. 'It really was very kind of you.'

'It was nothing,' I said, thinking nothing of the sort.

Not even an invitation in for a cup of coffee, I thought when I was sitting in the car once more. Lets me drive her all this way and not even invited inside.

But then there are lots of women like that, for whom men are just taxi-drivers they don't have to tip.

The heavy scent of the lady's Bajadi perfume was pulling quite a few funny faces at me. Some men aren't affected by it at all, but a woman's perfume smacks me right in the leather shorts. Arriving back at the Alex some twenty minutes later, I think I must have sniffed down every molecule of that woman's fragrance like a vacuum cleaner.

I called a friend of mine who worked at Dorlands, the advertising agency. Alex Sievers was someone I knew from the war.

'Alex. Are you still buying advertising space?'

'For as long as the job doesn't require one to have a brain.'

'It's always nice to talk to a man who enjoys his work.'

'Fortunately I enjoy the money a whole lot better.'

It went on like that for another couple of minutes until I asked Alex if he had a copy of that morning's *Beobachter*. I referred him to the page with Vogelmann's ad.

'What's this?' he said. 'I can't believe that there are people in your line of work who have finally staggered into the twentieth century.'

'That advertisement has appeared at least twice a week for quite a few weeks now,' I explained. 'What's a campaign like that cost?'

'With that many insertions there's bound to be some sort of discount. Listen, leave it with me. I know a couple of people on the *Beobachter*. I can probably find out for you.'

'I'd appreciate it, Alex.'

'You want to advertise yourself, maybe?'

'Sorry, Alex, but this is a case.'

'I get it. Spying on the competition, eh?'

'Something like that.'

I spent the rest of that afternoon reading Gestapo reports on Streicher and his *Der Stürmer* associates: of the Gauleiter's affair with one Anni Seitz, and others, which he conducted in secret from his wife Kunigunde; of his son Lothar's affair with an English girl called Mitford who was of noble birth; of *Stürmer* editor Ernst Hiemer's homosexuality; of *Stürmer* cartoonist Philippe Rupprecht's illegal activities after the war in Argentina; and of how the *Stürmer* team of writers included a man called Fritz Brand, who was really a Jew by the name of Jonas Wolk.

These reports made fascinating, salacious reading, of the sort that would no doubt have appealed to *Der Stürmer*'s own following, but they didn't bring me any nearer to establishing a connection between Streicher and the murders.

Sievers called back at around five, and said that Vogelmann's advertising was costing something like three or four hundred marks a month.

'When did he start spending that kind of mouse?'

'Since the beginning of July. Only he's not spending it, Bernie.'

'Don't tell me he's getting it for nothing.'

'No, somebody else is picking up the bill.'

'Oh? Who?'

'Well that's the funny thing, Bernie. Can you think of any reason why the Lange Publishing Company should be paying for a private investigator's advertising campaign?'

'Are you sure about that?'

'Absolutely.'

'That's very interesting, Alex. I owe you one.'

'Just make sure that if you ever decide to do some advertising it's me you speak to first, all right?'

'You bet.'

I put down the receiver and opened my diary. My account for work done on Frau Gertrude Lange's behalf was at least a week overdue. Glancing at my watch I thought I could just about beat the westbound traffic.

They had the painters in at the house in Herbertstrasse when I called, and Frau Lange's black maid complained bitterly about people coming and going all the time so that she was never off her feet. You wouldn't have thought it to look at her. She was even fatter than I remembered.

'You'll have to wait here in the hall while I go and see if she's available,' she told me. 'Everywhere else is being decorated. Don't touch anything, mind.' She flinched as an enormous crash echoed through the house and, mumbling about men with dirty overalls disrupting the place, she went off in search of her mistress, leaving me to tap my heels on the marble floor.

It seemed to make sense, their decorating the place. They probably did it every year, instead of spring cleaning. I ran my hand over an art-deco bronze of a leaping salmon that occupied the middle of a great round table. I might have enjoyed its tactile smoothness if the thing hadn't been covered in dust. I turned, grimacing, as the black cauldron waddled back into the hall. She grimaced back at me and then down at my feet.

'You see what your boots has gone and done to my clean floor?' she said pointing at the several black marks my heels had left.

I tutted with theatrical insincerity.

'Perhaps you can persuade her to buy a new one,' I said. I was certain she swore under her breath before telling me to follow her.

We went along the same hallway that was a couple of coats of paint above gloomy, to the double doors of the sitting-room–office. Frau Lange, her chins and her dog were waiting for me on the same chaise longue, except that it had been recovered with a shade of material that was easy on the eye only if you had a piece of grit in there on which to concentrate. Having lots of money is no guarantee of good taste, but it can make the lack of it more glaringly obvious.

'Don't you own a telephone?' she boomed through her cigarette smoke like a fog-horn. I heard her chuckle as she added: 'I think you must have once been a debt-collector or something.' Then, realizing what she had said, she clutched at one of her sagging jowls. 'Oh God, I haven't paid your bill, have I?' She laughed again, and stood up. 'I'm most awfully sorry.'

'That's all right,' I said, watching her go to the desk and take out her cheque-book.

'And I haven't yet thanked you properly for the speedy way in which you handled things. I've told all my friends about how good you were.' She handed me the cheque. 'I've put a small bonus on there. I can't tell you how relieved I was to have done with that terrible man. In your letter you said that it appeared as if he had hanged himself, Herr Gunther. Saved somebody else the trouble, eh?' She laughed again, loudly, like an amateur actress performing rather too vigorously to be wholly credible. Her teeth were also false.

'That's one way of looking at it,' I said. I didn't see any point in telling her about my suspicion that Heydrich had had Klaus Hering killed with the aim of expediting my re-joining Kripo. Clients don't much care for loose ends. I'm not all that fond of them myself.

It was now that she remembered that her case had also happened to cost Bruno Stahlecker his life. She let her laughter subside, and fixing a more serious expression to her face she set about expressing her condolences. This also involved her cheque-book. For a moment I thought about saying something noble to do with the hazards of the profession, but then I thought of Bruno's widow and let her finish writing it.

'Very generous,' I said. 'I'll see that this gets to his wife and family.'

'Please do,' she said. 'And if there's anything else that I can do for them, you will let me know, won't you?'

I said that I would.

'There is something you can do for me, Herr Gunther,' she said. 'There are still the letters I gave you. My son asked me if those last few could be returned to him.'

'Yes, of course. I'd forgotten.' But what was that she said? Was it possible that she meant the letters I still held in the file back at my office were the only surviving letters? Or did she mean that Reinhard Lange already had the rest? In which case, how had he come by them? Certainly I had failed to find any more of the letters when I searched Hering's apartment. What had become of them?

'I'll drop them round myself,' I said. 'Thank goodness he has the rest of them back safely.'

'Yes, isn't it?' she said.

So there it was. He did have them.

I began to move towards the door. 'Well, I'd better be getting along, Frau Lange.' I waved the two cheques in the air and then slipped them into my wallet. 'Thanks for your generosity.'

'Not at all.'

I frowned as if something had occurred to me.

'There is one thing that puzzles me,' I said. 'Something I meant to ask you about. What interest does your company have in the Rolf Vogelmann Detective Agency?'

'Rolf Vogelmann?' she repeated uncomfortably.

'Yes. You see I learnt quite by accident that the Lange Publishing Company has been funding an advertising campaign for Rolf Vogelmann since July of this year. I was merely wondering why you should have hired me when you might with more reason have hired him?'

Frau Lange blinked deliberately and shook her head.

'I'm afraid that I have absolutely no idea.'

I shrugged and allowed myself a little smile. 'Well, as I say, it just puzzled me, that's all. Nothing important. Do you sign all the company cheques, Frau Lange? I mean, I just wondered if this might be something your son could have done on his own without informing you. Like buying that magazine you told me about. Now what was its name? *Urania.*'

Clearly embarrassed, Frau Lange's face was beginning to redden. She swallowed hard before answering.

'Reinhard has signing power over a limited bank account which is supposed to cover his expenses as a company director. However, I'm at a loss to explain what this might relate to, Herr Gunther.'

'Well, maybe he got tired of astrology. Maybe he decided to become a private investigator himself. To tell the truth, Frau Lange, there are times when a horoscope is as good a way of finding something out as any other.'

'I shall make a point of asking Reinhard about this when I

next see him. I'm indebted to you for the information. Would you mind telling me where you got it from?'

'The information? Sorry, I make it a strict rule never to breach confidentiality. I'm sure you understand.'

She nodded curtly, and bade me good evening.

Back in the hall the black cauldron was still simmering over her floor.

'You know what I'd recommend?' I said.

'What's that?' she said sullenly.

'I think you should give Frau Lange's son a call at his magazine. Maybe he can work up a magic spell to shift those marks.'

17

Friday, 21 October

When I first suggested the idea to Hildegard Steininger, she had been less than enthusiastic.

'Let me get this straight. You want to pose as my husband?'

'That's right.'

'In the first place, my husband is dead. And in the second you don't look anything like him, Herr Kommissar.'

'In the first place I'm counting on this man not knowing that the real Herr Steininger is dead; and in the second, I don't suppose that he would have any more idea of what your husband might have looked like than I do.'

'Exactly who is this Rolf Vogelmann, anyway?'

'An investigation like this one is nothing more than a search for a pattern, for a common factor. Here the common factor is that we've discovered Vogelmann was retained by the parents of two other girls.'

'Two other victims, you mean,' she said. 'I know that other girls have disappeared and then been found murdered, you know. There may be nothing about it in the papers, but one hears things all the time.'

'Two other victims, then,' I admitted.

'But surely that's just a coincidence. Listen, I can tell you that I've thought of doing it myself, you know, paying someone to look for my daughter. After all, you still haven't found a trace of her, have you?'

'That's true. But it may be more than just a coincidence. That's what I'd like to find out.'

'Supposing that he is involved. What could he hope to gain from it?'

'We're not necessarily talking about a rational person here. So I don't know that gain will come into the equation.'

'Well, it all sounds very dubious to me,' she said. 'I mean, how did he get in touch with these two families?'

'He didn't. They got in touch with him after seeing his newspaper advertisement.'

'Doesn't that show that if he is a common factor, then it's not been through his own making?'

'Perhaps he just wants it to look that way. I don't know. All the same I'd like to find out more, even if it's just to rule him out.'

She crossed her long legs and lit a cigarette.

'Will you do it?'

'Just answer this question first, Kommissar. And I want an honest answer. I'm tired of all the evasions. Do you think that Emmeline can still be alive?'

I sighed and then shook my head. 'I think she's dead.'

'Thank you.' There was silence for a moment. 'Is it dangerous, what you're asking me to do?'

'No, I don't think so.'

'Then I agree.'

Now, as we sat in Vogelmann's waiting-room in his offices on Nürnburgerstrasse, under the eye of his matronly secretary, Hildegard Steininger played the part of the worried wife to perfection, holding my hand, and occasionally smiling at me smiles of the kind that are normally reserved for a loved one. She was even wearing her wedding-ring. So was I. It felt strange, and tight, on my finger after so many years. I'd needed soap to slide it on.

Through the wall could be heard the sound of a piano being played.

'There's a music school next door,' explained Vogelmann's secretary. She smiled kindly and added: 'He won't keep you waiting for very long.' Five minutes later we were ushered into his office.

In my experience the private investigator is prone to several common ailments: flat feet, varicose veins, a bad back, alcoholism and, God forbid, venereal disease; but none of them, with the possible exception of the clap, is likely to influence adversely the impression he makes on a potential client. However, there is one disability, albeit a minor one, which if found in a sniffer must give the client pause for thought, and that is short-sightedness. If you are going to pay a man fifty marks a day to trace your missing grandmother, at the very least you want to feel confident that the man you are engaging to do the job is sufficiently eagle-eyed to find his own cuff-links. Spectacles of bottle-glass thickness such as those worn by Rolf Vogelmann must therefore be considered bad for business.

Ugliness, on the other hand, where it stops short of some particular and gross physical deformity, need be no professional disadvantage, and so Vogelmann, whose unpleasant aspect was something more general, was probably able to peck at some sort of a living. I say peck, and I choose my words carefully, because with his unruly comb of curly red hair, his broad beak of a nose and his great breast-plate of a chest, Vogelmann resembled a breed of prehistoric cockerel, and one that had positively begged for extinction.

Hitching his trousers on to his chest, Vogelmann strode round the desk on big policeman's feet to shake our hands. He walked as if he had just dismounted a bicycle.

'Rolf Vogelmann, pleased to meet you both,' he said in a high, strangulated sort of voice, and with a thick Berlin accent.

'Steininger,' I said. 'And this is my wife Hildegard.'

Vogelmann pointed at two armchairs that were ranged in front of a large desk-table, and I heard his shoes squeak as he followed us back across the rug. There wasn't much in the way of furniture. A hat stand, a drinks trolley, a long and battered-looking sofa and, behind it, a table against the wall with a couple of lamps and several piles of books.

'It's good of you to see us this quickly,' Hildegard said graciously.

Vogelmann sat down and faced us. Even with a metre of desk between us I could still detect his yoghurt-curdling breath.

'Well, when your husband mentioned that your daughter was missing, naturally I assumed there would be some urgency.' He wiped a pad of paper with the flat of his hand and picked up a pencil. 'Exactly when did she go missing?'

'Thursday, 22 September,' I said. 'She was on her way to

dancing class in Potsdam and had left home – we live in Steglitz – at seven-thirty that evening. Her class was due to commence at eight, only she never arrived.' Hildegard's hand reached for mine, and I squeezed it comfortingly.

Vogelmann nodded. 'Almost a month, then,' he said ruminatively. 'And the police –?'

'The police?' I said bitterly. 'The police do nothing. We hear nothing. There is nothing in the papers. And yet one hears rumours that other girls of Emmeline's age have also disappeared.' I paused. 'And that they have been murdered.'

'That is almost certainly the case,' he said, straightening the knot in his cheap woollen tie. 'The official reason for the press moratorium on the reporting of these disappearances and homicides is that the police wish to avoid a panic. Also, they don't wish to encourage all the cranks which a case like this has a habit of producing. But the real reason is that they are simply embarrassed at their own persistent inability to capture this man.'

I felt Hildegard squeeze my hand more tightly.

'Herr Vogelmann,' she said, 'it's not knowing what's happened to her that is so hard to bear. If we could just be sure of whether or not –'

'I understand, Frau Steininger.' He looked at me. 'Am I to take it then that you wish me to try and find her?'

'Would you, Herr Vogelmann?' I said. 'We saw your advertisement in the *Beobachter*, and really, you're our last hope. We're tired of just sitting back and waiting for something to happen. Aren't we, darling?'

'Yes. Yes, we are.'

'Do you have a photograph of your daughter?'

Hildegard opened her handbag and handed him a copy of the picture that she had earlier given to Deubel.

Vogelmann regarded it dispassionately. 'Pretty. How did she travel to Potsdam?'

'By train.'

'And you believe that she must have disappeared somewhere between your house in Steglitz and the dancing school, is that right?' I nodded. 'Any problems at home?'

'None,' Hildegard said firmly.

'At school, then?'

We both shook our heads and Vogelmann scribbled a few notes.

'Any boyfriends?'

I looked across at Hildegard.

'I don't think so,' she said. 'I've searched her room, and there's nothing to indicate that she had been seeing any boys.'

Vogelmann nodded sullenly and then was subject to a brief fit of coughing for which he apologized through the material of his handkerchief, and which left his face as red as his hair.

'After four weeks, you'll have checked with all her relations and schoolfriends that she hasn't been staying with them.' He wiped his mouth with his handkerchief.

'Naturally,' Hildegard said stiffly.

'We've asked everywhere,' I said. 'I've been along every metre of that journey looking for her and found nothing.' This was almost literally true.

'What was she wearing when she disappeared?'

Hildegard described her clothes.

'What about money?'

'A few marks. Her savings were untouched.'

'All right. I'll ask around and see what I can find out. You had better give me your address.'

I dictated it for him, and added the telephone number. When he'd finished writing he stood up, arched his back painfully, and then walked around a bit with his hands thrust deep into his pockets like an awkward schoolboy. By now I had guessed him to be no more than forty.

'Go home and wait to hear from me. I'll be in touch in a couple of days, or earlier if I find something.'

We stood up to leave.

'What do you think are the chances of finding her alive?' Hildegard said.

Vogelmann shrugged dismally. 'I've got to admit that they're not good. But I will do my best.'

'What's your first move?' I said, curious.

He checked the knot of his tie again, and stretched his

Adam's apple over the collar stud. I held my breath as he turned to face me.

'Well, I'll start by getting some copies made of your daughter's photograph. And then put them into circulation. This city has a lot of runaways, you know. There are a few children who don't much care for the Hitler Youth and that sort of thing. I'll make a start in that direction, Herr Steininger.' He put his hand on my shoulder and accompanied us to the door.

'Thank you,' said Hildegard. 'You've been most kind, Herr Vogelmann.'

I smiled and nodded politely. He bowed his head, and as Hildegard passed out of the door in front of me I caught him glancing down at her legs. You couldn't blame him. In her beige wool bolero, dotted foulard blouse and burgundy wool skirt, she looked like a year's worth of war reparations. It felt good just pretending to be married to her.

I shook Vogelmann's hand and followed Hildegard outside, thinking to myself that if I were really her husband I would be driving her home to undress her and take her to bed.

It was an elegantly erotic daydream of silk and lace that I was conjuring up for myself as we left Vogelmann's offices and went out into the street. Hildegard's sexual appeal was something altogether more streamlined than steamy imaginings of bouncing breasts and buttocks. All the same, I knew that my little husband fantasy was short on probability since, in all likelihood, the real Herr Steininger, had he been alive, would almost certainly have driven his beautiful young wife home for nothing more stimulating than a cup of fresh coffee before returning to the bank where he worked. The simple fact of the matter is that a man who wakes alone will think of having a woman just as surely as a man who wakes with a wife will think of having breakfast.

'So what did you make of him?' she said when we were in the car driving back to Steglitz. 'I thought he wasn't as bad as he looked. In fact, he was quite sympathetic, really. Certainly no worse than your own men, Kommissar. I can't imagine why we bothered.'

I let her go on like that for a minute or two.

'It struck you as perfectly normal that there were so many obvious questions that he didn't ask?'

She sighed. 'Like what?'

'He never mentioned his fee.'

'I dare say that if he thought we couldn't have afforded it, then he would have brought it up. And by the way, don't expect me to take care of the account for this little experiment of yours.'

I told her that Kripo would pay for everything.

Seeing the distinctive dark-yellow of a cigarette-vending van, I pulled up and got out of the car. I bought a couple of packs and threw one in the glove-box. I tapped one out for her, then myself and lit us both.

'It didn't seem strange that he also neglected to ask how old Emmeline was, which school she attended, what the name of her dancing teacher was, where I worked, that sort of thing?'

She blew smoke out of both nostrils like an angry bull. 'Not especially,' she said. 'At least, not until you mentioned it.' She thumped the dashboard and swore. 'But what if he had asked which school Emmeline goes to? What would you have done if he'd turned up there and found out that my real husband is dead? I'd like to know that.'

'He wouldn't have.'

'You seem very sure of that. How do you know?'

'Because I know how private detectives operate. They don't like to walk right in after the police and ask all the same questions. Usually they like to come at a thing from the other side. Walk round it a bit before they see an opening.'

'So you think that this Rolf Vogelmann is suspicious?'

'Yes, I do. Enough to warrant detailing a man to keep an eye on his premises.'

She swore again, rather more loudly this time.

'That's the second time,' I said. 'What's the matter with you?'

'Why should anything be the matter? No indeed. Single ladies never mind people giving out their addresses and telephone numbers to those whom the police believe to be suspicious. That's what makes living on one's own so exciting. My daughter is missing, probably murdered, and now I have to worry that that horrible man might drop round one evening for a little chat about her.' She was so angry she almost sucked the tobacco out of the cigarette paper. But even so, this time when we arrived at her apartment in Lepsius Strasse, she invited me inside.

I sat down on the sofa and listened to the sound of her urinating in the bathroom. It seemed strangely out of character for her not to be at all self-conscious about such a thing. Perhaps she didn't care if I heard or not. I'm not sure that she even bothered to close the bathroom door.

When she came back into the room she asked me peremptorily for another cigarette. Leaning forwards I waved one at her which she snatched from my fingers. She lit herself with the table lighter, and puffed like a trooper in the trenches. I watched her with interest as she paced up and down in front of me, the very image of parental anxiety. I selected a cigarette myself, and tugged a book of matches from my waistcoat pocket. Hildegard glanced fiercely at me as I bent my head towards the flame.

'I thought detectives were supposed to be able to light matches with their thumbnails.'

'Only the careless kind, who don't pay five marks for a manicure,' I said yawning.

I guessed that she was working up to something, but had no more idea of what it could be than I had of Hitler's taste in soft-furnishings. I took another good look at her.

She was tall – taller than the average man, and in her early thirties, but with the knock-knees and turned–in toes of a girl half her age. There wasn't much of a chest to speak of, and even less behind. The nose was maybe a bit too broad, the lips a shade too thick, and the cornflower-blue eyes rather too close together; and with the possible exception of her temper, there was certainly nothing delicate about her. But there was no doubting her long-limbed beauty which had something in common with the fastest of fillies out at the Hoppegarten. Probably she was just as difficult to hold on the rein; and if you ever managed to climb into the saddle, you could have done no more than hope that you got the trip as far as the winning-post.

'Can't you see that I'm scared?' she said, stamping her foot on the polished wood floor. 'I don't want to be on my own now.'

'Where is your son Paul?'

'He's gone back to his boarding-school. Anyway, he's only ten, so I can't see him coming to my assistance, can you?' She dropped on to the sofa beside me.

'Well I don't mind sleeping in his room for a few nights,' I said, 'if you really are scared.'

'Would you?' she said happily.

'Sure,' I said, and privately congratulated myself. 'It would be my pleasure.'

'I don't want it to be your pleasure,' she said, with just a trace of a smile, 'I want it to be your duty.'

For a moment I almost forgot why I was there. I might even have thought that she had forgotten. It was only when I saw the tear in the corner of her eye that I realized she really was afraid.

18

'I don't get it,' said Korsch. 'What about Streicher and his bunch? Are we still investigating them or not?'

'Yes,' I said. 'But until the Gestapo surveillance throws up something of interest to us, there's not a lot we can do in that direction.'

'So what do you want us to do while you're looking after the widow?' said Becker, who was on the edge of allowing himself a smile I might have found irritating. 'That is, apart from checking the Gestapo reports.'

I decided not to be too sensitive about the matter. That would have been suspicious in itself.

'Korsch,' I said, 'I want you to keep your eye on the Gestapo inquiry. Incidentally, how's your man getting on with Vogelmann?'

He shook his head. 'There's not a lot to report, sir. This Vogelmann hardly ever leaves his office. Not much of a detective if you ask me.'

'It certainly doesn't look like it,' I said. 'Becker, I want you to find me a girl.' He grinned and looked down at the toe of his shoe. 'That shouldn't be too difficult for you.'

'Any particular kind of girl, sir?'

'Aged about fifteen or sixteen, blonde, blue-eyed, BdM and,' I said, feeding him the line, 'preferably a virgin.'

'That last part might be a bit difficult, sir.'

'She'll have to have plenty of nerve.'

'Are you thinking of staking her out, sir?'

'I believe it's always been the best way to hunt tiger.'

'Sometimes the goat gets killed though, sir,' said Korsch.

'As I said, this girl will have to have guts. I want her to know as much as possible. If she is going to risk her life then she ought to know why she's doing it.'

'Where exactly are we going to do this, sir?' said Becker.

'You tell me. Think about a few places where our man might notice her. A place where we can watch her without being seen ourselves.' Korsch was frowning. 'What's troubling you?'

He shook his head with slow distaste. 'I don't like it, sir. Using a young girl as bait. It's inhuman.'

'What do you suggest we use? A piece of cheese?'

'A main road,' Becker said, thinking out loud. 'Somewhere like Hohenzollerndamm, but with more cars, to increase our chances of him seeing her.'

'Honestly, sir, don't you think it's just a bit risky?'

'Of course it is. But what do we really know about this bastard? He drives a car, he wears a uniform, he has an Austrian or Bavarian accent. After that everything is a maybe. I don't have to remind you both that we are running out of time. That Heydrich has given me less than four weeks to solve this case. Well, we need to get closer, and we need to do it quickly. The only way is to take the initiative, to select his next victim for him.'

'But we might wait for ever,' said Korsch.

'I didn't say that it would be easy. You hunt tiger and you can end up sleeping in a tree.'

'What about the girl?' Korsch continued. 'You don't propose to keep her at it night and day, do you?'

'She can do it in the afternoons,' said Becker. 'Afternoons and early evenings. Not in the dark, so we can make sure he sees her, and we see him.'

'You're getting the idea.'

'But where does Vogelmann fit in?'

'I don't know. A feeling in my socks, that's all. Maybe it's nothing, but I just want to check it out.'

Becker smiled. 'A bull has to trust a few hunches now and then,' he said.

I recognized my own uninspired rhetoric. 'We'll make a detective out of you yet,' I told him.

She listened to her Gigli gramophone records with the avidity of someone who is about to go deaf, offering and requiring no more conversation than a railway ticket-collector. By now I had realized that Hildegard Steininger was about as self-contained as a fountain-pen, and I figured that she probably preferred the kind of man who could think of himself as little more than a blank sheet of writing paper. And yet, almost in spite of her, I continued to find her attractive. For my taste she was too much concerned with the shade of her gold-spun hair, the length of her fingernails and the state of her teeth, which she was forever brushing. Too vain by half, and too selfish twice over. Given a choice between pleasing herself and pleasing someone else she would have hoped that pleasing herself would have made everyone happy. That she should have thought that one would almost certainly result from the other was for her as simple a reaction as a knee jerking under a patella-hammer.

It was my sixth night staying at her apartment, and as usual she had cooked a dinner that was nearly inedible.

'You don't have to eat it, you know,' she had said. 'I was never much of a cook.'

'I was never much of a dinner guest,' I had replied, and eaten most of it, not for politeness' sake, but because I was hungry and had learnt in the trenches not to be too fussy about my food.

Now she closed the gramophone cabinet and yawned.

'I'm going to bed,' she said.

I tossed aside the book I was reading and said that I was going to turn in myself.

In Paul's bedroom I spent a few minutes studying the map of Spain that was pinned to the boy's wall, documenting the fortunes of the Condor Legions, before turning out the light. It seemed that every German schoolboy these days wanted to be a fighter-pilot. I was just settling down when there was a knock at the door.

'May I come in?' she said, hovering naked in the doorway. For a moment or two she just stood there, framed in the light from the hallway like some marvellous madonna, almost as if she were allowing me to assess her proportions. My chest and scrotum tightening, I watched her walk gracefully towards me.

Whereas her head and back were small, her legs were so long that she seemed to have been created by a draughtsman of genius. One hand covered her sex and this small shyness excited me very much. I allowed it for a short time while I looked upon the rounded simple volumes of her breasts. These were lightly, almost invisibly nippled, and the size of perfect nectarines.

I leant forwards, pushed that modest hand away, and then, taking hold of her smooth flanks, I pressed my mouth against the sleek filaments that mantled her sex. Standing up to kiss her I felt her hand reach down urgently for me, and winced as she peeled me back. It was too rough to be polite, to be tender, and so I responded by pushing her face first on to the bed, pulling her cool buttocks towards me and moulding her into a position that pleased me. She cried out at the moment when I plunged into her body, and her long thighs trembled wonderfully as we played out our noisy pantomime to its barnstorming denouement.

We slept until dawn came creeping through the thin material of the curtains. Awake before her, I was struck by her colour, which was every bit as cool as her awakening expression which changed not a bit as she sought to find my penis with her mouth. And then, turning on to her back, she pulled herself up the bed and laid her head on the pillow, her thighs yawning open so that I could see where life begins, and again I licked and kissed her there before acquainting it with the full rank of my ardour, pressing myself into her body until I thought that only my head and shoulders would remain unconsumed.

Finally, when there was nothing left in either of us, she wrapped herself round me and wept until I thought that she would melt.

19

Saturday, 29 October

'I thought you'd like the idea.'

'I'm not sure that I don't. Just give me a second to swill it around my head.'

'You don't want her hanging around somewhere just for the hell of it. He'll smell that shit in minutes and won't go near her. It's got to look natural.'

I nodded without a great deal of conviction and tried to smile at the BdM girl Becker had found. She was an extraordinarily pretty adolescent and I wasn't sure what Becker had been more impressed with, her bravery or her breasts.

'Come on, sir, you know what it's like,' he said. 'These girls are always hanging around the *Der Stürmer* display cases on street corners. They get a cheap thrill reading about Jewish doctors interfering with mesmerized German virgins. Look at it this way. Not only will it stop her from getting bored, but also, if Streicher or his people are involved, then they're more than likely going to take notice of her here, in front of one of these Stürmerkästen, than anywhere else.'

I stared uncomfortably at the elaborate, red-painted case, probably built by some loyal readers, with its vivid slogans proclaiming: 'German Women: The Jews are your Destruction', and the three double-page spreads from the paper under glass. It was bad enough to ask a girl to act as bait, without having to expose her to this kind of trash as well.

'I suppose you're right, Becker.'

'You know I am. Look at her. She's reading it already. I swear she likes it.'

'What's her name?'

'Ulrike.'

I walked over to the Stürmerkästen where she was standing, singing quietly to herself.

'You know what to do, Ulrike?' I said quietly, not looking at her now that I was beside her, but staring at the Fips cartoon with its mandatory ugly Jew. No one could look like that, I thought. The nose was as big as a sheep's muzzle.

'Yes, sir,' she said brightly.

'There are lots of policemen around. You can't see them, but they are all watching you. Understand?' I saw her head nod in the reflection on the glass. 'You're a very brave girl.'

At that she started to sing again, only louder, and I realized that it was the Hitler Youth song:

> 'Our flag see before us fly,
> Our flag means an age without strife,
> Our flag leads us to eternity,
> Our flag means more to us than life.'

I walked back to where Becker was standing and got back into the car.

'She's quite a girl, isn't she, sir?'

'She certainly is. Just make sure that you keep your flippers off her, do you hear?'

He was all innocence. 'Come on, sir, you don't think I'd try to bird that one, do you?' He got into the driving seat and started the engine.

'I think you'd fuck your great-grandmother, if you really want my opinion.' I glanced over each shoulder. 'Where are your men?'

'Sergeant Hingsen's on the first floor of that apartment building there,' he said, 'and I've got a couple of men on the street. One is tidying up the graveyard on the corner, and the other's cleaning windows over there. If our man does show up, we'll have him.'

'Do the girl's parents know about this?'

'Yes.'

'Rather public-spirited of them to give their permission, wouldn't you say?'

'They didn't exactly do that, sir. Ulrike informed them that she had volunteered to do this in the service of the Führer and the Fatherland. She said that it would be unpatriotic to try and stop her. So they didn't have much choice in the matter. She's a forceful sort of girl.'

'I can imagine.'

'Quite a swimmer, too, by all accounts. A future Olympic prospect, her teacher reckons.'

'Well, let's just hope for a bit of rain in case she has to try and swim her way out of trouble.'

I heard the bell in the hall and went to the window. Pulling it up I leant out to see who was working the bell-pull. Even three storeys up I could recognize Vogelmann's head of distinctive red hair.

'That's a very common thing to do,' said Hildegard. 'Lean out of a window like a fishwife.'

'As it happens, I might just have caught a fish. It's Vogelmann. And he's brought a friend.'

'Well, you had better go and let them in, hadn't you?'

I walked out on to the landing and operated the lever that pulled the chain to open the street door, and watched the two men climb up the stairs. Neither one of them said anything.

Vogelmann came into Hildegard's apartment wearing his best undertaker's face, which was a blessing since the grim set to his halitosic mouth meant that, for a while at least, it stayed mercifully shut. The man with him was shorter than Vogelmann by a head, and in his mid-thirties, with fair hair, blue eyes and an intense, even academic air about him. Vogelmann waited until we were all seated before introducing the other man as Dr Otto Rahn, and promised to say more about him presently. Then he sighed loudly and shook his head.

'I'm afraid that I have had no luck in the search for your daughter Emmeline,' he said. 'I've asked everyone I could possibly have asked, and looked everywhere I could possibly have looked. With no result. It has been most disappointing.' He paused, and added: 'Of course, I realize that my own disappointment must count as nothing besides your own. However, I thought I might at least find some trace of her.

'If there was anything, anything at all, that gave some clue as to what might have become of her, then I would feel justified in recommending to you that I continue with my inquiries. But there's nothing that gives me any confidence that I wouldn't be wasting your time and money.'

I nodded with slow resignation. 'Thank you for being so honest, Herr Vogelmann.'

'At least you can say we tried, Herr Steininger,' Vogelmann said. 'I'm not exaggerating when I say that I have exhausted all the usual methods of inquiry.' He stopped to clear his throat and, excusing himself, dabbed at his mouth with a handkerchief.

'I hesitate to suggest this to you, Herr and Frau Steininger, and please don't think me facetious, but when the usual has proved itself to be unhelpful, there can surely be no harm in resorting to the unusual.'

'I rather thought that was why we consulted you in the first place,' Hildegard said stiffly. 'The usual, as you put it, was something that we expected from the police.'

Vogelmann smiled awkwardly. 'I've expressed it badly,' he said. 'I should perhaps have been talking in terms of the ordinary and the extraordinary.'

The other man, Otto Rahn, came to Vogelmann's assistance.

'What Herr Vogelmann is trying to suggest, with as much good taste as he can in the circumstances, is that you consider enlisting the services of a medium to help you find your daughter.' His accent was educated and he spoke with the speed of a man from somewhere like Frankfurt.

'A medium?' I said. 'You mean spiritualism?' I shrugged. 'We're not believers in that sort of thing.' I wanted to hear what Rahn might have to say in order to sell us on the idea.

He smiled patiently. 'These days it's hardly a matter of belief. Spiritualism is now more of a science. There have been some quite amazing developments since the war, especially in the last decade.'

'But isn't this illegal?' I asked meekly. 'I'm sure I read somewhere that Count Helldorf had banned all professional fortune-telling in Berlin, why, as long ago as 1934.'

Rahn was smooth and not at all deflected by my choice of phrase.

'You're very well-informed, Herr Steininger. And you're right, the Police President did ban them. Since then, however, the situation has been satisfactorily resolved, and racially sound practitioners in the psychic sciences are incorporated in the Independent Professions sections of the German Labour Front. It was only ever the mixed races, the Jews and the gypsies, that gave the psychic sciences a bad name. Why, these days the Führer himself employs a professional astrologer. So you see, things have come a long way since Nostradamus.'

Vogelmann nodded and chuckled quietly.

So this was the reason Reinhard Lange was sponsoring Vogelmann's advertising campaign, I thought. To drum up a little business for the floating wine-glass trade. It looked like quite a neat operation too. Your detective failed to find your missing person, after which, through the mediation of Otto Rahn, you were passed on to an apparently higher power. This service probably resulted in your paying several times as much for the privilege of finding out what was already obvious: that your loved one slept with the angels.

Yes indeed, I thought, a neat piece of theatre. I was going to enjoy putting these people away. You can sometimes forgive a man who works a line, but not the ones who prey on the grief and suffering of others. That was like stealing the cushions off a pair of crutches.

'Peter,' said Hildegard, 'I don't see that we really have much to lose.'

'No, I suppose not.'

'I'm so glad you think so,' said Vogelmann. 'One always hesitates to recommend such a thing, but I think that in this case, there is really little or no alternative.'

'What will it cost?'

'This is Emmeline's life we're talking about,' Hildegard snapped. 'How can you mention money?'

'The cost is very reasonable,' said Rahn. 'I'm quite sure you'll be entirely satisfied. But let's talk about that at a later date. The most important thing is that you meet someone who can help you.

'There is a man, a very great and gifted man, who is

203

possessed of enormous psychic ability. He might be able to help. This man, as the last descendant of a long line of German men of wisdom, has an ancestral-clairvoyant memory that is quite unique in our time.'

'He sounds wonderful,' Hildegard breathed.

'He is,' said Vogelmann.

'Then I will arrange for you to meet him,' said Rahn. 'I happen to know that he is free this coming Thursday. Will you be available in the evening?'

'Yes. We'll be available.'

Rahn took out a notebook and started writing. When he'd finished he tore out the sheet and handed it to me.

'Here is the address. Shall we say eight o'clock? Unless you hear from me before then?' I nodded. 'Excellent.'

Vogelmann stood up to leave while Rahn bent and searched for something in his briefcase. He handed Hildegard a magazine.

'Perhaps this might also be of interest to you,' he said.

I saw them out and when I came back I found her engrossed in the magazine. I didn't need to look at the front cover to know that it was Reinhard Lange's *Urania*. Nor did I need to speak to Hildegard to know that she was convinced Otto Rahn was genuine.

20

Thursday, 3 November

The Resident Registration Office turned up an Otto Rahn, formerly of Michelstadt near Frankfurt, now living at Tiergartenstrasse 8a, Berlin West 35.

VC1, Criminal Records, on the other hand, had no trace of him.

Nor did VC2, the department that compiled the Wanted Persons List. I was just about to leave when the department director, an SS Sturmbannführer by the name of Baum, called me over to his office.

'Kommissar, did I hear you asking that officer about somebody called Otto Rahn?' he asked.

I told him that I was interested in finding out everything I could about Otto Rahn.

'Which department are you with?'

'The Murder Commission. He might be able to assist us with an inquiry.'

'So you don't actually suspect him of having committed a crime?'

Sensing that the Sturmbannführer knew something about an Otto Rahn, I decided to cover my tracks a little.

'Good grief, no,' I said. 'As I say, it's just that he may be able to put us in contact with a valuable witness. Why? Do you know someone by that name?'

'Yes, I do, as a matter of fact,' he said. 'He's more of an acquaintance really. There is an Otto Rahn who's in the SS.'

The old Hotel Prinz Albrecht Strasse was an unremarkable four-storey building of arched windows and mock Corinthian pillars, with two long, dictator-sized balconies on the first floor, surmounted by an enormous ornate clock. Its seventy rooms meant that it had never been in the same league as the big hotels like the Bristol or the Adlon, which was probably how it came to be taken over by the SS. Now called SS-Haus, and situated next door to Gestapo headquarters at number eight, it was also headquarters to Heinrich Himmler in his capacity as Reichsführer-SS.

In the Personnel Records Department on the second floor, I showed them my warrant and explained my mission.

'I'm required by the SD to obtain a security clearance for a member of the SS in order that he may be considered for promotion to General Heydrich's personal staff.'

The SS corporal on duty stiffened at the mention of Heydrich's name.

'How can I help?' he said eagerly.

'I require to see the man's file. His name is Otto Rahn.'

The corporal asked me to wait, and then went into the next room where he searched for the appropriate filing-cabinet.

'Here you are,' he said, returning after a few minutes with the file. 'I'm afraid that I'll have to ask you to examine it here. A file may be removed from this office only with the written approval of the Reichsführer himself.'

'Naturally I knew that,' I said coldly. 'But I'm sure I'll just need to take a quick look at it. This is only a formal security check.' I stepped away and stood at a lectern on the far side of the office, where I opened the file to examine its contents. It made interesting reading.

SS Unterscharführer Otto Rahn; born 18 February 1904 at Michelstadt in Odenwald; studied philology at the University of Heidelberg, graduating in 1928; joined SS, March 1936; promoted SS, Unterscharführer, April 1936; posted SS-Deaths Head Division 'Oberbayern' Dachau Concentration Camp, September 1937; seconded to Race and Resettlement Office, December 1938; public speaker and author of *Crusade Against the Grail* (1933) amd *Lucifer's Servants* (1937).

There followed several pages of medical notes and character assessments, and these included an evaluation from one SS-Gruppenführer Theodor Eicke which described Rahn as 'diligent, although given to some eccentricities'. By my reckoning that could have covered just about anything, from murder to the length of his hair.

I returned Rahn's file to the desk corporal and made my way out of the building. Otto Rahn.

The more I discovered about him, the less inclined I was to believe that he was merely working some elaborate confidence trick. Here was a man interested in something else besides money. A man for whom the word 'fanatic' did not seem to be inappropriate. Driving back to Steglitz, I passed Rahn's house on Tiergartenstrasse, and I don't thnk I would have been surprised to see the Scarlet Woman and the Great Beast of the Apocalypse come flying out the front door.

It was dark by the time we drove to Caspar-Theyss Strasse, which runs just south of Kurfürstendamm, on the edge of Grunewald. It was a quiet street of villas which stop only a little way short of being something more grand, and which are occupied largely by doctors and dentists. Number thirty-three, next to a small cottage-hospital, occupied the corner of Pauls-bornerstrasse, and was opposite a large florist where visitors to the hospital could buy their flowers.

There was a touch of the Gingerbread Man about the queer-looking house to which Rahn had invited us. The base-ment and ground-floor brickwork was painted brown, and on the first and second floors it was cream-coloured. A sep-tagonally shaped tower occupied the east side of the house, a timbered loggia surmounted by a balcony the centre portion, and on the west side, a moss-covered wooden gable overhung a couple of porthole windows.

'I hope you brought a clove of garlic with you,' I told Hildegard as I parked the car. I could see she didn't much care for the look of the place, but she remained obstinately silent, still convinced that everything was on the level.

We walked up to a wrought-iron gate that had been fashioned with a variety of zodiacal symbols, and I wondered what the two SS men standing underneath one of the garden's many spruce trees and smoking cigarettes made of it. This thought occupied me for only a second before I moved on to the more challenging question of what they and the several Party staff cars parked on the pavement were doing there.

Otto Rahn answered the door, greeting us with sympathetic warmth, and directed us into a cloakroom where he relieved us of our coats.

'Before we go in,' he said, 'I should explain that there are a number of other people here for this seance. Herr Weisthor's prowess as a clairvoyant has made him Germany's most important sage. I think I mentioned that a number of leading Party members are sympathetic to Herr Weisthor's work – incidentally, this is his home – and so apart from Herr Vogelmann and myself, one of the other guests here tonight will probably be familiar to you.'

Hildegard's jaw dropped. 'Not the Führer,' she said.

Rahn smiled. 'No, not he. But someone very close to him. He has requested that he be treated just like anyone else in order to facilitate a favourable atmosphere for the evening's contact. So I'm telling you now, in order that you won't be too surprised, that it is the Reichsführer-SS, Heinrich Himmler, to whom I am referring. No doubt you saw the security men outside and were wondering what was going on. The Reichsführer is a great patron of our work and has attended many seances.'

Emerging from the cloakroom, we went through a door soundproofed in button-backed padded green leather, and into a large and simply furnished L-shaped room. Across the thick green carpet was a round table at one end, and a group of about ten people standing over a sofa and a couple of armchairs at the other. The walls, where they were visible between the light oak panelling, were painted white, and the green curtains were all drawn. There was something classically German about this room, which was the same thing as saying that it was about as warm and friendly as a Swiss Army knife.

Rahn found us some drinks and introduced Hildegard and me to the room. I spotted Vogelmann's red head first of all, nodded to him and then searched for Himmler. Since there were no uniforms to be seen, he was rather difficult to spot in his dark, double-breasted suit. Taller than I had expected, and younger too – perhaps no more than thirty-seven or thirty-eight. When he spoke, he seemed a mild-mannered sort of man, and, apart from the enormous gold Rolex, my overall impression was of a man you would have taken for a headmaster rather than the head of the German secret police. And what was it about Swiss wristwatches that made them so attractive to men of power? But a wristwatch was not as attractive to this particular man of power as was Hildegard Steininger, it seemed, and the two of them were soon deep in conversation.

'Herr Weisthor will come out presently,' Rahn explained. 'He usually needs a period of quiet meditation before approaching the spirit world. Let me introduce you to Reinhard Lange. He's the proprietor of that magazine I left for your wife.'

'Ah yes, *Urania*.'

So there he was, short and plump, with a dimple in one of his chins and a pugnaciously pendant lower lip, as if daring you to smack him or kiss him. His fair hair was well-receded, although somewhat babyish about the ears. He had hardly any eyebrows to speak of, and the eyes themselves were half-closed, slitty even. Both of these features made him seem weak and inconstant, in a Nero-like sort of way. Possibly he was neither of these two things, although the strong smell of cologne that surrounded him, his self-satisfied air, and his slightly theatrical way of speaking, did nothing to correct my first impression of him. My line of work has made me a rapid and fairly accurate judge of character, and five minutes' conversation with Lange were enough to convince me that I had not been wrong about him. The man was a worthless little queer.

I excused myself and went to the lavatory I had seen beyond the cloakroom. I had already decided to return to Weisthor's house after the seance and see if the other rooms were any more interesting than the one we were in. There didn't appear to be a dog about the place, so it seemed that all I had to do was prepare my entry. I bolted the door behind me and set about releasing the window-catch. It was stiff and I had just managed to get it open when there was a knock at the door. It was Rahn.

'Herr Steininger? Are you in there?'

'I won't be a moment.'

'We'll be starting in a moment or two.'

'I'll be right there,' I said, and, leaving the window a couple of centimetres open, I flushed the toilet and went back to rejoin the rest of the guests.

Another man had come into the room, and I realized that this must be Weisthor. Aged about sixty-five, he wore a three-piece suit of light-brown flannel and carried an ornate, ivory-handled stick with strange carvings on its shaft, some of which matched his ring. Physically he resembled an older version of Himmler, with his small smudge of a moustache, hamster-like cheeks, dyspeptic mouth and receding chin; but he was stouter, and whereas the Reichsführer reminded you of a myopic rat, Weisthor had more of the beaver about his features, an effect that was accentuated by the gap between his two front teeth.

'You must be Herr Steininger,' he said, pumping my hand. 'Permit me to introduce myself. I am Karl Maria Weisthor, and I am delighted to have already had the pleasure of meeting your lovely wife.' He spoke very formally, and with a Viennese accent. 'In that at least you are a very fortunate man. Let us hope that I may be of service to you both before the evening has ended. Otto has told me of your missing daughter Emmeline, and of how the police and our good friend Rolf Vogelmann have been unable to find her. As I said to your wife, I am sure that the spirits of our ancient German ancestors will not desert us, and that they will tell us what has become of her, as they have told us of other things before.'

He turned and waved at the table. 'Shall we be seated?' he said. 'Herr Steininger, you and your wife will sit on either side of me. Everyone will join hands, Herr Steininger. This will increase our conscious power. Try not to let go, no matter what you might see or hear, as it can cause the link to be broken. Do you both understand?'

We nodded and took our seats. When the rest of the company had sat down, I noticed that Himmler had contrived to be sitting next to Hildegard, to whom he was paying close attention. It struck me that I would tell it differently, and that it would amuse Heydrich and Nebe if I told them I spent the evening holding hands with Heinrich Himmler. Thinking about it then I almost laughed, and to cover my half-smile I turned away from Weisthor and found myself looking at a tall, urbane, Siegfried-type wearing evening dress, with the kind of warm, sensitive manner that comes only of bathing in dragon's blood.

'My name is Kindermann,' he said sternly. 'Dr Lanz Kindermann, at your service, Herr Steininger.' He glanced down at my hand as if it had been a dirty dishcloth.

'Not the famous psychotherapist?' I said.

He smiled. 'I doubt that you could call me famous,' he said, but with some satisfaction all the same. 'Nevertheless, I thank you for the compliment.'

'And are you Austrian?'

'Yes. Why do you ask?'

'I like to know something about the men whose hands I hold,' I offered, and grasped his own firmly.

'In a moment,' said Weisthor, 'I shall ask our friend Otto to turn off the electric light. But first of all, I should like us all to close our eyes and to breathe deeply. The purpose of this is to relax. Only if we are relaxed will spirits feel comfortable enough to contact us and offer us the benefit of what they are able to see.

'It may help you to think of something peaceful, such as a flower or a formation of clouds.' He paused, so that the only sounds which could be heard were the deep breathing of the people around the table and the ticking of a clock on the mantelpiece. I heard Vogelmann clear his throat, which prompted Weisthor to speak again.

'Try and flow into the person next to you so that we may feel the power of the circle. When Otto turns off the light I shall go into trance and permit my body to be taken under the control of spirit. Spirit will control my speech, my every bodily function, so that I shall be in a vulnerable position.

Make no sudden noise or interruption. Speak gently if you wish to communicate with spirit, or allow Otto to speak for you.' He paused again. 'Otto? The lights, please.'

I heard Rahn stand up as if rousing himself from a deep sleep and creep across the carpet.

'From now on Weisthor will not speak unless he is under spirit,' he said. 'It will be my voice you hear speak to him in trance.' He turned off the light, and after a few seconds I heard him return to the circle.

I stared hard into the darkness at where Weisthor was sitting, but try as I might, I could see nothing but the strange shapes which play on the back of the retina when it is deprived of light. Whatever Weisthor said about flowers or clouds, I found it helped me to think of the Mauser automatic at my shoulder, and the nice formation of 9mm ammunition in the grip.

The first change that I was aware of was that of his breathing, which became progressively slower and deeper. After a while it was almost undetectable and, but for his grip, which had slackened considerably, I might have said he had disappeared.

Finally he spoke, but it was in a voice that made my flesh creep and my hair prickle.

'I have a wise king here from long, long ago,' he said, his grip tightening suddenly. 'From a time when three suns shone in the northern sky.' He uttered a long, sepulchral sigh. 'He suffered a terrible defeat in battle at the hands of Charlemagne and his Christian army.'

'Were you Saxon?' Rahn asked quietly.

'Aye, Saxon. The Franks called them pagans, and put them to death for it. Agonizing deaths, that were full of blood and pain.' He seemed to hesitate. 'It's difficult to say this. He says that blood must be paid for. He says that German paganism is grown strong again, and must be revenged on the Franks and their religion, in the name of the old gods.' Then he grunted almost as if he had been struck and went quiet again.

'Don't be alarmed,' Rahn murmured. 'Spirit can leave quite violently sometimes.'

After several minutes, Weisthor spoke again.

'Who are you?' he asked softly. 'A girl? Will you tell us your name, child? No? Come now –'

'Don't be afraid,' said Rahn. 'Please come forward to us.'

'Her name is Emmeline,' said Weisthor.

I heard Hildegard gasp.

'Is your name Emmeline Steininger?' Rahn asked. 'If so, then your mother and father are here to speak to you, child.'

'She says that she is not a child,' whispered Weisthor. 'And that one of these two people is not her real parent at all.'

I stiffened. Could it be genuine after all? Did Weisthor really have mediumistic powers?

'I'm her stepmother,' said Hildegard tremulously, and I wondered if she had recognized that Weisthor should have said that neither of us was Emmeline's real parent.

'She says that she misses her dancing. But especially she misses you both.'

'We miss you too, darling.'

'Where are you, Emmeline?' I asked. There was a long silence, and so I repeated the question.

'They killed her,' said Weisthor falteringly. 'And hid her somewhere.'

'Emmeline, you must try and help us,' said Rahn. 'Can you tell us anything about where they put you?'

'Yes, I'll tell them. She says that outside the window, there's a hill. At the bottom of the hill is a pretty waterfall. What's that? A cross, or maybe something else that's high, like a tower is on top of the hill.'

'The Kreuzberg?' I said.

'Is it the Kreuzberg?' Rahn asked.

'She doesn't know the name,' whispered Weisthor. 'Where's that? Oh how terrible. She says she's in a box. I'm sorry, Emmeline, but I don't think I can have heard you properly. Not in a box? A barrel? Yes, a barrel. A rotten smelly old barrel in an old cellar full of rotten old barrels.'

'Sounds like a brewery,' said Kindermann.

'Could you be referring to the Schultheiss Brewery?' said Rahn.

213

'She thinks that it must be, although it doesn't seem like a place where lots of people go. Some of the barrels are old and have holes in them. She can see out of one of them. No, my dear, it wouldn't be very good for holding beer, I quite agree.'

Hildegard whispered something that I failed to hear.

'Courage, dear lady,' Rahn said. 'Courage.' Then more loudly: 'Who was it that killed you, Emmeline? And can you tell us why?'

Weisthor groaned deeply. 'She doesn't know their names, but she thinks that it was for the Blood Mystery. How did you find out about that, Emmeline? That's one of the many thousands of things you learn about when you die, I see. They killed her like they kill their animals, and then her blood was mixed with the wine and the bread. She thinks that it must have been for religious rites, but not the sort she had ever seen before.'

'Emmeline,' said a voice which I thought must be Himmler's. 'Was it the Jews who murdered you? Was it Jews who used your blood?'

Another long silence.

'She doesn't know,' said Weisthor. 'They didn't say who or what they were. They didn't look like any of the pictures she's seen of Jews. What's that, my dear? She says that it might have been but she doesn't want to get anyone into trouble, no matter what they did to her. She says that if it was the Jews then they were just bad Jews, and that not all Jews would have approved of such a thing. She doesn't want to say any more about that. She just wants someone to go and get her out of that dirty barrel. Yes, I'm sure someone will organize it, Emmeline. Don't worry.'

'Tell her that I shall personally see to it that it happens tonight,' said Himmler. 'The child has my own word on that.'

'What's that you said? All right. Emmeline says to thank you for trying to help her. And she says to tell mother and father that she loves them very much indeed, but not to worry about her now. Nothing can bring her back. You should both get on with your lives and put what has happened behind you. Try and be happy. Emmeline has to go now.'

'Goodbye, Emmeline,' sobbed Hildegard.

'Goodbye,' I said.

Once again there was silence, but for the sound of the blood rushing in my ears. I was glad of the darkness because it hid my face, which must have shown my anger, and afforded me an opportunity to breathe my way back to a semblance of quiet sadness and resignation. If it hadn't been for the two or three minutes that elapsed from the end of Weisthor's performance and the raising of the lights, I think that I would have shot them all where they sat: Weisthor, Rahn, Vogelmann, Lange – shit, I'd have murdered the whole dirty lot of them just for the sheer satisfaction of it. I'd have made them take the barrel in their mouths and blown the backs of their heads on to each other's faces. An extra nostril for Himmler. A third eye-socket for Kindermann.

I was still breathing heavily when the lights went up again, but this was easily mistaken for grief. Hildegard's face was shiny with tears, which provoked Himmler to put his arm around her. Catching my eye he nodded grimly.

Weisthor was the last to get to his feet. He swayed for a moment as if he would fall, and Rahn took hold of him by the elbow. Weisthor smiled, and patted his friend's hand gratefully.

'I can see by your face, my dear lady, that your daughter came through.'

She nodded. 'I want to thank you, Herr Weisthor. Thank you so much for helping us.' She sniffed loudly and found her handkerchief.

'Karl, you were excellent tonight,' said Himmler. 'Quite remarkable.' There was a murmur of assent from the rest of the table, myself included. Himmler was still shaking his head in wonder. 'Quite, quite remarkable,' he repeated. 'You may all rest assured that I shall contact the proper authorities myself, and order that a squad of police be sent immediately to search the Schultheiss Brewery for the unfortunate child's body.' Himmler was staring at me now, and I nodded dumbly in response to what he was saying.

'But I don't doubt for a minute that they will find her there.

I have every confidence that what we have just heard was the child speaking to Karl in order that both your minds may now be put at rest. I think that the best thing for you to do now would be to go home and wait to hear from the police.'

'Yes, of course,' I said and, walking round the table, I took Hildegard by the hand and led her away from the Reichsführer's embrace. Then we shook hands with the assembled company, accepted their condolences and allowed Rahn to escort us to the door.

'What can one say?' he said with great gravitas. 'Naturally I am very sorry that Emmeline has passed on to the other side, but as the Reichsführer himself said, it's a blessing that now you can know for sure.'

'Yes,' Hildegard sniffed. 'It's best to know, I think.'

Rahn narrowed his eyes and looked slightly pained as he grasped me by the forearm.

'I think it's also best if for obvious reasons you were to say nothing of this evening's events to the police if they should come to say that they have indeed found her. I'm afraid that they might make things very awkward for you if you seemed to know that she had been found before they did themselves. As I'm sure you will appreciate, the police aren't very enlightened when it comes to understanding this sort of thing, and might ask you all sorts of difficult questions.' He shrugged. 'I mean, we all have questions concerning what comes to us from the other side. It is indeed an enigma to everyone, and one to which we have very few answers at this stage.'

'Yes, I can see how the police might prove to be awkward,' I said. 'You may depend on me to say nothing of what transpired this evening. My wife as well.'

'Herr Steininger, I knew you would understand.' He opened the front door. 'Please don't hesitate to contact us again if at some stage you would wish to contact your daughter. But I should leave it for a while. It doesn't do to summon spirit too regularly.'

We said goodbye again, and walked back to the car.

'Get me away from here, Bernie,' she hissed as I opened the door for her. By the time I had started the engine she was crying again, only this time it was with shock and horror.

'I can't believe people could be so – so *evil*,' she sobbed.

'I'm sorry you had to go through that,' I said. 'Really I am. I'd have given anything for you to have avoided it, but it was the only way.'

I drove to the end of the street and on to Bismarkplatz, a quiet intersection of suburban streets with a small patch of grass in the middle. It was only now that I realized how close we were to Frau Lange's house in Herbertstrasse. I spotted Korsch's car, and pulled up behind it.

'Bernie? Do you think that the police will find her there?'

'Yes, I think they will.'

'But how could he fake it and know where she is? How could he know those things about her? Her love of dancing?'

'Because he, or one of those others, put her there. Probably they spoke to Emmeline and asked her a few questions before they killed her. Just for the sake of authenticity.'

She blew her nose, and then looked up. 'Why have we stopped?'

'Because I'm going back there to take a look around. See if I can find out what their ugly little game is. The car parked in front of us is driven by one of my men. His name is Korsch, and he's going to drive you home.'

She nodded. 'Please be careful, Bernie,' she said breathlessly, her head dropping forwards on to her chest.

'Are you all right, Hildegard?'

She fumbled for the door-handle. 'I think I'm going to be sick.' She fell sideways towards the pavement, vomiting into the gutter and down her sleeve as she broke her fall with her hand. I jumped out of the car and ran round to the passenger door to help her, but Korsch was there before me, supporting her by the shoulders until she could draw breath again.

'Jesus Christ,' he said, 'what happened in there?'

Crouching down beside her I mopped the perspiration from Hildegard's face before wiping her mouth. She took the handkerchief from my hand and allowed Korsch to help her sit up again.

'It's a long story,' I said, 'and I'm afraid that it's going to have to wait awhile yet. I want you to take her home and then wait for me at the Alex. Get Becker there as well. I've a feeling we're going to be busy tonight.'

'I'm sorry,' said Hildegard. 'I'm all right now.' She smiled bravely. Korsch and I helped her out and, holding her by the waist, we walked her to Korsch's car.

'Be careful, sir,' he said as he got behind the driving wheel and started the engine. I told him not to worry.

After they had driven away, I waited in the car for half an hour or so, and then walked back down Caspar-Theyss Strasse. The wind was getting up a bit and a couple of times it rose to such a pitch in the trees that lined the dark street that, had I been of a rather more fanciful disposition, I might have imagined that it was something to do with what had taken place in Weisthor's house. Disturbing the spirits and that sort of thing. As it was I was possessed of a sense of danger which the wind moaning across the cloud-tumbling sky did nothing to alleviate, and indeed, this feeling was if anything made all the more acute by seeing the gingerbread house again.

By now the staff cars were gone from the pavement outside, but I nevertheless approached the garden with caution, in case the two SS men had remained behind, for whatever reason. Having satisfied myself that the house was not guarded, I tiptoed round to the side of the house, and to the lavatory window I had left unlocked. It was well that I stepped lightly, because the light was on and from inside the small room could be heard the unmistakable sound of a man straining on the toilet-bowl. Flattening myself in the shadows against the wall, I waited until he finished, and finally, after what seemed like ten or fifteen minutes, I heard the sound of the toilet flushing, and saw the light go off.

Several minutes passed before I judged it safe to go to the window and push it up the sash. But almost immediately upon entering the lavatory, I could have wished to have been else-where, or at least wearing a gas-mask, since the fecal smell that greeted my nostrils was such as would have turned the stomachs of a whole clinicful of proctologists. I suppose that's what bulls mean when they say that sometimes it's a rotten job. For my money, having to stand quietly in a toilet where someone has just achieved a bowel-movement of truly Gothic proportions is about as rotten as it can get.

The terrible smell was the main reason I decided to move out into the cloakroom rather more quickly than might have been safe, and I was almost seen by Weisthor himself as he trudged wearily past the open cloakroom door and across the hallway to a room on the opposite side.

'Quite a wind tonight,' said a voice, which I recognized as belonging to Otto Rahn.

'Yes,' Weisthor chuckled. 'It all added to the atmosphere, didn't it? Himmler will be especially pleased with this turn in the weather. No doubt he will ascribe all sorts of supernatural Wagnerian notions to it.'

'You were very good, Karl,' said Rahn. 'Even the Reichs-führer commented on it.'

'But you look tired,' said a third voice, which I took to be Kindermann's. 'You'd better let me take a look at you.'

I edged forward and looked through the gap between the cloakroom door and frame, Weisthor was taking off his jacket and hanging it over the back of a chair. Sitting down heavily, he allowed Kindermann to take his pulse. He seemed listless and pale, almost as if he really had been in contact with the spirit world. He seemed to hear my thoughts.

'Faking it is almost as tiring as doing it for real,' he said.

'Perhaps I should give you an injection,' said Kindermann. 'A little morphine to help you sleep.' Without waiting for a reply he produced a small bottle and a hypodermic syringe from a medical bag, and set about preparing the needle. 'After all, we don't want you feeling tired for the forthcoming Court of Honour, do we?'

'I shall want you there of course, Lanz,' said Weisthor, rolling back his own sleeve to reveal a forearm that was so bruised and scarred with puncture marks, that it looked as if he had been tattooed.

'I shan't be able to get through it without cocaine. I find it clarifies the mind wonderfully. And I shall need to be so transcendentally stimulated that the Reichsführer-SS will find what I have to say totally irresistible.'

219

'You know, for a moment back there I thought you were actually going to make the revelation tonight,' said Rahn. 'You really teased him with all of that stuff about the girl not wanting to get anyone into trouble. Well, frankly, he more or less believes it now.'

'Only when the time is right, my dear Otto,' said Weisthor. 'Only when the time is right. Think how much more dramatic it will be to him when I reveal it in Wewelsburg. Jewish complicity will have the force of spiritual revelation, and we will be done with this nonsense of his about respecting property and the rule of law. The Jews will get what's coming to them and there won't be one policeman to stop it.' He nodded at the syringe and watched impassively as Kindermann thrust the needle home, sighing with satisfaction as the plunger was depressed.

'And now, gentlemen, if you will kindly help an old man to his bed.'

I watched as they each took an arm and walked him up the creaking stairs.

It crossed my mind that if Kindermann or Rahn were planning to leave then they might want to put on a coat, and so I crept out of the cloakroom and went into the L-shaped room where the bogus seance had been staged, hiding behind the thick curtains in case either one of them should come in. But when they came downstairs again, they only stood in the hall and talked. I missed half of what they said, but the gist of it seemed to be that Reinhard Lange was reaching the end of his usefulness. Kindermann made a feeble attempt to apologize for his lover, but his heart didn't seem to be in it.

The smell in the lavatory was a hard act to follow, but what happened next was even more disgusting. I couldn't see exactly what took place, and there were no words to hear. But the sound of two men engaged in a homosexual act is unmistakable, and left me feeling utterly nauseated. When finally they had brought their filthy behaviour to its braying conclusion and left, chuckling like a couple of degenerate schoolboys, I felt weak enough to have to open a window for some fresh air.

In the study next door I helped myself to a large glass of

Weisthor's brandy, which worked a lot better than a chestful of Berlin air, and with the curtains drawn I even felt relaxed enough to switch on the desk-lamp and take a good long look around the room before searching the drawers and cabinets.

It was worth a look, too. Weisthor's taste in decoration was no less eccentric than mad King Ludwig's. There were strange-looking calendars, heraldic coats of arms, paintings of standing stones, Merlin, the Sword in the Stone, the Grail and the Knights Templar, and photographs of castles, Hitler, Himmler, and finally Weisthor himself, in uniform: first as an officer in some regiment of Austrian infantry; and then in the uniform of a senior officer in the SS.

Karl Weisthor was in the SS. I almost said it aloud, it seemed so fantastic. Nor was he merely an NCO like Otto Rahn, but judging from the number of pips on his collar, at least a brigadier. And something else too. Why had I not noticed it before – the physical similarity between Weisthor and Julius Streicher? It was true that Weisthor was perhaps ten years older than Streicher, but the description given by the little Jewish schoolgirl, by Sarah Hirsch, could just as easily have applied to Weisthor as to Streicher: both men were heavy, with not much hair, and a small moustache; and both men had strong southern accents. Austrian or Bavarian, she had said. Well Weisthor was from Vienna. I wondered if Otto Rahn could have been the man driving the car.

Everything seemed to fall in with what I already knew, and my overhearing the conversation in the hallway confirmed my earlier suspicion that the motive behind the killings was to throw blame on to Berlin's Jews. Yet somehow there still seemed to be more to it. There had been Himmler's involvement. Was I right in thinking that their secondary motive had been the enlistment of the Reichsführer-SS as a believer in Weisthor's powers, thereby ensuring the latter's power-base and prospects for advancement in the SS, perhaps even at the expense of Heydrich himself?

It was a fine piece of theorizing. Now all I needed to do was prove it, and the evidence would have to be watertight if Himmler was going to allow his own personal Rasputin to be sent up for multiple murder. The more so if it was likely to reveal the Reich's chief of police as the gullible victim of an elaborate hoax.

I started to search Weisthor's desk, thinking that even if I did find enough to nail Weisthor and his evil scheme, I wasn't about to make a pen-pal out of the man who was arguably the most powerful man in Germany. This was not a comfortable prospect.

It turned out that Weisthor was a meticulous man with his correspondence, and I found files of letters which included copies of those he had sent himself as well as those he had received. Sitting down at his desk I started to read them at random. If I was looking for typed-out admissions of guilt I was disappointed. Weisthor and his associates had developed that talent for euphemism that working in security or intelligence seems to encourage. These letters confirmed everything I knew, but they were so carefully phrased, and included several code-words, as to be open to more than one interpretation.

K. M. Wiligut Weisthor
Caspar-Theyss Strasse 33,
Berlin W.

To SS-Unterscharführer Otto Rahn,
Tiergartenstrasse 8a,
Berlin W.   8 July 1938

STRICTLY CONFIDENTIAL

Dear Otto,
It is as I had suspected. The Reichsführer informs me that a press embargo has been imposed by the Jew Heydrich in all matters relating to Project Krist. Without newspaper coverage there will be no legitimate way for us to know who is affected as a result of Project Krist activities. In order for us to be able to offer spiritual assistance to those who are affected, and thereby bring about our objective, we must quickly devise another means of being enabled legitimately to effect our involvement.

Have you any suggestions?

Heil Hitler,
Weisthor

222

Otto Rahn
Tiergartenstrasse 8a,
Berlin W.

To SS-Brigadeführer K. M. Weisthor
Berlin Grunewald   10 July 1938

Dear Brigadeführer,

I have given considerable thought to your letter and, with the assistance of SS-Hauptsturmführer Kindermann and SS-Sturmbannführer Anders, I believe that I have the solution.

Anders has some experience of police matters and is confident that in a situation created out of Project Krist, it would not be unusual for a citizen to solicit his own private agent of inquiry, police efficiency being what it is.

It is therefore proposed that through the offices and finance of our good friend Reinhard Lange, we purchase the services of a small private investigation agency, and then simply advertise in the newspapers. We are all of the opinion that the relevant parties will contact this same private detective who, after a decent interval to apparently exhaust his putative inquiries, will himself bring about our entry into this matter, by whatever means is deemed appropriate.

In the main such men are motivated only by money, and therefore, provided that our operative is sufficiently remunerated, he will believe only what he wishes to believe, namely that we are a group of cranks. Should at any stage he prove troublesome, I am certain that we will need only to remind him of the Reichsführer's interest in this matter to guarantee his silence.

I have drawn up a list of suitable candidates, and with your permission I should like to contact these as soon as possible.

Heil Hitler,
Yours,
Otto Rahn

K. M. Wiligut Weisthor
Caspar-Theyss Strasse 33, Berlin W.

To SS-Unterscharführer Otto Rahn
Tiergartenstrasse 8a, Berlin W.   30 July 1938

STRICTLY CONFIDENTIAL

Dear Otto,

I have learnt from Anders that the police are holding a Jew on suspicion of certain crimes. Why did it not occur to any of us that the police being what they are, they would frame some person, albeit a Jew, for these crimes? At the right time in our plan such an arrest would have been most helpful, but right now, before we have had a chance to demonstrate our power for the benefit of the Reichsführer, and hope to influence him accordingly, it is nothing short of a nuisance.

However, it occurs to me that we can actually turn this to our advantage. Another Project Krist incident while this Jew is incarcerated will not only effect this man's release, but will accordingly embarrass Heydrich very badly indeed. Please see to it.

Heil Hitler,
Weisthor

SS-Sturmbannführer Richard Anders,
Order of Knights Templar, Berlin
Lumenklub, Bayreutherstrasse 22 Berlin W.

To SS-Brigadeführer K. M. Weisthor
Berlin Grunewald   27 August 1938

STRICTLY CONFIDENTIAL

Dear Brigadeführer,

My inquiries have confirmed that Police Headquarters, Alexanderplatz, did indeed receive an anonymous telephone call. Moreover a conversation with the Reichsführer's adjutant, Karl Wolff, indicates that it was he, and not the Reichsführer, who made the said call. He very much dislikes misleading the police in this fashion, but he admits that he can see no other way of assisting with the inquiry and still preserve the necessity of the Reichsführer's anonymity.

Apparently Himmler is very impressed.

Heil Hitler,
Yours, Richard Anders

SS-Hauptstürmführer Dr Lanz Kindermann
Am Kleinen Wannsee
Berlin West

To Karl Maria Wiligut
Caspar-Theyss Strasse 33,
Berlin West   29 September

My dear Karl,
On a serious note first of all. Our friend Reinhard Lange has
started to give me cause for concern. Putting aside my own
feelings for him, I believe that he may be weakening in his
resolve to assist with the execution of Project Krist. That what
we are doing is in keeping with our ancient pagan heritage no
longer seems to impress him as something unpleasant but none
the less necessary. Whilst I do not for a moment believe that he
would ever betray us, I feel that he should no longer be a part of
those Project Krist activities which perforce must take place
within this clinic.

Otherwise I continue to rejoice in your ancient spiritual heir-
loom, and look forward to the day when we can continue to
investigate our ancestors through your autogenic clairvoyance.

Heil Hitler,
Yours, as ever,
Lanz

The Commandant,
SS-Brigadeführer Siegfried Taubert,
SS-School Haus,
Wewelsburg, near Paderborn,
Westphalia

To SS-Brigadeführer Weisthor
Caspar-Theyss Strasse 33,
Berlin Grunewald   3 October 1938

Herr Brigadeführer,
This is to confirm that the next Court of Honour will take place
here in Wewelsburg on the above dates. As usual security will

be tight and during the proceedings, beyond the usual methods of identification, a password will be required to gain admittance to the school house. At your own suggestion this is to be GOSLAR.

Attendance is deemed by the Reichsführer to be mandatory for all those officers and men listed below:

Reichsführer-SS Himmler
SS-Obergruppenführer Heydrich
SS-Obergruppenführer Heissmeyer
SS-Obergruppenführer Nebe
SS-Obergruppenführer Daluege
SS-Obergruppenführer Darre
SS-Gruppenführer Pohl
SS-Brigadeführer Taubert
SS-Brigadeführer Berger
SS-Brigadeführer Eicke
SS-Brigadeführer Weisthor
SS-Oberführer Wolff
SS-Sturmbannführer Anders
SS-Sturmbannführer von Oeynhausen
SS-Hauptsturmführer Kindermann
SS-Obersturmbannführer Diebitsch
SS-Obersturmbannführer von Knobelsdorff
SS-Obersturmbannführer Klein
SS-Obersturmbannführer Lasch
SS-Unterscharführer Rahn
Landbaumeister Bartels
Professor Wilhelm Todt

Heil Hitler,
Taubert

There were many other letters, but I had already risked too much by staying as long as I had. More than that, I realized that, for perhaps the first time since coming out of the trenches in 1918, I was afraid.

21

Friday, 4 November

Driving from Weisthor's house to the Alex, I tried to make some sense out of what I had discovered.

Vogelmann's part was explained, and to some extent that of Reinhard Lange. And perhaps Kindermann's clinic was where they had killed the girls. What better place to kill someone than a hospital, where people were always coming and going feet first. Certainly his letter to Weisthor seemed to indicate as much.

There was a frightening ingenuity in Weisthor's solution. After murdering the girls, all of whom had been selected for their Aryan looks, their bodies were hidden so carefully as to be virtually impossible to find: the more so when one took into account the lack of police manpower available to investigate something as routine as a missing person. By the time the police realized that there was a mass-murderer stalking the streets of Berlin, they were more concerned with keeping things quiet so that their failure to catch the killer did not look incompetent – for at least as long as it took to find a convenient scapegoat, such as Josef Kahn.

But what of Heydrich and Nebe, I wondered. Was their attendance at this SS Court of Honour deemed mandatory merely by virtue of their senior rank? After all, the SS had its factions just like any other organization. Daluege, for instance, the head of Orpo, like his opposite number Arthur Nebe, felt as ill-disposed to Himmler and Heydrich as they felt towards him. And quite clearly of course, Weisthor and his faction were antagonistic towards 'the Jew Heydrich'. Heydrich, a Jew. It was one of those neat pieces of counter-propaganda that relies on a massive contradiction to sound convincing. I'd heard this rumour before, as had most of the bulls around the Alex, and like them I knew where it originated: Admiral Canaris, head of the Abwehr, German Military Intelligence, was Heydrich's most bitter opponent, and certainly the most powerful one.

Or was there some other reason why Heydrich was going to Wewelsburg in a few days? Nothing to do with him was ever quite what it seemed to be, although I didn't doubt for a minute that he would enjoy the prospect of Himmler's embarrassment. For him it would be nice thick icing on the cake that had as its main ingredient the arrest of Weisthor and the other anti-Heydrich conspirators within the SS.

To prove it, however, I was going to need something else besides Weisthor's papers. Something more eloquent and unequivocal, that would convince the Reichsführer himself.

It was then that I thought of Reinhard Lange. The softest excrescence on the maculate body of Weisthor's plot, it certainly wasn't going to require a clean and sharp curette to cut him away. I had just the dirty, ragged thumbnail that would do the job. I still had two of his letters to Lanz Kindermann.

Back at the Alex I went straight to the duty sergeant's desk and found Korsch and Becker waiting for me, with Professor Illmann and Sergeant Gollner.

'Another call?'

'Yes, sir,' said Gollner.

'Right. Let's get going.'

From the outside the Schultheiss Brewery in Kreuzberg, with its uniform red brick, numerous towers and turrets, as well as the fair-sized garden, made it seem more like a school than a brewery. But for the smell, which even at two a.m. was strong enough to pinch the nostrils, you might have expected to find rooms full of desks instead of beer-barrels. We stopped next to the tent-shaped gatehouse.

'Police,' Becker yelled at the nightwatchman, who seemed to like a beer himself. His stomach was so big I doubt he could have reached the pockets of his overalls, even if he had wanted to. 'Where do you keep the old beer-barrels?'

'What, you mean the empties?'

'Not exactly. I mean the ones that probably need a bit of mending.'

The man touched his forehead in a sort of salute.

'Right you are, sir. I know exactly what you mean. This way, if you please.'

We got out of the cars and followed him back up the road we had driven along. After only a short way we ducked through a green door in the wall of the brewery and went down a long and narrow passageway.

'Don't you keep that door locked?' I said.

'No need,' said the nightwatchman. 'Nothing worth stealing here. The beer's kept behind the gate.'

There was an old cellar with a couple of centuries of filth on the ceiling and the floor. A bare bulb on the wall added a touch of yellow to the gloom.

'Here you are then,' said the man. 'I guess this must be what you're looking for. This is where they puts the barrels as needs repairing. Only a lot of them never get repaired. Some of these haven't been moved in ten years.'

'Shit,' said Korsch. 'There must be nearly a hundred of them.'

'At least,' laughed our guide.

'Well, we'd better get started then, hadn't we?' I said.

'What exactly are you looking for?'

'A bottle-opener,' said Becker. 'Now be a good fellow and run along, will you?' The man sneered, said something under his breath and then waddled off, much to Becker's amusement.

It was Illmann who found her. He didn't even take the lid off.

'Here. This one. It's been moved. Recently. And the lid's a different colour from the rest.' He lifted the lid, took a deep breath and then shone his torch inside. 'It's her all right.'

I came over to where he was standing and took a look for myself, and one for Hildegard. I'd seen enough photographs of Emmeline around the apartment to recognize her immediately.

'Get her out of there as soon as you can, Professor.'

Illmann looked at me strangely and then nodded. Perhaps he heard something in my tone that made him think my

interest was more than just professional. He waved in the
police photographer.

'Becker,' I said.

'Yes, sir?'

'I need you to come with me.'

On the way to Reinhard Lange's address we called in at my
office to collect his letters. I poured us both a large glass of
schnapps and explained something of what had transpired that
evening.

'Lange's the weak link. I heard them say so. What's more,
he's a lemon-sucker.' I drained the glass and poured another,
inhaling deeply of it to increase the effect, my lips tingling as I
held it on my palate for a while before swallowing. I shuddered
a little as I let it slip down my backbone and said: 'I want you
to work a Vice-squad line on him.'

'Yes? How heavy?'

'Like a fucking waltzer.'

Becker grinned and finished his own drink. 'Roll him out
flat? I get the idea.' He opened his jacket and took out a short
rubber truncheon which he tapped enthusiastically on the
palm of his hand. 'I'll stroke him with this.'

'Well, I hope you know more about using that than you do
that Parabellum you carry. I want this fellow alive. Scared
shitless, but alive. To answer questions. You get it?'

'Don't worry,' he said. 'I'm an expert with this little india
rubber. I'll just break the skin, you'll see. The bones we can
leave until another time you give the word.'

'I do believe you like this, don't you? Scaring the piss out of
people.'

Becker laughed. 'Don't you?'

The house was on Lützowufer-Strasse, overlooking the
Landwehr Canal and within earshot of the zoo, where some
of Hitler's relations could be heard complaining about the
standard of accommodation. It was an elegant, three-storey
Wilhelmine building, orange-painted and with a big square
oriel window on the first floor. Becker started to pull the bell
as if he was doing it on piecework. When he got tired of that

he started on the door knocker. Eventually a light came on in the hall and we heard the scrape of a bolt.

The door opened on the chain and I saw Lange's pale face peer nervously round the side.

'Police,' said Becker. 'Open up.'

'What is happening?' he swallowed. 'What do you want?'

Becker took a step backwards. 'Mind out, sir,' he said, and then stabbed at the door with the sole of his boot. I heard Lange squeal as Becker kicked it again. At the third attempt the door flew open with a great splintering noise to reveal Lange hurrying up the stairs in his pyjamas.

Becker went after him.

'Don't shoot him, for Christ's sake,' I yelled at Becker.

'Oh God, help,' Lange gurgled as Becker caught him by the bare ankle and started to drag him back. Twisting round he tried to kick himself free of Becker's grip, but it was to no avail, and as Becker pulled so Lange bounced down the stairs on his fat behind. When he hit the floor Becker gripped at his face and stretched each cheek towards his ears.

'When I say open the door, you open the fucking door, right?' Then he put his whole hand over Lange's face and banged his head hard on the stair. 'You got that, queer?' Lange protested loudly, and Becker caught hold of some of his hair and slapped him twice, hard across the face. 'I said, have you got that, queer?'

'Yes,' he screamed.

'That's enough,' I said pulling him by the shoulder. He stood up breathing heavily, and grinned at me.

'You said a waltzer, sir.'

'I'll tell you when he needs some more of the same.'

Lange wiped his bleeding lip and inspected the blood that smeared the back of his hand. There were tears in his eyes but he still managed to summon up some indignation.

'Look here,' he yelled, 'what the hell is this all about? What do you mean by barging in here like this?'

'Tell him,' I said.

Becker grabbed the collar of Lange's silk dressing-gown and twisted it against his pudgy neck. 'It's a pink triangle for you, my fat little fellow,' he said. 'A pink triangle with bar if the letters to your bottom-stroking friend Kindermann are anything to go by.'

Lange wrenched Becker's hand away from his neck and stared bitterly at him. 'I don't know what you're talking about,' he hissed. 'Pink triangle? What does that mean, for God's sake?'

'Paragraph 175 of the German Penal Code,' I said.

Becker quoted the section off by heart: 'Any male who indulges in criminally indecent activities with another male, or who allows himself to participate in such activities, will be punished with gaol.' He cuffed him playfully on the cheek with the backs of his fingers. 'That means you're under arrest, you fat butt-fucker.'

'But it's preposterous. I never wrote any letters to anyone. And I'm not a homosexual.'

'You're not a homosexual,' Becker sneered, 'and I don't piss out of my prick.' From his jacket pocket he produced the two letters I'd given him, and brandished them in front of Lange's face. 'And I suppose you wrote these to the tooth-fairy?'

Lange snatched at the letters and missed.

'Bad manners,' Becker said, cuffing him again, only harder.

'Where did you get those?'

'I gave them to him.'

Lange looked at me, and then looked again. 'Wait a minute,' he said. 'I know you. You're Steininger. You were there tonight, at –' He stopped himself from saying where he'd seen me.

'That's right, I was at Weisthor's little party. I know quite a bit of what's been going on. And you're going to help me with the rest.'

'You're wasting your time, whoever you are. I'm not going to tell you anything.'

I nodded at Becker, who started to hit him again. I watched dispassionately as first he coshed him across the knees and ankles, and then lightly once, on the ear, hating myself for keeping alive the best traditions of the Gestapo, and for the cold, dehumanized brutality I felt inside my guts. I told him to stop.

Waiting for Lange to stop sobbing I walked around a bit, peering through doors. In complete contrast to the exterior, the inside of Lange's house was anything but traditional. The furniture, rugs and paintings, of which there were many, were all in the most expensive modern style – the kind that's easier to look at than to live with.

When eventually I saw that Lange had drawn himself together a bit, I said: 'This is quite a place. Not my taste perhaps, but then, I'm a little old-fashioned. You know, one of those awkward people with rounded joints, the type that puts personal comfort ahead of the worship of geometry. But I'll bet you're really comfortable here. How do you think he'll like the tank at the Alex, Becker?'

'What, the lock-up? Very geometric, sir. All those iron bars.'

'Not forgetting all those bohemian types who'll be in there and give Berlin its world-famous night-life. The rapists, the murderers, the thieves, the drunks – they get a lot of drunks in the tank, throwing-up everywhere –'

'It's really awful, sir, that's right.'

'You know, Becker, I don't think we can put someone like Herr Lange in there. I don't think he would find it at all to his liking, do you?'

'You bastards.'

'I don't think he'd last the night, sir. Especially if we were to find him something special to wear from his wardrobe. Something artistic, as befits a man of Herr Lange's sensitivity. Perhaps even a little make-up, eh, sir? He'd look real nice with a bit of lipstick and rouge.' He chuckled enthusiastically, a natural sadist.

'I think you had better talk to me, Herr Lange,' I said.

'You don't scare me, you bastards. Do you hear? You don't scare me.'

'That's very unfortunate. Because unlike Kriminalassistant Becker here, I don't particularly enjoy the prospect of human suffering. But I'm afraid I have no choice. I'd like to do this straight, but quite frankly I just don't have the time.'

We dragged him upstairs to the bedroom where Becker

selected an outfit from Lange's walk-in wardrobe. When he found some rouge and lipstick Lange roared loudly and took a swing at me.

'No,' he yelled. 'I won't wear this.'

I caught his fist and twisted his arm behind him.

'You snivelling little coward. Damn you, Lange, you'll wear it and like it or so help me we'll hang you upside down and cut your throat, like all those girls your friends have murdered. And then maybe we'll just dump your carcass in a beer-barrel, or an old trunk, and see how your mother feels about identifying you after six weeks.' I handcuffed him and Becker started with the make-up. When he'd finished, Oscar Wilde by comparison would have seemed as unassuming and conservative as a draper's assistant from Hanover.

'Come on,' I growled. 'Let's get this Kit-Kat showgirl back to her hotel.'

We had not exaggerated about the night tank at the Alex. It's probably the same in every big city police station. But since the Alex is a very big city police station indeed, it followed that the tank there is also very big. In fact it is huge, as big as an average cinema theatre, except that there are no seats. Nor are there any bunks, or windows, or ventilation. There's just the dirty floor, the dirty latrine buckets, the dirty bars, the dirty people and the lice. The Gestapo kept a lot of detainees there for whom there was no room at Prinz Albrecht Strasse. Orpo put the night's drunks in there to fight, puke, and sleep it off. Kripo used the place like the Gestapo used the canal: as a toilet for its human refuse. A terrible place for a human being. Even one like Reinhard Lange. I had to keep reminding myself of what it was that he and his friends had done, of Emmeline Steininger, sitting in that barrel like so many rotten potatoes. Some of the prisoners whistled and blew kisses when they saw us bring him down, and Lange turned pale with fright.

'My God, you're not going to leave me here,' he said, clutching at my arm.

'Then unpack it,' I said. 'Weisthor, Rahn, Kindermann. A signed statement, and you can get a nice cell to yourself.'

'I can't, I can't. You don't know what they'll do to me.'

'No,' I said, and nodded at the men behind the bars, 'but I know what they'll do to you.'

The lock-up sergeant opened the enormous heavy cage and stood back as Becker pushed him into the tank.

His cries were still ringing in my ears by the time I got back to Steglitz.

Hildegard lay asleep on the sofa, her hair spread across the cushion like the dorsal fin of some exotic golden fish. I sat down, ran my hand across its smooth silkiness, and then kissed her forehead, catching the drink on her breath as I did so. Stirring, her eyes blinked open, sad and crusted with tears. She put her hand on my cheek and then on to the back of my neck, pulling me down to her mouth.

'I have to talk to you,' I said, holding back.

She pressed her finger against my lips. 'I know she's dead,' she said. 'I've done all my crying. There's no more water in the well.'

She smiled sadly, and I kissed each eyelid tenderly, smoothing her scented hair with the palm of my hand, nuzzling at her ear, chewing the side of her neck as her arms held me close, and closer still.

'You've had a ghastly evening too,' she said gently. 'Haven't you, darling?'

'Ghastly,' I said.

'I was worried about you going back to that awful house.'

'Let's not talk about it.'

'Put me to bed, Bernie.'

She put her arms around my neck and I gathered her up, folding her against my body like an invalid and carrying her into the bedroom. I sat her down on the edge of the bed and started to unbutton her blouse. When that was off she sighed and fell back against the quilt: slightly drunk I thought, unzipping her skirt and tugging it smoothly down her stockinged legs. Pulling down her slip I kissed her small breasts, her stomach and then the inside of her thighs. But her pants seemed to be too tight, or caught between her buttocks, and resisted my pulling. I asked her to lift her bottom.

'Tear them,' she said.

'What?'

'Tear them off. Hurt me, Bernie. Use me.' She spoke with breathless urgency, her thighs opening and closing like the jaws of some enormous praying mantis.

'Hildegard –'

She struck me hard across the mouth.

'Listen, damn you. Hurt me when I tell you.'

I caught her wrist as she struck again.

'I've had enough for one evening.' I caught her other arm. 'Stop it.'

'Please, you must.'

I shook my head, but her legs wrapped around my waist and my kidneys winced as her strong thighs squeezed tight.

'Stop it, for God's sake.'

'Hit me, you stupid ugly bastard. Did I tell you that you were stupid, too? A typical bone-headed bull. If you were a man you'd rape me. But you haven't got it in you, have you?'

'If it's a sense of grief you're after, then we'll take a drive down to the morgue.' I shook my head and pushed her thighs apart and then away from me. 'But not like this. It should be with love.'

She stopped writhing and for a moment seemed to recognize the truth of what I was saying. Smiling, then raising her mouth to me, she spat in my face.

After that there was nothing for it but to leave.

There was a knot in my stomach that was as cold and lonely as my apartment on Fasanenstrasse, and almost immediately I arrived home again I enlisted a bottle of brandy in dissolving it. Someone once said that happiness is that which is negative, the mere abolition of desire and the extinction of pain. The brandy helped a little. But before I dropped off to sleep, still wearing my overcoat and sitting in my armchair, I think I realized just how positively I had been affected.

22

Sunday, 6 November

Survival, especially in these difficult times, has to count as some sort of an achievement. It's not something that comes easily. Life in Nazi Germany demands that you keep working at it. But, having done that much, you're left with the problem of giving it some purpose. After all, what good is health and security if your life has no meaning?

This wasn't just me feeling sorry for myself. Like a lot of other people I genuinely believe that there is always someone who is worse off. In this case however, I knew it for a fact. The Jews were already persecuted, but if Weisthor had his way their suffering was about to be taken to a new extreme. In which case what did that say about them and us together? In what condition was that likely to leave Germany?

It's true, I told myself, that it was not my concern, and that the Jews had brought it on themselves: but even if that were the case, what was our pleasure beside their pain? Was our life any sweeter at their expense? Did my freedom feel any better as a result of their persecution?

The more I thought about it, the more I realized the urgency not only of stopping the killings, but also of frustrating Weisthor's declared aim of bringing hell down on Jewish heads, and the more I felt that to do otherwise would leave me degraded in equal measure.

I'm no knight in shining armour. Just a weather-beaten man in a crumpled overcoat on a street corner with only a grey idea of something you might as well go ahead and call Morality. Sure, I'm none too scrupulous about the things that might benefit my pocket, and I could no more inspire a bunch of young thugs to do good works than I could stand up and sing a solo in the church choir. But of one thing I was sure. I was through looking at my fingernails when there were thieves in the store.

*

I tossed the pile of letters on to the table in front of me.

'We found these when we searched your house,' I said.

A very tired and dishevelled Reinhard Lange regarded them without much interest.

'Perhaps you'd care to tell me how these came to be in your possession?'

'They're mine,' he shrugged. 'I don't deny it.' He sighed and dropped his head on to his hands. 'Look, I've signed your statement. What more do you want? I've cooperated, haven't I?'

'We're nearly finished, Reinhard. There's just a loose end or two I want tied up. Like who killed Klaus Hering.'

'I don't know what you're talking about.'

'You've got a short memory. He was blackmailing your mother with these letters which he stole from your lover, who also happened to be his employer. He thought she'd be better for the money, I guess. Well, to cut a long story short, your mother hired a private investigator to find out who was squeezing her. That person was me. This was before I went back to being a bull at the Alex. She's a shrewd lady, your mother, Reinhard. Pity you didn't inherit some of that from her. Anyway, she thought it possible that you and whoever was blackmailing her might be sexually involved. And so when I found out the name, she wanted you to decide what to do next. Of course she wasn't to know that you'd already acquired a private investigator in the ugly shape of Rolf Vogelmann. Or at least, Otto Rahn had, using money you provided. Coincidentally, when Rahn was looking around for a business to buy into, he even wrote to me. We never had the pleasure of discussing his proposition, so it took me quite a while to remember his name. Anyway, that's just by the by.

'When your mother told you that Hering was blackmailing her, naturally you discussed the matter with Dr Kindermann, and he recommended dealing with the matter yourselves. You and Otto Rahn. After all, what's one more wet-job when you've done so many?'

'I never killed anyone, I told you that.'

'But you went along with killing Hering, didn't you? I

expect you drove the car. Probably you even helped Kinder-mann string up Hering's dead body and made it look like suicide.'

'No, it's not true.'

'Wearing their SS uniforms, were they?'

He frowned and shook his head. 'How could you know that?'

'I found an SS cap badge sticking in the flesh of Hering's palm. I'll bet he put up quite a struggle. Tell me, did the man in the car put up much of a fight? The man wearing the eyepatch. The one watching Hering's apartment. He had to be killed too, didn't he? Just in case he identified you.'

'No –'

'All nice and neat. Kill him, and make it look like Hering did it, and then get Hering to hang himself in a fit of remorse. Not forgetting to take away the letters of course. Who killed the man in the car? Was that your idea?'

'No, I didn't want to be there.'

I grabbed him by the lapels, picked him off his chair and started to slap him. 'Come on, I've had just about enough of your whining. Tell me who killed him or I'll have you shot within the hour.'

'Lanz did it. With Rahn. Otto held his arms while Kinder-mann – he stabbed him. It was horrible. Horrible.'

I let him back down on the chair. He collapsed forward on to the table and started to sob into his forearm.

'You know, Reinhard, you're in a pretty tight spot,' I said, lighting a cigarette. 'Being there makes you an accomplice to murder. And then there's you knowing about the murders of all these girls.'

'I told you,' he sniffed miserably, 'they would have killed me. I never went along with it, but I was afraid not to.'

'That doesn't explain how you got into this in the first place.' I picked up Lange's statement and glanced over it.

'Don't think I haven't asked myself the same question.'

'And did you come up with any answers?'

'A man I admired. A man I believed in. He convinced me that what we were doing was for the good of Germany. That it was our duty. It was Kindermann who persuaded me.'

239

'They're not going to like that in court, Reinhard. Kindermann doesn't play a very convincing Eve to your Adam.'

'But it's true, I tell you.'

'That may be so, but we're fresh out of fig-leaves. You want a defence, you better think of something to improve on that. That's good legal advice, you can depend on it. And let me tell you something, you're going to need all the good advice you can get. Because the way I see it, you're the only one who's likely to need a lawyer.'

'What do you mean?'

'I'll be straight with you, Reinhard. I've got enough in this statement of yours to send you straight to the block. But the rest of them, I don't know. They're all SS, acquainted with the Reichsführer. Weisthor's a personal friend of Himmler's, and, well, I worry, Reinhard. I worry that you'll be the scapegoat. That all of them will get away with it in order to avoid a scandal. Of course, they'll probably have to resign from the SS, but nothing more than that. You'll be the one who loses his head.'

'No, it can't be true.'

I nodded.

'Now if there was just something else besides your statement. Something that could let you off the hook on the murder charge. Of course, you'd have to take your chances on the Para 175. But you might get away with five years in a KZ, instead of an outright death sentence. You'd still have a chance.' I paused. 'So how about it, Reinhard?'

'All right,' he said after a minute, 'there is something.'

'Talk to me.'

He started hesitantly, not quite sure whether or not he was right to trust me. I wasn't sure myself.

'Lanz is Austrian, from Salzburg.'

'That much I guessed.'

'He read medicine in Vienna. When he graduated he specialized in nervous diseases and took up a post at the Salzburg Mental Asylum. Which was where he met Weisthor. Or Wiligut, as he called himself in those days.'

'Was he a doctor too?'

'God, no. He was a patient. By profession a soldier in the Austrian army. But he is also the last in a long line of German wise men which dates back to prehistoric times. Weisthor possesses ancestral clairvoyant memory which enables him to describe the lives and religious practices of the early German pagans.'

'How very useful.'

'Pagans who worshipped the Germanic god Krist, a religion which was later stolen by the Jews as the new gospel of Jesus.'

'Did they report this theft?' I lit another cigarette.

'You wanted to know,' said Lange.

'No, no. Please go on. I'm listening.'

'Weisthor studied runes, of which the swastika is one of the basic forms. In fact, crystal shapes such as the pyramid are all rune types, solar symbols. That's where the word "crystal" comes from.'

'You don't say.'

'Well, in the early 1920s Weisthor began to exhibit signs of paranoid schizophrenia, believing that he was being victimized by Catholics, Jews and Freemasons. This followed the death of his son, which meant that the line of the Wiligut wise men was broken. He blamed his wife and as time went by, became increasingly violent. Finally he tried to strangle her and was later certified insane. On several occasions during his confinement he tried to murder other inmates. But gradually, under the influence of drug treatment, his mind was brought under control.'

'And Kindermann was his doctor?'

'Yes, until Weisthor's discharge in 1932.'

'I don't get it. Kindermann knew Weisthor was a spinner and let him out?'

'Lanz's approach to psychotherapy is anti-Freudian, and he saw in Jung's work material for the history and culture of a race. His field of research has been to investigate the human unconscious mind for spiritual strata that might make possible a reconstruction of the pre-history of cultures. That's how he came to work with Weisthor. Lanz saw in him the key to his own branch of Jungian psychotherapy, which will, he hopes, enable him to set up, with Himmler's blessing, his own version of a Goering Research Institute. That's another psychotherapeutic –'

'Yes, I know it.'

'Well, at first the research was genuine. But then he discovered that Weisthor was a fake, that he was using his so-called ancestral clairvoyance as a way of projecting the importance of his ancestors in the eyes of Himmler. But by then it was too late. And there was no price that Lanz would not have paid to make sure of getting his institute.'

'What does he need an institute for? He's got the clinic, hasn't he?'

'That's not enough for Lanz. In his own field he wants to be remembered in the same breath as Freud and Jung.'

'What about Otto Rahn?'

'Gifted academically, but really little more than a ruthless fanatic. He was a guard in Dachau for a while. That's the kind of man he is.' He stopped and chewed his fingernail. 'Might I have one of those cigarettes, please?'

I tossed him the packet and watched him light one with a hand that trembled as if he had a high fever. To see him smoke it, you would have thought it was pure protein.

'Is that it?'

He shook his head. 'Kindermann still has Weisthor's medical case history, which proves his insanity. Lanz used to say that it was his insurance, to guarantee Weisthor's loyalty. You see, Himmler can't abide mental illness. Some nonsense about racial health. So if he were ever to get hold of that case history, then –'

'– then the game would be well and truly up.'

'So what's the plan, sir?'

'Himmler, Heydrich, Nebe – they've all gone to this SS Court of Honour at Wewelsburg.'

'Where the hell is Wewelsburg?' Becker said.

'It's quite near Paderborn,' said Korsch.

'I propose to go after them. See if I can't expose Weisthor

242

and the whole dirty business right in front of Himmler. I'll take Lange along for the ride, just for evidentiary purposes.'

Korsch stood up and went to the door. 'Right, sir. I'll get the car.'

'I'm afraid not. I want you two to stay here.'

Becker groaned loudly. 'But that's ridiculous, it really is, sir. It's asking for trouble.'

'It may not quite go the way I'm planning. Don't forget that this Weisthor character is Himmler's friend. I doubt that the Reichsführer will take too kindly to my revelations. Worse still, he may dismiss them altogether, in which case it would be better if there was only me to take the heat. After all, he can hardly kick me off the force, since I'm only on it for as long as this case lasts and then I'm back to my own business.

'But you two have careers ahead of you. Not very promising careers, it's true.' I grinned. 'All the same, it would be a shame for you both to earn Himmler's displeasure when I can just as easily do that on my own.'

Korsch exchanged a short look with Becker, and then replied: 'Come on, sir, don't give us that cold cabbage. It's dangerous, what you're planning. We know it, and you know it too.'

'Not only that,' Becker said, 'but how will you get there with a prisoner? Who'll drive the car?'

'That's right, sir. It's over three hundred kilometres to Wewelsburg.'

'I'll take a staff car.'

'Suppose Lange tries something on the way?'

'He'll be handcuffed, so I doubt I'll have any trouble from him.' I shook my head and collected my hat and coat from the rack. 'I'm sorry, boys, but that's the way it's got to be.' I walked to the door.

'Sir?' said Korsch. He held out his hand. I shook it. Then I shook Becker's. Then I went to collect my prisoner.

Kindermann's clinic looked just as neat and well-behaved as it had the first time I'd been there, in late August. If anything, it seemed quieter, with no rooks in the trees and no boat on the lake to disturb them. There was just the sound of the wind and the dead leaves it blew across the path like so many flying locusts.

I placed my hand in the small of Lange's back and pushed him firmly towards the front door.

'This is most embarrassing,' he said. 'Coming here in handcuffs, like a common criminal. I'm well known here, you know.'

'A common criminal is what you are, Lange. Want me to put a towel over your ugly head?' I pushed him again. 'Listen, it's only my good nature that stops me from marching you in there with your prick hanging out of your trousers.'

'What about my civil rights?'

'Shit, where have you been for the last five years? This is Nazi Germany, not ancient Athens. Now shut your fucking mouth.'

A nurse met us in the hallway. She started to say hallo to Lange and then saw the handcuffs. I flapped my ID in front of her startled features.

'Police,' I said. 'I have a warrant to search Dr Kindermann's office.' This was true: I'd signed it myself. Only the nurse had been in the same holiday camp as Lange.

'I don't think you can just walk in there,' she said. 'I'll have to –'

'Lady, a few weeks ago that little swastika you see on my identity card there was considered sufficient authority for German troops to march into the Sudetenland. So you can bet it will let me march into the good doctor's underpants if I want it to.' I shoved Lange forward again. 'Come on, Reinhard, show me the way.'

Kindermann's office was at the back of the clinic. As an apartment in town it would have been considered to be on the small side, but as a doctor's private room it was just fine. There was a long, low couch, a nice walnut desk, a couple of big modern paintings of the kind that look like the inside of a monkey's mind, and enough expensively bound books to explain the country's shoe-leather shortage.

'Take a seat where I can keep an eye on you, Reinhard,' I

told him. 'And don't make any sudden moves. I scare easily and then get violent to cover my embarrassment. What's the word the rattle-doctors use for that?' There was a large filing cabinet by the window. I opened it and started to leaf through Kindermann's files. 'Compensatory behaviour,' I said. 'That's two words, but I guess that's what it is all right.

'You know, you wouldn't believe some of the names that your friend Kindermann has treated. This filing cabinet reads like the guest list at a Reich Chancellery gala night. Wait a minute, this looks like your file.' I picked it out and tossed it on to his lap. 'Why don't you see what he wrote about you, Reinhard? Perhaps it will explain how you got yourself in with these bastards in the first place.'

He stared at the unopened file.

'It really is very simple,' he said quietly. 'As I explained to you earlier on, I became interested in the psychic sciences as a result of my friendship with Dr Kindermann.' He raised his face to me challengingly.

'I'll tell you why you got yourself involved,' I said, grinning back at him. 'You were bored. With all your money you don't know what to be at next. That's the trouble with your kind, the kind that's born into money. You never learn its value. They knew that, Reinhard, and they played you for Johann Simple.'

'It won't work, Gunther. You're talking rubbish.'

'Am I? You've read the file then. You'll know that for sure.'

'A patient ought never to see his doctor's case notes. It would be unethical of me to even open this.'

'It occurs to me that you've seen a lot more than just your doctor's case notes, Reinhard. And Kindermann learnt his ethics with the Holy Inquisition.'

I turned back to the filing cabinet and fell silent as I came across another name I recognized. The name of a girl I had once wasted a couple of months trying to find. A girl who had once been important to me. I'll admit that I was even in love with her. The job is like that sometimes. A person vanishes without trace, the world moves on, and you find a piece of information that at the right time would have cracked the case wide open. Aside of the obvious irritation you feel at remembering

245

how wide of the mark you'd really been, mostly you learn to live with it. My business doesn't exactly suit those who are disposed to be neat. Being a private investigator leaves you holding more loose ends than a blind carpet-weaver. All the same, I wouldn't be human if I didn't admit to finding some satisfaction in tying them off. Yet this name, the name of the girl that Arthur Nebe had mentioned to me all those weeks ago when we met late one night in the ruins of the Reichstag, meant so much more than just satisfaction in finding a belated solution to an enigma. There are times when discovery has the force of revelation.

'The bastard,' said Lange, turning the pages of his own case notes.

'I was thinking the same thing myself.'

'"A neurotic effeminate",' he quoted. 'Me. How could he think such a thing about me?'

I moved down to the next drawer, only half listening to what he was saying.

'You tell me, he's your friend.'

'How could he say these things? I don't believe it.'

'Come on, Reinhard. You know how it is when you swim with the sharks. You've got to expect to get your balls bitten once in a while.'

'I'll kill him,' he said, flinging the case notes across the office.

'Not before I do,' I said, finding Weisthor's file at last. I slammed the drawer shut. 'Right. I've got it. Now we can get out of this place.'

I was about to reach for the door-handle when a heavy revolver came through the door, followed closely by Lanz Kindermann.

'Would you mind telling me what the hell's going on here?'

I stepped back into the room. 'Well, this is a pleasant surprise,' I said. 'We were just talking about you. We thought you might have gone to your Bible class in Wewelsburg. Incidentally, I'd be careful with that gun if I were you. My men have got this place under surveillance. They're very loyal, you know. That's the way we are in the police these days. I'd hate to think what they'd do if they found out that some harm had come to me.'

Kindermann glanced at Lange, who hadn't moved, and then at the files under my arm.

'I don't know what your game is, Herr Steininger, if that is your real name, but I think that you had better put those down on the desk and raise your hands, don't you?'

I laid the files down on the desk and started to say something about having a warrant, but Reinhard Lange had already taken the initiative, if that's what you call it when you're misguided enough to throw yourself on to a man who is holding a ·45-calibre pistol cocked on you. His first three or four words of bellowing outrage ended abruptly as the deafening gunshot blasted the side of his neck away. Gurgling horribly, Lange twisted around like a whirling dervish, grasping frantically at his neck with his still-manacled hands, and decorating the wallpaper with red roses as he fell to the floor.

Kindermann's hands were better suited to the violin than something as big as the ·45, and with the hammer down you need a carpenter's forefinger to work a trigger that heavy, so there was plenty of time for me to collect the bust of Dante that sat on Kindermann's desk and smash it into several pieces against the side of his head.

With Kindermann unconscious, I looked round to where Lange had curled himself into the corner. With his bloody forearm pressed against what remained of his jugular, he stayed alive for only a minute or so, and then died without speaking another word.

I removed the handcuffs and was transferring them to the groaning Kindermann when, summoned by the shot, two nurses burst into the office and stared in terror at the scene that met their eyes. I wiped my hands on Kindermann's necktie and then went over to the desk.

'Before you ask, your boss here just shot his pansy friend.' I picked up the telephone. 'Operator, get me Police Headquarters, Alexanderplatz, please.' I watched one nurse search for Lange's pulse and the other help Kindermann on to the couch as I waited to be connected.

'He's dead,' said the first nurse. Both of them stared suspiciously at me.

'This is Kommissar Gunther,' I said to the operator at the Alex. 'Connect me with Kriminalassistant Korsch or Becker in the Murder Commission as quickly as possible, if you please.' After another short wait Becker came on to the line.

'I'm at Kindermann's clinic,' I explained. 'We stopped to pick up the medical case history on Weisthor and Lange managed to get himself killed. He lost his temper and a piece of his neck. Kindermann was carrying a lighter.'

'Want me to organize the meat wagon?'

'That's the general idea, yes. Only I won't be here when it comes. I'm sticking to my original plan, except that now I'm taking Kindermann along with me instead of Lange.'

'All right, sir. Leave it to me. Oh, incidentally, Frau Steininger called.'

'Did she leave a message?'

'No, sir.'

'Nothing at all?'

'No, sir. Sir, you know what that one needs, if you don't mind me saying?'

'Try and surprise me.'

'I reckon that she needs –'

'On second thoughts, don't bother.'

'Well, you know the type, sir.'

'Not exactly, Becker, no. But while I'm driving I'll certainly give it some thought. You can depend on it.'

I drove west out of Berlin, following the yellow signs indicating long-distance traffic, heading towards Potsdam and beyond it, to Hanover.

The autobahn branches off from the Berlin circular road at Lehnin, leaving the old town of Brandenburg to the north, and beyond Zeisar, the ancient town of the Bishops of Brandenburg, the road runs west in a straight line.

After a while I was aware of Kindermann sitting upright in the back seat of the Mercedes.

'Where are we going?' he said dully.

I glanced over my right shoulder. With his hands manacled behind his back I didn't think he'd be stupid enough to try hitting me with his head. Especially now it was bandaged, something the two nurses from the clinic had insisted on doing before allowing me to drive the doctor away.

'Don't you recognize the road?' I said. 'We're on our way to a little town south of Paderborn. Wewelsburg. I'm sure you know it. I didn't think you would want to miss your SS Court of Honour on my account.' Out of the corner of my eye I saw him smile and settle back in the rear seat, or at least, as well as he was able to.

'That suits me fine.'

'You know, you've really inconvenienced me, Herr Doktor. Shooting my star witness like that. He was going to give a special performance for Himmler. It's lucky he made a written statement back at the Alex. And, of course, you'll have to understudy.'

He laughed. 'And what makes you think I'll take to that role?'

'I'd hate to think what might happen if you were to disappoint me.'

'Looking at you, I'd say you were used to being disappointed.'

'Perhaps. But I doubt my disappointment will even compare with Himmler's.'

'My life is in no danger from the Reichsführer, I can assure you.'

'I wouldn't place too much reliance on your rank or your uniform if I were you, Hauptsturmführer. You'll shoot just as easily as Ernst Röhm and all those SA men did.'

'I knew Röhm quite well,' he said smoothly. 'We were good friends. It may interest you to know that that's a fact which is well-known to Himmler, with all that such a relationship implies.'

'You're saying he knows you're a queer?'

'Certainly. If I survived the Night of Long Knives, I think

I can manage to cope with whatever inconvenience you've arranged for me, don't you?'

'The Reichsführer will be pleased to read Lange's letters, then. If only to confirm what he already knows. Never underestimate the importance to a policeman of confirming information. I dare say he knows all about Weisthor's insanity as well, right?'

'What was insanity ten years ago merely counts as a treatable nervous disorder today. Psychotherapy has come a long way in a short time. Do you seriously believe that Herr Weisthor can be the first senior SS officer to be treated? I'm a consultant at a special orthopaedic hospital at Hohenlychen, near Ravensbruck concentration camp, where many SS staff officers are treated for the prevailing euphemism that describes mental illness. You know, you surprise me. As a policeman you ought to know how skilled the Reich is in the practice of such convenient hypocrisies. Here you are hurrying to create a great big firework display for the Reichsführer with a couple of rather damp little crackers. He will be disappointed.'

'I like listening to you, Kindermann. I always like to see another man's work. I bet you're great with all those rich widows who bring their menstrual depressions to your fancy clinic. Tell me, for how many of them do you prescribe cocaine?'

'Cocaine hydrochloride has always been used as a stimulant to combat the more extreme cases of depression.'

'How do you stop them becoming addicted?'

'It's true there is always that risk. One has to be watchful for any sign of drug dependency. That's my job.' He paused. 'Why do you ask?'

'Just curious, Herr Doktor. That's my job.'

At Hohenwarhe, north of Magdeburg, we crossed the Elbe by a bridge, beyond which, on the right, could be seen the lights of the almost completed Rothensee Ship Elevator, designed to connect the Elbe with the Mittelland Canal some twenty metres above it. Soon we had passed into the next state of Niedersachsen, and at Helmstedt we stopped for a rest, and to pick up some petroleum.

It was getting dark and looking at my watch I saw that it was almost seven o'clock. Having chained one of Kindermann's hands to the door handle, I allowed him to take a pee, and attended to my own needs at a short distance. Then I pushed the spare wheel into the back seat beside Kindermann and handcuffed it to his left wrist, which left one hand free. The Mercedes is a big car, however, and he was far enough behind me not to worry about. All the same, I removed the Walther from my shoulder-holster, showed it to him and then laid it beside me on the big bench seat.

'You'll be more comfortable like that,' I said. 'But so much as pick your nose and you'll get this.' I started the car and drove on.

'What is the hurry?' Kindermann said exasperatedly. 'I fail to understand why you're doing this. You could just as easily stage your performance on Monday, when everyone arrives back in Berlin. I really don't see the need to drive all this way.'

'It'll be too late by then, Kindermann. Too late to stop the special pogrom that your friend Weisthor's got planned for Berlin's Jews. Project Krist, isn't that what it's called?'

'Ah, you know about that do you? You have been busy. Don't tell me that you're a Jew-lover.'

'Let's just say that I don't much care for lynch-law, and rule by the mob. That's why I became a policeman.'

'To uphold justice?'

'If you want to call it that, yes.'

'You're deluding yourself. What rules is force. Human will. And to build that collective will it must be given a focus. What we are doing is no more than a child does with a magnifying-glass when it concentrates the light of the sun on to a sheet of paper and causes it to catch alight. We are merely using a power that already exists. Justice would be a wonderful thing were it not for men. Herr –? Look here, what is your name?'

'The name is Gunther, and you can spare me the Party propaganda.'

'These are facts, Gunther, not propaganda. You're an anachronism, do you know that? You are out of your time.'

'From the little history I know it seems to me that justice is never very fashionable, Kindermann. If I'm out of my time, if I'm out of step with the will of the people, as you describe it, then I'm glad. The difference between us is that whereas you wish to use their will, I want to see it curbed.'

'You're the worst kind of idealist: you're naïve. Do you really think that you can stop what's happening to the Jews? You've missed that boat. The newspapers already have the story about Jewish ritual murder in Berlin. I doubt that Himmler and Heydrich could prevent what is going on even if they wanted to.'

'I might not be able to stop it,' I said, 'but perhaps I can try and get it postponed.'

'And even if you do manage to persuade Himmler to consider your evidence, do you seriously think that he'll welcome his stupidity being made public? I doubt you'll get much in the way of justice from the Reichsführer-SS. He'll just sweep it under the carpet and in a short while it will all be forgotten. As will the Jews. You mark my words. People in this country have very short memories.'

'Not me,' I said. 'I never forget. I'm a fucking elephant. Take this other patient of yours, for instance.' I picked up one of the two files I had brought with me from Kindermann's office and tossed it back over the seat. 'You see, until quite recently I was a private detective. And what do you know? It turns out that even though you're a lump of shit we have something in common. Your patient there was a client of mine.'

He switched on the courtesy light and picked up the file.

'Yes, I remember her.'

'A couple of years ago, she disappeared. It so happens she was in the vicinity of your clinic at the time. I know that because she parked my car near there. Tell me, Herr Doktor, what does your friend Jung have to say about coincidence?'

'Er . . . meaningful coincidence, I suppose you mean. It's a principle he calls synchronicity: that a certain apparently coincidental event might be meaningful according to an unconscious knowledge linking a physical event with a psychic condition. It's quite difficult to explain in terms that you would understand. But I fail to see how this coincidence could be meaning-ful.'

'No, of course you don't. You have no knowledge of my unconscious. Perhaps that's just as well.'

He was quiet for a long while after that.

North of Brunswick we crossed the Mittelland Canal, where the autobahn ended, and I drove south-west towards Hildes-heim and Hamelin.

'Not far now,' I said across my shoulder. There was no reply. I pulled off the main road and drove slowly for several minutes down a narrow path that led into an area of woodland.

I stopped the car and looked around. Kindermann was dozing quietly. With a trembling hand I lit a cigarette and got out. A strong wind was blowing now and an electrical storm was firing silver lifelines across the rumbling black sky. Maybe they were for Kindermann.

After a minute or two I leant back across the front seat and picked up my gun. Then I opened the rear door and shook Kindermann by the shoulder.

'Come on,' I said, handing him the key to the handcuffs, 'we're going to stretch our legs again.' I pointed down the path which lay before us, illuminated by the big headlights of the Mercedes. We walked to the edge of the beam where I stopped.

'Right that's far enough,' I said. He turned to face me. 'Synchronicity. I like that. A nice fancy word for something that's been gnawing at my guts for a long time. I'm a private man, Kindermann. Doing what I do makes me value my own privacy all the more. For instance, I would never ever write my home telephone number on the back of my business card. Not unless that someone was very special to me. So when I asked Reinhard Lange's mother just how she came to hire me in the first place instead of some other fellow, she showed me just such a card, which she got out of Reinhard's jacket pocket before sending his suit to the cleaners. Naturally I began to start thinking. When she saw the card she was worried that he might be in trouble, and mentioned it to him. He said that he picked it off your desk. I wonder if he had a reason for doing that. Perhaps not. We'll never know, I guess. But whatever the reason, that card put my client in your office on the day she disappeared and was never seen again. Now how's that for synchronicity?'

'Look, Gunther, it was an accident, what happened. She was an addict.'

'And how did she get that way?'

'I'd been treating her for depression. She'd lost her job. A relationship had ended. She needed cocaine more than seemed apparent at the time. There was absolutely no way of knowing just by looking at her. By the time I realized she was getting used to the drug, it was too late.'

'What happened?'

'One afternoon she just turned up at the clinic. In the neighbourhood, she said, and feeling low. There was a job she was going for, an important job, and she felt that she could get it if I gave her a little help. At first I refused. But she was a very persuasive woman, and finally I agreed. I left her alone for a short while. I think she hadn't used it in a long time, and had less tolerance to her usual dose. She must have aspirated on her own vomit.'

I said nothing. It was the wrong context for it to mean anything anymore. Revenge is not sweet. Its true flavour is bitter, since pity is the most probable aftertaste.

'What are you going to do?' he said nervously. 'You're not going to kill me, surely. Look, it was an accident. You can't kill a man for that, can you?'

'No,' I said. 'I can't. Not for that.' I saw him breathe a sigh of relief and walk towards me. 'In a civilized society you don't shoot a man in cold blood.'

Except that this was Hitler's Germany, and no more civilized than the very pagans venerated by Weisthor and Himmler.

'But for the murders of all those poor bloody girls, somebody has to,' I said.

I pointed the gun at his head and pulled the trigger once; and then several times more.

From the narrow winding road, Wewelsburg looked like a

fairly typical Westphalian peasant village, with as many shrines to the Virgin Mary on the walls and grass verges as there were pieces of farm-machinery left lying outside the half-timbered, fairy-story houses. I knew I was in for something weird when I decided to stop at one of these and ask for directions to the SS-School. The flying griffins, runic symbols and ancient words of German that were carved or painted in gold on the black window casements and lintels put me in mind of witches and wizards, and so I was almost prepared for the hideous sight that presented itself at the front door, wreathed in an atmosphere of wood smoke and frying veal.

The girl was young, no more than twenty-five and but for the huge cancer eating away at one whole side of her face, you might have said that she was attractive. I hesitated for no more than a second, but it was enough to draw her anger.

'Well? What are you staring at?' she demanded, her distended mouth, widening to a grimace that showed her blackened teeth, and the edge of something darker and more corrupt. 'And what time is this to be calling? What is it that you want?'

'I'm sorry to disturb you,' I said, concentrating on the side of her face that was unmarked by the disease, 'but I'm a little lost, and I was hoping you could direct me to the SS-School.'

'There's no school in Wewelsburg,' she said, eyeing me suspiciously.

'The SS-School,' I repeated weakly. 'I was told it was somewhere hereabouts.'

'Oh that,' she snapped, and turning in her doorway she pointed to where the road dipped down a hill. 'There is your way. The road bends right and left for a short way before you see a narrower road with a railing rising up a slope to your left.' Laughing scornfully, she added, 'The school, as you call it, is up there.' And with that she slammed the door shut in my face.

It was good to be out of the city, I told myself walking back to the Mercedes. Country people have so much more time for the ordinary pleasantries.

I found the road with the railing, and steered the big car up the slope and on to a cobbled esplanade.

It was easy enough to see now why the girl with the piece of coal in her mouth had been so amused, for what met my eyes was no more what one would normally have recognized as a schoolhouse, than a zoo was a pet-shop, or a cathedral a meeting hall. Himmler's schoolhouse was in reality a decent-sized castle, complete with domed towers, one of which loomed over the esplanade like the helmeted head of some enormous Prussian soldier.

I drew up next to a small church a short distance away from the several troop trucks and staff cars that were parked outside what looked like the castle guard-house on the eastern side. For a moment the storm lit up the entire sky and I had a spectral black-and-white view of the whole of the castle.

By any standard it was an impressive-looking place, with rather more of the horror film about it than was entirely comfortable a proposition for the intendant trespasser. This so-called schoolhouse looked like home from home for Dracula, Frankenstein, Orlac and a whole forestful of Wolfmen – the sort of occasion where I might have been prompted to re-load my pistol with nine millimetre cloves of snub-nosed garlic.

Almost certainly there were enough real-life monsters in the Wewelsburg Castle without having to worry about the more fanciful ones, and I didn't doubt that Himmler could have given Doctor X quite a few pointers.

But could I trust Heydrich? I thought about this for quite a while. Finally I decided that I could almost certainly trust him to be ambitious, and since I was effectively providing him with the means of destroying an enemy in the shape of Weisthor, I had no real alternative but to put myself and my information in his murdering white hands.

The little church bell in the clock-tower was striking midnight as I steered the Mercedes to the edge of the esplanade and beyond it, the bridge curving left across the empty moat towards the castle gate.

An SS trooper emerged from a stone sentry-box to glance at my papers and to wave me on.

In front of the wooden gate I stopped and sounded the car horn a couple of times. There were lights on all over the castle, and it didn't seem likely that I'd be waking anyone, dead or alive. A small door in the gate swung open and an SS corporal came outside to speak to me. After scrutinizing my papers in his torchlight, he allowed me to step through the door and into the arched gateway where once again I repeated my story and presented my papers, only this time it was for the benefit of a young lieutenant apparently in command of the guard-duty.

There is only one way to deal effectively with arrogant young SS officers who look as though they've been specially issued with the right shade of blue eyes and fair hair, and that is to outdo them for arrogance. So I thought of the man I had killed that evening, and fixed the lieutenant with the sort of cold, supercilious stare that would have crushed a Hohenzollern prince.

'I am Kommissar Gunther,' I rapped at him, 'and I'm here on extremely pressing Sipo business affecting Reich security, which requires the immediate attention of General Heydrich. Please inform him at once that I am here. You'll find that he is expecting me, even to the extent that he has seen fit to provide me with the password to the castle during these Court of Honour proceedings.' I uttered the word and watched the lieutenant's arrogance pay homage to my own.

'Let me stress the delicacy of my mission, lieutenant,' I said, lowering my voice. 'It is imperative that at this stage only General Heydrich or his aide be informed of my presence here in the castle. It is quite possible that Communist spies may already have infiltrated these proceedings. Do you understand?'

The lieutenant nodded curtly and ducked back into his office to make the telephone call, while I walked to the edge of the cobbled courtyard that lay open to the cold night sky.

The castle seemed smaller from the inside, with three roofed wings joined by three towers, two of them domed, and the short but wider third, castellated and furnished with a flagpole where an SS penant fluttered noisily in the strengthening wind.

The lieutenant came back and to my surprise stood to

attention with a click of his heels. I guessed that this probably had more to do with what Heydrich or his aide had said than with my own commanding personality.

'Kommissar Gunther,' he said respectfully, 'the general is finishing dinner and asks you to wait in the sitting-room. That is in the west tower. Would you please follow me? The corporal will attend to your vehicle.'

'Thank you, Lieutenant,' I said, 'but first I have to remove some important documents that I left on the front seat.'

Having recovered my briefcase, which contained Weisthor's medical case-history, Lange's statement and the Lange–Kindermann letters, I followed the lieutenant across the cobbled courtyard towards the west wing. From somewhere to our left could be heard the sound of men singing.

'Sounds like quite a party,' I said coldly. My escort grunted without much enthusiasm. Any kind of party is better than late-night guard-duty in November. We went through a heavy oak door and entered the great hall.

All German castles should be so Gothic; every Teutonic warlord should live and strut in such a place; each inquisitorial Aryan bully should surround himself with as many emblems of unsparing tyranny. Aside from the great heavy rugs, the thick tapestries and the dull paintings, there were enough suits of armour, musket-stands and wall-mounted cutlery to have fought a war with King Gustavus Adolphus and the whole Swedish army.

In contrast, the sitting-room, which we reached by a wooden spiral staircase, was furnished plainly and commanded a spectacular view of a small airfield's landing lights a couple of kilometres away.

'Help yourself to a drink,' said the lieutenant, opening the cabinet. 'If there's anything else you need, sir, just ring the bell.' Then he clicked his heels again and disappeared back down the staircase.

I poured myself a large brandy and tossed it straight back. I was tired after the long drive. With another glass in my hand I sat stiffly in an armchair and closed my eyes. I could still see the startled expression on Kindermann's face as the first bullet struck between the eyes. Weisthor would be missing him and his bag of drugs badly by now, I thought. I could have used an armful myself.

I sipped some more of the brandy. Ten minutes passed and I felt my head nodding.

I fell asleep and my nightmare's terrifying gallop brought me before beast men, preachers of death, scarlet judges and the outcasts of paradise.

23

Monday, 7 November

By the time I finished telling Heydrich my story the general's normally pale features were flushed with excitement.

'I congratulate you, Gunther,' he said. 'This is much more than I had expected. And your timing is perfect. Don't you agree, Nebe?'

'Yes indeed, General.'

'It may surprise you, Gunther,' Heydrich said, 'but Reichsführer Himmler and myself are currently in favour of maintaining police protection for Jewish property, if only for reasons of public order and commerce. You let a mob run riot on the streets and it won't just be Jewish shops that are looted, it will be German ones too. To say nothing of the fact that the damage will have to be made good by German insurance companies. Goering will be beside himself. And who can blame him? The whole idea makes a mockery of any economic planning.

'But as you say, Gunther, were Himmler to be convinced by Weisthor's scheme then he would certainly be inclined to waive that police protection. In which case I should have to go along with that position. So we have to be careful how we handle this. Himmler is a fool, but he's a dangerous fool. We have to expose Weisthor unequivocally, and in front of as many witnesses as possible.' He paused. 'Nebe?'

The Reichskriminaldirektor stroked the side of his long nose and nodded thoughtfully.

'We shouldn't mention Himmler's involvement at all, if we can possibly avoid it, General,' he said. 'I'm all for exposing Weisthor in front of witnesses. I don't want that dirty bastard to get away with it. But at the same time we should avoid embarrassing the Reichsführer in front of the senior SS staff. He'll forgive us destroying Weisthor, but he won't forgive us making an ass of him.'

'I agree,' said Heydrich. He thought for a moment. 'This is Sipo section six, isn't it?' Nebe nodded. 'Where's the nearest SD main provincial station to Wewelsburg?'

'Bielefeld,' Nebe replied.

'Right. I want you to telephone them immediately. Have them send a full company of men here by dawn.' He smiled thinly. 'Just in case Weisthor manages to make this Jew allegation against me stick. I don't like this place. Weisthor has lots of friends here in Wewelsburg. He even officiates at some of the ludicrous SS wedding ceremonies that take place here. So we might need to mount a show of force.'

'The castle commandant, Taubert, was in Sipo prior to this posting,' said Nebe. 'I'm pretty certain we can trust him.'

'Good. But don't tell him about Weisthor. Just stick to Gunther's original story about KPD infiltrators and have him keep a detachment of men on full alert. And while you're about it, you'd better have him organize a bed for the Kommissar. By God, he's earned it.'

'The room next to mine is free, General. I think it's the Henry I of Saxony Room.' Nebe grinned.

'Madness,' Heydrich laughed. 'I'm in the King Arthur and the Grail Room. But who knows? Perhaps today I shall at least defeat Morgana le Fay.'

The courtroom was on the ground floor of the west wing. With the door to one of the adjoining rooms open a crack, I had a perfect view of what went on in there.

The room itself was over forty metres long, with a bare, polished wooden floor, panelled walls and a high ceiling complete with oak beams and carved gargoyles. Dominating was a long oak table that was surrounded on all four sides with high-backed leather chairs, on each of which was a silver disk and what I presumed to be the name of the SS officer who was entitled to sit there. With the black uniforms and all the ritualistic ceremony that attended the commencement of the court proceedings, it was like spying on a meeting of the Grand Lodge of Freemasons.

First on the agenda that morning was the Reichsführer's approval of plans for the development of the derelict north tower. These were presented by Landbaumeister Bartels, a fat, owlish little man who sat between Weisthor and Rahn. Weisthor himself seemed nervous and was quite obviously feeling the lack of his cocaine.

When the Reichsführer asked him his opinion of the plans, Weisthor stammered his answer: 'In, er . . . in terms of the, er . . . cult importance of the . . . er . . . castle,' he said, 'and, er . . . its magical importance in any, er . . . in any future conflict between, er . . . East and West, er . . .'

Heydrich interrupted, and it was immediately apparent that it was not to help the Brigadeführer.

'Reichsführer,' he said coolly, 'since this is a court, and since we are all of us listening to the Brigadeführer with enormous fascination, it would I believe be unfair to you all to permit him to go any further without acquainting you of the very serious charges that have to be made against him and his colleague, Unterscharführer Rahn.'

'What charges are these?' said Himmler with some distaste. 'I know nothing of any charges pending against Weisthor. Nor even of any investigation affecting him.'

'That is because there was no investigation of Weisthor. However, a completely separate inquiry has revealed Weisthor's principal role in an odious conspiracy that has resulted in the perverted murders of seven innocent German schoolgirls.'

'Reichsführer,' roared Weisthor, 'I protest. This is monstrous.'

'I quite agree,' said Heydrich, 'and you are the monster.'

Weisthor rose to his feet, his whole body shaking.

'You lying little kike,' he spat.

Heydrich merely smiled a lazy little smile. 'Kommissar,' he said loudly, 'would you please come in here now?'

I walked slowly into the room, my shoes sounding on the wooden floor like some nervous actor about to audition for a play. Every head turned as I came in, and as fifty of the most powerful men in Germany focused their eyes on me, I could have wished to have been anywhere else but there. Weisthor's jaw dropped as Himmler half rose to his feet.

'What is the meaning of this?' Himmler growled.

'Some of you probably know this gentleman as Herr Steininger,' Heydrich said smoothly, 'the father of one of the murdered girls. Except that he is nothing of the kind. He works for me. Tell them who you really are, Gunther.'

'Kriminalkommissar Bernhard Gunther, Murder Commission, Berlin-Alexanderplatz.'

'And tell these officers, if you will, why you have come here.'

'To arrest one Karl Maria Weisthor, also known as Karl Maria Wiligut, also known as Jarl Widar; Otto Rahn; and Richard Anders, all for the murders of seven girls in Berlin between 23 May and 29 September 1938.'

'Liar,' Rahn shouted, jumping to his feet, along with another officer whom I supposed to be Anders.

'Sit down,' said Himmler. 'I take it that you believe that you can prove this, Kommissar?' If I'd been Karl Marx himself he couldn't have regarded me with more hatred.

'I believe I can, sir, yes.'

'This had better not be one of your tricks, Heydrich,' Himmler said.

'A trick, Reichsführer?' he said innocently. 'If it's tricks you're looking for, these two evil men had them all. They sought to pass themselves off as mediums, to persuade weaker-minded people that it was the spirits who were informing them where the bodies of the girls they themselves had murdered were hidden away. And but for Kommissar Gunther here, they would have attempted the same insane trick with this company of officers.'

'Reichsführer,' Weisthor spluttered, 'this is utterly preposterous.'

'Where is the proof you mentioned, Heydrich?'

'I said insane. I meant exactly that. Naturally there is no one here who could have fallen for such a ludicrous scheme as theirs. However, it is characteristic of those who are insane to believe in the right of what they are doing.' He retrieved the file containing Weisthor's medical case history from underneath his sheaf of papers and laid it in front of Himmler.

'These are the medical case notes of Karl Maria Wiligut, also known as Karl Maria Weisthor, which until recently were in the possession of his doctor, Hauptsturmführer Lanz Kindermann –'

'No,' yelled Weisthor, and lunged for the file.

'Restrain that man,' screamed Himmler. Immediately the two officers standing beside Weisthor caught him by the arms. Rahn reached for his holster, only I was quicker, working the Mauser's slide as I laid the muzzle against his head.

'Touch it and I'll ventilate your brain,' I said, and then relieved him of his gun.

Heydrich carried on, apparently undisturbed by any of this commotion. You had to hand it to him: he was as cool as a North Sea salmon, and just as slippery.

'In November 1924, Wiligut was committed to a lunatic asylum in Salzburg for the attempted murder of his wife. Upon examination he was declared insane and remained institutionalized under the care of Dr Kindermann until 1932. Following his release he changed his name to Weisthor, and the rest you undoubtedly know, Reichsführer.'

Himmler glanced at the file for a minute or so. Finally he sighed and said: 'Is this true, Karl?'

Weisthor, held between two SS officers, shook his head.

'I swear it's a lie, on my honour as a gentleman and an officer.'

'Roll up his left sleeve,' I said. 'The man is a drug addict. For years Kindermann has been giving him cocaine and morphine.'

Himmler nodded at the men holding Weisthor, and when they revealed his horribly black-and-blue forearm, I added: 'If you're still not convinced, I have a twenty-page statement made by Reinhard Lange.'

Himmler kept on nodding. He stepped round his chair to stand in front of his Brigadeführer, the sage of the SS, and slapped him hard across the face, then again.

'Get him out of my sight,' he said. 'He is confined to

quarters until further notice. Rahn. Anders. That goes for you too.' He raised his voice to an almost hysterical pitch. 'Get out, I say. You are no longer members of this order. All three of you will return your Deaths Head rings, your daggers and your swords. I shall decide what to do with you later.'

Arthur Nebe called the guard that was waiting in readiness and, when they appeared, ordered them to escort the three men to their rooms.

By now almost every SS officer at the table was open-mouthed with astonishment. Only Heydrich stayed calm, his long face betraying no more sign of the undoubted satisfaction he was feeling at the sight of his enemies' rout than if he had been made of wax.

With Weisthor, Rahn and Anders sent out under guard, all eyes were now on Himmler. Unfortunately, his eyes were very much on me, and I holstered my gun feeling that the drama had yet to end. For several uncomfortable seconds he simply stared, no doubt remembering how at Weisthor's house I had seen him, the Reichsführer-SS and Chief of the German Police, gullible, fooled, sold – fallible. For the man who saw himself in the role of the Nazi Pope to Hitler's Antichrist, it was too much to bear. Placing himself close enough to me to smell the cologne on his closely shaven, punctilious little face, and blinking furiously, his mouth twisted into a rictus of hatred, he kicked me hard on the shin.

I grunted with pain, but stood still, almost to attention.

'You've ruined everything,' he said, shaking. 'Everything. Do you hear?'

'I did my job,' I growled. I think he might have booted me again but for Heydrich's timely interruption.

'I can certainly vouch for that,' he said. 'Perhaps, under the circumstances, it would be best if this court were postponed for an hour or so, at least until you've had a chance to recover your composure, Reichsführer. The discovery of so gross a treason within a forum that is as close to the Reichsführer's heart as this one will doubtless have come as a profound shock to him. As indeed it has been to us all.'

There was a murmur of agreement at these remarks, and

265

Himmler seemed to regain control of himself. Colouring a little, possibly with some embarrassment, he twitched and nodded curtly.

'You're quite right, Heydrich,' he muttered. 'A terrible shock. Yes indeed. I must apologize to you, Kommissar. As you say, you merely did your duty. Well done.' And with that he turned on his not inconsiderable heel and marched smartly out of the room, accompanied by several of his officers.

Heydrich started to smile a slow, curling sort of smile that got no further than the corner of his mouth. Then his eyes found mine and steered me towards the other door. Arthur Nebe followed, leaving the remaining officers to talk loudly among themselves.

'It's not many men who live to receive a personal apology from Heinrich Himmler,' Heydrich said when the three of us were alone in the castle library.

I rubbed my shin painfully. 'Well, I'm sure I'll make a note of that in my diary tonight,' I said. 'It's all I've ever dreamed of.'

'Incidentally, you didn't mention what happened to Kindermann.'

'Let's just say that he was shot while trying to escape,' I said. 'I'm sure that you of all people must know what I mean.'

'That's unfortunate. He could still have been useful to us.'

'He got what a murderer properly has coming to him. Someone had to. I don't suppose any of those other bastards will ever get theirs. The SS brotherhood and all that, eh?' I paused and lit a cigarette. 'What will happen to them?'

'You can depend on it that they're finished in the SS. You heard Himmler say so himself.'

'Well, how ghastly for them all.' I turned to Nebe. 'Come on, Arthur. Will Weisthor get anywhere near a courtroom or a guillotine?'

'I don't like it any more than you do,' he said grimly. 'But Weisthor is too close to Himmler. He knows too much.'

Heydrich pursed his lips. 'Otto Rahn, on the other hand, is merely an NCO. I don't think the Reichsführer would mind if some sort of accident were to befall him.'

I shook my head bitterly.

'Well, at least there's an end to their dirty little plot. At least we'll be spared another pogrom, for a while anyway.'

Heydrich looked uncomfortable now. Nebe got up and looked out of the library window.

'For Christ's sake,' I yelled, 'you don't mean to say that it's going to go ahead?' Heydrich winced visibly. 'Look, we all know that the Jews had nothing to do with the murders.'

'Oh yes,' he said brightly, 'that's certain. And they won't be blamed, you have my word on it. I can assure you that –'

'Tell him,' said Nebe. 'He deserves to know.'

Heydrich thought for a moment, and then stood up. He pulled a book from off the shelf and examined it negligently.

'Yes, you're right, Nebe. I believe he probably does.'

'Tell me what?'

'We received a telex before the Court convened this morning,' said Heydrich. 'By sheer coincidence, a young Jewish fanatic has made an attempt on the life of a German diplomat in Paris. Apparently he wished to protest against the treatment of Polish Jews in Germany. The Führer has sent his own personal physician to France, but it is not expected that our man will live.

'As a result, Goebbels is already lobbying the Führer that if this diplomat should die then certain spontaneous expressions of German public outrage be permitted against Jews throughout the Reich.'

'And you'll all look the other way, is that it?'

'I don't approve of lawlessness,' said Heydrich.

'Weisthor gets his pogrom after all. You bastards.'

'Not a pogrom,' Heydrich insisted. 'Looting will not be permitted. Jewish property will merely be destroyed. The police will ensure that there is no plunder. And nothing will be permitted which in any way endangers the security of German life or property.'

'How can you control a mob?'

'Directives will be issued. Offenders will be apprehended and dealt with.'

'Directives?' I flung my cigarettes against the bookcase. 'For a mob? That's a good one.'

'Every police chief in Germany will receive a telex with guidelines.'

Suddenly I felt very tired. I wanted to go home, to be taken away from all of this. Just talking about such a thing made me feel dirty and dishonest. I had failed. But what was infinitely worse, it didn't seem as if I'd ever been meant to succeed.

A coincidence, Heydrich had called it. But a meaningful coincidence, according to Jung's idea? No. It couldn't be. There was no meaning in anything, anymore.

24

Thursday, 10 November

'Spontaneous expressions of the German people's anger': that was how the radio put it.

I was angry all right, but there was nothing spontaneous about it. I'd had all night to get worked up. A night in which I'd heard windows breaking, and obscene shouts echoing up the street, and smelt the smoke of burning buildings. Shame kept me indoors. But in the morning which came bright and sunny through my curtains I felt I had to go out and take a look for myself.

I don't suppose I shall ever forget it.

Ever since 1933, a broken window had been something of an occupational hazard for any Jewish business, as synonymous with Nazism as a jackboot, or a swastika. This time, however, it was something altogether different, something much more systematic than the occasional vandalism of a few drunken SA thugs. On this occasion there had occurred a veritable Walpurgisnacht of destruction.

Glass lay everywhere, like the pieces of a huge, icy jigsaw cast down to the earth in a fit of pique by some ill-tempered prince of crystal.

Only a few metres from the front door to my building were a couple of dress shops where I saw a snail's long, silvery trail rising high above a tailor's dummy, while a giant spider's web threatened to envelope another in razor-sharp gossamer.

Further on, at the corner of Kurfürstendamm, I came across an enormous mirror that lay in a hundred pieces, presenting shattered images of myself that ground and cracked underfoot as I picked my way along the street.

For those like Weisthor and Rahn, who believed in some symbolic connection between crystal and some ancient Germanic Christ from which it derived its name, this sight must have seemed exciting enough. But for a glazier it must have looked like a licence to print money, and there were lots of people out sightseeing who said as much.

At the northern end of Fasanenstrasse the synagogue close to the S-Bahn railway was still smouldering, a gutted, blackened ruin of charred beams and burned-out walls. I'm no clairvoyant but I can say that every honest man who saw it was thinking the same thing I was. How many more buildings would end up the same way before Hitler was finished with us?

There were storm-troopers – a couple of truck-loads of them in the next street – and they were testing some more window-panes with their boots. Cautiously deciding to go another way, I was just about to turn back when I heard a voice I half-recognized.

'Get out of here, you Jewish bastards,' the young man yelled.

It was Bruno Stahlecker's fourteen-year-old son Heinrich, dressed up in the uniform of the motorized Hitler Youth. I caught sight of him just as he hurled a large stone through another shop window. He laughed delightedly at his own handiwork and said: 'Fucking Jews.' Looking around for the approval of his young comrades he saw me instead.

As I walked over to him I thought of all the things I would have said to him if I had been his father, but when I was close to him, I smiled. I felt more like giving him a good jaw-whistler with the back of my hand.

'Hallo, Heinrich.'

His fine blue eyes looked at me with sullen suspicion.

'I suppose you think you can tell me off,' he said, 'just because you were a friend of my father's.'

'Me? I don't give a shit what you do.'

'Oh? So what do you want?'

I shrugged and offered him a cigarette. He took one and I lit us both. Then I threw him the box of matches. 'Here,' I said, 'you might need these tonight. Maybe you could try the Jewish Hospital.'

'See? You are going to give me a lecture.'

'On the contrary. I came to tell you that I found the men who murdered your father.'

'You did?' Some of Heinrich's friends who were now busy looting the clothes shop yelled to him to come and help. 'I won't be long,' he called back to them. Then he said to me: 'Where are they? The men who killed my father.'

'One of them is dead. I shot him myself.'

'Good. Good.'

'I don't know what is going to happen to the other two. That all depends, really.'

'On what?'

'On the SS. Whether they decide to court-martial them or not.' I watched his handsome young face crease with puzzlement. 'Oh, didn't I tell you? Yes, these men, the ones who murdered your father in such a cowardly fashion, they were all SS officers. You see, they had to kill him because he would probably have tried to stop them breaking the law. They were evil men, you see, Heinrich, and your father always did his best to put away evil men. He was a damned good policeman.' I waved my hand at all the broken windows. 'I wonder what he would have thought of all this?'

Heinrich hesitated, a lump rising in his throat as he considered the implications of what I had told him.

'It wasn't – it wasn't the Jews who killed him then?'

'The Jews? Good gracious no.' I laughed. 'Where on earth did you get such an idea? It was never the Jews. I shouldn't believe everything you read in *Der Stürmer*, you know.'

It was with a considerable want of alacrity that Heinrich returned to his friends when he and I had finished speaking. I smiled grimly at this sight, reflecting that propaganda works both ways.

Almost a week had passed since I'd seen Hildegard. On my return from Wewelsburg I tried telephoning her a couple of times, but she was never there, or at least she never answered. Finally I decided to drive over and see her.

Driving south on Kaiserallee, through Wilmersdorf and Friedenau, I saw more of the same destruction, more of the

271

same spontaneous expressions of the people's rage: shop signs carrying Jewish names torn down, and new anti-Semitic slogans freshly painted everywhere; and always the police standing by, doing nothing to prevent a shop being looted or to protect its owner from being beaten-up. Close to Waghäuselerstrasse I passed another synagogue ablaze, the fire-service watching to make sure the flames didn't spread to any of the adjoining buildings.

It was not the best day to be thinking of myself.

I parked close to her apartment building on Lepsius Strasse, let myself in through the main door with the street key she had given me, and walked up to the third floor. I used the door knocker. I could have let myself in but somehow I didn't think she'd appreciate that, considering the circumstances of our last meeting.

After a while I heard footsteps and the door was opened by a young SS major. He could have been something straight out of one of Irma Hanke's racial-theory classes: pale blond hair, blue eyes and a jaw that looked like it had been set in concrete. His tunic was unbuttoned, his tie was loose and it didn't look like he was there to sell copies of the SS magazine.

'Who is it, darling?' I heard Hildegard call. I watched her walk towards the door, still searching for something in her handbag, not looking up until she was only a few metres away.

She was wearing a black tweed suit, a silvery crêpe blouse and a black feathered hat that plumed off the front of her head like smoke from a burning building. It was an image that I find hard to put out of my mind. When she saw me she stopped, her perfectly lipsticked mouth slackening a little as she tried to think of something to say.

It didn't need much explaining. That's the thing about being a detective: I catch on real fast. I didn't need a reason why. Perhaps he made a better job of slapping her around than I had, him being in the SS and all. Whatever the reason, they made a handsome-looking couple, which was the way they faced me off, Hildegard threading her arm eloquently through his.

I nodded slowly, wondering whether I should mention catching her stepdaughter's murderers, but when she didn't ask, I smiled philosophically, just kept nodding, and then handed her back the keys.

I was half way down the stairs when I heard her call after me: 'I'm sorry, Bernie. Really I am.'

I walked south to the Botanical Gardens. The pale autumn sky was filled with the exodus of millions of leaves, deported by the wind to distant corners of the city, away from the branches which had once given life. Here and there, stone-faced men worked with slow concentration to control this arboreal diaspora, burning the dead from ash, oak, elm, beech, sycamore, maple, horse-chestnut, lime and weeping-willow, the acrid grey smoke hanging in the air like the last breath of lost souls. But always there were more, and more still, so that the burning middens seemed never to grow any smaller, and as I stood and watched the glowing embers of the fires, and breathed the hot gas of deciduous death, it seemed to me that I could taste the very end of everything.

Author's Note

Otto Rahn and Karl Maria Weisthor resigned from the SS in February 1939. Rahn, an experienced outdoors traveller, died from exposure while walking in the mountains near Kufstein less than one month afterwards. The circumstances of his death have never been properly explained. Weisthor was retired to the town of Goslar where he was cared for by the SS until the end of the war. He died in 1946.

A public tribunal, consisting of six Gauleiters, was convened on 13 February 1940, for the purpose of investigating the conduct of Julius Streicher. The Party tribunal concluded that Streicher was 'unfit for human leadership', and the Gauleiter of Franconia retired from public duties.

The *Kristallnacht* pogrom of 9 and 10 November 1938 resulted in 100 Jewish deaths, 177 synagogues burnt down and the destruction of 7,000 Jewish businesses. It has been estimated that the amount of glass destroyed was equal to half the annual plate-glass production of Belgium, whence it had originally been imported. Damages were estimated to be in the hundreds of millions of dollars. Where insurance monies were paid to Jews, these were confiscated as compensation for the murder of the German diplomat, von Rath, in Paris. This fine totalled $250 million.

READ MORE IN PENGUIN

In every corner of the world, on every subject under the sun, Penguin represents quality and variety – the very best in publishing today.

For complete information about books available from Penguin – including Puffins, Penguin Classics and Arkana – and how to order them, write to us at the appropriate address below. Please note that for copyright reasons the selection of books varies from country to country.

In the United Kingdom: Please write to *Dept. EP, Penguin Books Ltd, Bath Road, Harmondsworth, West Drayton, Middlesex UB7 0DA*

In the United States: Please write to *Consumer Sales, Penguin USA, P.O. Box 999, Dept. 17109, Bergenfield, New Jersey 07621-0120.* VISA and MasterCard holders call 1-800-253-6476 to order Penguin titles

In Canada: Please write to *Penguin Books Canada Ltd, 10 Alcorn Avenue, Suite 300, Toronto, Ontario M4V 3B2*

In Australia: Please write to *Penguin Books Australia Ltd, P.O. Box 257, Ringwood, Victoria 3134*

In New Zealand: Please write to *Penguin Books (NZ) Ltd, Private Bag 102902, North Shore Mail Centre, Auckland 10*

In India: Please write to *Penguin Books India Pvt Ltd, 706 Eros Apartments, 56 Nehru Place, New Delhi 110 019*

In the Netherlands: Please write to *Penguin Books Netherlands bv, Postbus 3507, NL-1001 AH Amsterdam*

In Germany: Please write to *Penguin Books Deutschland GmbH, Metzlerstrasse 26, 60594 Frankfurt am Main*

In Spain: Please write to *Penguin Books S. A., Bravo Murillo 19, 1° B, 28015 Madrid*

In Italy: Please write to *Penguin Italia s.r.l., Via Felice Casati 20, I–20124 Milano*

In France: Please write to *Penguin France S. A., 17 rue Lejeune, F–31000 Toulouse*

In Japan: Please write to *Penguin Books Japan, Ishikiribashi Building, 2–5–4, Suido, Bunkyo-ku, Tokyo 112*

In Greece: Please write to *Penguin Hellas Ltd, Dimocritou 3, GR–106 71 Athens*

In South Africa: Please write to *Longman Penguin Southern Africa (Pty) Ltd, Private Bag X08, Bertsham 2013*

READ MORE IN PENGUIN

A SELECTION OF CRIME AND MYSTERY

Devices and Desires P. D. James

When Commander Adam Dalgliesh becomes involved in the hunt for the killer in a remote area of the Norfolk coast, he finds himself caught up in the dangerous secrets of the headland community. And then one moonlit night it becomes chillingly apparent that there is more than one killer at work in Larsoken ...

Gallowglass Barbara Vine

When Sandor saves little Joe from the path of a London tube train he claims his life for himself. In adoration and gratitude, Joe willingly offers himself to him, becoming Sandor's *gallowglass*, servant to the chief. 'Of all living writers, she can enter most convincingly into the criminal, or even pathological, mind' – *Sunday Times*

Death among the Dons Janet Neel

'*Death among the Dons* is probably the best crime novel set in a women's college since Dorothy Sayers's *Gaudy Night*' – T. J. Binyon. 'Janet Neel sets her nerve-tingling plot in a wonderfully alive and intelligent collegiate milieu' – *Sunday Times*

Pleading Guilty Scott Turow

Gage and Griswell is a large law firm with an even larger problem: $5.6 million has suddenly vanished from the coffers of its largest client. 'Extravagant with danger, sex and especially money – and full of surprises to the end' – *Independent on Sunday*

The Big Sleep Raymond Chandler

Millionaire General Sternwood, a paralysed old man, is already two-thirds dead. He has two beautiful daughters – one a gambler, the other a degenerate – and an elusive adventurer as a son-in-law. The General is being blackmailed, and Marlowe's assignment is to get the blackmailer off his back. As it turns out, there's a lot more at stake ...

BY THE SAME AUTHOR

March Violets

In the third year of the Reich the future was casting strange shadows . . .

Berlin, 1936. The city was full of March Violets, late converts to National Socialism in the early and prosperous years of the rule of Germany's Great Persuader – Adolf Hitler. For Bernie Gunther business was booming, especially in the missing-persons field. But somehow he couldn't bring himself to like it.

So, when Ruhr industrialist Hermann Six hired him to find the men who had murdered his daughter and son-in-law and walked away with a priceless necklace, Gunther was glad for the variety. And when Ilse Rudel, the UFA Film Studio's Aryan ice goddess, stepped out of a dark sports car in the millionaire's drive, he realized suddenly why people envied men as rich as Hermann Six . . .

'Fast-paced, laconic, unpredictable and witty' – *Evening Standard*

BY THE SAME AUTHOR

A German Requiem

Guilty of a list of war crimes as long as your arm, perhaps Emil Becker deserves to die. But should he hang for the crime he is charged with?

Convinced his old Kripo colleague is innocent, Bernie Gunther leaves the seedy ruins of Berlin, 1947, for prosperous Vienna, where Becker is held for the murder of an American Nazi-hunter. There, at the home of the new Powers' bureaucracies, he finds a façade masking hideous hypocrisy. The Americans have a new enemy and in the name of anti-communism new alignments have formed – alignments built of suspicion, treachery, double and triple dealing, that make many of the wartime atrocities look lily-white by comparison . . .

'A *tour de force* thriller of the highest quality' – *Sunday Telegraph*

also published:

Berlin Noir
An Omnibus